Travel Page

Every publication from Rippple Books has this special page to document where the book travels, who has it and when.

Dixon Grace
1.9.7
Hamburg

Alexa Camouro

Rippple
Books

First published in 2013 by
Rippple Books

Editor: Estelle Raschka
Cover design: Claudia Bode
Layout: Susanne Hock

Rippple Books
Postfach 304263
20325 Hamburg
Germany
www.rippplebooks.com

A CIP catalogue record for this book is available from the British Library.

ISBN: 978-3-9814585-9-6

The room is rectangular. Not very big, but it feels big because there's just one table and two chairs. Plastic chairs in black, a metal table with a vinyl covering that looks sticky, that's stained with the rings of coffee cups and water glasses.

The usual standard stuff in a room that's mostly off-limits. Nothing fancy or comfortable or aesthetically pleasing.

"Function over form," she says softly, looking down at the floor and seeing small holes where a chair – a special chair – could be bolted down.

She's sitting in one of the black plastic chairs, slouching really, arms folded, and wearing clothes thrown over her baggy sleeping underwear; her sleeping costume, as Astrid would call it.

They hadn't allowed her to get dressed. No bra. No shoes. Not even a chance for a morning pee.

What a way to wake up, she thinks. But where was Ben? Why hadn't he been there when they came, when they stormed in with helmets on and automatic weapons raised? Oh, but he'll be pissed all right. They kicked the door down.

This makes her smile, then she shakes her head.

Come on, she tells herself. The room. Focus on the room. It's about four metres by three by three. So, an area of twelve square, volume of thirty-six cubic. Like the business class section of a plane, roomy and high-ceilinged. No. The ceiling's too high. Because all those plane designers are little people, building claustrophobic cabins with tight seats and limited leg room, big enough for them but no one else. Kids maybe.

She knows this. She toured the interiors department, had a class with six Hobbit-sized cabin designers. For the first lesson, they even sat in two lines of three, one behind the other, chairs close together and shoulders almost touching, like they were on a flight somewhere.

She laughs a little.

Stop it, she says to herself. The room. Concentrate. That mirror on the wall. They're watching.

She decides the room is more swimming pool than airplane

1

interior. An upside-down pool, replete with greyish-blue walls and a metallic, chemical smell. Chlorine dried by the sun; the backyard pool of a foreclosed house left to rot in a Melbourne suburb. The result of a financial bubble bursting, some sub-division contracting company going bankrupt, the houses half-built, with all those young couples now riddled with debt and living with their parents again, or bunking in a caravan in front of a friend's house. The Australian dream gone horribly wrong.

That's better, she thinks. Run with that. Feel the sadness and loss. The anger. All those people drowning in an ocean of debt, the way I'm drowning in this upside-down pool. All those people who went after something and failed, or had it taken away from them, wrestled away at gun-point, woken at dawn by half a dozen guys in riot gear who shout "keine Bewegung" when you're still asleep, then cuff you and haul you away. And you can't shout or protest because your mouth is still furry with sleep and you're somewhere between dreamland and reality and you'd been having the nicest dream of empty beaches and softly peeling waves and gulls squawking and you could almost taste the salt of the water on your tongue and that's the place where you most want to be.

Not here. Not in this room. Not even in this country.

Having lost the focus, she rubs at her wrists, to try again.

She wonders why they cuffed her, like she's some criminal mastermind they chased halfway across Europe; some massive deployment that required the coordination of police forces from several countries. Car chases, jumping out of trains at high speed, false IDs, disguises, Swiss bank accounts, that sort of thing.

And she wonders why they said nothing, except "keine Bewegung." Didn't say what she's done, just barged in and dragged her from the bed. Some slight act of mercy meant she had a millisecond to throw on pants and a shirt.

Then cuffed.

At least they didn't use those plastic handcuffs, she thinks. The ones which cut off the circulation and leave red welts that take years to disappear, making people think you tried to commit suicide once. So, that works in their favour. Old-fashioned, dangling, S&M cuffs. And they weren't rough, either. Another plus. They were just ... brisk. Yeah, that's it. Brisk. In a hurry, as if someone was timing them. A training drill.

She shakes her head. "This must be some kind of mistake," she says to the mirror.

2

God, I look awful, she thinks, running her hands through her still sleep-matted hair.

She hates the stringy feel of the blonde dye job. And it needs to be re-dyed.

She runs her hands through it again, nearly pulling the hair from its roots. What it needs, she thinks, is a double wash and a hundred brush strokes. Double wash and a hundred brush strokes. The way mum had done it. Brush out all the crap, brush the blonde away, get back to the roots. Such beautiful hair, until she cut it all off and left.

She starts to cry. She focuses harder. The memories, the loss, all the things she missed out on, things she didn't get.

Real tears come and she doesn't wipe them away. They run down her cheeks and drip onto her shirt.

The door opens. She sits up straight and gathers herself.

"Morgen."

He's a big man, and he seems to fill the room, breathing in deeply and sucking the air out of it. He's a bit paunchy, heavy all over, but not fat. Solid. She wonders if he was an athlete when he was younger. He has that filled out look of a guy who played a lot of sport, then was happy to stop going to training, to let himself go. Now, he's kilos in three figures. A muscular lump.

He's dressed in new cheap clothes, the kind of stuff that hangs on massive racks at discount department stores. Stuff that's sorted by colour and always on sale. Clothes made of plastic. On him, they don't fit exactly right, and the colours don't suit him, certainly not that yellow pullover. It makes her think someone else bought the clothes for him, or ordered them from an online catalogue. A wife dressing her husband the way she wants him to look.

He closes the door, then stands at the table, almost readying himself to sit down, like he doesn't quite trust the structural integrity of that little plastic chair. He has a thin blue dossier in his right hand and some kind of book or magazine. He places both on the table. She sees it's a book of logic problems, with a pen hooked into the cover. There's a folded corner, half-way through, marking the page and puzzle he's up to. Nearly every page has been dog-eared, making the top of the book fan open slightly.

The man sits down slowly. The chair slides on the floor a little, but holds.

"Wie geht's?" he asks.

"What am I doing here? What's going on?"

"Moment. Moment."

He zips down the ill-fitting yellow pullover and plucks a pair of glasses from the pocket of his shirt. He has big hands, meaty and swollen, with a couple of the knuckles bulging; fingers once dislocated and not quite put back into place, maybe snapping them in himself and getting it wrong.

Heroin addict hands, she thinks. But he's no addict.

She does not want to be touched by those hands.

He puts his glasses on, pushes the book of logic problems somewhat reluctantly aside and flips open the dossier. He smoothes his moustache with a massive index finger as he reads, or pretends to read. His moustache is perfectly trimmed to the corners of his mouth.

"Australierin," he says.

"Pardon?"

"You are from Australia."

"Yes."

He looks up, thick brown eyebrows almost knitted together. "Sie sprechen Deutsch, oder?"

"What?"

"Do you speak German?"

"Sorry. No."

"Why not?" he asks, checking the dossier again. A finger taps against the paper. "You are here since nearly two years."

"Well, excuse me," she says. "I never got the chance to start. And every time I tried, people spoke back to me in English."

"Yes. Blame us for that. It is the fault of us that you cannot speak our language."

"Uh-huh. You got that right."

He grunts and goes back to the dossier. She sees his eyes move to the book of logic problems.

"You do them in English?"

"Hmm."

"That's a good way to practice. For learning, I mean."

"I am willing to work at a new language," he says, without looking up.

"Yeah, but English is the world's most illogical language. There's all these rules, then all these exceptions to the rules."

"I do not understand."

4

"I'm rambling. Sorry." She gestures at the book, happy to have something to talk about, a focus. "But those are tricky, because of the double negatives and the double meanings."

He checks the dossier and looks up. "You are English teacher."

"And that's also why I never learned German. I speak English all day."

"Is no excuse."

"I guess not. Have I been arrested by the language police?"

"That is not funny." He spreads his arms in order to signify the room they're in, and says, "All this, is no joke."

"I know."

"And, Miss Dixon, do you know why you are here?"

She laughs.

This makes him angry. "Why are you laughing?"

"I'm sorry. It's just so old fashioned, to call someone Miss with their first name. So Victorian, or deep south America a hundred years ago."

"I do not follow."

"Ah, I get it. You think Dixon's my surname."

"That is how it is written here. Grace Dixon."

"It's wrong," she says. "Why do you people always get my name wrong? It's Dixon Grace."

"No. It is Grace Dixon. Because it is here in the file."

She laughs incredulously. "Yeah. Sure. Your freaking file is right and I'm wrong. I told the git in the foreign office several times that Grace is my surname and still he put it down like this. Same with my bank card, and my insurance card. Why would you all think you'd know my name better than me? Such arrogance."

The man crosses his big forearms tightly, like an oversized kid in a huff. "This is not a good start."

"I guess I got hauled out of the wrong side of the bed this morning."

"Miss Grace."

"You can call me Dixon."

"I will not. Miss Grace, do you know why you are here?"

"I asked you the same question," she says. "I don't have a clue, logic or otherwise."

"This is very serious."

"I agree with you on that. It's definitely a serious room, with some serious-looking bolt holes in the floor, and a serious mirror which some serious people are probably looking through." She waves at them. "And it's definitely a serious matter when you arrest someone for no reason."

"We have a reason."

"What is it?"

"A source."

"To hell with that," she says. "I don't want to hear any of it. I want to contact my embassy. Now."

"We contacted them."

"That's great, but I want to contact them. There is no reason for me to be here. I've led the life of a saint in Germany."

"Please. Calm down."

"I'm calm. I'm seeing nothing but yellow sun. Maybe on a different day with you, I'd be seeing red."

He tugs self-consciously at the yellow pullover, zipping it up, then down, then rubbing his forehead and retreating to the dossier. He lets out a loud sigh.

"My name is Kriminaloberkommissar Gerd Schultze. I work in LKA5."

"Ell car aah phoonph?"

"Landeskriminalamt."

"Is that where I am?

"Yes," Schultze says. "Wirtschaftskriminalität."

"Love the compound nouns, but it's all Greek to me."

"You should learn German then," he shouts. Then he controls himself, clearly aware there are people watching and judging. He even gives the mirror a brief, apologetic glance. "My department is responsible for economic crime."

"Like insider trading, that sort of stuff?"

"Sometimes, yes."

She shrugs. "I don't have any shares. And I paid all my taxes last year. This year too. Paying ahead like a good citizen. I have an accountant who organised that for me."

"Very smart. The tax system here is complex." Schultze checks the dossier again. "Especially when you are selbstständig."

"Right, a freelancer. It was the only visa I could get. But in the end, I didn't get it. They gave it to someone called Grace Dixon. Never met her. Maybe she's the one you want."

A smile stretches below Schultze's moustache, a thin line of relative exasperation that breaks long parentheses at each corner of his mouth, bracketing the hair.

"I read that Australians like to joke," he says, sounding very informed, "but this is serious. Can you be serious?"

"Sure. Of course. I've got nothing but respect for the police. I've done nothing wrong and I've got no idea why I'm here." She speaks to the mirror. "Can we make this quick? I've got classes to teach."

"Ahem, the crime is Wirtschaftsdelikt," Schultze says formally. "Economic spying."

"Economic spying? Do you mean corporate espionage?"

Schultze snaps his fingers. "That is it. I made a direct translation."

"And you're sure you've got the right person?"

"Our source named you."

Dixon crosses her arms and sits back. "Who was that exactly?"

"I cannot say."

"Ben?"

Schultze looks at the dossier.

"Because he wasn't there when the cavalry arrived," Dixon says. "He must've left when I was asleep. Rather convenient, don't you think?"

"We need to stay on the topic. I will ask you some questions and you will answer them."

"I wouldn't believe a word he says."

"Who?"

"Ben. Benjamin Steckdorf. He called this in, didn't he?"

"No, he did not," Schultze says, and Dixon decides that he's lying. "Now, my questions."

"Let's go. Get it over with. Are you recording this?"

"We are."

"Filming it too?" She runs her hands through her hair and checks herself in the mirror. "I look terrible. That's really brutal, you know, to pull someone out of bed before they've even had a shower and brushed their teeth. Do you treat your wife like this? Are you married, Gerd?"

"Kriminaloberkommissar Schultze."

She watches Schultze play with the wedding ring, pushing it up to his big knuckle and twirling it a few times.

"You'll never get that off," she says. "I hope you love your wife because that marriage is forever. Or you'll have to chop your finger off. What did you do to your fingers anyway? They look wrecked."

"Handball," he says, looking at them. "But we must talk about you."

7

"That's big here, isn't it? I have some friends who play basketball and I went to watch a game. They always have to play on these rubber floors. They're so dusty, the players slip all over the place and twist their ankles. It's dangerous."

"They are handball courts, not basketball courts."

"That's right. Because a real basketball court is made of wood."

"Look, we must focus on why you are here."

She shifts in the chair. "I'm sorry, Gerd. I'm cranky when I get up too early. When I don't get my morning shower and coffee. I'm a girl who likes routine."

Schultze claps his hands together once. "Right. Miss Grace, what do you know about planes?"

"Airplanes?" she says, shrugging. "They fly, sometimes crash. They never have enough leg room, not even for little old me. And they're an awful thing to sit in for the twenty-four hour trip to Australia."

"You teach at the ... uh ... at the big plane company across the Elbe."

"You mean Flussair?"

He grimaces, and nods once.

"You can't say the name?"

"No."

"Hah." In a mock serious tone, "Yes, Mr Schultze. I teach at the big plane company on the other side of the river. Isn't that well said? No one will ever know."

"When did you start there?"

"Almost a year ago. My language school organises classes there." Sarcastically, "Can I say the name of the school?"

Schultze checks the dossier. "Multilinga."

"Why can we say that name and not Flussair?"

"Because I say so."

"Hah. You don't scare me," Dixon says roughly. She just keeps herself from jumping up and attacking Schultze. Not to hurt him, but to show him that she could take him down, easily.

"I only want answers. And facts."

Dixon nods slowly. "They know already, don't they? And they want to keep their name out of the press, out of the police files. Keep everything nice and clean."

"I am right. You know a lot about this."

"And so I should. According to you, I'm a corporate spy."

"You admit it."

8

"More Aussie humour, I'm afraid. You've got the wrong Dixon Grace, or Grace Dixon, or whoever. The wrong girl."

Schultze clasps his fingers together, seeming to restrain himself. Dixon wishes he would get up and try something. He looks like he wants to.

Come on, lard bucket, she thinks. Try me.

Schultze taps the table three times with that combined fist, which is the size of a small pumpkin.

"Grace Treya Dixon," he says, reading from the dossier. "Sorry. Dixon Treya Grace. Born in Narooma, New South Wales. Female. Twenty-six years old."

"Wow. You must fly through those logic problems."

The very faint sound of a woman laughing makes Dixon look at the mirror.

"What kind of name is Treya?"

"It's my middle name. Would you like to call me Miss Treya?"

"You are very rude," Schultze says. "This name, are you a native?"

"A what?"

"A native from Australia."

"Do you mean an Aborigine?"

"Yes." Nodding with embarrassment and avoiding Dixon's eyes, "Yes."

"I'm not. It's Indian. Sanskrit, actually. It means walking in three paths."

"You are Indian," Schultze says, pouncing on the fact. He takes the pen from his logic problems book and makes a note in the file. The pen seems to get lost in his big hand.

"My grandmother is, but I'm Australian. And that means I get to call my embassy to ask for support."

"Ah," a big index finger in the air, and a moustache smiling, "but you say you did nothing wrong."

"Which is precisely why I want to call my embassy, so I can get out of here and get on with my life."

"Please, calm yourself."

She takes a deep breath. She knows she's pushing it, knows she has to, up to a certain point. She also knows that she has rights.

"You don't seem to think this is a mistake," she says.

Schultze has something of a hopeless look on his face, like he's powerless to the facts. "I only know what I know," he declares. "Now, you came to Germany in January last year. May I ask why?"

"Obviously to steal secrets from plane company X." She sighs and lowers her voice. "I have a friend here. We met at school in Narooma. She was an exchange student."

"Astrid Thielen."

"How do you know that?"

"It is in the file."

"So you got her name right."

"You registered at her apartment," Schultze says, also reading out the date and address.

"Yeah, so I stayed with her for a bit, then I took a room in a shared flat in the Portuguese Quarter. It was really cramped. Bathroom was a closet. It was awful."

"And you moved in with Benjamin Steckdorf in January of this year."

"Why are you repeating this?" Dixon asks. "You're not exactly the world's greatest interrogator."

"I wish to establish the facts."

"For a crime I have nothing to do with?"

The door opens and a woman enters.

The field is half the size of a regular cricket field, and it's square rather than oval. A converted soccer field. They've put up nets on both sides, strung up on flag poles, to stop the balls going into the tennis courts to the north and the car park to the south. It helps, as does the five-euro fine for hitting the ball out of the field. But there's still been search parties sent out for balls hit into the bushes to the east and west.

It's all quite ridiculous really. Miniature cricket being played by adults.

Surprisingly, there's a turf wicket; the grass cut as short as it can go and then rolled. After the first innings, the roller was brought out again, with four guys sitting on it for extra weight. It looks like they rotate the pitch, never using the same strip twice, and today's wicket is much closer to the car park boundary than the tennis courts. Every batsman is trying to hit the ball towards that shorter boundary. The captain of the fielding team has loaded that side with fielders. Three batsmen have already been caught on that side, and there was a run-out, more the result of a language problem than a mix-up; one player shouting in English, the other in Hindi, then both in German. By the time they'd decided on a common form of communication, one of them had to trudge back to the tiny dugout and clubhouse, which is two pergola tents duct-taped together.

Sure, not quite a clubhouse, on the not-quite oval, with twenty-two not-quite cricketers in not-quite whites. But she's finding it fun to watch, to be reminded.

It's a lovely day, in a leafy suburb in the west of Hamburg.

Good to be out of the city, she thinks to herself.

She's sitting on a blanket with her back against the fence, close enough to the small gaggle of WAGs to hear their conversation, if not necessarily understand it. They seem friendly, and she'd like to sit with them, but will wait to be invited.

She reads, looking up each time a ball is bowled. While the quality of the cricket is questionable, the spirit is right, and they're all having a great time. They're savouring this small pocket of the familiar they've carved – and rolled – in this unfamiliar and foreign land. This place

11

where they are temporary, uprooted and wanting to go home, and perhaps wanted to go home. The Indians, Sri Lankans and Pakistanis, that is. The Aussies, the South Africans and the Brits are able to blend in. There is one especially loud Aussie in a blue hat who shouts encouragement after every single ball.

Yet all the players are in white, or off-white, and are keenly chasing the red leather ball, knowing to shine it on one side to get some swing, even if none of the bowlers are skilled enough to get any swing. Keeping the ball on the pitch seems challenging enough. The committed shining leaves long red streaks near the right pocket of their pants and on the right bum cheek. It all looks right, sounds right, like cricket should. They've got the gear, they walk in with the bowler, they clap each delivery – "Bowling Sanjay" – or in the case of the loud-mouthed Aussie, hold brief motivational seminars. The guys in the slips bite their nails, adjust their tackle and converse before crouching down to be ready to catch a snick that will surely fall short because they are standing too far back for such a slow bowler. And the batsman keeps swinging big, trying to send the ball into the car park despite the five-euro fine, but misses each time, to the oohs and aahs of the fielders.

It is all very entertaining, and she likes the memories it brings back: sitting with Miranda under the summer sun, perving on the young guys in her dad's team. Back then, the oval was an oval, and massive, and the ball moved so fast it was impossible to keep up with the action. It was nicer to lie back on the blanket, stare up at the blue sky and gossip with her sister, and bitch about their mother.

She watches a couple of deliveries, missing Miranda, wondering how she's doing. And she wants more than just the superficial lines spoken on the telephone, or those thin emails and veiled status updates. She resolves to write her a letter when she gets home.

She misses her dad too. And Laz. After six months, a bit of homesickness is finally kicking in.

There are shouts of jubilation from the pitch. Sanjay has struck. Or is it Jasnay? Either way, a batsman is walking back to the tent, shaking his head and shouting at the umpire as he departs. She checks the clubhouse tents. Another player, already padded up, takes a protector from the kit bag and shoves it down the front of his pants, manoeuvring it and dipping his knees a few times to get everything nice and comfortable.

The new batsman pats his teammate on the back as he heads for the middle. He executes a few high knee kicks, to loosen up, and swings his arms in big circles, holding the bat; all the usual bluster to make the bowling team worry he'll hit everything out of the park. Dixon thinks he'll be lucky to get bat on ball. She watches him take middle from the umpire, mark the line with his running shoe and do a quick one-eighty to check the field placing. They're all on the car park side. He bangs the bat loudly against the soft turf wicket. The bowler, renewed by the breakthrough, strides in purposefully. The fielders shuffle forward. The ball pitches short and wide. The batsman straight-arms it, letting it go outside the off stump. The fielders clap, the Aussie yells, and the ball is thrown from wicketkeeper to slip to gully to cover to mid-off and back to the bowler, getting dropped a couple of times on the way.

She laughs softly and goes back to the book she's labouring through.

Time passes. A few runs are scored, mostly from wides and byes. A hawk circles the field. She manages to get through a few more pages. She almost falls asleep.

"What are you reading?"

"Huh?"

She looks up and sees a tall guy, rather good-looking. He has his hands in the pockets of his creased white pants, the collar of his shirt turned up. He's also wearing one of the pretentious knitted wool vests, which has an elaborate emblem stitched in blue and green near his left shoulder: a shield, the club's moniker, some kind of bird. The vest makes him look pompous and a little fat.

"The book," he says. "What is it?"

She flips it closed to look at the cover, as if she can't really believe she's reading it. He looks at it too.

"*Stasiland*," he says. "Is that about what I think it is?"

"East Germany, yeah." She tosses the book aside, not bothering to mark the page. "It's by an Aussie author. My roommate gave it to me, and now I'm forced to read it."

"Are you Australian?"

"Yes."

He laughs, his hands lifting a little in the pockets, flaring the pants. "Then none of us were right," he says, and she's picked out his accent as British. The high-brow intonation of some superior kid from a good family who went to private school and who still calls his mother mumsy.

"Right about what?"

"Sorry, but uh, I, my teammates and I, we were discussing where you might be from."

"And? What was the consensus?"

"The sub-continent, somewhere. But I went for a wild choice and said South America."

"Why would I be watching the cricket then?"

"That's what Sree said."

She looks at the field as a ball is bowled. "The cricket not worth watching? The game's totally boring, so you make a betting pool about the one spectator."

"It's not like that. It was just good fun." He sighs, in a faux friendly, warm way. "I started it, to concoct a way to come over and talk to you."

"You could've just come over and said hello," she says. "I don't like guys who give me lines."

This makes him adjust his footing, and he turns slightly to watch the cricket. Another batsman gets out.

"Oh no," he says. "That's pretty much the end of us."

"There are still four wickets left."

"Our tail doesn't exactly wag. The guys still to come are learning. And it doesn't really matter, because it's just an intra-club game. It's all for fun."

"It looks like fun."

"The league games are more serious."

"I saw you bat," she says. "You did all right."

"Thanks, but I was desperately unlucky. I gave us a good start, but it all went downhill after I got out. I made thirty-eight. I was seeing it like a basketball. Hit some wonderful pull shots."

"All to the short boundary?"

"Erm, a couple went that way, I think. But then one delivery hit a hole in the pitch and bowled me. There was nothing I could do."

"Tough luck," she says, without any sympathy.

"That's cricket." He turns to her again. "Are you enjoying the book, reading about the new old Germany? Or the old new Germany?"

She gives it a glance. "You know what, I'm no expert on East Germany, but I think it's rubbish. And I'm only a dozen pages in. It's like reading a tabloid. Sensationalist journalism. Take all the bad parts and magnify them, and ignore anything good. I guess you know all about that kind of tabloid stuff, being a Brit."

"I'm not British."

"You sound it."

"I'm German," he says proudly. "I was educated in England."

"You must've been to use a word like educated."

Again the shuffling of feet. "Excuse me if I speak the Queen's English."

"May God save her."

There comes the sound of clapping from the field. The players congregate together and start walking for the tents.

"Afternoon tea," he says. "Would you like a cup?"

"Definitely."

He extends a hand to help her up. "I'm Ben."

"Dixon."

He pulls her up and they shake hands once standing.

"That's a nice name," he says.

"Yeah, I like it."

They start walking towards the tents.

"Are you hungry as well?" he asks. "Afternoon tea here is a bit like lunching at the United Nations cafeteria."

"It looks more like a medical tent for the wounded."

"Wounded pride, perhaps."

"Sounds like junior cricket, minus the pushy parents and tears."

He smiles. She sees he has a nice smile, when he smiles for real.

"So, how did you end up here?" he asks.

The front of the school is crowded. There's a lot of reuniting going on, a lot of hugging between girls and high-fiving between boys. She sneers at their behaviour, all these idiots running up to their friends like they haven't seen each other all summer, when they actually were all together for pretty much the whole summer. She sees one group of girls going through a dramatic reunion, with a few of them crying; she saw them yesterday at the beach.

She's jealous, wishing she had such a group to hide in. One of the crowd. Normal.

She hangs back, looking for familiar faces, forcing herself to smile and say hello, even to all the people she knows don't like her. She takes in the various increases in breast size, which crotches of the boys are bulging just slightly more. Now in their uniforms again, allowing for comparison to last year, everyone looks a little bigger, a little taller, a bit more filled out. Some of the boys have turned into men during the last two months, as if they spent the summer in a laboratory.

She's in year eleven now, upper school. And everyone in her year is intent on making a good impression, determined to start the year well.

As agreed, she lets Misty walk ahead. She's in year twelve, after all. This will be Misty's one and only year to rule the school. Dixon watches her sister, fighting her envy and dismissing her sympathy. There'll be high-pressure exams, decision-making for university, the school formal. And there'll be parties too, all-nighters held at farms off the highway when the parents are away for some agricultural show. She hopes she won't get dragged along. Misty will be front and centre, but Dixon would rather spend the evenings working on her short game than go to parties and be forced to drink. More fun would be to hit bucket after bucket with her massive driver, watching the white specks disappear into the darkness, with the added satisfaction of hitting the balls out of sight. She's convinced Misty would rather do that too. But the boys don't leave her alone.

Poor little Miranda, she thinks, hating her. Always the centre of attention. Look at the boys trailing behind her.

She sneers in her sister's direction.

Poor Miranda, the topic of every dinner-table conversation in their house, and this morning's drive to school. What's Miranda going to do? Which university will she attend? What will she study?

Dixon knows her sister has no intention of going to university. She wants to be a model and a golf pro.

Stupid bitch, she thinks to herself, watching her sister sway that glorious arse of hers towards her clique. The girls engage in double-cheek kiss-hellos. All very cool and superior. As they walk towards the entrance, elbows locked, the younger kids part, like a guard of honour, and the boys stare and salivate.

Dixon grunts. Yes, she's jealous, but she still doesn't want to be Misty, or be like Misty. She isn't looking forward to next year when she will be in year twelve and all the pressure and attention will be on her. But she won't have that boy-magnet rear or the ultra-cool clique. She can just do her thing until it's all blessedly over.

She's sick of school, sick of all the same kids she's known her whole life, of all the games and rituals and expectations. She wants a bigger place, a more expansive world, somewhere exotic. A place where she can disappear, or even better, completely reinvent herself.

"Hey, Dixie."

"Hi, Shaz."

They share a quick hug.

"Have a good summer?" Shaz asks.

"We were both at the beach yesterday."

"Can you believe it's over? The summer was, like, so fast gone."

"Yep. Another looong year to go."

"You going to the beach after school?"

"Probably. If it stays hot."

"Then I'll see you there. Or in class."

Shaz runs ahead, to another melodramatic meet-up with a few long-lost friends she saw yesterday.

"Stupid bitch," Dixon says.

She walks off to the side of the groups, under the shade of a tree. It's hot, and bound to be stuffy in the classrooms.

It's a beautiful day. In the car on the way to school, her mother had crapped on and on about what a wonderful day it was, letting loose some pathetic wisdom – like she was reading straight from a self-help book nestled in her lap – that the conditions of the first day of school set the precedent for all the days that followed. Dixon knew it was false optimism, the kind of forced positivity her mother had mastered long ago, aimed specifically at Miranda, but at Dixon too. Both girls, both in upper secondary school, both at key points in their lives, both the potential target for predators and teenage boys only interested in one thing. And her mother had used a golf analogy to make it stick, even though she didn't play, and both girls weren't listening.

"Like a triple bogie on the first hole," she'd said. "You spend the rest of your round trying to recover from it. Miranda, I'm talking to you. Stuff up now and you'll spend the rest of your life trying to recover from your mistakes."

Heavy words, Dixon thought then, and thinks now, standing in the shade. Why did mum always have to be such a drama queen? All this planning for the future, this hardcore decision-making. We're teenagers. If Misty wants to, she can go out and have fun, and sleep around if she's careful about it. And I should be allowed to raise a little hell. Isn't that what being a teenager is all about? Experimenting, pushing the limits and having a good time? Take some risks, play some practical jokes, steal the odd magazine from the newsagent just to see if you can. Mum won't have it. Study, study, study.

Her father is more understanding, more forgiving, the voice of laconic reason in the household. His solution for everything is to go out and play nine holes, on the more peaceful back nine of Narooma Golf Club, out in the woods and not on the fancy front nine along the windswept cliffs. For Dixon, golf has always been the solution as well, because her mother never comes along.

Someone taps her shoulder.

Dixon turns to the girl with the long blonde hair. "What?"

"Um, excuse me. Hi. I'm looking for the administration building."

"You don't wanna go to school here. Run while you've got the chance."

The pretty girl frowns. She has very pale skin and eyebrows so blonde it's like they're not even there. "Joking, right?"

"Where are you from?" Dixon asks. "You got a totally weird accent."

"Germany."

"Really? Wow. The other side of planet."

"I'm on exchange for a year. My name's Astrid."

"What a nice name. Be prepared to meet a lot of Sharons and Kylies

18

and Jodies." Dixon snickers through her nose. "But Astrid sounds like something from outer space. Astrid. Asteroid. A star."

"Um, the administration building?" Astrid asks, looking at Dixon like she's a fruitcake.

"Follow me," Dixon says. "That's exactly where I'm headed. My moronic mother enrolled me in calculus and trig and I've gotta get out of it. Rearrange my whole schedule."

They start walking, weaving between the groups. These boys make no effort to part or let them through. Quite a few of them deliberately try to get in their way. Dixon shoves them aside.

"Ignore the wildlife," she says. "Narooma Neanderthals. A thriving species here. They'll love you if you throw them a bunch of bananas."

"Do you know all of them?" Astrid asks, lowering her head so strands of her blonde hair fall forward, veiling her face.

"Most of them, unfortunately. I try to forget their names, but they're imprinted on my brain. This is a district school, for the whole area. But I went to pre-school with some of these dicks, then primary school, and now high school. The funny thing is, they haven't changed at all since I first met them. They just got taller."

This makes Astrid laugh, even if she looks like she's not sure she should.

"My name's Dixon. But everyone calls me Dixie."

They reach the admin building and walk inside.

The woman enters carrying a large cup of coffee, a half-litre thermos with a handle and a top that has a small waft of steam leaking through the mouth hole. She's tall and lean, with long brown hair parted just left of the middle and hanging loose. The slightly wavy hair frames her face, makes her look rather unruly and disorganised, as if every morning she whacks her alarm clock with a fist, throws on whatever is lying on the floor from last night, fills up the thermos cup and heads out the door. Her face is elongated and rounded, like an upright olive, and she's got the deep, leathery tan that results from growing up on the coast; skin that's tanned by the sun and burnt by the wind. Broad shoulders giving shape to a tight white blouse, long legs in unironed business pants, and her whole body moving with the kind of loose-limbed confidence of someone who knows how to handle herself.

"Moin," she says, slurping coffee.

Schultze turns in his chair, but doesn't stand up. "Wer sind Sie?"

"Korner." She peers over his shoulder to look at the dossier.

"Abteilung?"

"LKA7," she murmurs, as if it means nothing. She puts down her cup, but continues to stand as there's no extra chair. She grins as she says, "Grace Dixon?"

"The file's wrong. My name's Dixon Grace."

Korner nods.

"We established that already," Schultze says.

"After a whole hour of questioning?" She tilts her head slightly towards the mirror. "I was admiring your technique from the cleverly concealed control room."

"Wer sind Sie?" Schultze demands.

Korner ignores him. "Dixon, I'm Kriminalhauptkommissar Babette Korner. I'll be leading this investigation."

"Leading?" Schultze stands up. "Who has said this?"

Korner quickly grabs the vacant chair, bringing it around the corner of the table so she sits at a right angle to Dixon. She takes the dossier as well, and slurps some more coffee.

"That is my chair."

"Sorry, but the music stopped." Korner blows on the lid of the coffee cup, blowing through the hole and creating a deep hollow sound, like a windpipe.

"Please," Schultze says. "That is my chair. I am questioning Miss Grace."

"Not anymore. So, Dixon, do you need anything?"

"A big coffee like you've got. A shower. Some real clothes. Some shoes. To call my embassy. To get out of here."

Korner holds up her hand. "Okay, okay. Slow down. Let's start with a coffee." She turns. "What's your name again?"

"Kriminaloberkommissar Schultze."

"These long titles are such a mouthful," she says to Dixon. "You should see our business cards." Back to Schultze, "Well, while you're getting yourself a chair, get a coffee for Dixon as well. She's a visiting national from Australia. Show her some respect."

"We shall see about this." Schultze opens the door and exits the room.

"Don't you just love German men," Korner says, almost apologetically. "Not exactly gifted in the charm department." To the mirror, "Yeah, you heard me right." To Dixon, "But they do respect authority and rank. I outrank him, you see. Just. And I'm from Staatsschutz."

"What's that?"

"National security."

"He told me this was economic something or other."

"Wirtschaftsdelikt. He speaks wonderful English, doesn't he? Yes, corporate espionage, that's what we've been told, but I think it's bigger than that." A sip of coffee. Dixon waits. "Relax. We've got some time. Schultze will be a while, but so will the coffee. Right now, he's sitting at his desk. He'll call his boss, and his boss will call my boss, and it'll travel back along the line until Schultze realises he'll be assisting this investigation. Then, because he's a German man and he'll be pissed off, he'll look in my file to see if he can find something on me he can use. He'll learn I'm from East Germany and when he comes back in the jokes will start. The Stasi and Trabi jokes. West Germany as bankrolling superhero. Don't worry. I'm immune to it. You have to be to survive here." To the mirror again, "Yeah, you heard that right too. I know the deal." To Dixon, "It's like some conversational game we have to play. The rules of east-west engagement. So, are you a corporate spy?"

"What? No, absolutely not. Like I keep telling you, I have no idea where this is all coming from."

"Maybe your boyfriend," Korner says, pushing some strands of hair behind her ear, opening up her face. Her profile is jagged but interesting, dominated by a long nose that looks like it's been broken once or twice.

"Ben? Your partner already dismissed that idea."

"He's not my partner. We're from different departments. But Ben, he works at Flussair. He was on the inside."

"So, you can say the company's name?"

"In here, yes."

This makes Dixon smile, then she catches herself. "Do you think Ben's the spy?" she asks.

Korner shrugs. "I need to talk with him, take a peek inside his soul to see if he's got the make-up for it. You know, the right character. The balls, and the motivation. Corporate spies and insiders are always motivated by something specific. Money, revenge, celebrity. Something like that."

"He has enough money," Dixon says.

"Rich family, I know. Maybe he didn't have the courage to break up with you. German men are intimidated by strong women. The problem is, that makes it hard for us to have long term relationships. Us strong women, I mean. And from what I've read and heard, Ben sounds a bit soft to me. Blankenese family, father in the Hamburg Senate. He never had to struggle or fight, never had to work a part-time job as a teenager. He got everything without ever having to suffer. But you, Dixon, you were in the police once, in Australia."

"How do you know that?"

"I did some research while Schultze was trying to get your name right." After a sip of coffee, "You were police. A tough one, I bet. I think Ben couldn't quite handle you, couldn't control you. Am I right? Maybe he made up all this corporate spying stuff just to end the relationship."

"Break up with me by getting me arrested?"

"Stranger things have happened. Motivation makes people do strange things. And if someone's weak and they want to achieve a goal, they'll normally take the easiest route to get there." She shakes

22

her head. The hair comes loose from behind her ears. "I could tell you stories, of my break-ups and those of my friends. The length these guys went to just to get out of the relationships." Another shake. "Ben doesn't strike me as someone who likes confrontation."

"That's true."

Korner lets these words hang in the air. She sips her coffee, the cup going a little higher each time as she gets closer to the bottom. She smiles at the mirror, and waves once.

Dixon pulls her chair closer to the table. "You know, I have to say, your English is very good."

"Thank you," Korner says. "I spent a lot of time abroad. I was in the army. Schultze probably knows that too now. I'll smack him if he tries to make any Nazi jokes. So, I was in Yugoslavia, the Balkans, Afghanistan for a few months. A lot of work with NATO, which is why I spoke English all the time. It was good work, challenging stuff, and it felt like we were doing something worthwhile, something that would make a difference. But there reaches a point when you get too old to be sleeping in dusty tents under the illusions of saving the world. Afghanistan was the last straw. I just couldn't tolerate what was happening to the women there, to girls, and that it's been happening like that for hundreds of years."

Dixon nods, feeling a sense of kinship with Korner, but not willing to say so. She also gets the feeling that Korner is telling more about herself to be ingratiating.

"And when you're in the army and working in places like that," Korner continues, "you don't get to have any real relationships. Everyone in the army's a bit too fucked up by what's going on, and everyone back home doesn't really understand it. How was your relationship with Ben?"

Dixon rubs her hands together. Her fingers are cold, the skin dry. She slides her fingers under her thighs to warm them up.

"I won't lie," she says, "but I also don't want to get Ben in trouble. I don't think he's trying to sabotage our relationship, and I don't think he's a spy or an insider or whatever you want to call him. If you want my opinion, he's probably trying to score some points, to get ahead at work."

Korner drains her mug as she waits for Dixon to finish. But when Dixon doesn't say anything more, she's forced to prompt her: "Go on, please."

"It was dying," Dixon admits, and she smiles, thinking about it.

"Our relationship. Like a plane that's lost an engine and is slowly falling to earth. Everyone knows it's gonna crash, but it seems to take forever for it to happen."

"Good analogy."

"We'd got to that awful point," Dixon continues, "where you're like two roomies, but sharing a bed. Two old friends running a household. Every conversation is domestic. We're out of sponges. It's your turn to take out the garbage. Please don't leave the toilet seat up. We've got Lars and Mirna's baby shower on Saturday. That kind of stuff. Sex once a week, if that."

"Why didn't you end it?"

"I was going to. Soon. My plan was to go back to Australia for Christmas, and use that as the break-up point. My biggest worry was that Ben would come running after me at the airport and we'd have some awful Hollywood moment."

Korner laughs. "One problem. It's only September. You were going to keep at it until Christmas?"

"I know. It's pathetic. I'm also not too good with confrontation. I don't like hurting people."

"Were you planning to come back?"

Dixon shrugs. "That I hadn't decided yet. I don't know. I'm still not sure." She looks around the room. "Actually, now I'm sure. You lock me up for no reason. Why would I want to keep living in a country where that happens?"

Again, Korner waits for Dixon to continue, and this time she does, without needing coercion.

"I thought I might try somewhere else in Europe. Somewhere warmer. Spain, Portugal, maybe Croatia."

"Ah, another foreigner complaining about the Hamburg weather."

"I only hear the locals complaining. I like the weather here. It's much better than people think. I just want something new. Being an English teacher pretty much opens up all of Europe for work."

"You don't like it here?"

"I was loving it up until this morning."

Korner leans forward, with her elbows on the table and both hands around her empty thermos cup. "I've seen this before," she says. "You work as a freelancer at a company, you get told certain things, then you just tell them to friends and family without really knowing the significance or the importance."

Dixon raises one eyebrow. "Spying through ignorance?"

"I'm not implying that you're stupid. Really not. But it happens sometimes. Companies that want information prey on people like you."

"Like me? Idiots, yeah?"

"No," Korner says, smiling, "I mean people working temporarily in companies, as consultants or English teachers or temp workers." She takes a deep breath. "Look. There's something you need to understand. Information is the new commodity. There are immense and complicated networks for the trading of secret company information. And not just for new products and technologies, but to anticipate stock prices and investment options. A little insider tip can make some people very rich, like knowing the next cards in blackjack or if the referee will give a player a red card. Maybe one sentence you said, that slipped out innocently in normal conversation in a bar, was heard by someone who knew the right people and traded the information. Maybe you let something slip about the new navigation technology."

"I signed a secrecy agreement," Dixon says loudly. "I never talked with anyone about work. That was the deal."

"Not even with Ben?"

"Okay, a bit, at the start, to get me up to speed so I could run the classes better. But that was superficial stuff, info about the company and what they've already done. We didn't talk about any top secret stuff. We didn't talk at all really, except about raised and lowered toilet seats, and the lack of sponges. Unless someone used that information to make a pile of money investing in sponge stocks."

Korner smiles again, revealing a mouth of interesting-looking teeth; white, but none of them entirely straight, as if she'd worn braces as a kid, but they hadn't quite done the job.

"You seem like a smart girl," Korner says. "I didn't mean to insult your intelligence before. How did you end up in here?"

"In Hamburg?"

"In here."

"You tell me," Dixon says, putting her hands in the air, palms up. "I was sleeping soundly when a battalion of guys in riot gear were suddenly in the bedroom. And me without a rape whistle to blow."

"They didn't touch you," Korner says angrily.

"No, just pointed automatic weapons in front of my eyeballs."

"Where was Ben?"

"Dunno." Dixon strokes her hands through her stiff hair. She pulls it back to make a ponytail, but without anything to secure it lets it drop. "Sometimes he goes running before work. Or he runs to work, along the river to Teufelsbrück, to catch the ferry. He says it makes a good impression." Sarcastically, "That he's a get-ahead kind of guy."

"But you were asleep."

"Today is the one day of the week that I don't have early-morning classes, which is also why I was really pissed to be woken up by the Hamburg Army. I work a week of donut days. Classes in mornings, classes in the evenings and a big hole in between. Except today. So, thanks for ruining it for me."

"Sounds tough," Korner says.

"It's not that bad. I like it. It means I can enjoy the days. I can go for a walk around the Alster at three on a Thursday when everyone else is at work."

"When most people are at work," Korner corrects. "How's the pay?"

"All right. Multilinga doesn't pay big money, but they have clients who cancel their classes a lot, because their employees have to work rather than sit in a meeting room learning English. We get paid for classes cancelled too late."

"Earning money doing nothing."

"Right."

Korner clears her throat. "I checked your, hmm, your bank account. Quite healthy. You don't pay rent?"

"Ben owns the apartment. I mean, his family does."

"I know," Korner says confidently, like she knows everything, every minute detail of Dixon's life.

"Moving in together was his idea," Dixon says. "And I did it as much for the apartment as for him. His family doesn't like me very much. I think they've got something against foreigners. Last Christmas, his mother crapped on and on about some local girl Ben grew up with, dropped her name into every conversation. And kept mentioning that she was doing very well for herself. Ugh."

The door opens. Schultze enters, carrying two cups. Another man, younger, follows him in with a chair, drops it, then leaves, closing the door behind him.

"Welcome back," Korner says. "Did you go all the way to Italy to get that coffee?"

"I had something to check," Schultze replies, grinning evilly as he sits down. "Questions of Staatssicherheit. Oh, I mean Staatsschutz."

"Funny." Korner slides the cup to Dixon. "See? I told you. Straight away with the East Germany jokes."

"I don't get it," Dixon says, sipping.

"Staatssicherheit was the Stasi, the secret police in the GDR."

"They spied on everyone," Schultze says.

"How does my file look?" Korner asks him.

"How should I know? So, where are we? I am involved in this investigation. Equal involved. It includes both our departments."

Korner nods. "Excellent. Very good. We'll have comic relief and someone who can get us coffee and extra chairs if we need them."

Dixon laughs.

"Quiet," Schultze says. "I do not understand why you take this not serious."

"Like I keep telling you," Dixon says, voice raising. "I've done nothing wrong. When this is over, when you've all apologised to me, with a formal apology from your bosses upstairs, and maybe when I've sued the Hamburg Police for wrongful arrest and for withholding my rights, and when I'm lying on a beach back home, this will all make a great travel yarn. It'll be funny, one day. How I was arrested in Hamburg for, hah, being a corporate spy. What a fantastic story. The only problem is, no one will believe it."

Korner claps her hands together and says, "Good. If you're innocent, then this will all be over quickly. And you can make your classes today and fly home when you're ready. Kriminaloberkommissar Schultze, where shall we start?"

"She can tell us how she did it, who she did it for and why."

"That sounds easy." Another clap. "Straight and to the point. What's the English idiom? An elephant in a toy shop?"

"A bull in a China shop," Dixon says.

"That's it. So, care to answer his question? How, who and why?"

"I don't know what you want to hear," Dixon says, again raising her hands in innocence. "You're barking so far up the wrong tree. I'm an English teacher. I work for Multilinga. They give me books to use, but they're crap. I often tailor my classes to the needs of the students. I like teaching English. I enjoy the contact with the students, meeting new people. Very rarely is there a dickhead in a class. Hamburg has surprisingly few dickheads."

"Dickhead?" Schultze echoes.

"There's one in this room," Korner says.

"Is that English slang for criminal?" Schultze asks.

"Yes, yes it is. Let's go with that." To Dixon, "Tell us about Ben. You said the relationship was dying, but I want to know how you met. In an English class? Was he your student?"

"His English is too good for that," Dixon says. "He went to school in England. Boarding school, then to London for university."

"I know."

"Why did you ask then?"

"To see if you'd tell the truth."

Dixon sneers. "Why would I lie?"

"It's just a little police trick. But you probably know all about them. So, how did you meet?"

"You don't know that?"

"No."

"We met at the cricket," Dixon says, enjoying the memory.

"Is that a bar?" Schultze asks.

"It's a sport." Dixon just stops herself from adding, you dickhead.

Korner gives Schultze's beefy forearm a condescending pat. "If you like, you could go and spend some time with that file. I'm sure we've got something on cricket. You can never do enough background reading, right?"

"I do not like your tone."

"No, you don't like my rank. Or my black belt in karate. Or my six months dodging land mines and car bombs in the Afghanistan wilderness. Or the fact that I was born in Darss. Or … Mensch. This would be so much easier without you, Schultze."

"I am staying."

"Until lunch break, yeah?" Korner looks at Dixon, who's smiling at their exchange. "I know what cricket is. The British soldiers played it with the Afghani kids, to gain their acceptance. Do they play here in Hamburg?"

"There are a few teams."

"Hamburg was controlled by the British," Schultze says, "after the war."

"Most of the guys are from India," Dixon explains. "Engineers, working at Flussair."

"Please do not say the company's name."

"Fuck you. What will you do arrest me?" Calming herself and

28

talking to Korner, "Ben was one of a handful of Germans in his team. Most of them were still learning, but he could play."

"How did you end up there?" Korner asks.

"At the cricket?" Dixon sips her coffee. It tastes like boiled battery acid, but she takes another sip, buying herself some time, getting the story together. "I'd been here about six months, but I was having trouble making friends. And I wasn't getting along with Astrid. We didn't really click like we did at school. She'd changed. A lot. She was always too busy, and she didn't seem to want to take me into her circle. Whenever I was with her friends, they were so cold towards me, like they were interviewing me for a job they'd already promised to someone else."

Korner nods, knowing exactly what Dixon means.

"It takes time to make friends here," Schultze says, "but once you make a friend here, that is a friend for life."

"That's bullshit," Korner counters. "Don't listen to him, Dixon. That's just a Hamburg excuse for being cold and rude to people. I don't understand why they can't just be friendly from the start. Why should it take years to make a friendship? Like it's some kind of hazing process."

"Hazing?" Schultze echoes. "What is this word?"

"That's why you went to the cricket, Dixon," Korner continues. "To meet people. Expats."

"Yeah. I thought there'd be some Aussies there, maybe some Kiwis. But there was only one. And he was terrible at cricket, wouldn't be allowed to join beach cricket in Narooma. The Indians and Sri Lankans were much nicer."

"You are Indian," Schultze says.

"No," Dixon replies heatedly. "We've been down this road already. My grandmother is from India. I am Australian."

"It's okay, Dixon," Korner says. "Ignore him."

"Hard to do. He fills the room and won't shut up."

"Back to Ben," Korner prompts. "The cricket."

"I got along well with the Indians and their families. I kept going to the cricket in Flottbek, when I had nothing better to do. It was easy to meet people there. I got to know Ben during afternoon tea break."

Korner turns to Schultze. "That's one of the traditions of cricket. To stop in the middle of the afternoon for a cup of tea."

Schultze giggles. "Only the British would do such a thing."

The office has a large desk with half a dozen chairs around it, making the room seem more a place for group meetings than job interviews. Despite the chairs, the desk is set up like this is someone's office, with a flat-screen monitor, a sparkling white keyboard and mouse, and the scattered papers and notes of work half done. He also has the sense that he is invading, occupying someone else's space, and perhaps that person is on the other side of the door, waiting for him to leave.

He walks to the window and checks his watch. His meeting started five minutes ago.

That's annoying. Not that he has anything to do today, anywhere to be, but he still likes to keep to a schedule; as limited as it has become.

Nathan Channar stands on the top floor of this new circular building on Poonamallee High Road and stares down at the tongue of land on the other side of the Cooum River. He thinks Chintadripet looks vastly different from this vantage point, prosperous and busy, affluent almost, with the poverty hidden by the distance and height. It doesn't look anything like the neighbourhood he knew as a child, not from up here.

Even that world is changing, he thinks.

Humble beginnings, the boy from Chintadripet, plucked from the filthy streets and destined for superstardom. That had always been a key component of his story; his hero's narrative, the sports marketing people had called it. Yes, starting from the lowest possible rung, that had always been mentioned in newspaper articles and television reports, as if he were the example everyone could look to, that everyone could cite. But now, that same description, his decrepit roots and tainted upbringing, was being used as an explanation, to make people understand why one of India's fringe talents had done what he'd done. The early hardships, the lack of education, the envy and hate of those well-off, the desire for fast money and status, the desperate attempt to get ahead. That's what they said about him now. And not even the best sports marketing people could change that narrative.

Ever since March he has wanted to disappear. Some days, he finds it hard to get out of bed. He just can't face the people on the street, their dirty looks and vile remarks. Greedy, that's what the newspapers had said. Out of his depth and looking for profit and money because he lacked the necessary talent to break into the national eleven. An opportunist, they'd called him; a greedy, selfish opportunist.

So he had wanted more. Is that so bad? More for his family, for other children growing up like him, down there in Chintadripet.

The difference between there and here is still so great, he thinks, and he's suddenly overcome with the urge to trash the office, to throw chairs through the windows and walk out with the computer under his arm.

He shakes his head in that slight, admonishing way people do when they're alone, when their regrets and mistakes collapse on top of them and there's no chance for distraction.

He wants to open a window and jump.

Because there's nothing left for him. No cricket, no training, no team meals, no tours. No schedules. All of it undone and destroyed by a few innocent words. They just slipped out, answers to a stranger's questions when his mind was elsewhere.

Did the captain plan to bat or bowl? Bat.

How does the pitch look? Firm.

Do you think you'll make runs today? Yes.

Innocent, superfluous stuff, making polite conversation with a fan who even asked for his autograph afterwards. The kind of chatter that was banal dressing room small talk and which all cricket fans regularly engage in.

It ruined his fledging career.

He laughs viciously, hating himself.

He's startled by the glass doors being swept open. A girl in a stylish grey and blue skirt-suit enters briskly. The skirt-suit is figure hugging, very western, as if she's the personal assistant for the CEO of some enormous American corporation. Or even the secretary for the head of MI5. She's got that exotic spy girl strut, that generous lift of arse and breast that the hopes of the nation could rest on; the broad shoulders that would look as slender and sexy in a fur coat as a bullet-proof vest.

Nathan smiles, very glad for the distraction.

"Mr Marawar will see you now," she says. "Please come with me."

"This isn't his office?"

31

She smiles. "This way, please."

He follows her, trying not to stare, but again, the distraction is good. He walks with his hands in the pockets of his pants, the bottom half of what was his India national team formal suit. They took all his suit jackets and blazers, all the gear and memorabilia, such as it was. They were trying to wipe away all trace of him, to get rid of the stain in order to keep themselves clean. All he had left was this one pair of pants. He's worn them almost every day, hanging onto the semblance of what was, to the person he was; and it meant he's spent many days in the preceding months pondering what might have been.

"I know that Mr Marawar is very much looking forward to meeting you," the girl says, and he's delighted that she's talking again, to him no less. "He's a great admirer of you."

"Ah, really?" Nathan clears his throat. "Still? Even with all that, uh, well, that happened?"

"Of course."

A short hallway connects the room he waited in with Marawar's office. Glass all the way. He sees other people working, hunched over desks or leaning back in chairs as they talk on the phone. Every person is wearing a headset, and they all look very engaged in what they're doing. He wonders if he can do that too: wear a suit, put in nine hours a day, submit to the whims and targets of an overseer.

"At least it's a schedule," he mutters.

"Pardon?"

"Nothing. Good to see everyone so busy."

They reach the end of the hall. The girl presses a button and the large door opens, releasing a gaseous hiss and swinging wide like the door to a vault. She smiles and tilts her head.

"In you go. He won't bite."

"Will you escort me out later?" he asks playfully.

She pivots and walks down the hall. "I think you can find your own way out," she says over her shoulder.

Nathan watches her walk, but the door is automatic and starts to swing shut. He steps inside and the door closes behind him with a low-toned thunk.

He's alone.

This office is twice the size of the one he waited in, and the desk is massive. The room is shaped like a half moon, with floor-to-ceiling windows curving in a perfect arc, offering a breathtaking view of

Chennai. He wants to go up to the windows, starting at the very left of the room, and slowly walk the half circle, to take it all in. His city, his hometown, so impoverished when he was a child, but now growing, changing and improving. Half the city under construction.

Look at all the cranes, he thinks. And nearly every one of them has the Nayakall brand. That giant N that everyone in Chennai knows.

He can't move. He's still standing just inside the room. He could lean backwards against the closed door.

He's overwhelmed by the thought that an extended family from Chintadripet could live quite comfortably in this office.

The sound of a toilet flushing makes him turn.

"Ah, Nathan," Marawar says, wiping his hands on a towel that he then lobs into the basket near the small kitchenette. "You're finally here."

Nathan steps forward to take Marawar's proffered hand. It's still slightly damp.

"Devan Marawar. Please, call me Devan." He moves around the huge glass desk. "Did you find it all right? I would think so. You have home field advantage."

Nathan edges towards the desk, unsure whether to sit or not. He puts his hands behind his back.

"This building wasn't here when I was a child," he says, trying to sound humble, still not able to shake the narrative the sports marketing people had schooled him on.

"The area's changing," Marawar says as he eases into his high-backed chair. "Every single day, it's changing. If you come back in a year, you won't recognise it. Take a seat. Would you like something to drink?"

"I'm fine, thank you," Nathan says, sitting down. He crosses one leg over the other and waits for Marawar to talk.

"Just a moment," Marawar says. He busies himself at the computer, typing slowly, every now and then looking up at the screen.

It gives Nathan the chance to take him in. He thinks Devan Marawar looks smaller in person, but that's probably because he's only ever seen him on television and in photographs. Once, someone pointed Marawar out to him at a cricket function, but it was across a large, packed hall, and he didn't get a good look; it was hard to see over all those lanky fast-bowlers and around those puffed-up association people, squeezed into suits several sizes too small. The man in front of him is slight and rather weak-looking. He's surprisingly young up close, with a smooth face and soft, deceptive eyes.

Nathan is very good with eyes. As a batsman, he had the knack of knowing what the bowler might do just by looking in his eyes. And he also knew when he had got on top of a bowler, by the defeat and disappointment that came through in the eyes.

He finds it hard to read Marawar's eyes.

Nathan's gaze shifts to the window, to seething, changing Chennai down below.

He misses cricket, badly. The competition and possibilities. The cunning and guile. You go out and bat for your team, and it's you against the rest of them. There is no tougher test of character, so he thinks. He even misses all the travel, the sharing of hotel rooms and the long dinners with local officials. He misses the glorious feeling of hitting the ball in the centre of the bat, timing it so perfectly that the contact isn't even felt, and it's like caressing the ball to the boundary.

"Sorry about the lifetime ban," Marawar says, moving the keyboard aside.

"So am I."

"Sounds like they want to make an example of you. Well, they wanted to. Make you a scapegoat. They can put it all onto one person and start again. Especially with the IPL having such a good start."

"I don't like twenty-twenty," Nathan says. "It's silly cricket."

"I agree, but the money involved ... scandalous." Pointing a finger at Nathan, "Of course, it's great for the cricketers. I think the IPL's a good move. There's a lot of big sponsorship money floating around the IPL, for next year too. Naming rights, merchandising rights, TV rights. A lot of money and a lot of people with vested interests in the results."

Marawar talks very quickly, making it hard for Nathan to keep up. But that last sentence resonates with him.

"Are you implying it's fixed?" Nathan asks.

With a smile, Marawar says, "You tell me."

"I never fixed matches," Nathan says angrily, but then calms himself down. "I apologise. I'm having some trouble. I'm not in a very good place without my cricket."

"I know. I know. It was what you defined yourself by, and now it's gone."

Nathan nods.

"I saw you bat last year, in the tour match in Sussex."

"Yes?"

"Poetry. You batted just beautifully. It was wonderful to watch, and it was a shame I couldn't stay."

"I made a century," Nathan says. "Not that it matters anymore."

"No, not then and not now. You were definitely born at the wrong time, Nathan. India has an abundance of good batsmen. A golden generation. Tendulkar, Dravid, Sehwag."

"And all the others on the fringes, who are good enough, but can't get their chance."

"Like you. You couldn't break in either." Marawar laughs. "You should've paid someone to break Tendulkar's hands."

Nathan takes great offence to this. "Excuse me? I would never have done that."

"No, of course not. Still, I think it's a shame you never got your chance."

"Nothing can change that now."

Marawar gives him another smile, this one sympathetic and encouraging, and just slightly patronising, but Nathan sees that the eyes give nothing away.

"What will you do now?" Marawar asks. "Without your cricket."

"I'm looking for a new challenge."

"Did you spend all night thinking up that line? I know you need something new to define yourself by. Dinesh told me."

"Do you know Dinesh? Are you also from Chennai?"

Marawar ignores the question. "I know you've contacted him, asking about coaching opportunities." Talking at a rapid rate, "You think because he was your coach that he'd still be connected and would help you out. Nathan, you need wise up to your situation. You'll never do anything with cricket again. That's over for you. When you understand that, and accept it, then you can move onto a new challenge."

"I appreciate you taking the time to see me."

"Don't flatter me. We are not so different, you and I. I'm not some king sitting on a throne. I'm building something. I'm getting my hands dirty, for India." Pointing at the city below, "And I started down there with you. In the muck."

"I didn't know that."

"Everyone thinks that when you wear a suit and control a company that you were born in a suit, that someone gave you the company on a silver platter. That's not how it was for me. I worked and I struggled. And more than anything, I compromised."

"I know you're a busy man," Nathan says defensively. "I very much appreciate this meeting."

"You have Dinesh to thank for that. You see, Nathan, business is all about knowing the right people, and trusting the people you know. I trust Dinesh and Dinesh trusts you, and now we are sitting here discussing the future of India, the future of Nathan Channar. Connections, networks and trust. That's what businesses are built on." After a breath, "Innovation is people-driven. You can mechanise a factory every way you want, but you still need people to innovate. This is where the Americans and the British have got it wrong. They think production and industry is technical, that everything should be automated and outsourced. But machines can't innovate or invent. Machines can't imagine. You need people for that. Good people. Smart people. Local people you can trust." Marawar pauses and raises a finger. "Nathan, that's why Germany has such a powerful economy. They know that it takes people to make great things. They invest in their people."

Nathan nods, not really following, not keeping up with the whirlwind of words, not really sure what this high-powered businessman has in mind for him, and just not able to read his eyes. Bodyguard? he wonders. Security maybe? Chauffeur? He marvels again at where he's sitting, getting the slightest sour taste of disgust in his mouth as he remembers he grew up in an apartment a quarter of the size of this office.

He finds it difficult to believe that Devan Marawar did as well.

"India needs people," Marawar continues. "We've got a billion of them, but we're not getting the most out of them. Not even close. There is incredible potential here. Human potential. We need to do what the Germans have done."

"Innovate?" Nathan offers.

"Yes," with Marawar tapping the glass desk for emphasis, "yes, innovate. But to do that we first need to educate. We need to invest in our own people. Unlock all of that potential."

"I see."

"What do you know about Nayakall, Nathan?"

After all the preaching and ranting, the high-speed delivery, this question takes Nathan by surprise.

"Well, I'll be honest. Not that much. I know you're involved in

36

construction. Hospitals and schools. I admire that. Office buildings too, and factories." With a gesture towards the windows, "All those cranes."

"Did Dinesh tell you that? Yes, we do all of that. We're involved mostly at the investment level, getting money together for construction projects. Of course, we own a lot of the companies that do the planning, development and building, but my focus is investment. That's how economies work, Nathan. You don't need an MBA to understand it. You get the money, you build something that's needed. You employ people to do it, pay them well, they spend their money, the country grows. You've got your boom. Chennai is one of the fastest growing cities in the world. We've got all this money circulating here, employing people, paying people, building things the city needs. A few more decades, and with the right developments and investments, this city could rival London, New York or any of the European capitals. And those places, Nathan, that's old power. They're in decline, living on theoretical money. Their time is over. It's our time now. Because the power is shifting. A modern India has the potential to become the world's dominant economic power."

Marawar lets these emphatic words hang in the air. He sits back in his chair, satisfied and slightly winded.

Nathan doesn't know how to respond, because he disagrees, and it's clear that Marawar doesn't want to hear anything contrary to what he's just said. Nathan sees a different future for India, one very much like the present. As part of the India cricket squad, he'd had to make all those visits to the slums, to shake the hands of children who played in shit-coloured rivers, to take the dirty, broken pens and sign scraps of garbage, while every single one of those children were wishing the cricket star in front of them was actually Sachin Tendulkar or Rahul Dravid, and not Nathan Channar. He thinks there is no hope for India, no chance to become an industrial power. The cranes are just cranes, turning the old into the new so it can quickly become the old again. And this is the life in the city, he reminds himself. Out in the countryside, they're still ploughing their fields by hand, still giving daughters away for marriage before they bleed, still living ten to a room in small shanty huts.

He wants to say all this to Marawar, to make him understand how India really is outside of this massive office; the reality of the street down below.

"Well?" Marawar asks. "What do you think?"

"How can I contribute?" Nathan is determined not to let Dinesh down.

"You don't seem like the office type. You're too good looking for that. And I can see that you're restless after just ten minutes in that chair."

"I spent nearly my whole life in cricket nets and on ovals."

"Chasing a red leather ball, what a noble pursuit. Look where that got you. Sorry. I don't mean to offend you or belittle your achievements. Listen to me, Nathan. Here's what I think. I think you're sitting here for all the same reasons I'm sitting here. Because you and I, we are not that different."

"How so?"

"Like me, you want more for India," Marawar says, as if he's stating the obvious. "I can see it. Maybe you can't put into words like I can. Not yet. But you want more, for yourself and everyone else. And let me tell you more about you. You're a victim, Nathan, a victim of this country's backwardness, of all the out-of-date processes and ideas. You're the scapegoat for a group of dusty officials who want to keep things the way they are. And you're like me. From the street. I also think about all the little children in India. They're dreaming of being cricket stars when they should be dreaming of being engineers and architects and doctors and teachers. They should be dreaming much bigger than eleven players on a field chasing a red ball. Because that, Nathan, is a limited, selfish dream. They should be dreaming about making this country great." Sweeping an arm towards the windows, to Chennai spread out below, which Nathan knows is still a seething, stinking dung-pile of a city despite the developments, "There's so much potential out there, and it's going to waste. How many brilliant, innovative minds aren't being harnessed? All the boys and girls not getting the education they need, the education they want? And then there are those who get it and leave. You see it with boys going overseas to study. They want to get out of here. They study abroad and stay there. That's their goal. To escape. But it's wrong. It is so wrong, Nathan, and we need to change that. They should be here, working for India. For Nayakall."

Nathan is moved. Marawar's words are reaching some place deep inside him. It makes him shift in the chair. He uncrosses his legs and sits up straight, then leans forward and looks at Marawar. Suddenly,

Nathan doesn't want to let Marawar down. He would now go in and bat for Marawar, as he would for Dinesh. Stand under the broiling sun and dodge bouncers and bumpers, face down the whole attack.

"I know you love your country," Marawar says. "It needs our help. Don't you agree?"

"Yes," Nathan says softly, unsure how to word his feelings. "I want to help. The poor people here. Every day I see it. Especially the children." After a solemn pause, "The children, it's their expression that hurts the most. They've lost hope before they start school. You can see it in their eyes. They see no future. What I want to say is that they see a future that is nothing for them. It's not the future they want. Or it's a future that doesn't include them."

Marawar smiles warmly. Nathan thinks he sees the eyes relax, a veil dropping.

"Dinesh was right," Marawar says. "He's an excellent judge of character. Always was. He works for me now. I would do anything for that man."

"What does he do at Nayakall? I didn't see him in the office."

"He's not here," Marawar says. "Dinesh is a pilgrim."

"I don't follow you."

"Well, he was in imports, but he's changed to exports. He was doing what I want you to do."

"And that is?" Nathan asks.

"Home field advantage. I want you to bring the Indians home."

She sits outside, wrapped in a heavy blanket. She faces the sun, which is low in the sky and shimmering off the lake. It makes her squint as she watches the people walking past. They look back at her, with quizzical expressions; they're wondering, and discussing with each other, why she's sitting outside on this sub-zero day. And maybe why she's alone, because no one else is. It's all old couples and families, and they're very rugged up.

She ignores the people staring at her, because it's nice to sit outside. If there's one thing she's come to really dislike during her short time in Germany, it's that every room is stuffy and overheated, to the point that the windows fog up with steaming people and steaming breath, and everyone starts to yawn. It's as if they all grew up fearing drafts, that their parents told them that fresh air was bad.

So, she's happy to sit outside, because she's already discovered it's a royal pain going inside during winter: all the clothing has to come off until you're standing there in a shirt with your jacket, two pullovers and scarf hooked over your arms, and the air so thick you want to run for the nearest exit.

And it's not even that cold today, she thinks. The sun is out, spring is coming. So why isn't anyone smiling?

The promenade in front of the small harbour is empty, save for a couple of strolling oldies in matching jackets and a few families with jump-suited toddlers. One group of parents is standing in a tight ring, smoking cigarettes and talking while their kids play around the fountain, some game of their own devising. The parents look like dour people, low-to-middle class, but comfortably well-off. She's marvelled at that these first few months; even the lower classes have it good in Germany.

She takes a sip of her weak, lukewarm coffee and ponders what the parents might be talking about. Just from looking at them, their lives seem to unfold in front of her, their conversation with it: suburban houses, Opels, beer bought by the crate, big screen televisions, mundane but well-paid jobs, the heat cranked up as far as it will go and all the windows closed. Maybe secrets and affairs and lies, the usual stuff that entertains settled suburbanites. Not forgetting the reality TV gossip, all those casting shows and sing-offs that the Germans can't seem to get enough of.

Still, it's very nice to be here, in this small lakeside town; to be out of Hamburg and Astrid's cramped, stuffy flat. She needs to find somewhere else to live. Or go away every weekend like this, to a small village and stay in a teenager-packed youth hostel and have everyone stare at her because she's alone. That's one way to do it. Treat Astrid's apartment as a place to sleep during the week.

No, she thinks. I need to find a room.

She spies a small, middle-aged woman walking along the promenade. Her darkish complexion and lack of stature – plus her lack of a companion – make people stare at her. Dixon even hears the rubbing of hands on glass behind her, and she turns to see a window-seated couple, their heads in two circles of rubbed-away mist. Like porthole windows on a ship. Both people stare at the woman, who is now walking towards Dixon. Up close, it's hard to tell how old she is. She could be anywhere from forty to sixty, or perhaps even older. Her skin is smooth and delicate, her brown hair cut short. She's pretty, Dixon thinks, and must've been very pretty when she was younger. The slightly horn-rimmed glasses make her look bookish and intellectual.

"Hello," she says. With a gesture towards a chair, "May I?"

"Of course. Are you Sara?"

"Yes."

"Good. I thought I was at the wrong place."

As Sara wraps a blanket around her, she looks in the direction of the café. "The Germans," she says, "they certainly like to stare."

"And they hate the cold."

"It would make one wonder why they wanted to conquer Russia, a very cold place with nothing to stare at."

Sara sits down. Even with the blanket around her, she seems very small in the chair.

"But you're not even wearing a hat," Dixon says. "Don't you feel the cold?"

"I've got used to it over the years."

"I'm struggling a bit. Not so much with the winter, but with the winter culture."

"Well, it will be warm in a few weeks," Sara says, taking off her glasses to give them a wipe. "It can be quite beautiful here in the spring."

"Yeah, but everyone gives me a hard time because I'm from

Australia. They just don't get it that I would choose to spend the winter here. 'Oh, you're from Australia. How can you stand it here?' I'm sick of hearing that."

"Without the weather, Germans wouldn't have any small talk. They may not have any conversation at all. Come the summer and they'll be complaining that it's far too hot, or raining too much, or not enough."

Dixon points at the group of parents, still standing in a tight ring and smoking. "I bet they're talking about the weather."

"Or cleverly working the weather into whatever the conversation topic is."

Dixon laughs.

"Did you manage to find it all right?" Sara plucks the menu that's jammed between the sugar dispenser and the salt and pepper shakers. "Waren, and the café."

"Sure. Easy. I took the train here last night. It was a bit hairy, but I got here."

"Hairy? I haven't heard that expression for a while. Did you feel unsafe on the train?"

"No. It was a regional train, to Rostock," Dixon says. "Packed to the nines. Like, people swinging from the ceilings and sitting on top of each other. I chatted with a few people and they said they do the trip every weekend. Hamburg to Rostock on Friday, then back to Hamburg on Sunday evening. I think everyone on the train was doing that."

Sara nods. "Azubis, probably. There aren't that many opportunities in the new Germany, for education positions, traineeships and such. Don't be fooled by this lovely little town. The region is suffering. Unemployment is high and a lot of people leave in order to get work. Those kids on the train, they have their education or work in Hamburg, but they can't afford to live there. Maybe they take a room somewhere, or sleep on a sofa, and go home every weekend."

"Maybe. But this train, it was like a long, rolling toilet. People drinking and smoking and making out. They treated the train like it was some derelict building about to be demolished. I guess it'll be the same on the way back tomorrow."

"Not very German, is it?"

"In a way," Dixon says, "it was rather refreshing. To see them letting their hair down a bit. They're teenagers and young adults. Why shouldn't they enjoy themselves?"

"You didn't feel scared?"

Dixon shakes her head. "It's got nothing on tram ninety-six to St Kilda on a Friday night. That's scary."

"I've never felt safer than in Germany."

"Agreed."

"And it's nice here, isn't it?" Sara says. "They do quaint village very well."

"I like it."

"I try to spend some weekends here, when I have the time. A university colleague has a holiday apartment on the lake. May I ask where you are staying?"

"At the youth hostel." Dixon points. "Down there somewhere, about twenty minutes walk. On another lake. A lot of lakes here. Do they freeze over so people can ice skate on them?"

"It has to be very cold for that. Ten below for weeks on end." Sara offers a cheeky smile. "Imagine all the conversation it would generate."

Dixon laughs again.

"How are you finding it in Hamburg?" Sara asks.

"Yeah, good. Nice city. Love the harbour, all the cranes and the big ships. And it's great that you can walk everywhere, or take the train. One thing I hate about Australia is that you can't live there without a car. Even in Melbourne, which has decent public transport, except at night. A car is necessary. The cities are too spread out. All these suburbs. Everyone wanting a slice of the Australian dream, even when they can't afford it."

"A house. With a garden."

"Which means the whole city is basically suburbs, an ever-expanding hive of sub-divisions."

"What about work and your visa?"

"The work was easy," Dixon says, with a shrug. "I came at the right time, at the start of the year when companies have money to throw at employee education. But mostly I'm teaching the unemployed at Multilinga. The necessary tour of duty for the new teachers."

"And your visa?"

"All in order. I thought it would be majorly hard, but it was just time-consuming. Took a whole day, of waiting. And the waiting room wasn't the nicest place to be."

"Were you the only white person in there?" Sara asks. "The only Australian?"

"I went with an American girl, also a newbie at Multilinga. I'm glad we went together because some of the women in the waiting room really stared at us. It was rather uncomfortable."

"You should feel sorry for them."

"I should?" Dixon asks, turning to Sara. "Yeah, I guess I should. We looked at the floor the whole time, waiting for our numbers to be called. And there were times when no numbers were called for like an hour. It was hell."

They lapse into silence. The waitress finally braves the cold and comes out to take their order. They both ask for coffees. Dixon decides on a slice of apple cake with whipped cream. The waitress practically runs back inside.

"We can share it," Dixon says. "Make it feel like we're only taking on half the calories."

"Good idea. But you look like you're doing all right in that regard."

"I am? Thanks. It's a leftover from Melbourne. Last year I was really in shape. Had to be."

Sara nods. "You were in the police in Melbourne."

"That's right. Did you get my whole life story?"

"Some. I would like to know what happened."

"You don't know that part? The attacks?"

"It's difficult to decipher the news as it's broadcast from Australia," Sara says. "What's written and reported in your newspapers always has some kind of angle, a subjective point of view, as if they're trying to convince the public things happen in a certain way, perpetuated by certain people."

"Well said."

"When was that? Last year?"

"That's when it was first reported," Dixon says. "But the newspapers made it out to be an isolated incident, and that the Indian students were at fault. I got to know some students there, did some investigating, really stuck my nose in where it wasn't wanted. Those students said it's been going on for years. No one ever went to the police, and if they did, the police just shrugged and looked the other way."

"I can understand the students," Sara says. "They didn't want to make any trouble."

"Yeah, they were scared, of reprisals and other attacks. They just wanted to get their degrees and leave. It was like they were being bullied in high school. 'We'll get youse if youse dob us in.' Ugh. I hate people like that. Bullies. The police is full of them."

"Is that why you decided to leave?"

After a pause, Dixon says, "I couldn't do anything. I couldn't help those kids. All of my investigating was basically me educating myself."

The waitress scurries towards them. She serves the two coffees and the cake, her hands shaking with the cold. She doesn't wait to see if they want anything else and jogs back inside.

"How thin is her skin?" Dixon asks, sipping the coffee, which again is far from hot.

"The Germans are very good people," Sara says. "They're not all cold inside."

Dixon takes another sip, drinking up before the coffee gets cold. "I think I've just figured out why they turn the heat up full blast. It's to keep their coffees warm. They just don't seem to understand the concept of hot drink."

"You need to ask for it hot," Sara says, taking a spoonful of cake. "Hmm. This is good. Homemade."

Dixon also spoons some cake into her mouth, with a generous amount of cream. "With quitting the police, I hadn't planned it. The whole thing with the Indian students was a jading experience. The attacks, that these poor kids were targeted, that there was no one who could help them and they just let themselves be bullied. I couldn't protect them. They couldn't even protect themselves."

"What did you do?"

"I took some time off, went home to Narooma. Played a lot of golf with my dad. He was glad I'd quit the force. He never liked it that I was a cop."

"And now you're here," Sara says. "I think that's a very good thing. It all turned out for the best."

"I hope so. But I'm not even thirty and I've already changed careers three times."

"Be happy about that. You've had experiences, and those experiences have shaped you. A lot of German people your age are still studying. I've got PhD students who are almost middle-aged."

"My roommate is in that boat too. Still studying, but not quite middle-aged."

"To be what?"

"A lawyer.

Sara grins.

"Astrid doesn't think it's funny at all. She walks through the world with her head down."

"Be kind to her," Sara says. "And support her. It's always useful to know a lawyer."

Dixon has some more cake. "This is yummy. That's one thing I really like here. The quality of things, especially the food. It's really good, and it's affordable."

"This country has a lot of plus points. You'll learn about them in time."

"How long have you been here?"

"Nearly twenty years," Sara says, and her voice is rather wistful. "I came here as a graduate student not long after the Berlin Wall fell. I was studying in Edinburgh at the time and had just finished my degree. Back then, it looked like Berlin was the place to be, where history was being made. I was right. It was an incredible time."

"I'd like to see Berlin. I'll come visit you. You can show me the city."

"You may visit, but I won't be your tour guide. Berlin's a city you need to discover for yourself."

Dixon is taken aback by this. "Um, okay, well, I'll come and maybe we can share a piece of cake in one of the cafés."

"That's a good idea. And the coffee will be hot, I promise."

They fall into silence again. The cake is almost finished.

"So, Sara?" Dixon doesn't quite know how to start. "How's this going to work?"

"What do you mean?"

"Are you just going to keep an eye on me, make sure I don't get in any trouble?"

"You strike me as a girl who can take care of herself. Finish the cake and we'll take a walk around the lake. I don't want to talk here."

Korner's mobile rings. She looks at the screen, then stands up. She answers the phone as she exits the room.

Dixon eyes Schultze, despising him. "How much longer is this gonna take?"

"We are at the start," he says. "There is still very much to cover."

"Can I ask you something?" She decides to see if she can push him, make him respond. "Where did you learn your English? Because, I'm sorry, but it's just awful. You sound like one of those robotic announcement voices at airports and train stations."

Schultze turns slightly red, but it's difficult to tell if it's from anger or embarrassment. "I learned from the fifth class. I think I speak English very good."

"Believe me. You need help. You sound so ... German. Do they run classes here?"

"We do not have time for learning."

"Just for arresting and interrogating innocent people. I guess that makes up the main part of your work day. Am I right?"

"No," Schultze says, viciously shaking his head, as if trying to shake out whatever violent thoughts he might be having towards Dixon. "We do research. Paper and more paper."

Dixon sits back in her chair, realising she probably won't be able to provoke him. He's a desk jockey, she decides. Probably doesn't even know how to use a gun.

"You are bad teacher," Schultze says.

"Excuse me. Why do you say that?"

"Teacher should help student."

"You're not my student. And your English is getting worse with each sentence."

"Ach, verdammt noch mal," Schultze shouts at the mirror.

"Whoa, and now it's so bad it's turning into German." Satisfied she's pissed him off, she changes her tone. "Hey, Gerd, sorry. Here's a tip for free. You should watch TV. Or movies. Watch in English with English subtitles. It's a great way to learn. That's what I tell my students. Children's television is even better, because the language is simple. You can watch with your kids."

47

"I want not to sound American."

Dixon nods. "I agree with you there. Nothing worse than someone talking in a foreign language with a put-on accent. Ben sounds like such a goose with his British accent. Like he's royalty. Ugh. I told him about it, but he wouldn't listen. I said, 'Just relax and speak how you normally speak.' And he'd say, 'This is how I speak,' all stuck up and proper. What an idiot."

"Your relationship, with Herr Steckdorf, was not well?"

"Wasn't good, you mean? I guess you missed that part, when you went to read up on your colleague. Yeah, bad, awful, beating a dead horse. I think I've been in it for the rent-free apartment for the last few months. Such a great view, overlooking the Elbe and the harbour. That terrace is fantastic. I don't know how many nights I sat out there. Even in winter."

Schultze seems to have lost his bluster. "Please," he says, speaking as if deflating, "say more."

"Ben was on the road a lot, travelling for business. To Toulouse and Seattle, sometimes to China and India. I don't really know what he does exactly, when he's travelling. He never talked about it. Top-secret stuff. But he complained about the travelling a lot. Really, a lot. With that accent, we'd call him a whinging Pom back home. He went on and on about the airports and hotels and cramped planes, waiting in lines, flying economy. I told him to put some pressure on the interior designers to make the cabins bigger. But he said the airlines are to blame. They're the ones jamming in as many seats as will fit. And cutting flights so every plane is packed."

Schultze clears his throat. "Yes. Now, this top-secret stuff."

"I told you. Ben never spoke about it."

"But you had access to it, on his computer."

"He doesn't have one," Dixon says, shrugging. "He has a company notebook, and a tablet I think, but he never brought them home. And if he did, I never saw them. I do know he's not allowed to bring them home. My HR dragons told me that." Leaning close to confide, "One of my classes, with fire-breathing women."

"I am right. You are bad teacher."

"I'm not. I'm just reacting to this stupid situation. What would you do in my position?"

"I would cooperate and answer the questions. I would treat the ... Kommissar with complete respect. If I am innocent, it is over quickly."

"I am innocent," Dixon replies. "But you don't think so. You don't even have any evidence. You have a source, and that's probably someone trying to save his own skin. I have rights, you know. This isn't Saudi Arabia or Iran. This is Germany. I have rights."

"This is a very serious crime."

Dixon cocks her head to one side, showing Schultze her striking profile, that collection of inherited features she knows look very good together: her grandmother's broad forehead and high cheekbones, her mother's small, straight nose and sturdy chin, her father's blue eyes and upward turning mouth, ready to smile, ready to laugh. Even hauled out of bed without a shower, she knows it's a good combination.

She sees Schultze swallow. He's got a very big Adam's apple. There's the weakness, she thinks.

"You're a liar, Gerd," she says. "You haven't called the embassy. You said that you did, but you didn't. That's gonna be bad news for you when this is all over. I haven't been in Germany for very long, but I know that things don't get swept under the rug here without someone taking the fall. Your colleague outranks you, so she's safe. Sounds like her department's more powerful than yours too. National security pretty much trumps everything. You're screwed. Arresting the wrong person, lying to them, falsifying everything. You're a kangaroo in the headlights, Gerd, waiting to be hit by a road train."

"Please answer the question."

"I'll have your head on a platter when this is over," Dixon continues. Then she abruptly changes her tone. "No. Sorry. I take that back. My grandmother taught me never to wish anything bad on someone. Um, I hope you stay in exactly the same position as now, unchanged, all the days the same, and you can do your logic problems on the way to work and wait for your pension day. Your kids go to university. Snow at Christmas. Everyone's happy."

Schultze crosses his arms angrily. "What about the secrets? Herr Steckdorf's computer."

"It wasn't me," Dixon shouts, angry now. Then to the mirror, "Didn't you get that before? I saw no secrets, I looked at no computer. There was no corporate fucking espionage. All right? Hook me up to a polygraph if you want. Give me truth serum. Water-board me. Bolt my chair to the floor and let fatso wail at me. It won't change a thing, because I haven't done anything wrong."

"Miss Grace, please."

She's really shouting now and slapping the table for emphasis: "I demand to call my embassy." Another slap. "Astrid is a paralegal. I demand to call her too. I have the right to legal representation."

She goes to slap the table again, but Schultze rises from his chair and grabs her left wrist. She lets him get a good grip, then pulls her left arm towards her. She gets a fistful of the yellow pullover with her right hand and levers Schultze's weight forward over the edge of the table, bringing him down so he's belly-first on the table, his big feet dangling in the air. She keeps him there with her own bodyweight and gets her right hand around his neck, the fingers gripping the skin on the side and the thumb pressing against his Adam's apple. Schultze struggles and gasps.

"Hilfe," he just manages to shout.

The door opens. Korner stands there, holding a box with both hands. She has a surprised and curious look on her face as she takes in the scene. Her head cocks slightly.

Dixon and Schultze both look at Korner. Nobody moves for a few seconds.

"Is this a bad time?" Korner asks.

Dixon lets go of Schultze's neck and the big man falls back into his chair. He rubs at his throat and gasps. He lets out a few very loud coughs.

"That was a big mistake," he says.

Korner places the box on the table, but doesn't sit down. She grips the sides of the box with her hands.

"Everything all right, Dixon?" she asks.

"He started it. He attacked me. I just defended myself, instinctively."

"She is crazy," Schultze says.

"Be quiet," Korner orders. To Dixon, "We'll pretend it never happened."

"There's a lot of pretending going on in here," Dixon says. "He lied to me about calling the embassy."

"I know. I'm sorry for that. Conservative Germany strikes again. We need to be sure we've got the right person before we start bothering the nice people who stamp Australian student visas." Korner rummages in the box. "We found some things in the apartment. I want to ask you about them."

"Fire away. Planted evidence is about as useful as no evidence. Lawyer please."

"Answer the questions," Schultze shouts.

"You fucking liar," Dixon shouts back. "And you call yourself police. Shame on you."

Like a referee with two boxers, Korner holds up calming hands, one for Schultze and one for Dixon.

"That's enough," she says. "There's no need to shout. Kriminaloberkommissar Schultze, you will restrain yourself and act in a professional manner."

"Now just a moment," Schultze says, rising from the chair.

Korner pushes him back into it, rather roughly. "Maybe you should use your powers of observation and logic while I ask Dixon about some of the items in this box, okay?"

Schultz tries to peer inside, but Korner moves the box away from him, closer to Dixon. She pulls out a pink mobile phone and places it on the table.

"Is this yours?" Korner asks.

"Yes."

Schultze scoffs. "My daughter has a handy like that. She is nine years."

"Last warning," Korner says, pointing at him. "Don't make me dismiss you." She holds the phone in front of Dixon. "I want to know about some of the numbers saved."

"Sure. I've got nothing to hide. Let's make it snappy."

Korner manipulates the screen and shows it to Dixon. "Who is Olga-one?"

Dixon licks her dry lips.

"Ja," Schultze says emphatically. "There is something to hide."

"You know something," Dixon says, "I'm really starting to not like you, and I like everybody." She turns to Korner. "It doesn't matter now, because it's over with Ben. Olga-one is actually Ole. I had a short affair with him during the summer. It ended a couple of weeks ago."

"Ole who?" Korner asks.

"Lessinger. Ole Lessinger. One of my former students, and ... and Ben's boss."

Korner and Schultze exchange a glance.

"It meant nothing," Dixon adds. "The affair. I was glad to end it."

"Yes, but that means you were close to the head of Ben's department. Navigation and guidance systems. And very close to Ben."

"Yeah. I guess that's worth about twenty years in prison, isn't it? Knowing people. Ooooo. Lock her up. She fucks around."

Korner smiles. "This is the department with the leak."

"It's also a department that has hundreds of employees, all of them with access to technology and secrets that I have absolutely no access to. Don't you think it's more likely the spy is someone in the department? Come on, Gerd, it's logic. Surely. It could be Ben or Ole, or any of them. I never got near that department. My classes take place in meeting rooms on the other side of the premises."

"What about Ole?" Korner asks. "Did you talk shop with him?"

"He was a one-to-one student. The department heads can do that. They don't want to sit in classes with their underlings. Ole and I talked sports and ate lunch. He plays golf."

"And so do you?"

"Yes, but I haven't played here much because you need this license thingy."

"A Platzreife."

"Right. Only in Germany do you need a license to play golf. To pass a written and practical test. I played off ten when I was in high school, and I used to hit from the men's tees."

"Ten?" Korner says. "That's impressive."

"Do you play?"

"Not with a handicap of ten."

Dixon tries to smile. "Maybe we can play when this is all over. But I don't have my bag here, and I don't have this platz-thingy."

"We must get back to Ole and the affair," Schultze says.

"Gladly, but there's not much to say. The lessons were over by the time the affair started. And that only lasted a few weeks anyway. A summer fling. Ole told me that the company was very conservative. He couldn't get caught sleeping with one of the English teachers, or a colleague's girlfriend. He'd be ruined."

"Why Olga-one?" Korner asks.

"Come on. So Ben wouldn't find out. Or maybe so obvious that he would find out. Ben's soft, but he's a very jealous type. Didn't like me ever talking with other guys. I think he couldn't imagine me possibly liking anyone more than him. Or even instead of him. I guess I should be glad you arrested me. It got me out of that relationship. Thanks for that. But you can't tell anyone I had an affair with Ole. I don't want to mess up his life."

"Were you in love with him?"

"With Ole? He's more than old enough to be my father. No, not love. But I … admired him."

"Why?"

"Because he's all the things Ben thinks he himself is but isn't."

Korner takes a look inside the dossier. "Are you close with your father? Steven Grace."

"Why do you ask?"

"Well, like you said, Ole was older than you." With a glance at Schultze, "You don't need to be a logic expert to figure out that maybe you were looking for a replacement, because your father's on the other side of the world."

"What a pathetic attempt at psychology," Dixon says. "Ole and dad are way different. And Ole was in shape. He ran the marathon this year. Anyway, I think I got involved with him as a way of ending it with Ben. If only I'd known it would've been easier just to get arrested."

"Ben didn't know about the affair?"

"Nuh. He's too caught up in his own world. For Ben, it's Ben and only Ben." Dixon lets out a loud breath. "Maybe Ben's the spy you want. If not him, then it's definitely an inside job. Don't you see that?"

Schultze frowns and shakes his head.

"Well, I never got close enough to steal anything," Dixon continues. "When I teach there, I'm in meeting rooms miles from the NAG department, and I can't bring anything with me except my books and a pen. No computer, no USB sticks. Nothing."

"NAG?" Schultze asks.

"Navigation and guidance. That's what they call it. Boy, you must look at the answers to solve those logic problems."

"So you do know something."

"Wow, Gerd, the acronym. Lock me away for that."

Korner is still holding the phone and playing with it. "Did you have this with you?"

"My phone? Had to, in case there was a cancellation. Or a room change, which happened a lot. You can get lost over there. The place is huge. But I turned the phone off during my classes."

"Where were the lessons with Ole Lessinger?" Korner asks. "In his office?"

"Nope. Lunch lessons. We met in the cafeteria."

"What did you talk about?"

"I told you," Dixon shouts. "Sports. Golf. Boating."

"Boating? That's new."

"He has a yacht in the Wedel harbour. Well, it's more boat than yacht."

Korner finally sits down. She leans back and crosses her legs. "Is that where you met?"

"Sometimes. When Ben was away on business trips. I think it was only a couple of times. Not exactly the heated, lusty affair you might be thinking it was. We talked a lot. His marriage is a mess. I met his wife at the company's summer festival. She's a demon."

"Why have you been at this festival?" Schultze asks.

Dixon stares at Schultze and shakes her head. "Not the brightest bulb in the interrogation lamp, are you?" Very slowly and patronisingly, "I'm the girlfriend of one of the employees. Benjamin Steckdorf. Would you like me to spell his name? At the festival, WAGs were allowed. Hah. The WAGs of NAG."

"I do not follow."

"Wives and girlfriends," Korner says. "Maybe you should take a break."

"Nein."

"I'm telling you to take a break."

Schultze runs his tongue along the top row of his teeth. With the moustache, the gesture makes him look briefly hideous.

"I will watch from the observation room," he says, standing up.

"Do that."

"Ich hasse Ossi Frauen," he says as he leaves the room.

"I heard that," Korner says. "And I'll be reporting it to your boss."

The door closes, leaving Dixon alone in the room with Korner. Well, sort of alone. Dixon doesn't know how many people are watching from behind the mirror. With Schultze gone, the room feels much more spacious and airy.

"In the male department," Korner says, "this city is going backwards. Maybe it's a late reaction to having a gay mayor for so long. They all start behaving like cavemen again."

"Now there I disagree with you. A lot of the German men I've met, I've found them completely girly and vain. It's like at some point they all became convinced they had to be like David Beckham to get ahead, to get girls to like them."

Korner laughs.

"Really," Dixon continues. "I went to the gym in the winter. The smells coming from the men's changing rooms, you wouldn't believe it. Ben sometimes came with me and he always took twice as long to have a shower and get dressed."

"The metrosexual generation."

"Probably our fault. Or Beckham's. I hate it. Nothing says insecure more than a person who takes ages to get ready."

"Easy for you to say. They pulled you out of bed and you still look fabulous."

Dixon self-consciously plays with her hair, avoiding the mirror. "I look like something a dozen cats dragged in."

"I think you're way out of Ben's league," Korner observes.

"I reckon he might say the opposite. But we got along well enough at the start."

"How did it start?" Korner asks, taking the kind of tone she thinks a friend would take when discussing a relationship. "After meeting at the cricket, did he go after you?"

Dixon lets out a short chuckle. "Slowly. It took ages. Maybe he was trying to bore me into submission. Date after date, with nothing happening. It was like with Astrid's friends. I thought I was being interviewed for a position. There's not a lot of fire in a courtship that comes across as a series of job interviews. So, after we met at the cricket, I kept going, when there were games to watch. Eventually, after a couple of weeks, he asked me to have dinner with him. He made it sound formal and special, and I really dressed up for it, but he took me to this burger joint in the Schanze. It was packed. We had to sit at the bar and shout at each other. Mata Hari, I think it was called."

"Hatari. I know it. There's one around the corner from my apartment in Ottensen."

"The burgers were massive," Dixon goes on. "American style, in a roll the size of Gerd's fist. I could only eat half of it. Ben had this weird pizza-looking thing."

"Flammkuchen."

"Yeah, I think that's it."

"And then?"

"Nothing. He walked me home, even kept his distance from me. Another date a week later. Then another. Finally I was invited up to his apartment and we went from there. Spent a weekend in London too. It felt a bit like we were on some pre-planned schedule. The progress being ticked off on an Excel spreadsheet."

"Was it good?"

Dixon tilts her head towards the mirror. "Shall I go into graphic detail so all the boys in there can whack off?"

"Best not to. The floor's already sticky enough."

This makes Dixon smile. She's starting to like Korner, even though she knows Korner is just trying to win her trust and all of that other stuff from the interrogator's basic handbook. She decides to let her.

"May I call you Babette?" she asks, relaxing into the plastic chair, trying to show that her guard is dropping.

"Of course. Until the Kriminaloberkommissar comes back. I've got to be formal with him. Keep him on the leash. And when I say good, I mean the relationship, not the sex."

"It was fun at the start," Dixon says. "It always is, isn't it? You think you'll never run out of things to learn about the other person, but soon you do. Life takes over and the fire slowly burns out. Now that I talk about it, I think Ben was just after a good trophy wife. As part of his resume. Only family men get ahead at Flussair."

"Did you ever see him at work?"

Dixon shakes her head. "Different schedules. My morning classes started early, and the evening classes finished late."

"Was he jealous of you having lunch with Ole?"

"Not at all. He encouraged it, kept telling me to put in good words for him. And I think he didn't consider Ole to be any competition for Ben the mega-stud."

"Sounds like he really wants to get ahead."

"He won't," Dixon says, letting satisfaction creep into her voice. "He's not leadership material. Ole already said that to me. And I could see it watching Ben play cricket. He wanted to be the leader, to be captain, but he didn't have the necessary qualities to make people follow him."

"I know what you mean."

"Do you? In cricket, being captain is a very important role. It's not like soccer, where the best player gets to wear a fancy armband. It's like on a ship. A captain, in command, with a crew who all look up to you and who are willing to follow you to the end. Ben likes to think he's that kind of person, a leader of men, a taker of responsibility, but he's not even close."

"Sometimes people want things for themselves, but they just can't get them."

"True. My sister, Miranda, she wanted to be a golf pro, but she wasn't good enough. Whenever it got tight, she screwed up. Didn't have the mettle."

"What did she do instead?"

"She became an instructor," Dixon says, missing her sister, hoping that she'll see her soon. "For beginners and kids. She was a model for while, when she was at university. She's beautiful, but unfortunately not quite tall enough."

Korner sits forward and looks into the box. She takes her time, moving items around until finding what she wants. It's a photograph. She places it on the table and turns it so Dixon sees it the right way up.

"Who's this?" Korner asks, pointing. "We checked your other photos. She's not in your family."

"That's Sara. A friend."

"Are you at the cricket?"

"That was taken in Berlin," Dixon says. "On the grass in front of the government building."

Korner takes a closer look. "Ah, the Reichstag. Of course. Who is she?"

"Like I said, a friend." She tries to make it sound like Sara is off limits, but adds, "She's my minder in Germany. Someone my grandmother knows. Laz knows a lot of people and she was worried I might get into trouble here in Germany. She put some feelers out into her network and came up with Sara. She's a professor at the university there. Post-colonial studies."

Korner looks thoughtfully at the smiling Sara in the photograph, here in sunglasses rather than her usual, slightly horn-rimmed spectacles.

"What's her full name?"

"Why do you want to know?"

"She's interesting for us," Korner says flatly.

"Because she's Indian?"

"Have you heard of a company called Nayakall?"

Dixon takes a moment to think. "No."

"It's a big holding company. One of the companies they own is Aerospace India. Plane construction. Started about five years ago, with small aircraft, local stuff." Korner pauses, letting the information sink in. "But, they've taken some pretty big steps forward in the last few years. They're now getting into passenger planes, to supply the airlines in Asia and the Middle East."

"And this means what?"

"We believe Nayakall might be receiving the inside information stolen from Flussair."

"Ah, I get it," Dixon says. "Because Sara's Indian and the company is too, then she must be involved. And me as well, with my Indian grandmother. We all must be in it. Indian mafia. Does this qualify as racial profiling?"

"I just want to get the facts straight."

"Like Gerd and his puzzles, yeah? Figure out what isn't the answer in order to get the answer. Narrow down the possibilities. Well, you've got some work to do. There are hundreds of Indians living in Hamburg. Thousands probably. You'll have to talk with all of them. Arrest them, why not? One of us is bound to be connected to India Spaceshuttles, or whatever they're called."

Annoyed, Korner runs her hands through her hair, tucking it behind her ears. "Just tell me her name."

"You don't know it? How can you know if she's connected if you don't know her name?"

"Dixon, I'm losing patience with this," Korner says, her face suddenly hard. "You're in this room until I say you can leave. Do you understand that? You can shout for lawyers, but you will not get one until I say so. I suggest you start cooperating."

Dixon looks at the photograph, of her and Sara sitting on the Reichstag lawn. They're both sitting cross-legged, like they're meditating, but they're both laughing.

"That was a fun trip. Sara's really funny. You wouldn't expect it, to look at her. But she's funny."

"When was the photo taken?"

"Autumn. Last year. We hadn't seen each other for a while. I'd got settled in Hamburg and didn't really need her help any more. But it was great to catch up."

"Did Ben take the photo?"

"He wasn't there. I went to Berlin on my own."

"Who took it then?"

Dixon raises her eyebrows. "Do you want me to say it was some guy from Nayakall?"

"I just want you to tell me the truth."

"Fine. It was one of Sara's PhD students. That's what she does mainly, supervise PhDs. She travels a lot, supervises for other universities too. A couple in Europe. One in India. She's something of a doyen in post-colonial studies. Very smart."

Korner picks up the photo and waves it a little. "Why do have a print? All of your photos are prints. But everything's digital these days."

"I'm a bit behind," Dixon admits. "I'm not very good with computers. That whole phase has kind of passed me by. I was something of a wild teenager, stuffed up my last two years of school. Didn't get into university, and only got into dental school because of Laz. She knew some people there. That's how I ended up in Melbourne. But dental hygiene wasn't really my thing, so I joined the police. That was great."

"Stop stalling," Korner says, holding up the photograph. "Name."

Dixon decides it's time to play ball. "Saraswati Mittal," she says, as if confessing to a big secret. "Professor Doctor Saraswati Mittal. But you're wasting your time, and mine."

Korner stands up. "I'll be back in a minute."

"Can I have something to eat?" Dixon asks. "I'm starving. Maybe another coffee, or a cup of tea."

"Soon enough. And I want to know who Olga-two is."

"That's another story. Feed me and I'll tell it."

"All right. When I'm back," Korner says, and she leaves the room.

She rides, keeping as far to the right as possible, hitting every drain. The dangerous Elbchaussee is packed with cars. It's a single-lane boulevard, on the hill above the river, and lined with beautiful houses and villas. It would be an enjoyable ride if not for the drivers treating the road like a double-lane highway.

She pedals hard, flying down the hill beside Jenisch Park to Teufelsbrück, then blessedly getting onto the bike path that follows the Elbe. Here, she slows down, cruising and weaving between the people. A few times she has to brake in order to avoid slamming into a zigzagging dog that's not on a leash; or worse, a zigzagging dog that is on a leash, one of those extension leashes, with the owner completely oblivious to the dog's movements. It's difficult to get around these small tangles of mutts, leashes entwined, the owners chatting together and seeming vaguely apologetic. But she does so with a smile on her face, because it's a lovely evening, sunny and warm, with plenty of daylight left, too. She marvels again that these summer days just never seem to end. And she thinks it's good to see so many people out, the post-work crowd bleary-eyed from another day spent indoors. They are gladly unshackled and free to enjoy the evening. They're wrestling with their dogs, drinking beers in the restaurants that line the path, running, walking, cycling, stopping to buy ice cream from a van.

She pedals on, enjoying the ride, slaloming down the path towards the small Blankenese harbour. The tide has gone out, leaving the boats stranded on the riverbed's silty brown sand. She pictures Ole's boat, also stuck, and smiles, glad that they won't go sailing.

She thinks again of how to end it with Ole, how to bring the subject up and let him down easy. There can't be a scene, she knows that, and she thinks Ole knows that too. She's got what she needed from the relationship and there's no point stringing him along anymore. He has a wife. Kids, house, car and boat. And a reputation. He will want to protect all of that.

So she hopes. Better, she thinks, is to get him to end it, to make him understand what he's putting at risk. Then, she could play the heart-broken victim.

But she knows it would be better to take control.

A man on a racing bike whizzes past. He's fully spandexed, his yellow look-at-me jacket glowing.

She's happy with her hybrid, Ben's old bike. It's just a little too big for her, even with the seat as low as it can go. It makes her fully extend her leg when the pedal is at its lowest point, and she has to tilt the bike to get on or off. But it's easy to ride and fast.

Ben is letting her borrow the bike. She sneers thinking about this. He didn't give it to her. He's lending it, and he repeatedly emphasised this after taking delivery of a new mountain bike earlier in the year. But that bike just sits in the apartment, unused, the chain still impeccably clean and never oiled. That bothers her, even if it meant she gets to use this good bike. He spends the money on the bike, but never uses it. Why buy it at all? Ben has a cellar full of stuff like that, toys and whims. And she knows his bedroom in the family house in Blankenese is the same.

She looks up at the houses of the Treppenviertel, the intricate maze wedged onto the hill. Steckdorf Manor is up there somewhere, on the top, with its river views, wooden floors and high ceilings; with all that furniture that looks like it was chosen from a country living magazine. *Fox Hunters Monthly*, or something vile like that. The pastoral and horsy prints hanging on the walls. The antlers. The grand piano that's never been played. All the rooms that don't get used. An army of vases, all full with fresh flowers. And lording over it all is Frau Steckdorf, who doesn't let Dixon call her anything but Frau Steckdorf, the queen in her massive, lifeless hive. Maybe more black widow than queen bee, Dixon thinks. Ready to bed her husband one last time and then devour him.

Just the thought of the house makes her feel ill; simply riding along the river here knowing that the house is so close by. She's only been there once, for Christmas last year, and she never wants to go back.

Anger makes her pedal harder, to put Blankenese behind her.

That Christmas Eve with the Steckdorf family. The enormous villa with the enormous tree that the family stood around while the staff decorated. But Dixon had got involved in the decorating, feeling more kinship with the help than with the Steckdorf snobs.

She hasn't been there since Christmas. Frau Steckdorf clearly didn't approve of her, had been firmly against Dixon moving with Ben into the family's "city dwelling," to use Frau Steckdorf's high-brow

English, and had rather viciously and repeatedly dropped the name of some girl called Ingrid. This former girlfriend of Ben's was still living in the area and "doing very, very well for herself," Frau Steckdorf had said. "Looking better and better every year. Improving with age like a fine wine."

She's starting to sweat with the effort of pedalling. Sweating with anger.

She leaves the exorbitant rents of the Treppenviertel behind and passes a rustic, down-home caravan park that's more her speed. She would have preferred sitting around a campfire here on Christmas Eve, and waking up in a cosy caravan on Christmas morning, rather than in that asylum on the hill. She thinks there's something creepy about the Steckdorf villa, beyond the scary residents. All those empty rooms and long hallways freak her out, but she thinks it goes deeper than that. Something primal. When they had arrived for Christmas dinner, bearing gifts and alcohol, she had stood in front of the villa, gobsmacked by its size and opulence. All she could wonder was: what does this place cost? Four, maybe five million euros? Or more? She was too scared to ask. On the footpath, near the security gate, there was a collection of small brass squares. She was standing on them, and took a step back. Each one had a name, a date and the camp the person had been transported to. She had asked Ben what they were, and he had dismissively said, "Memorials."

The bike path starts to narrow and there are fewer people around. The river is still on the left and there are trees and forest to her right. She suddenly feels that she is outside of the city, away from the traffic, noise and stress, and this is a good feeling. Up ahead, there are twin chimneys, letting out wisps of smoke that trail towards the west. There'll be plenty of light later, but she decides to take the train back. This is enough exercise for one day.

The sun is high and warm. She wonders again why all the locals complain about the weather. She found June and July wonderful, like two months of long weekends. There were cricket matches, barbecues and garden parties, and trips to Sylt, Sankt Peter Ording and Heiligenhafen. She'd taken kite-surfing lessons, run barefoot on the beach, played golf with a crappy set of rental clubs on an expensive pitch and putt course, swum in the North and Baltic Seas. It was never too hot, and when it rained, it made for a refreshing change. And she'd had so much free time. With all her students taking holidays, her lessons had dried up. Work became more an inconvenience she had to schedule her holidays around. The lessons were picking up again now, with school just about to start.

She wants more summer. She doesn't want winter, and she certainly doesn't want to spend Christmas at Steckdorf Manor.

I'm going home for Christmas, she decides. Frau Fuckedoff can sit on her big Christmas tree and rotate, or have her servants rotate her.

The image makes her laugh, and she's happy with her decision. End it with Ole, end it with Ben. Sever all ties and go.

The path comes to an abrupt end. There's only some stairs and a special ramp for pushing bicycles. She manages to get off the bike and starts climbing the stairs. She's leg-weary from the ride, a bit saddle-sore too, but at least she knows she's had some exercise.

At the top of the hill, she has to double back to the main road, riding briefly into the stiff easterly. There's still a bit of riding to do, through the urban sprawl of Wedel. There's traffic again, noise and stress, and she keeps to the bike path, stopping at the red lights like the locals do.

Having only been here a few times, the way is vaguely familiar. She follows the signs to the Wedel Harbour, scooting down a short hill to arrive at the Willkomm Höft, where they play the national anthem for every ship entering or departing the Hamburg harbour.

"The anthem of the ship's country," Ole had once told her. "Not the anthem of Germany."

She skirts the road to get to the west end of the harbour, following a dike where sheep are grazing. There are a few people flying kites, and specks of walkers with their dogs. Along the dike path, she sees quite a few roller-bladers.

At the Sailors Inn, she locks her bike and walks down to the pier.

She's nervous, hating confrontation.

Keep it clean, she thinks to herself. No broken hearts. No running away to Mexico together.

The wood of the pier creaks under her sneakers. The boats are low, some nestled on the sand and slightly tilted. Most of the boats are covered in tarps. She knows from Ole that those boats just sit there all year round.

She sees Ole sitting at the back of his boat with his face to the sun. It's a small, wood-panelled skiff, a hobby boat, more dinghy than boat, and perhaps more useful as a word than a vessel. "Yes, I own a boat," and there would be no need to show pictures. It's still a good, truthful boast. Ole has already swapped his business suit for boating attire, the local uniform of polo shirt, baggy linen shorts and canvas shoes without socks. Sitting there, it looks like he's patiently waiting for the tide to come in so he can take a relaxing twilight sail.

She slows her walk, not wanting to disturb him.

She thinks he looks good, tanned and fit, a decade younger than he is, and comfortable with himself and all that he has. He looks thankful, content. His feet are perched on the big door handle of the cabin. In that cabin, down two narrow steps, there's a pull down single bunk held firm by a pair of chains. When they had once managed to get themselves onto it, she had thought it would break. She won't be doing that again, or bending over the small fold-out table that smells of fish.

She gives the railing a tentative knock. Ole turns, alcohol-free beer in hand.

"Dixie. I thought you weren't coming."

"Permission to come aboard, skipper."

Ole laughs. "You are something. Well, hop on. But we're not going anywhere. I'm due for dinner at twenty-hundred."

"You better start fishing. Catch something to feed the troops."

He laughs again, a little more than necessary. Just laughing because he feels so good.

"Not many women in this world make me smile like you do, Dixie," he says.

She walks the gangway and he helps her onto the boat.

"With a more substantial vessel, Mr Lessinger, you could head out to the Med and start importing new women. There's plenty of them in Libya and Tunisia and Algeria who want out. You could sell them on and make a profit."

His face turns sour. "Arab spring. They're going to overrun us soon."

"Don't talk like that, Ole. You sound like Frau Stinkdorf. I mean, Frau Steckdorf."

"Ben's mother?"

Dixon nods. "She who crawled out of the primordial goo of the rivers of hell."

"Ha-ha. Beer?"

"Alcohol-free? What's the point? Anyway, I can't stay long and neither can you. Ben's flying back tonight."

"Really? That changed." Ole sits back down, but the back of the boat is cramped with the two of them and he doesn't put his feet up on the door handle. He can't.

"He's coming back a day early," she says. "I guess he misses me too much."

"Awww. Liar."

Dixon leans against the cabin and sighs. She's struck by inspiration. "Look, Ole," she begins. "I think he knows. About us. He's been checking my phone and ..."

"You think he knows? What does that mean?"

"I don't know." Shrugging, like none of it's her fault, "I think he suspects something. Not necessarily you, but he thinks I've got someone else."

"Who cares?"

"You do, Ole. Think about it." She paces the back of the boat, taking a half-step and turning. "It's not worth risking. You know how much Ben wants your job."

"He'll never get it," Ole says, taking a long drink and grimacing after, like it is actually alcoholic beer.

"He still wants it, and he'll happily step on you in the process. You don't want to give him any potential ammunition to shoot you with."

"I don't care. You're worth it."

"I am not," Dixon says. "Really, I'm not. And don't start that again. I'm not sailing off into the sunset with you in this thing. We wouldn't even make it to the North Sea. You'd need to tempt me with a yacht ten times the size. Something with a deck I can lie on in a bikini while we island-hop down the coast of Croatia."

Ole grins broadly, and also a little sadly. "A beautiful vision."

"But it's no reality. If Ben finds out about us, and can prove it, you'll lose a lot. You'll lose everything."

"I will gain you."

"No, you won't. I've thought about this a lot the last few days. I'm not going to be that woman."

"What woman?"

"The woman you throw everything away for. Then in six months you make me walk the plank off this boat because you made a mistake. And you blame me for it. I don't want that hanging over my head for the rest of my life."

Ole takes another long drink. He grimaces again, making his

65

round face more lined than usual and the tendons flex at the neck; all of it giving away his age. Dixon can't help but think he looks old when he's sad, a few years from the retirement he doesn't want. He doesn't look anything like the man she cheered for at the Hamburg Marathon back in May. He'd looked younger then, happy, a cap on his balding head, his face bobbing between the bodies of the huge crowd of runners.

The bottle is empty. Ole drops it on the wooden floor of the boat. It rolls to a corner.

"So why even start?" he asks.

"You came after me," Dixon says, not willing to back off. She's come too far now, and it's almost done.

"You were my teacher."

"And I was close to reporting you for harassment when I was your teacher."

"Seems like a long time ago, now." With a sigh, "I never wanted the lessons. I just wanted to spend time with you, get to know you."

"So you faked bad English?"

He nods, proud of himself.

"Sneaky," she says. "You need to be good to be bad."

"You used to wait for me in my office, and then we walked to lunch together. Remember? That was a good time. I guess not for you. You were paid to be there."

"Are you gonna call me a whore? I won't stand for that Ole. I'll punch a hole in your boat and make it sink. Well, it'll sink when the tide comes in."

Ole chuckles, sadly. Dixon hopes to hell that the old man won't cry.

"Everything's a joke to you," he says. "I'm a joke."

"You're not. It's just not gonna work. Not if Ben knows. He will bring you down, Ole. He's been plotting it for months, and this is just what he needs. I think you're smart enough to know what all that means. There's too much at stake."

Stop rambling, she orders herself.

Ole stands up slowly. "I like what I do," he says, weakly and without conviction. "I like my life. I love my children. But I don't love my wife. With or without you, that's going to end, some day. The company is keeping us together."

"So, you do understand what's at stake."

"I could change companies," he suggests.

"At your age?"

His shoulders drop. "That is an awful thing to say."

"Sorry. I didn't mean it like that."

He breathes in and out, his runner's lungs inflating impressively. "But you're right," he concedes. "I'm too old for a new position. And a second divorce? Another wife who takes everything? No thanks. And two children still in high school. If I'm lucky, I might end up living on this boat."

"You know, and don't take this the wrong way, but a lot of people in Australia are retired, or semi-retired. At your, um, age."

"You said that once, in a nice way. It's hard to believe. All those people still able to work and they don't. What do they do with their time?"

"Sit in the sun and worry if their money will last as long as they live."

"I don't want that." He checks his watch, then gives his balding head a disillusioned rub. "I better start."

"You all right?"

"Yes. I'll leave first."

But he doesn't seem to know how to. He looks around the back of the boat, like he's searching for something. He nods a couple of times, taking in his situation, all the things he can't find on this small boat. He gives up and grabs the railing to lift himself out.

"I'm sorry, Ole. I..."

He waves a hand at her and turns his back as he walks down the gangway and onto the pier. That hurts her; that he doesn't look back. Between the trees, she sees him get into his black Audi and drive away. Not once does he look towards her, still standing on the back of the boat and leaning against the cabin door.

She hears water lapping against the side of the boat, the tide coming in.

Behind her, she tries the handle and the door opens. Inside, she sees that Ole has left his suit in a neat, folded pile on the short bench. In his haste to leave, he has also left his leather attaché case.

She checks the pier once more. It's empty. She enters the cabin and flips open the attaché case. There's a notebook inside.

"What?" She turns her head so the wind isn't rushing past her ears. "Speak up, old man."

"I asked what you're gonna hit."

"Not sure, dad," she says, flipping through her irons. "All my distances are screwed up."

"You're just out of practice. It'll all come back." His soft, crinkly smile makes her heart melt. "It's just great to have you back, Dixie."

"A surprise cameo."

"More than that, I hope."

They share a moment, father and daughter. Dixon's trying to calculate how many times they've played golf together, stood on the cliff-side tee of this third hole and debated tactics, discussed life and laughed.

"It's not polite to stare," she says playfully. "You taught me that."

"He-he. Yep. But, I gotta say, you've changed, Dixie."

"Changed? How?"

"Dunno. You look harder. On the inside. I guess you have to be in the police."

"Yeah. Right."

She looks towards the green. It's about a hundred and fifty from the back of the tee to the middle of the green, from the blue markers that Steve always insisted they hit off, even when she and Miranda were kids and they could barely hit further than the ladies' tee.

"Okay, Captain Guru," Dixon says. "Give me some advice."

"He-he. There's no doubt in my mind that you'll hit for the green. In fact, I'm suggesting you should."

The pin is placed way left, making it even harder to the judge the distance. Plus, with the wind howling, once the ball gets up in the air, anything could happen.

So many variables, she thinks, including my lost ability.

The wind is gusting from the north-east. She feels the force of it buffeting her left shoulder. She considers playing a controlled draw, but doesn't think she's able to today. Safer would be to lay it over the cliff and let the wind blow it back. But she doesn't want to be at the mercy of the wind. Of course, if she hits it straight, she knows the wind will grab hold of the ball and she'll end up on the fourth fairway, which is where Miranda's training group is now. All four of them having played for safety – Dixon bets they're all under Misty's instructions – hitting, flubbing and doffing to the right in order to avoid the chasm.

Steve sees her looking at Miranda. "Don't shout," he says. "She'll let us play through at the next tee. She knows what she's doing."

"She better. Otherwise, we'll be out here until it's dark."

They both watch Miranda, who's not playing herself, work with the group. She gives some tips to the next learner about to hit. He takes three very robotic practice swings, finally lines up to hit the ball, stares at it for an eternity, then swings and misses. He goes through the routine again.

"Oh, gawd," Dixon groans. "Was I ever that bad?"

"You used to struggle with this hole. And you really hated making mistakes, especially with putting. You went through a handful of putters before you were ten."

"You kept giving me one for my birthday, and for Christmas. I thought that was the deal. I'd break it and you'd buy me one."

"He-he."

"And you never bought me one that worked."

"One went over this cliff, if I remember rightly."

"Timed to perfection," Dixon says, "a day before my twelfth birthday."

"You're lucky I was so generous."

"Not anymore?"

Steve pulls an iron from his bag. "You don't need my help. Haven't needed it for ages." He coughs once. "I'm gonna hit a lazy eight. You?"

"I don't think I'll make the distance with the driver."

"Just play your normal game. Take a short iron. Punch it low so the wind can't do too much to it. Swing easy."

"Yeah, yeah, yeah."

"You're much stronger now than when you were a teenager," Steve says, looking at her, with not quite the admiration she wants. "More filled out."

"Excellent. I've finally become the tomboy you always wanted."

"That's not what I mean."

Dixon gestures towards the green. "Misty's the one that's filled out.

I'm in shape. All the aikido classes, the training. Pumping iron in the weight room with all the boys. Breaking heads in St Kilda on Friday nights."

Steve uses his tee to dig dirt and grass out of the eight iron's grooves. "I don't wanna hear all that."

"Relax. Most of the time it's all writing tickets and reports."

"You like it?" Steve asks, still digging and cleaning.

"Nuh." She flips through her irons again. She takes the six half way out, then slides it back in. "Okay, a bit. But I certainly don't like wearing those ultra-tight sports bras. Ugh. I can barely breathe in them. At the end of the shift, it's like taking off a corset."

"I thought you looked good in your uniform."

"That's nice of you to say, but I looked like a pre-teen lesbian. That's what they want. They made us wear those fucking bras from the start. We couldn't be policing the streets of Melbourne with our tits hanging out."

"He-he. Good to hear you've got your sense of humour back. I was worried about you. Laz and Misty were too."

"The terrible trio banding together to solve all my problems again, right?" she says sarcastically.

"We're on your side."

"I'm all right. I'll confess, dad. It's been a tough year. Sometimes, it feels really good to break some heads, especially when you cuff some real dickhead who you know has made life miserable for some people. There's a warm fuzzy in that, like arresting the school bully. But pretty soon that same dickhead is back on the street making life miserable for others. And there are just too many people you can't help."

"The students you talked about?"

"Yeah." She pulls an iron from the bag. "So, I think I'll hit a hyperactive five to complement your lazy eight."

Miranda's group is still on the green, putting and missing and walking all over each others' lines. Miranda holds the flag, her body leaning slightly against the wind. Even from this distance, Dixon thinks that her sister's looking a bit on the plump side; a bit more milk bottle than hourglass, though she would never tell her that.

"No doubt about it," Dixon says, "the worse you are at golf, the longer it takes."

"We all gotta start somewhere."

"Okay. Oo-ah hurra, they're off the green. You're up, Gully."

"I don't field there anymore," Steve says as he takes a broken tee from the ground. "Don't have the reflexes. And I'm scared to play in me glasses and have some rocking cut shot hit me in the face."

"Where does that leave you?"

Teeing his ball up, "Out on the boundary. Fine leg and long on. Pretty soon I'll be fielding at left-right-out. But I'm still making runs."

"Batting with your glasses on."

"Yep, and a helmet too, these days. It keeps me sane. Cricket and golf. Since ... and I'm just swinging and getting lucky."

"You lie," Dixon says.

He addresses the ball, takes half a back swing and follows through all the way around, slow and easy. The ball starts left, with good height, heading for the Tasman Sea. But then it slowly drifts with the wind and plonks on the green a couple of metres from the pin.

"See? Still swinging and getting lucky. In my previous life, I must have been a very good boy. Or girl."

"That's bullshit, dad. I saw the board in the clubhouse. You're hitting off twelve."

"Too much time on me hands, I guess."

"It's been three years, dad."

Steve walks a few paces away from the tee, then back again. "I know. I know. Don't start with me, Dixie."

Dixon decides to hit off the grass, without a tee. She drops her ball and takes her stance.

"Now, concentrate on what you're doing," Steve says. "Not on the ball or the shot. Anything else. Let your mind go."

She's heard it before, but it's still comforting to hear her dad say these things. For focus, she thinks of her mother, who she remembers as being more milk bottle than hourglass. She thinks Misty should get herself into shape to stop reminding them of what they've lost.

She swings and makes good contact, but catches the ball a bit fat. How appropriate, she thinks, as the ball sails through the air. Its path is low, and she has a brief flash of worry, that the ball won't make it – a worry that encapsulates her entire childhood – but it clears the chasm and trickles into the front bunker.

"Crap," she says, relieved. "Sand."

"Get up and down in two and you've got yourself a par."

"My father, the constant gardener and mathematical genius."

She slams the five iron angrily into her bag. They grab their buggies and start walking towards the green. The golf shoes pinch at her little toes as she walks. Boot feet, she thinks, flattened out and broad.

She's glad that's over.

"How is the business anyway?" she asks.

"Can't complain," Steve says, the wind blowing his shoulder-length blonde hair all around his face. Not yet fifty, he still has a head full of hair, just starting to fade to white.

"You need a haircut."

He runs a hand through it. "No, thanks."

Dixon guesses he still hasn't cut it since he'd had to shave it all off, three years ago, when he picked up lice in India; that awful journey when he went to bring her mother home and brought back a whole lot of bugs as well.

She sniffs.

"You all right?"

"Yeah." She sniffs again, giving her dad a sad smile.

They walk a bit in silence, then Steve says, "Business is good. I hired a couple of guys. Bernie at the bank, you remember him? His son, Bryce, he was a class below you."

"You're asking the wrong daughter, dad. For me, high school's a blur of stolen cars, failed exams and lost dreams."

"I recall you played some pretty good golf."

She mimics his nasal, grainy voice, "Kept me sane."

"He-he. Anyway, Bernie convinced me to take some bank credit, build up the business. Expand, you know. It's going well. Aussies, we love our gardens."

"You mean we love trying to outdo each other with our gardens."

"That too."

They reach the green.

Dixon takes out her sand-wedge. "I'm jealous, Gully. Of your life and your lie. Can we swap balls?"

"No."

"I guess you always wished I had a pair."

"He-he. Okay, okay," Steve says. "Maybe at the start I would've been happy to have a boy. I had all these visions of afternoons in the cricket nets and going surfing and playing golf."

"You did all that with me."

"Yep, and it was great." Pointing at her, then towards the fourth tee, "You and Misty, you grew up to be tougher and more honest and reliable than any of the blokes around here, than any fellas I ever met."

"Don't get emotional on me, old man," she says. "You're not allowed to turn soft on me in old age. You're supposed to be my rock."

He gestures towards the bunker. "Come on. Spoon it out and tap it in."

She takes the rake into the bunker with her. She places it to the side and takes her stance, digging her feet in.

"Strong wrists, loose arms," Steve says.

"Quiet, please!"

"And don't think."

Again, she focuses on her mother, remembering those awful drives to school; those fifteen minute therapy sessions, one-way therapy, with only her mother speaking. She thinks of all the cages in their backyard, the sickly rabbits and winged birds. All the assorted milk bottles for feeding orphaned animals. Her mother caring more about some motherless joey than about her or Misty.

"Ugh," she grunts.

Her anger makes her tighten her grip on the sand-wedge. She swings and takes a good amount of sand, getting the required lift and not feeling the contact. The sand rains down on the green while the ball lands and dribbles to the hole, stopping a metre short.

"Lovely shot, Dixie," Steve says. "You always had a good short game."

"Yeah," she says, raking the bunker, "once you finally bought me a putter that worked."

Steve is smiling as he lines up his putt. He doesn't bother taking the flag out, or with practice swings. He misses the hole, barely, and taps in for his par using the back of his putter. He gives the flag a yank, pulling out his ball as well.

"That's a penalty," Dixon says, walking onto the green. "Putting with the flag in."

"You can dock me shot a hole if you like."

"I don't want your charity, Gully. The last time I played was ... Easter. When I was here."

Steve holds the flag and steps away from the hole. "How long are you planning to stay?" he asks, trying not to sound lonely. "Till new year?"

"Trying to get rid of me?"

"Not at all. But you just showed up, out of the blue."

"Well said that," Dixon says, lining up her putt. "Out of the blue. Out of uniform."

She takes her stance and lifts the putter, but Steve speaks: "You quit?"

"I was gonna tell you and Misty tonight." She puts the distraction to good use, clearing her mind and holing her putt. "Yes!"

Steve stays where he is, still holding the flag. "Dixie, what the hell does that mean?"

"It means we both made par."

"I'm serious."

Dixon leans her putter against her leg and rearranges her ponytail, undoing the hair band then securing it tighter so the wind doesn't blow her hair loose. It's the same practiced movement she's done several times a day for the last few years, and she almost feels the need to finish the action by putting her police hat on her head.

"Talk, girl," Steve orders. "Explain yourself."

She retrieves her ball from the hole and walks off the green. Steve replaces the flag and follows her.

"I'm well out of it," she says. "I'd had enough. The whole episode with the Indian students. That was the last straw." Placing her putter in her bag and turning to Steve, "In fact, it was the first and last straw. The only straw. I couldn't help them, dad. I couldn't change anything. And not just them. All the other people in Melbourne. I couldn't help them. I'm ticketing some guy for speeding while in the house across the street, some kiddie fiddler's getting his jollies behind closed doors. Or a beast is laying into his wife. And worst of all, nobody on the force cares. Okay, some of them do, but a lot of them are mercenaries. Guerrillas, the soldier and ape kind."

"Maybe you just need to cool off here for a few weeks," Steve suggests.

"That won't change anything. I quit in September."

"What? Why didn't you say something?"

"I told Laz," Dixon says apologetically. "She promised not to talk, and she didn't. Old Lazarus is made of stone."

"But you didn't tell me." Steve slides his putter into his bag, grabs the handle of his buggy and starts walking for the fourth tee.

Dixon hustles to catch up with him.

"Jesus, Dixie," he says harshly. "I thought you had it together."

"I did. I do. It fell apart for a while, but I'm good now."

Steve grunts.

"I'm serious, dad. After those attacks and the protests, I got to know some of the Indian students, did some investigating. These kids have been getting tormented for years, beaten and robbed. They just never reported it. It's like the playground mentality. A city full of bullies, and I couldn't stop any of it. Those students, they're good kids, dad. They just want an education, what they can't get back home. And when they're finished, they want to go back to India and build up their country. I really admire them for that."

Steve stops. "You're not going to India."

"No way," Dixon says, stopping too. "Promise, cross my heart."

"Good."

"But I do want to travel. Get a worldly education, like you did."

"Yeah? And mow lawns?"

"Teach English."

"Hah. What do you know about teaching?"

"I looked into it already," Dixon says. "Had a Skype interview. I'm all set up. Just need to get there."

"Where?"

"Germany. Hamburg. You remember Astrid?"

Steve runs a hand through his hair. "Vaguely."

"High school. The girl with the long blonde hair. Me getting arrested for borrowing a car. Doesn't that ring a bell?"

"You took the blame, to help her out."

"I didn't want her to get deported."

"Didn't she go home anyway?"

Dixon nods. "But the cops were all over me for borrowing the car. See what I mean? There's no justice in the world. Astrid ended up staying with Laz until she went home."

"Nothing happened. The McDougalls are still there. So, what about Astrid?"

"She's living in Hamburg. I'm gonna stay with her, and teach English."

"Just like that?"

"Yep. And I won't need to carry a gun or wear a sports bra."

Steve starts walking again. "Look, Dixie," he says. "You're an adult. You can do whatever you want. Go to Hamburg, teach English, travel around Europe. But just promise me you won't go to India."

Dixon holds up her right hand. "I promise, father."

"He-he," but this time the laughter is sad and empty.

They reach the fourth tee. Miranda and her training group are all squeezed onto the one bench.

"What took you so long?" she asks. "Did Dixie send half a dozen balls to a watery grave?"

He sits in a corner sofa in the open plan room and sips his tea. A few people are scattered around the room: all men, all travelling alone, all reeking of money. Some are in suits, others in thawbs, those long white wrap-around bed sheets, replete with ghutrah and agal. He thinks they look a little bit silly; not exactly the most ideal airport attire, especially if blending in is a priority. Yet, he would be the first to admit that the thawb is very practical in the heat. Having donned one during a recent visit to the Kingdom, he knows this for a fact. He felt ridiculous, but was surprisingly cool and comfortable. He didn't go for the tea towel on the head during that visit, because it reminded him of his mother, who was a dishwasher for the better part of her life. Was, he thinks, smiling. Now she runs a luxury bed & breakfast in Goa, thanks to his investment.

Since he started working for Nayakall, all the Prasads have done well for themselves, have taken big steps forward and risen through society's levels. It makes him feel very good to distribute his wealth amongst his family, but only when they put it to use: start a company or service, or open a B&B like his mother did. When it came to his investments, he had a very clear rule – there was to be no wasting of his money.

There's rather a lot of tapping at keyboards and quiet murmuring into phones, but the lounge is mostly peaceful, the heavy furniture absorbing the sounds. He finds it relaxing to sit here, to sip tea and ponder the lives of the men sitting nearby. What thoughts and ideals do they hold close to their hearts? What place do they long for? What kind of future do they see? He laughs softly to himself. And why are you walking around in a bed sheet?

He knows why, but he also knows the benefit of anonymity, of making yourself part of the furniture so you don't stand out. That's why he wore the thawb in the Kingdom, to blend in. He adapts his clothing and habits to wherever he is. These are the lessons from the road he has learned over several years of criss-crossing the globe; all that time spent waiting and observing. The many hours and days spent alone with his thoughts. Watching people, watching how they interact and do business, and identifying their mistakes and weaknesses.

It's good to sit inside the lounge, to have this space, this respite. On the other side of the entrance, the airport is a seething throng of humanity, populated by almost every nationality the world has to offer: sub-Saharan Africans with few possessions, but with the hollow eyes and future-less stares of people who have escaped something and don't know where they will end up next; tanned Europeans in branded clothing, their hands clutching duty-free bags filled with boxed alcohol and bricks of cigarettes; bum-bag wearing Americans waddling like ducks and fanning themselves with their passports while complaining that no one speaks English; smiling Australians with skin like leather and sunglasses perched on their heads, and all of them in summer clothes; Asians sleeping on spread-out newspaper and hugging their luggage; whorish-looking Russian girls in heels so high it looks like they're walking on stilts; and that colourless, anonymous horde going up and down the mall, or sitting on plastic chairs, staring blankly and bleary-eyed at nothing, killing the time until their connection.

He's glad that's outside and that he's not among them.

He checks his watch. She's fifteen minutes late. That bothers him, though it could be a delay of some kind, so not her fault. But he has a flight to catch, another meeting in another airport lounge in another country. When you have something that people want, he thinks, they should be coming to you, arriving on time or earlier, to show their respect and level of interest. Tardiness is bad for business.

He takes out his tablet, to prepare. Her lateness will cut the presentation short. He decides to get straight to the point, without the usual pampering and small talk. He notices that, using his tablet, he now blends in with the other men in the lounge. The only difference is he doesn't reek of wealth like they do; at least not of inherited wealth. He has earned everything he has. His charcoal suit is tailored, his shirt silk and his tie in a firm Windsor knot. With tablet in hand, it all looks good and right. But he was not born into wealth, and he's aware that all the designer clothes, weighty airport lounge cards and first class tickets won't change that. Inherited wealth has its particular kind of snobbery, and it has an innate ability to recognise it in others. There were times in his life when he struggled and went hungry, when he suffered and toiled and dreamed of bigger things. That's why his shoulders are hunched a little bit forward in his tailored suit, why he

78

always counts his change and why he attempts humility and invisibility in surroundings such as this one. It's also why he doesn't like people who don't keep to scheduled appointments.

His tablet tells him that his eleven o'clock in Dubai is Zamira Omenova, from Kyrgyzstan. Another blind date meeting. He opens the presentation file to have it ready to show the moment she enters. If she enters, he thinks, checking his watch again. He reads the material prepared on Ms Omenova. It's brief. She's non-government, an independent contractor, some kind of consultant for various companies. She's a go-between for exchanges between the companies that want to remain anonymous and the suppliers of the special products those companies want.

There's no picture.

He's dealt with this type before. Fishermen. Or in this case, a fisherwoman, in search of the bait that will help some other company land a big fish. If that's the case, he decides, she won't need much convincing; just first contact, a run-through of the technology available and a handshake. How it actually works won't be her concern. In fact, it would probably all go over her head. She'll be interested in availability and price, but the actual negotiations are the second step and he'll have nothing to do with them. He's here to make contact. In an hour, he'll be flying somewhere else for another such meeting.

This exotic, country-hopping lifestyle is a long way from the dusty cricket nets of Chennai.

He has much to be thankful for, and seldom does a day pass when he's not aware of this.

A small woman passes through the lounge's double doors. She flanked by two bodyguards, both a head and a half taller then she is. Every single man in the room turns to look at her, as if she has invaded their domain. But she walks with purpose, sensible heels clicking.

He stands to greet her. Zamira Omenova is nothing like he expected. She is small, middle-aged and fragile-looking. Her black hair is cut short, in a bowl, but parted to reveal a flat forehead and opening up her round, Mongolian face even more. He had expected some striding six-foot sexpot, a girl raised in a lab who could pilot a helicopter and strangle a man with her legs. A girl who could assemble a sniper rifle blindfolded, speak a dozen languages and wear lingerie with a trench coat.

He blinks a few times. Too many in-flights movies, he thinks.

She comes up to him and stops. "You are Mr Dinesh Prasad?"

"Yes," he says, feeling suddenly protective of this tiny woman from central Asia. "Please, call me Dinesh."

They shake hands. Once her hand is free, she gives a slight wave of dismissal. The two bodyguards drift towards the buffet.

"I apologise," she says, as she sits down. "I was detained. At immigration hall."

Her English is halting and heavily accented. From experience, Dinesh decides to speak slowly.

"It can be very busy here," he says, sitting as well. "Many people coming and going. Where have you come from this morning?"

"I say not," she says, her round face expressionless. She leans back and crosses her legs. The massive armchair seems to envelop her.

"Shall we start then?" Dinesh asks.

"Please. Show."

Glad to be spared small talk, and on the clock now because she was late, Dinesh gets right to it. He sits forward in the sofa and holds the tablet so she can see the screen and he can manipulate it.

"You are familiar with what we do, yes?"

She nods once.

"And you know it's top secret. We don't just give this information to anyone."

"I sign agreement," she says angrily.

"Yes, good. That's standard procedure. Everyone must do that, because we are protective of our products."

"When product work. Show."

Dinesh taps the screen, opening the presentation. The first slide has the heading DRONE NAVIGATION. He flicks to the next slide, which is a picture of a fighter jet in flight. Through the glass, it's clear that there is no pilot.

"We have developed technology for advanced pilot-less flying," Dinesh says softly. "This jet is just an example. The technology can be used for all kinds of aircraft and in lots of different situations. Any weather as well. We first developed it to assist in dangerous rescue missions. In the Himalayas, for example."

"Rescue not interesting. Military yes, frozen mountain climber no."

"Well, it certainly has military applications," Dinesh says, smiling. He jumps ahead to a few slides with other military examples. "As you can see, it's especially good for defence and scouting."

"Yes. Yes. I want."

"Can you be more specific?"

"I want this," she says pointing at the screen. "Where come technology from?"

"Aerospace India. The headquarters are on the outskirts of Chennai."

She grins, showing long, thin teeth. "This I not believe. Fly-by-wire be western technology. India not capable."

Dinesh puts the tablet on the sofa and sits back. "You should do more research before wasting my time with a meeting like this," he says, keeping his voice calm and even, and still talking slowly for her benefit. "Your opinion of India is out of date."

"Yes?"

"Most certainly yes. Aerospace India has been developing this technology over the last five years. Other companies have already successfully used it."

"You disclose this information not."

"Because we are very protective of our technology and we greatly respect the discretion of our clients. They don't want their names in the press and we comply with that."

"But India is backward land."

"Again, your opinion is out of date. There has been a move, spearheaded by my company, to bring educated, high-potential Indians back home. Aerospace India is a good example. Many of our engineers worked at Boeing and Bombardier and other aircraft manufacturers, or were interns. They have brought their expertise and experience to Aerospace India. This cutting-edge technology," with a gesture to the tablet, "has come off our drawing board."

"Is good speech," she says, looking like she's enjoying the exchange, "but Indians building high-tech plane like Kazakhs making supercar."

She follows this comment with a loud, deep-toned laugh, making the men look at her again and scowl in her direction.

"You're welcome to visit the plant," Dinesh says, sneaking a look at his watch. "You and your client, or clients. You could even go to the testing ground to see the technology in action. Better than that, given the right planning, we could have you pilot a drone aircraft."

"I want do that."

"It's child's play. Like a computer game."

She nods a few times, then uses both hands to part her hair away from her forehead. "You sell to all?" she asks.

"Of course not. We have a very limited target group. We are fully aware that, in the wrong hands, this technology can have negative applications. We are focused on saving lives."

"Yes, saving lives," she echoes.

"This is very useful technology, game-changing technology. A dangerous mission can be carried out without putting pilots and crew in harm's way. Imagine a passenger plane being hijacked. Like nine-eleven. The hijackers can be prevented from controlling the plane. This technology had been designed and developed specifically for safety and security purposes."

"Yes, security." She's all smiles as she stands up. "I want."

Dinesh stands up as well. They shake hands.

"I come to India," she says. "Bring money, take tech."

"Excellent."

"We make drone flight together," she declares, like they're planning to fly to the moon.

"That sounds very good, but you won't be dealing directly with me at Aerospace India. I'm just the messenger."

She is disappointed by this.

"Once you're there," Dinesh adds quickly, understanding the importance she places in hierarchy, "you'll be dealing with people from a higher level than me. That I can assure you."

"Very good. Mr Prasad, good day."

She walks towards the exit, beckoning the guards with a flick of her right hand. They put down their half finished plates and slump after her, one on either side.

Dinesh sits back down and pours some tea. It's still warm. The pot has been sitting on a grill with three candles underneath. Another glance at his watch assures him he has a few minutes to collect himself, and to wonder just who Ms Omenova might be fronting for. It's out of his hands now and best not to think about it.

What he chooses to focus on is this: if the deal goes through, his commission will be around five million rupees.

Olga, she thinks, alone in the room and requiring a focus. Poor Olga. Lucky Olga. Olga whose life I fixed.

She stares at the mirror and plays with her hair.

Olga who also had a blonde rinse, but not anymore.

The door opens. Schultze enters, talking on his mobile phone. He hangs up, lowers himself carefully into the chair and flips the blue dossier open.

"Who was that?" Dixon asks.

"Colleague."

"Babette?"

"Who?"

"Kriminal-whatever Korner. The woman who was in here with us? Your boss?"

"She is not my boss," Schultze says, his big index finger moving across the page as he reads.

"Why don't you like her? She seems really nice to me. Professional too."

"It is a long story."

"Does it start in 1961?"

This makes Schultze look up. "So you know something about history."

"Didn't you see the photograph? I took a trip to Berlin. The year got stuck in my head because it's the same year my mum was born."

"Your mother," Schultze says, going back to the dossier.

"I did a bit of a wall tour," Dixon continues, reminiscing brightly, then catching herself and toning it down a little. "It was fascinating. I rented a bike for the day and followed the outline of bricks in the street. You know, the bricks that mark the old borderline?"

"And?"

She crosses her arms and tries to look through the mirror. "I found it hard to believe it had happened. I remember learning about it at school, but I didn't really get it. It didn't sink in until I saw it. The wall. The Berlin Wall."

"You have seen the tourist attraction," Schultze says. "You have seen not the real wall."

83

Dixon looks around the room. "You people seem to like building enclosures. To keep people in, or others out."

"You know nothing of this country."

"Educate me then. Tell me about your country. Tell me all about innocent until proven guilty. Tell me everything about the fair fucking legal system."

"Silence."

"Oh, and what'll you do? Lock me up? You already did that. Wrongly. So, I'm gonna speak my mind. Get it all on the record."

"Enough." Schultze clears his throat loudly. "Your mother. Gaurika Grace."

"Rika. Everyone called her Rika."

"She died in," checking the dossier, "2006. In India. Please, tell me about that."

"No. It's got nothing to do with this and I don't want to talk about it."

"Why not?"

Dixon shakes her head. "You idiot. Why do you think?"

"For me, the connection is clear," Schultze persists. "She was in India. Your contact in Berlin is Indian. Your heritage, your family. You have been spy for an Indian company."

"Brilliant," she says, giving Schultze an ironic slow clap. "Exceptional police work. Case closed. Look out India, because Germany's coming."

"Your mother died in," again looking at the dossier, "Uttarakhand. Where is this place?"

"No idea. I've never been to India. I think that's where Laz came from."

Schultze looks at her, his bushy eyebrows raised.

"That's not in your precious little file? Laz is my grandmother. Yes, she's Indian, but she's lived most of her life in Australia. Mum went to Uttarakhand to chase up her roots." She takes a deep breath and swallows a sob. "Mum had something of a mid-life crisis. She fell apart, had all these stupid ideas of divorcing my dad and running off to India to find herself. A spiritual journey, she said. But we all called it a selfish journey. Rika, like always, doing things just for Rika."

"How did she die?"

"You're brutal, you know that," she says, really hating him. "In India, the spiritual suddenly became very physical. She caught Dengue

84

fever and ... and she died from it. The country's a mess. God. Dengue fever. Like something from the Middle Ages."

She starts to cry and lowers her head, really feeling it this time. What hurts the most is the sense of abandonment, that even when her mother was there, she wasn't. Running away to India was simply the icing on the cake.

"Do you need a Tempo?" Schultze asks.

"A what? You've lost me."

"A Tempo." He reaches into his back pocket and produces a small packet of tissues. He offers her one.

"Thanks."

She takes a tissue and blows her nose, grimacing as she does so because his broad arse has been sitting on the packet all this time.

"Welcome," he says, and Dixon gets from him the feeling that he's very satisfied with the interrogation so far. He's even sneaking looks at the mirror, just to show his confidence and drive home his advantage.

"Can we change the subject?" she asks.

"No."

She sniffs loudly. "I miss her."

While Schultze reads more in the dossier – a copybook pausing technique designed to make her sweat, she assumes – her mother is foremost in her thoughts. She can't decide if she's just lied or not. Does she miss her? she wonders. Come on. Reach deep down inside yourself and find where the honesty is hidden. Yes. No. There's no chance to fix anything, that's what's missing. A chance to turn things around. But then, there were those few moments when mum was all there. And it was the rarity of such moments that made them so telling.

"Miss Grace? Miss Grace?"

"Huh?"

"Did you hear what I said?"

"Sorry, no. Some idiot reminded me that my mum's gone, and she's never coming back. How's your mother, Gerd?"

"I said that we wait now for confirmation from your contact in Berlin. Frau Korner is doing that work."

"I hope she's not going all the way to Berlin to do it. I've already been in here long enough."

"But with that confirmation," Schultze says, voice rising, "you will be in very much trouble."

"Right. Power up the electric chair. Fry me."

"Miss Grace, please, do not shout."

"You're the one shouting."

She wipes her eyes and pulls herself together. After finger-combing her hair a few times, she's got a renewed focus: double-wash and a hundred brush strokes. Eighteen holes of golf, then a swim in the ocean. That's the life.

"When this is over," she says, "I'm getting on the first plane out of here. Today, if I can manage it."

Schultze smiles. "Good."

"Excuse me?"

"There is no chance," he says, looking very pleased with himself, "but if you are free, I hope you leave."

She's stunned. "Wow. Like, big wow. First I'm arrested, then I get deported because I'm not welcome here. I tell you, the colour of this room just turned a deep shade of red. Time to trim that moustache a little, Gerd?"

"That is not what I mean."

"What then? No foreigners allowed?" she asks, grateful that this ridiculous excuse for a detective is giving her something to focus on.

"No," with an uncomfortable glance at the mirror, "I did not say that."

"It certainly sounded that way. You know, I found all that Germany-the-fatherland crap during the World Cup last year pretty terrifying. Those crowds on Heiligengeistfeld, waving flags and singing the anthem at the top of their lungs, and drinking copious amounts of beer. It all could've turned ugly, given the right motivation."

"Why can we not be proud of who we are?"

"That depends. Are you gonna start shipping foreigners out? Starting with me?"

Schultze sits forward. "No. You understand not correct. What I want to say is ... that people ... they shall appreciate to live here. We welcome everyone, but nobody ever thank us. We are the strongest economy in Europe. We always must give money to other countries, take in Polish, Czech and all other workers from east Europe. Everyone takes advantage of Germany. But we say nothing, because if we say something, all these people say bad things about us."

"You've given me plenty of bad things to say about you."

"Germany pays for Europe," Schultze says, now firmly into his rant. "Always pay. We pay for East Germany too. And we do not have anything. No gold, no oil, no land. We do not rape our land like you do. Yes, I know about the mining in Australia. I see documentary. You have resource, but all we have is people. We educate our people."

"Not the police," Dixon says snidely.

But Schultze ignores her. "We make things," he continues, louder than before. "Technology and industry. We work hard. We do not sit in the sun and drink ouzo like the Greeks, and complain and complain, say Germany, give us more money. No. We work. When the economy is down, we work harder."

"Me too," Dixon says. "I work hard. I don't drink ouzo, and the sun never shines here."

Schultze calms himself a little. "You are a criminal. You will go to prison."

"Why are you so convinced about that? You don't have a shred of evidence."

"I have ... Aussage," Schultze declares. "I do not know the English word. A person, she says it is you."

"A testimony. A statement. That's your evidence? That's one person's word against another. That won't hold up in court."

"The testimony is worth much."

"Of course it is, and me being a second-generation Indian, with a friend in Berlin who's Indian, and teaching English at Flussair." She knocks the table with her fist. "Case closed. She gets life."

"Please, be calm. And do not use the company's name."

"Who made this statement anyway?" Dixon asks.

"Frau Steckdorf."

She laughs incredulously. "Well, that just brilliant. Hole in one. I wouldn't believe a word she says if I were you. The woman is pure evil."

Schultze bristles. "The Steckdorfs are one of the most prominent families in Hamburg. Herr Steckdorf is the third generation of his family to serve in the Hamburg Senate."

"Ah," nodding, "that's why you believe them. They're big and powerful. Because the rich and famous never tell lies. Which makes me wonder if you have political aspirations. Am I guessing right? Do you need to kiss the right arses? You strike me as an arse kisser. A bootlick, a lapdog. I saw your type all the time in the force, grovelling to get ahead."

"Frau Steckdorf says ..."

"My God, that woman's a piece of work," Dixon says with vigour. "The nerve of her. Well, here's my testimony. Frau Steckdorf pays her staff cash. No contract, no benefits or insurances. It's all under the table. And she pays them peanuts and treats them like slaves." She takes a seething breath. "And that villa ..."

"What about it?"

"I would really, really like to know how they got it. The circumstances and what they paid, if they paid anything."

"Now, you have lost me."

"Come on," Dixon says encouragingly, "you're all up into research and puzzles. Solve this one. Dig into the records on Steckdorf Manor. Ugh. It's probably untraceable, all the loose ends neatly tied. But check out the staff for yourself. What do you call it? Black work?"

"Schwarzarbeit."

"Right. That's a crime, isn't it? Shouldn't your riot squad be breaking down her door?"

"Frau Steckdorf has been very cooperative. She says that you used the computer of Benjamin at Christmas. She saw you."

Dixon throws up her hands. "Oh, please. Is this for real? See that girl using a computer, she's a spy, has to be. Because only spies know how to use computers. That fucking woman. She is going down when I get out of here." Another seething breath, this time to calm herself. "Look, I was sending photos home to my family. White Christmas and all that. A real tree with candles on it, decorated by the Steckdorf slaves. And like I already told your boss, I'm not that good with computers. I asked Ben to help me with it. And it was just a tablet. I don't think there was anything important on it except a few thousands photos of Ben." Leaning forward to disclose a secret, "He's pretty vain."

"Yes, but, we still have this ... how do you call it?"

"Statement."

Schultze nods. "We have the statement from Frau Steckdorf. With her sign."

"Her signature."

"Correct."

"What a good citizen she is. But how did she find out?"

"It is irrelevant."

"Maybe she's got someone on the inside. Or you questioned the Steckdorfs for background information, and the beast of the house was only too eager to come forward and make a damning statement. She probably went straight to Ingrid afterwards, to tell her the wonderful news that Ben is single again." She sighs angrily. "I'm so glad I'm out of the family. But, when I'm out of here, I'll be paying Frau Stinkdorf a visit."

"Frau Steckdorf. That is not a good idea," Schultze says. "You have no chance anyway."

Dixon slaps the table with both hands and stands up. "This is all rubbish," she shouts at the mirror. "You've got nothing. I want a lawyer. I want to call my embassy."

"Miss Grace."

"I want to be out of here in the next ten minutes. I want to be on the next flight back to Australia."

"Miss Grace."

"Shut it, Uncle Fritz," Dixon says, turning to him. "You wanna try attacking me again? Come on. I'll have ya."

But Schultze remains slouched in the chair.

"This has gone on long enough." Pacing the room as she shouts, "I'm willing to cooperate, but I have my limits. I'm not staying here because of Frau Fuckedoff's statement. I'm also an Australian national and I don't deserve to be treated this way."

"Miss Grace. Ole Lessinger is dead."

She stops pacing. "What? He's what?"

"He was found this morning. On his boat. In the cabin. Dead."

"You're kidding me?" She falls into the chair, shocked, all her energy and bravado gone.

"This is no joke," Schultze says. "We found your fingerprints on the boat. On the door handle to the cabin."

"Yeah. Sure. I was there a few weeks ago."

"Where were you last night between ten and twelve?"

She stares at him, wanting to pound his big melon head into the table. She laughs softly, bitterly.

"Answer the question," Schultze orders.

"So that's on me as well. Did Frau Steckdorf give a statement? Is she your star witness?"

"Is not necessary." Schultze checks the dossier. "You have black belt in aikido."

"I took you down, didn't I? I'd do it again, gladly."

"Lessinger was ... erwürgt," Schultze says, putting his big hands to his own throat. "Eh, eh, no air."

"Strangled. He was strangled?" Dixon asks. "Then my fingerprints must be all over his neck, surely."

"We believe the murder had hand shoes."

Dixon shakes her head. "You really need lessons. The murderer wore gloves."

"Yes," Schultze says, embarrassed and offended. "We believe the murderer wore gloves."

"And I happen to own a pair of gloves. It must've been me. Or is there some kind of Indian connection to this too? Were the gloves made in India?"

"Please, answer the question." Schultze is starting to look exasperated. His forehead is just slightly shiny and damp. "Where were you last night?"

"At home."

"Witness?"

"I was alone. In bed."

"Where was Benjamin Steckdorf?"

Dixon shrugs. "At work, I think. Maybe fucking Ingrid. Or strangling Ole. Or plotting my demise with the bitch of Blankenese."

"Benjamin Steckdorf says he was at work."

"So why did you ask me?"

"He has alibi," Schultze says. "But you, no alibi. And your prints on door handle. Do you not see how bad it is for you? There is nobody else it can be."

"It's logic, isn't it?"

Schultze smiles. "Yes. It is why you cannot leave. This are very serious crimes. Economic spying ..."

"Corporate espionage. At the very least get it right. For the record."

"Corporate espionage and murder," Schultze says emphatically.

"Great. Fantastic." She raises her right hand, as if taking an oath. "I swear I didn't do it. But what's the point? You don't believe me."

"I do not."

She stretches and yawns, refusing to be sad for Ole. "And now?"

"Now you confess."

"Can't we have some more police brutality first? You can beat my confession out of me."

"I will not."

She points at the floor. "You can always bolt me down, so I can't fight back. Would you like to do that?"

Schultze turns slightly red. "Certainly not."

"Do you like the rough stuff, Gerd? I've had that experience before. The big bullies like to be slapped around."

"Why killed you Ole?" Schultze bursts out, flustered.

"I didn't kill him. What's my motive? What could possibly be my motive?"

"You wanted to cover yourself. You knew he was on the boat. You arranged to meet him there."

"Okay. Witnesses? There are always people in the Sailors Inn. The barflies there would've seen something."

"We are questioning people."

"Good luck with that," Dixon says. "But I haven't spoken to Ole for weeks. Not since I ended it in August."

"How did he react?"

Dixon stares at the table. She counts the dirty rings. Fourteen.

"Miss Grace?"

"He wasn't that broken up about it," she says. "He knew what was on the line. He didn't want to risk anything. Ole's not a risk-taker. Well, he wasn't. God. I can't believe he's dead. Who'd want to kill him? Was it maybe a robbery gone wrong? Anything stolen?"

"We are still investigating."

"Why tell me this now? Did you know all along?" Dixon thinks she might cry again. "That was the call. When you came in."

"Yes," Schultze says. "We confirmed the match of your fingerprints."

"Ole's whole family left prints on the boat. Maybe it was one of them. A jealous wife," she suggests, "or something."

Schultze closes the dossier and clasps his hands together. "It is all very clear to me. You started the relationship with Herr Lessinger in order to get the information. Then, once you had it, you killed him to cover yourself."

"I thought I got the information from Ben's tablet at Christmas?"

"That too."

"Fantastic theory. But I'm just an English teacher."

"And a former police officer with a black belt in aikido."

"Doesn't that work in my favour?" Dixon asks. "I'm on your side. I was in the force. And check my record. I never hurt anybody. I never even fired my gun. That was one of the reasons I quit. I couldn't hurt people, not even the criminals who really deserved it."

"You had no problem hurting me."

"That was self-defence. You attacked me."

"You murdered Herr Lessinger."

"I did not!" Dixon shouts, and she starts to cry.

The door opens. Korner enters.

"Schultze, you didn't hurt her, I hope," she says.

"I did not touch her," Schultze says, holding up his meaty hands.

Korner sits down. "Good." Facing Dixon, and leaning forward with her elbows on her knees, "I guess you know about Ole Lessinger. The good detective here playing the ace with his first card."

Schultze grunts angrily.

"Dixon?" Korner asks with genuine concern. "Are you all right?"

Nodding and wiping away the tears, she says, "It's all too much."

"I know. I know."

"Can I use the bathroom, please?"

"Of course. Schultze? Will you do the honours?"

"Nein."

"Then get someone," Korner orders.

Schultze gestures towards the mirror. After a few seconds, the door opens and a woman in a black cap walks in. Dixon stands and follows her out of the room.

They get off the bus at the Whale Motor Inn. As the bus pulls away, the boys sitting on the back seat bang against the rear window and blow fish-mouths to get their attention.

"Ugh," Dixon grunts. "So sophisticated, aren't they?"

"Like in kindergarten," Astrid says.

"It's your fault. They're goin berko because of you."

"Berko?"

"Crazy. Insane. Off ya rocker."

"Oh," Astrid says. "The slang here is really weird."

"And so are the people. What you're witnessing here in Narooma is de-evolution. The boys and men are evolving backwards. In a few more years, they'll be swinging from the trees again." She points down Bowen Street. "This's the way."

Their heavy school backpacks bounce on their shoulders as they walk; all those new books and reams of printouts. On the street, the locals greet each other and stop to converse while the tourists wander aimlessly, bored, with nothing to do and the caravan park too cramped for relaxing.

"Where are we going?" Astrid asks.

"You'll see."

"Is this the café you talked about?"

"How do you know that?"

"You told me this morning."

Dixon stops walking. "I did? Yeah, I guess I did. You really listen. I better be more careful what I say."

"It's because of the language."

"All that ocker slang?" Dixon starts walking again. "Strine, that is. Like this. The rhine in spine fawls minely on the pline."

Astrid laughs.

"Must be bloody hard for you," Dixon says. "With the language and all."

"It is. I must concentrate so hard. And then I'm really tired at night."

"At least you'll ace your German class. Ace Astrid. That's a good nickname for you. From now on, you are Ace."

93

"I'm not taking German," Astrid says, looking not as pleased with the nickname as Dixon.

"Wunderbar. Du kannst mich helfen."

"Du kannst mir helfen."

"Mir. Right. See? You're already helping. I need you, Ace."

Dixon opens the gate and leads the way down the path.

"Is this it?" Astrid asks.

"Yep."

"But this looks like a house. There's not even a sign out the front."

"You're right," Dixon says, her voice sinister and conniving. "It's a trap. I'm luring you to your death. You'll be kept here to do all of my homework for the whole year while I play golf after school instead. Bwu-ha-ha."

Astrid stops just short of the steps.

"I'm kidding, Ace. You're totally safe here. It's a secret lair. A sanctuary. The only place in the whole town, in the whole freaking region, where sanity prevails and the people are super nice to each other. Come on."

Astrid takes the steps slowly.

"Laz bought the house ages ago," Dixon continues. "Turned the living room and kitchen into a café. She made the master bedroom a day-care centre. And there are a few rooms for people to stay in. Bunk beds. For women in trouble, that sort of thing. A refuge, a hideout." She points across the street. "And so conveniently located not far from Narooma's cop shop."

"Cop shop? Like for photocopying?"

Dixon laughs. "Good one. Nah, it's the police station."

"Oh."

"Come on," Dixon says, swinging the fly-screen open. "Laz makes great muffins."

The main door is already open, to let in the afternoon breeze. Inside, in the short hallway, there's the usual collection of prams, half a dozen of them, parked side by side, like cars. There's also a neat line up of shoes, placed under or next to the wearer's pram.

Dixon kicks her sneakers off. "House rules. No shoes indoors."

Astrid complies, slipping her backpack off, then bending down to untie her laces. Dixon sees that Astrid has rather big feet, with those red anklet socks making her look like a clown in training. Or the daughter of a clown.

Dixon laughs to herself.

"What's so funny?" Astrid asks.

"Nothing. I like your socks. Revolutionary red. Very cool."

Astrid holds her shoes with fingers hooked under the heels. "Do I have to hang them up?"

"They smell that bad?"

"To keep the spiders out. My host family keeps ... telling me to do this."

"Leave em," Dixon says. "No spiders in here. Laz hates them. She gets the house sprayed every couple of months, to protect the kids as well."

"Okay." Astrid places her shoes next to her backpack, neatly.

A chorus of laughter comes from the living room.

"Seven hens a-cackling," Dixon sings, rolling her eyes.

"What?"

"Let's hope one of them doesn't laugh so hard she lays an egg."

Dixon leads the way in. All the women present turn to look, their laughter dying down. There are six of them, gathered around a table littered with empty coffee cups and glasses. A couple of women have indulged in cake or muffins, with the empty plates still on the table. On the floor, there is a large rug with three infants in similar poses; slight variations of rolling on their backs with their feet and hands in the air.

"Hi," Dixon says, attempting to greet everyone at once. "S'up, Laz?"

Dixon's grandmother is leaning next to the counter, looking relaxed and tired. Her smooth, brown hair is plaited into two long, rather girlish pigtails. She's wearing a white blouse over a purple dress, and her feet are bare. She has both arms crossed in front of her and could easily pass for Dixon's mother.

"Looks like you made it through the first day," she says.

"Yep. Only a couple hundred to go," Dixon replies. "Whoopee."

"Learn anything good?"

"Just more laws of the jungle." Raising her hands in the air, "All hail the alpha male."

The women laugh.

"Still keeping the status quo," one says.

"Men on top," Laz quips, and the women laugh some more.

As Astrid sits down to play with the babies, Dixon moves behind the counter and helps herself. She puts a chocolate muffin on one plate and a blueberry muffin on another.

"You lousy thief," Laz says.

"Nuh-uh, Lazzle Dazzle," Dixon says. "This is women's liberation. I'm a woman and I'm liberating these muffins from oppression."

Laz shakes her head, but she's smiling. "Taught too well."

"Your fault."

"You can have one each. Then you can go out the back and do your homework on the veranda."

Dixon shrugs, holding a plate in each hand. "It's the first day of school. We don't have any homework."

"Aren't you going to introduce your friend?" Laz asks, looking down at Astrid, who's more interested in cooing and tickling the babies.

"That's Astrid," Dixon says. "From Germany. We met this morning. I've recruited her as my German tutor."

"Hi," Astrid says, waving from the rug. The three babies are now swarming around her, loving the attention, perhaps starved of it.

"Very nice to meet you, Astrid," Laz says, bowing her head a little.

"She's from Lübeck," Dixon says. "On exchange for a year. Cool, huh? She's staying with a host family."

"Which family?" Laz asks.

"The McDougalls," Astrid says, gently pushing the infants away so she can stand up. One baby begins to cry. "They have a house down near the marina. On Riverside Drive."

The women tut and harrumph. Glances are exchanged and two women put their heads together to whisper. The mother of the crying baby reaches down and scoops the child up.

"You're always welcome here," Laz says, and her voice has the firm sound of a declaration, something that could be written in stone.

"Okay."

"Anytime you're feeling lonely or maybe a bit unsafe, you can come here."

Astrid takes a few steps backwards off the rug. "Uh, thanks."

"The café shuts down in the evenings," Dixon says, sidling up next to Astrid, plates in hand. "But Laz is always here. Aren't you, Laz?"

She nods. "There's a bell at the front door. You can come in the middle of the night if you're in trouble or need some support. I'm here, or someone will be here who can help."

Astrid looks a bit confused, somewhat confronted. She looks like she wants to speak, but just nods.

"Come on, Ace," Dixon says. "Let's do our homework on the veranda, like good girls."

Astrid retrieves her backpack.

"You won't need that." Dixon gestures with her head towards the back of the house. "The veranda's really nice. We can have a smoke."

"Dixie, no smoking," Laz shouts. "You know the rules. I put an alarm up."

"Crap," Dixon says to Astrid. "She thinks of everything."

"I don't smoke."

"Me neither. I just say it to rile her up."

They walk down the hallway, passing a few closed doors and a few open ones. Someone is singing in the shower. One door has a collection of colourful pictures on it. There's a lot of noise coming from behind that door.

"The day-care centre," Dixon explains. "Laz set it up for me and Misty so my mum could continue working. She's a vet."

"Yes, you said that already."

"Wow. You really do listen. Anyhoo, all the other women in town wanted to use it too, so they could work and get a break from their screaming brats."

"Mrs McDougall doesn't work," Astrid says softly. "She's always at home. She doesn't even go outside."

On the veranda, Dixon puts the plates on the plastic table.

"Is it all right there?" she asks, falling into a plastic chair.

Astrid nods and sits down as well. She takes in the garden. "This is beautiful."

Between the lush plants and tall trees, a few women are spread out, working, some on hands and knees.

"It gets a lot of love," Dixon says. "Laz lets women stay here for free under the condition they work, in the garden or in the house. She always recommends the garden first. She says it's good for the soul, especially if you're suffering. To plant something and help it grow."

Astrid watches the women work, her eyes moving from one to the other, but stopping at a woman who's lovingly trimming a rose bush.

"Gardening helps you take your mind off the bad stuff," Dixon continues. "My dad helps out sometimes, with equipment and plants and what not. He's a landscape gardener, but he's not allowed to set foot in this garden. He consults from afar."

"How come?"

"The whole property is man-free, except the day-care centre. Baby boys are allowed."

"Why are there no men?"

"Laz wanted it that way. House rules. I'm down with it. Which muffin do you want?"

Astrid selects blueberry and uses her thumb and forefinger to pull off a morsel from the top. "Hmm. Lecker."

"I told you. The best muffins in town. Maybe in the world, but I'm not worldly enough yet to compare." Sighing, "One day."

"Mrs McDougall is a terrible cook."

"Yeah? Come here and eat. And that muffin's sugar-free. Everything Laz makes is sugar-free."

"Can I ask you something?"

"Sure."

"How old is she?"

"Laz? Fifty," tilting her head, chewing and thinking, "something. Two or three. I remember her fiftieth birthday party. A couple of years ago."

"She looks so young." Astrid looks at the woman trimming the rose bush. "Is she, you know, Aboriginal?"

"No. Hah. She's Indian." Dixon lowers her voice. "The woman you're staring at, she's Aboriginal. Half, I think. Maybe a quarter. You should probably stop staring."

Astrid catches herself, and turns in her chair. "Sorry. She's the first Aboriginal I saw."

"Thought the place would be full of them, eh?" Dixon says. "Probably was, two or so hundred years ago. Don't go there."

"Okay. Is Laz married? She doesn't have a bindi."

Through a mouthful of muffin, Dixon says, "A wha?"

"A bindi." Astrid puts a finger between her eyebrows. "The little red dot Indian women have. I learned about it at school."

"Oh, dunno. She never had one. She was married. Terrible story."

Astrid pulls her knees under her chin, the heels of her sizeable feet on the edge of the plastic chair. She looks at Dixon, wanting her to continue.

"We should be talking about you," Dixon says. "The exotic blonde bombshell from the other side of the world who got the whole school talking today."

"My life's not that interesting."

"Please. You're like a Bond girl in waiting."

"Tell me about Laz."

"You really want to know?" Dixon asks.

Astrid nods.

"Okay. Yeah, so, Laz came here in the sixties, right? My mum was already born." Dixon pauses briefly, looking at the garden. "I don't know the full story, but I know that Laz was married twice. She had my mum when she was fifteen."

"Oh my God."

"Yeah. Can you imagine that? Me and you, already married to some joker, with a kid. That's how it is in India. Arranged marriages and all that. So Laz told me."

"Is Laz an Indian word for grandmother?" Astrid asks. She nibbles at some more muffin, delicately pulling the paper away.

"It's her name. Laranya. Everyone calls her Laz. We always did. Never called her gran or nana or something like that. I sometimes call her Lazarus, you know, just to piss her off. But she likes it now. Craps on about being raised from the dead."

"The Book of Johannes."

"Astrid says what now?"

"Um, the Book of John. I had Bible studies at school. That was the idea of my parents."

"Uncool," Dixon says. "Forced to learn fairytales." She takes a mouthful of muffin and talks through it uncouthly: "So, Laz got married when she was, like, twelve. Her parents gave her away, which I gotta say is definitely a whole lot worse than your parents making you do Bible studies. She was promised to some family, to some guy she didn't even know. Like it was a business deal."

"Where is he?" Astrid asks. "No men are allowed here."

Dixon shrugs. "Freak knows. In India, I guess. Somewhere. If he's still alive. The marriage didn't work out. Laz told me her new family rejected her, sent her back, like some faulty product they'd ordered in the post. 'A bartered cow that gave poisoned milk,' to quote the great Lazarus."

"That's awful."

"Sure is, and the shafted family wanted a refund. It's bad news in India when a wife's rejected. Bad for everyone involved, but it was especially bad for Laz. I can see it, though. I can see the whole thing. There's no way Laz, even at the age of twelve, would let herself be some family's slave. She's too independent. Too strong."

Her muffin finished, Astrid rests her chin on her knees. "It's amazing to think things like that happen in the world," she says. "I have a friend in Lübeck. She's Turkish. She's scared she will be forced to marry. And her life has so many limits."

"From your point of view," Dixon says, "and mine. She'd be welcome here. She could plant something in the garden."

"Maybe. Finish the story."

"Woah. Very direct. Yes, ma'am. Where was I?"

"India. The marriage that went wrong."

Dixon shakes her head. "Ace, you are simply the world's greatest listener. Possibly Narooma's one and only listener." She chuckles a couple of times. "So Laz was sent home, and this brought mega shame on her family. She was pregnant too. With my mum. She lived in the doghouse for a while. Her family had to get rid of her, to restore their honour or something, because there was still a bunch of other daughters to marry off. She was given to someone in the family. A second or third cousin. He was a doctor and they came to Australia. Lived in Canberra."

"What a story," Astrid says. "What a life."

"Laz's amazing."

"Where is he now?"

"He died. Before I was born. Heart attack. Another unhealthy doctor." She turns to Astrid. "Why is that, Ace? You know, a dentist has bad teeth, a doctor smokes and drinks. A vet can talk to animals but not to people. But he did have money stashed away and Laz got all of it. She moved here, bought this house and turned it into a café."

"Wow."

"Yeah, she gets this incredible tale, this amazing life, and all I get is boring old Narooma. Take you, Ace. You're from the other side of the planet. And now you're here. You've already done something amazing. But not me. Ugh. I want so much more than this little coastal village."

"But it's beautiful here," Astrid exclaims. "It's paradise."

"Yeah," Dixon concedes, "but it's dull. Okay. The people in this house are pretty good. The golf course rocks. Love the beach. But I hate school. Hate it so much. I can't believe I've got two more years to go."

"Do you want to go to university?"

"Dunno. You?"

Astrid nods. "I want to be a lawyer."

"You're too pretty for that. None of the judges will take you seriously, unless you're in a beauty contest."

"I'm not pretty," Astrid says, her pale skin blushing.

"You were definitely the hot topic at school today. But that could've been just because you're fresh meat. Someone they've never seen before."

"Dixie, you are the only person who talked to me. Thanks for that. Everyone else was rude."

Dixon looks a little guilty. "My fault, I guess. The black-listed bad girl. None of the boys talk to me either. They're intimidated. And they also know about this place and my direct link to it. Although, that doesn't stop them from pawing all over Misty."

"She's really pretty," Astrid says.

"Yeah. Don't you just hate her?"

Astrid looks around the garden. She seems to relax a bit more into the chair, now resting her cheek on her knees and facing Dixon.

"Why is this wonderful place bad?" she asks.

"The café?" Dixon snorts. "You'll find out eventually. This house, and Laz, not at the top of the Narooma popularity tree. Especially among the male species."

They both turn to the garden. The women have moved around a bit. Two have stopped to talk. One of them is pregnant and she doesn't look to be much older than Dixon and Astrid.

"You homesick?" Dixon asks, finishing her muffin.

"A little." Astrid is thoughtful for a moment. "I didn't expect it to be so different here."

"It's too boring. Too quiet. Where's the life? Where's the variation?"

"It is quiet," Astrid says, nodding. "I thought Lübeck was sleepy."

"When you're back, I'll come and visit you."

"Promise?"

"Promise," Dixon says. "Wherever you are in Germany, one day I'll come and sleep on your sofa."

Astrid holds out her hand. They shake.

"But maybe I'll wait until you're a high-powered lawyer," Dixon says, "living in some huge house. Then I can have my own room."

"You can stay as long as you want. I want to study in Hamburg."

"Thanks, Ace. Hamburg, huh? That sounds sufficiently exotic."

"It's a fantastic city. The Beatles started there."

"Oh yeah? Done." Dixon stands up. "You want another muffin?"

Astrid nods. "And something to drink, please?"

"I'll make some tea. Laz has fantastic herbal tea, all grown right here."

Dixon grabs the plates and heads into the house, leaving Astrid staring at the garden.

The hallways are empty, all the doors closed. The university is veiled in a ghostly pallor this Saturday night, the lights off, the chairs up on desks, the students nowhere to be seen.

She finds the workshop. There's a slither of light coming from underneath the door. She knocks, then enters. All five students look at her. They are studying together in a tight group, the table covered with open books.

"Hi," she says with a friendly wave. "I don't want to interrupt. I'm just looking for Musheer."

"Musheer who?" one asks.

"I don't have his last name." She checks the piece of paper in her hand. "Musheer P."

The other four boys go back to studying, but the one who asked the question keeps looking at her. His eyes are hard. He's a little older and seems to be their leader of sorts.

"Why do you want Musheer?" he asks.

"I just want to talk to him," she says, taking a few short steps inside. "About the attack."

"What attack?"

"You know what I mean," her voice harder now.

"Who are you? KKK?"

The boys snigger with laughter.

"My name is Dixon Grace. Constable Grace, of the Melbourne Police."

He sneers at this. "Don't the police usually wear uniforms?"

"I'm not working today. I'm doing ... I'm looking into the attack. I want to know why this happened and to find out who did it."

"Good luck."

"Are you Musheer P?"

He shakes his head. "Musheer is still in hospital."

"Which one?"

"A big one."

It's not going quite as she had planned. Walking down the endless, dark hallways, she hadn't factored in any kind of resistance. She'd thought they'd be more than willing to help her find the dickheads who attacked Musheer P. Now, they won't even tell her the hospital where he is recovering.

"Look," she says, softening her tone, "I want to help, somehow. Can any of you tell me about the attack? Did anyone see it? Please, any information you have would be helpful."

"Why are you talking in the singular? This has been going on for years."

A few more tentative steps, getting closer to the table. "Have you been targeted?" she asks.

He nods slowly, as do the other boys. They exchange glances, and their eyes have the communal softness of shared memories.

"We all have," he says, "at some point. It's part of the experience. The," with emphasis, "procedure. Maybe we don't get beaten to a pulp like Musheer, but something happens to us. Maybe we get robbed, or someone slashes the tires of our cars, if any of us has a car. Or someone paints graffiti on our house, where we live three to a room."

"What do they write?"

"Terrorist go home. Indians out. We grew here, you flew here. Stuff like that."

"Why don't you report it?"

He lets out a short laugh and turns to the other boys. "The policewoman wants me to report the graffiti." They all laugh. To Dixon, he says, "Great idea. Then we get beaten to a pulp like Musheer. That's what happens when we go to the police. Musheer went to you when he was robbed, and now he's in hospital."

"I would've helped him."

"Yes. I'm sure."

"But you're saying this is not an isolated incident?"

"It's a price to pay. The university is expensive, but acceptance costs much more."

She eyes him curiously, impressed with his smarts, liking him and wanting to protect him. She wants to protect all of them.

"I don't understand," she says.

"No. You don't. None of you do, in uniform or not. And that's the problem."

A few more steps. "Please. I want to understand."

The door opens. A man enters carrying a couple of plastic bags tied shut. The bags are shaped square by the take-out containers inside.

"Ah, we have a visitor," the man says, looking at Dixon warily. He's rather short, wearing a cheap suit that's one size too big. Or he bought it a while ago and has since lost weight. He appears to be slightly older than the students. "Who are you?" he asks.

"I'm investigating the attack on Musheer," she says, walking with him as he approaches the table. She feels a pressing and unexplainable need to stand close to him.

"I'm not Musheer," he says as he places the bags on the table. "I'm just a delivery boy. A messenger." To the students, "Who's hungry?"

The boys start clearing the table, marking books with scraps of paper before closing them. The containers are taken from the bags while one boy retrieves a short stack of paper plates and some plastic cutlery from a nearby counter.

Dixon gets the sense that they eat a lot of meals in here. She now feels like she's intruding, more so than when they were studying. This eating together comes across to her as being more intimate.

Two bottles of unbranded cola are placed on the table. Upside down over the neck of one bottle is a stack of plastic cups. Soon, dinner is set up, with the containers open and steam rising. The room fills with the aroma of curry and rice. The delivery boy sits down as well. The containers are passed around as the food is shared. One student pours six cups of cola. While clearly hungry, they take their time and eat slowly. They sit close together and knock elbows as they eat.

No one talks.

There's a small gap at the table. She takes a chair and places it in the gap. The elder student and the delivery boy shift their chairs just enough for her to join. But she isn't offered a plate or a drink.

"Looks good," she says.

"It is," the elder student replies.

"You look like you've earned it."

"Who are you anyway?" the delivery boy asks. "A detective?"

"I'm Constable Grace."

"Police?"

"Yes. I want to find the people who attacked Musheer." To the group, "I want to help you. I want you to stand up to these bullies, to stop the cycle."

Muffled, bitter laughter.

"You should fight them off," she adds.

"We're outnumbered," the elder says. "And anyway, who are you

105

to say this? You're the police. You're supposed to be protecting us. But you and all your police friends, you look the other way. You are not interested in us. You don't even believe us when we report a crime. You think we make it all up."

"I believe you," she says emphatically, and her voice echoes in the room. "I'm not looking the other way."

"You are one person."

"And you're not exactly Lara Croft," the delivery boy says, getting a chorus of laughter from the students. "You think you can take on the entire city?"

"At the very least let me help you guys."

"They don't need your help. And it sounds like they never wanted it anyway."

She turns to him. "Who are you? Do you work here?"

"I offered these fine young men jobs," the delivery boy says, still eating.

"Jobs? So what are you then? Delivery boy, messenger or recruiter?"

"I'd say a unique combination of all three."

"What kind of jobs?"

"Construction projects. Mechanical engineering. Aircraft. That sort of thing. We need smart kids."

"Who's we?"

"India."

"The whole country?" she asks incredulously. "You're from the government then?"

He laughs with his mouth full, covering his mouth with his hand, then swallows. "Governments don't have any power anymore," he says. "The fact that you're here proves that. Police, political leaders, officials, they can't do anything to change the world."

"So we should all stop trying? Thanks for making what I do every day sound unnecessary and useless."

"Your words, not mine," he says with smile. "You should get into business instead. Companies are where the real power is these days. It's companies that are changing the world."

"Not always for the better," she counters.

"True. Not every company is like Nayakall."

"Who?"

"It's an Indian company," he says. "One with very noble aspirations."

"And these guys are coming to work for you?"

106

"No, not for me," again with a smile, broader than before, and warmer, and it makes her shift in her chair. "I'm just the recruiter. But they will help change India for the better."

She watches them eat, considering this, feeling suddenly sad and helpless. A wave a grief washes over her and she fights hard to let it pass without it taking hold.

They smile, chewing. One takes a sip of coke.

She decides to change tack.

"While you're all so immersed in eating," she begins, "can I tell you a story?"

They exchange glances and nods. The expression on the recruiter's face is one of humour. He's expecting a funny story. She's keen to shock him, to draw him closer to her.

"My grandmother is from India," she says. "My mother ... she was born there too. And she died there. My father's Australian and I grew up here. Not in Melbourne. In Narooma."

"Where?" one boy asks.

She's surprised to hear a different student speak. It makes her think she's got their attention. "It's on the coast," she explains, trying not to sound condescending. "In New South Wales."

"I thought you were Aboriginal," another says.

"Have you ever seen an Aboriginal?" She tries to smile. "I got a lot of that when I was a kid. That's why I dyed my hair blonde when I first came to Melbourne. That was seven years ago. I haven't dyed it since. When I first got here, I worked as a secretary for a dentist. My grandmother organised that, knew some people here. I studied at night to become a dental hygienist. Don't laugh. You're all going to be engineers, but I screwed up in high school, failed pretty much everything, and that meant uni was out of reach for me. Dental school was the best I could do, and I was lucky to have that. My sister was already living here, studying sports science at La Trobe. I moved in with her."

She stops in order to gauge their level of attention.

"Would you like to get to the point of this story?" the recruiter asks. He's finished eating and is now sitting with his arms crossed, somewhat bored.

"In 2004, my sister was attacked. We were coming out of a bar on Chapel Street."

"Where's that?" one boy asks.

"In South Yarra. You guys need to get out more."

"Yes," the elder student says, "so we can get robbed in front of everybody and beaten in parking lots."

"Sorry," she says. "It was a Sunday evening. Not late. But you know the Sunday sessions, when people start pounding alcohol at lunch time."

There's a collective shrug of bemusement.

"We study on Sundays," the elder says.

"On Saturday nights too. Good for you. Well, there are worse things you can do. Nothing more boring than a bunch of pissed guys at six on a Sunday evening. Not much that's more dangerous either. They were moving down Chapel Street in large groups, you know, in herds, hunting. Misty and I had just had dinner with some friends and we were heading home. A group of guys followed us. Misty got all the looks in my family, and these guys went straight for her, got right up in her face. And this was on a crowded street. Everyone just turned the other way. No one tried to help. I pushed these guys away, but that just made them more aggressive. Misty decided to run for it, down this short path near the corner of Arthur Street. It follows the train line. That was a stupid thing to do, because it was dark and it was Sunday and there was no one down there. A couple of guys chased after her while two guys held onto me. I broke free and ran down the path as well. The guys who stayed behind were too drunk to run."

"What happened?" the recruiter asks, with a look of genuine concern on his face.

"I couldn't see Misty, but I could hear her muffled screaming. She was trying to shout with one of their hands on her mouth. I thought then that was disgusting enough. Having one of these hands on your mouth. Ugh. I tried to find her. I could hear the two guys, grunting and swearing. Some guy with a dog walked past me, oblivious to it all, even looking the other way. No, he knew what was going on. He just didn't care. I stopped to listen and heard one guy say, 'Me love you long time,' and his mate said, 'Nah, nah, it's like this. You veddy, veddy pleddy.' And they both laughed, like it was all some fucking joke." After a pause, "Then I saw them. The shadows on the ground next to a tree. I got closer. I could see Misty lying on her back, struggling. They'd lifted her dress over her head, muffling her with it. One of them pinned the dress down over her face with his knees. Like it was an expert move, you know."

Another pause. She looks from face to face. They've all finished eating. Every take-out container is empty. There's not a grain of rice left.

"I found a big piece of wood on the ground and picked it up. I've played golf since I could walk, and I gripped this thick stick like it was a driver." She shows them her interlocking golf grip. "I came up behind them and hit them as hard as I could. One in the head and the other in the leg. I think I broke his leg. Something snapped. He screamed in pain and rolled on the grass. The other guy was out cold. He had his pants and underwear around his ankles. Misty got to her feet and gave that guy a kick in the stomach. Kicked him again and again until I pulled her back. We ran down the path to William Street and jumped in a taxi."

"And?" the recruiter asks. "Did you go to the police?"

"Of course. We had to wait around for hours for a female constable. None of the men wanted to deal with us. They kept saying there were all these tests involved, to prove it was rape. I said that it wasn't rape. We were attacked. They looked at us like we'd brought it on ourselves. Okay. So we waited for the female constable. Misty was a mess. Nothing like that had ever happened to either one of us before. The experience really affected her. It changed her. A few weeks later, she dropped out of uni and moved back to Narooma."

"Did the police catch the guys?" the recruiter asks.

Dixon is surprised to see the students don't seem terribly touched by the story. But she has got the recruiter's attention.

"At the station, we made the report. Well, I did. Misty couldn't talk about it. At the end, the constable told me straight out that it was pointless. They couldn't do anything. We had no names, no evidence, no description. So, nothing happened. If anything, the constable said, I might get in trouble for hitting the two guys, if they bothered to go to the police."

"Sounds familiar," the elder says.

"You see? I do understand. But I also decided to do something about it."

"By joining the police?"

She nods. "Because I wanted to change things. To make a difference." She lets out an exasperated sigh. "But I was way wrong." To the recruiter, "When you talk about governments not having power, you're right, to a certain point. In the police, we spend more time writing parking and speeding tickets than catching bad guys. Anything to generate revenue. And plenty of the guys on the force are crooks, in big and small ways."

The recruiter smiles at her. "Your honesty is refreshing, but it's also useless. At least it's useless for these boys."

"I just wanted you all to know where I'm coming from," she says.

"Thank you for the story," the elder says. He starts cleaning up the table, but the other students take the cue and do it for him. The plates and containers are packed away, the table is wiped down, and the books come out again.

"We can all be affected by bad experiences," she says, sitting back, slightly drained. "And now that I told you what happened to me, I don't want to know where Musheer is. Maybe it's better he recovers and goes to work in India, like you guys."

"And what about you?" the recruiter asks. "Why keep policing streets that you can never make safe?"

"Good question." Then coyly, "Are you offering me a job as well?"

"Perhaps."

"I'm not an engineer."

"We need people with all sorts of skill sets."

She takes a deep breath. She wants to continue the conversation with the recruiter in private.

"Now, I don't know," she says. "I feel ... powerless. These attacks are wrong. I'm trying to put together a report, really comprehensive, but no one wants to look at it. I guess they hope you'll pack up and go home. Then it won't be a problem anymore."

"And now you really do understand," the elder says. "All we want is an education."

"Your sister packed up and went home as well," the recruiter says.

"She did. And I think that was the wrong thing to do."

"Well, that's what we're going to do," the elder says. "And it's right for us."

"We're not wanted here," another says, looking up from his open book. "We will graduate and return to India. To work for Nayakall."

"And our families will be taken care of," the elder adds.

"That's right," the recruiter says. "We take care of our own." To Dixon, "Maybe you're interested as well."

She smiles at him. "Give me your best offer."

He strides down the hallway, passing offices where his colleagues are working diligently. Every door is open, as part of Ole Lessinger's policy. It's unlike the other departments he's visited, where the colleagues work behind closed doors, making the office seem like a low-level civil service bureau, or a prison, and you have to knock on doors anytime you want to ask someone something, and when allowed to enter, you feel like you're the last person wanted in this forbidden domain.

He hates offices like that, and hopes to heaven and hell he doesn't end up in one. He's no fan of Lessinger – would be glad to see the old fart's head impaled on a long spear – but he does like the open-door policy. And when he's running this department, he decides, he will go a step further: get rid of all the walls and turn it into an open-plan office.

He's renovating as he heads towards Lessinger's office, which is the last door at the end of this hallway, and the one door that's always closed. Down with this wall, new desks for everyone, more comfortable chairs, more potted plants, a few high-quality espresso machines. Maybe a few cricket posters for motivation, and for not-so-subtle hints at the power of teamwork, with him as their admired and highly-respected captain.

He misses cricket. They're training indoors every Wednesday in Altona, and the distance isn't as far as it is to summer training in Klein Flottbek, saving him time, but it's just not the same. The plastic floor and the plastic ball, the way it skids and slides and swings, making batting impossible. Worse is trying to hit that yellow ball in a big multi-purpose gymnasium that has yellow walls. You can't see it, and then it clatters into the plastic stumps to the cheers of everyone watching.

It's just not cricket, he thinks. But the outdoor season is a good five months away. He's sure that next season the club will make him captain of the first team. He is absolutely certain of it, and it's why he keeps going to indoor training, to be a good club man and assert his leadership, so that the decision will, in the end, be a no-brainer for the club.

He's nervous, scared that Lessinger will ensure his transfer to

111

another department, some boring place where they push papers and every door is closed.

"No," he says out loud. Then to himself: I'm here for a promotion, because that's what I deserve.

Strangely, the hallway seems to extend, like some weird movie effect, the door moving into the distance. The sensation is not unlike what he feels when going out to bat, with the pitch far away. On that long walk, the opposition give you the evil eye, because they're keen for an early breakthrough.

Yes, he thinks, opening the batting against a fearsome bowling attack is more of a challenge than an end-of-year appraisal with Ole Lessinger. But the principles and metaphors are the same: take the shine off the ball and get your eye in, dodge the bouncers and let anything outside the off stump go through to the keeper.

He's a few minutes early, but knocks anyway, wanting to get this sordid ordeal over with; to get his promotion and run before anyone can take it away from him.

He knows his time has come. Lessinger will be full of praise and rewards.

"Enter," says a voice from behind the door.

He takes a deep breath. "Defence to attack. Let the crap go."

He opens the door. Lessinger looks up, but doesn't stand up.

"Ah, Benjamin, good. You're on time," Lessinger says. He gestures towards the man sitting on the small sofa. "This is Laurent Fournier. From HR."

"How do you do," Ben says, immediately not liking the person he's heard a lot of rumours about.

They shake hands, with Fournier remaining seated and reaching his hand up for Ben to grasp.

"He's why we're having the appraisal in English," Lessinger explains. "No problem for you, is it?"

"No, of course not. I was educated in England."

"That explains the accent," Lessinger says with a laugh.

"Maybe it is eh more of eh problem for me," Fournier says in a very strong French accent.

Ben tries to laugh politely.

"We'll keep it simple," Lessinger says. "And quick. Take a seat, Benjamin, so we can get started. I've got five more of these to knock off before lunch."

Ben sits. Unsure of his best position, he fidgets momentarily before deciding on left leg crossed over right, with his hands in his lap. He tries to appear calm, relaxed and in no way frightened of the coming attack. The chair is quite a long way from the desk, making him feel exposed.

Lessinger squints at his monitor, like he's reading the information for the first time. "Right. Benjamin Steckdorf. Second assistant team manager for navigation systems military. That's a mouthful. Maybe the first thing we can appraise is your job title."

"By removing the second assistant part?" Ben offers with a smile.

Lessinger's face is blank. "That's rather forward. Is that what you think this is all about? Getting promoted?"

"I was thinking ..."

"Look, Benjamin. We've got a pretty steep pyramid in place, you know that. There's not a lot of room at the top. Not even at mid-level, and you're a long way from that."

"I ... I didn't mean to assume. But, but I've been here for three years now, and I think I've done excellent work."

"Three years is nothing," Lessinger says, looking to Fournier for confirmation. The HR man replies with a bored nod.

"But my work ..."

"Yes, yes, as a team member. Management is another issue. It's a completely whole other issue entirely. You're not ready."

"I've already done it," Ben says, uncrossing his legs and sitting up straight. "I managed my team while Frank Krüttgen was on holiday."

Lessinger turns to Fournier. "Frank is the manager for navigation systems military."

Another bored nod.

"That was in," Lessinger taps at the keyboard and looks at the monitor, squinting again, inquisitive, "August. Summer downtime. More than half the team was on holiday in August. Family men, school holidays." To Fournier, "Not much happens here in August. Mostly, we let the kids play with the toys for a while."

The Frenchman lets out one slightly jovial chuckle.

"We tested the new fly-by-wire navigation," Ben says proudly. "In a helicopter."

"Like I said. Boys with toys. Went well?"

"You didn't read my report?"

"I think I glanced at it," Lessinger says dismissively. "But it was so long. Frank told me about it. Bring me up to speed."

"There are still some kinks to work out," Ben says, crossing his right leg over his left, "but the helicopter didn't crash. That was important. We kept it under control. When the weather improves, we want to test the system on a light aircraft."

"I know, I know. Frank told me all that. And those are Frank's projects, not yours. The aircraft test will be more meaningful than playing with helicopters during summer break. Frank's on top of things."

"Yes, he is." Ben sees Fournier look at his watch; the slightest movement of the Frenchman's right pinky to lift the left sleeve of his suit jacket coupled with a quick lowering of the eyes. He hates Fournier, and Lessinger, and Krüttgen. All the arseholes positioned at the top of the pyramid and who are not willing to make way for anyone.

"You did a lot of travelling this year," Lessinger says. "You're quite the jetsetter. Brazil, the States, France, China, India, Israel, Russia. You were all over the place. Were you ever here?"

"Well, it's like you just said. A lot of the members of my team, I mean, of the team are family oriented. They can't travel and they don't want to, and they always leave the company early to get home to their families. Being single, hard-working and committed to the company, the travelling always falls on me."

"Don't speak badly about your colleagues and superiors like that," Lessinger says angrily. "We're a family company. You should think about settling down as well."

"I want to make a career," Ben says.

"Marry that girlfriend of yours. I met her at the Christmas party. Something starting with D. Unusual name, can't remember it. Australian. Beautiful, I might add."

"Dixon."

Lessinger snaps his fingers. "Dixon. That's it. What a piece of work she is. Funny too." Turning to Fournier, "Gorgeous. Parfait dix. Perfect ten." Back to Ben, "You lucky boy. How did you pull that off?"

"Excuse me?"

"You should marry her. I would if I were you."

"We're seeing each other," Ben says, struck by Lessinger's candour and hating him for being attracted to Dixon. He decides to stake his claim, to make Lessinger back off before he gets any ideas. "We're moving in together in January."

"That's a good start," Lessinger says with a smile. "You know we highly value employees committed to family. It shows stability, a sense of the future."

"Reliability," Fournier adds, struggling to get the word out.

"Yes, indeed. We need people we can depend on, people here for the long term. Marry her, before she heads back to Australia. What does she do again?"

"She's an English teacher."

"Is that right?"

"She teaches classes here as well."

Lessinger's eyes brighten. "Might be time I brushed up on my grammar and vocab. Organise myself some single lessons."

Ben bristles at this. "Your English sounds perfectly good to me. You don't need any lessons."

"Neither do you," Lessinger counters.

There's an awkward silence, which Fournier ends. "Maybe I am the one who needs lessons," he says, sneaking another look at his watch.

Ben, who knows all about Fournier the Fornicator and the numerous harassment claims he's managed to shrug off, just keeps himself from shouting down this idea.

"Yes. So," Lessinger says, "let's wrap this up. Benjamin, how do you rate your performance this year? Be honest."

Now crossing his arms, "I think I performed very well. Thanks to my efforts, the various projects I worked on have taken big steps forward. I proved my leadership abilities in the summer and did a lot of hard travelling for the team. I also put in more hours than my contract requires."

Lessinger holds up a hand to make him stop. "That's very good. Thank you. And what do you see for yourself in the future? Apart from marrying that delicious Australian girl of yours."

"Like I said, I want to make a career." And he decides to take a risk. "I want to sit there, in your chair."

Lessinger looks both humoured and surprised. "Are you forgetting the pyramid? I don't think my position is in your future just yet. Three years, Benjamin, you've just started here. And you're skipping a few levels."

"That's nothing new for me. I skipped a year at school in England."

"That probably says more about the British education system than your intellect."

Fournier chuckles, enjoying the show.

"I think you should focus on your team," Lessinger says decisively. "I've got Frank lined up for a new project. Drone navigation."

"It's a very exciting project," Ben says, now attempting to be ingratiating, having failed miserably with taking a risk. He's getting the distinct impression that Lessinger doesn't like him.

"You sound like you want to be involved."

Ben nods. "I do."

"Hmm. Frank's going to lead the project," Lessinger says. "And that means his current position as team manager will open up. Do you think you should be considered for that?"

"I do. Yes, certainly."

"What about the drone navigation project?" Lessinger has a crafty look on his face. "I thought that's what you wanted. Or was it just my chair?"

"Are you offering me a choice?"

Lessinger moves his head from side to side. "Well, for argument's sake, let's say I am. What would you prefer, to be in the drone navigation team or team leader of navigation systems military?"

"That's an interesting question," Ben says, briefly giving it some thought. "I would take the leadership position."

"Would you?" With a casual wave, "It's all just talk anyway. I don't think you're leadership material. Do you?"

"I do."

"I do, I do, I do. Are we having an appraisal or are you auditioning for *Mamma Mia*?"

"Or practicing for eh his wedding," Fournier adds.

They both laugh.

"Sorry," Lessinger says, looking anything but apologetic. "Unprofessional, I know, and," with a glance at the clock behind him, "taking up too much time. Look, I'll discuss your profile with Frank during his appraisal. My feeling is you're best suited to a team member role, where we make use of your availability and flexibility, while we've still got it. But I'll listen to what Frank has to say, if he has anything to say." He taps at the keyboard and checks the monitor. "You're only thirty-two. You have plenty of time to get into management. Maybe you should do some evening courses, to learn more about management and get yourself ready. But for now, I think my chair remains well out of reach."

Disappointed, and not knowing what to say, and seething, Ben looks down at his hands.

"That's not what you came in here for, I know," Lessinger says in a fatherly tone. "Think about that over Christmas. Think about how you can balance your expectations with reality."

"Balance my expectations with reality," Ben echoes sarcastically, pissed off now. "Sounds like something from a self-help book."

"There's no need to talk like that. You should be grateful. You're very lucky to be working in navigation and guidance systems. This is where everyone wants to be." Pointing left, then right, "There are guys slaving in other departments dreaming of doing what you do, and a lot of them have been here for over twenty years."

"I didn't mean to sound disrespectful," Ben says, trying to keep his voice even. "I only want to impress upon you, on both of you, that I am ambitious."

"Noted. Now, we better bring this to an end. You'll be getting your Christmas bonus. Buy that lovely girlfriend of yours something nice. And have a good holiday."

Ben stands. I'm out, he thinks, without even scoring a run. Kept swinging and missing until I spooned one into the air for an easy catch. I should've just let everything go and waited.

"Thank you for your time," he manages to say. "And merry Christmas."

He shakes Lessinger's hand, then Fournier's, both men remaining seated.

They say something, but the words don't register. Then he's out of the office, closing the door behind him and trudging down the long hallway. And it's like that long, lonely walk back to the clubhouse, with everyone staring.

The seat is cold but clean. There's a lavenderish whiff in the air, maybe emitting from one of those air fresheners you plug into the wall. There's no graffiti, no grubby specks of chewing gum wedged into corners, no spiders, no shoe streaks on the floor. She thinks it might be possible to eat off the floor, but she most certainly doesn't want to. The floor is cold against her bare feet.

There are three extra rolls of toilet paper in this cubicle alone, stacked in a neat pyramid on top of the tank, plus an almost full roll on the holder.

It's good to have this moment of quiet, she thinks, to be out of the interrogation room and away from that idiot Schultze.

She wants so much to take him down, really slam his head against the table. The way he so blandly announced that Ole was dead, the arrogance of his accusations, his horrible pudgy hands. She wants to bolt him down in a chair and shave off his moustache with a rusty blade.

And he's a father, she thinks. A husband. He touches his wife with those hands, strokes his children's cheeks.

Focus, she tells herself. The cubicle.

She's reminded again how set Germans are on having clean bathrooms. During the last eighteen months, she's observed the local toilet culture with an almost scientific fascination, taking note of the etiquette and required behaviour. In public places, nearly all toilets are paid toilets, replete with a slot to drop in a coin. Or, there's an attendant in a lab coat with a little dish for dropping coins into, so you can pay what you think is best for the waste you've left behind; you'd want to wash those coins at the end of the day. Or the companies where she taught English, which had clean bathrooms but with little instruction cards for how to use a toilet brush. The unisex toilet at Multilinga has that too, a sign next to the brush, in six languages: "This is not decoration. You must use this." Not only had someone taken the time to make the sign and stick it to the wall, but had also translated it into all the languages offered by the school. That's what had amazed her, and it had the look of something that had required the work of several people. A toilet task force. A special team. Someone in that team had come up with the idea of laminating the sign, to keep it clean, or make it easier to clean. The first time she saw it, she wondered if there had been a meeting about it. Agenda point seven at the January staff meeting: toilet upkeep, with a crash course in how to use a toilet brush correctly.

She smiles, recalling how someone had written on that sign in permanent marker, "You'll never shit alone," in jocular reference to the smaller of Hamburg's two soccer teams, FC St Pauli. That same person had also drawn a skull-and-crossbones, the club's symbol, having got down on hands and knees next to the toilet to do so.

She's finished her business, but remains seated. She sees the guard pacing in front of the door, the shadow moving back and forth. Her boots squeak and leave skinny black streaks on the floor with each pivot, streaks that will surely by mopped away before the day is over.

One guard, she thinks, for a suspected murderer and corporate spy; for a person who required a riot squad to be arrested and brought in. That's certainly a bit lean, but it makes it easier. She wonders if they don't consider her any kind of a threat, that here in the LKA, she wouldn't dare try anything, or have any hope of escaping.

She takes a deep breath. She knows she can't go back into the interrogation room, to face Schultze and Korner. It's a waste of time, and now with Ole dead, she has one more loose end to tie. She has a feeling who killed him, a hunch, not necessarily the exact person, but the group behind it. But she can't tell any of that to Korner. And there's no way that Schultze will believe her. That demented ogre has already written and signed his report. In his head, he's on the train home, having moved onto the next logic problem.

No. She needs to get out of here, to find Ole's killer and prove her own innocence. Nothing will happen the longer she remains here. She needs to get proactive, because doing that will also show her innocence.

Action, she thinks. Act now.

She closes her eyes and visualises the guard. She listens to the steps, imagining the movement, where the guard puts her weight, which side she favours. Is she left-handed or right? Does she work out? Can she defend herself without pointing a gun?

I can take her, she thinks.

Her hands shaking a little, she pulls some toilet paper off the roll.

Eight squares. It's the double ply stuff, good quality, maybe from the brand with greatest name in toilet paper: Happy End. More Denglish gone wrong, she thinks with a smile. She folds it length-wise and wraps it around the knuckles of her left hand, like a bandage.

She wonders where the guard might be from. Turkey perhaps, or maybe further east. Syria, Iran, Iraq, first or second generation. If that's right, then she admires the guard for joining the police and trying to make a difference, and is already sorry for what she's about to do.

Again, she closes her eyes.

Details, details. She's not as tall as I am, but heavier, more buxom. That's a problem, because the clothes won't fit. When entering the toilet, she pushed the door open with her right hand, and used that hand and her right foot to hold it open for me. She placed her jacket next to the basin just before I entered the cubicle. Her gun is holstered at the small of her back, to be grabbed by her right hand when necessary. She's chewing gum. She seems bored by this kind of work. I think she wants to be out working the streets, trying to nail some real wanker rather than escorting suspects to the toilet. Good for her. Brown hair, tied in a ponytail that is poking out the backside of her cap, just above the Velcro strap. The hair band is white. The black cap has a skull-and-crossbones on it.

"Finished?" the guard shouts.

"Almost."

She thinks it's strange that the guard is wearing an FC St Pauli cap, because the left-wing fans make no secret of their disregard for authority and often clash with the Hamburg police. She remembers the incredible numbers of police in riot gear, the vans and water cannons lined up on Budapester Strasse, for some of St Pauli's home games. That situation is made even more weird by the fact that plenty of those St Pauli ultras are really key account managers and desk jockeys and office ants who don brown hoodies for home matches and pretend to be hardcore left-wingers for the afternoon.

Mental diversion, she tells herself.

"Where are you from?" she asks, her voice echoing.

"Germany," the guard says, with anger. "Why does everyone ask me that?"

"Sorry."

"Come on. Time's up."

She stands and pulls up her tracksuit pants. The toilet paper is tight around her left knuckles and holds firm when she makes a fist. She turns to flush and sees that there's no sign next to the toilet brush. She assumes the LKA recruits are schooled in bathroom etiquette at basic training.

She flushes, lowers the lid and grabs the toilet brush. It drips on the floor. She takes one last, relaxing breath and reaches for the door handle.

The adrenalin builds. She feels suddenly more alive than she has in months.

The door opens towards her, swinging on superbly-engineered hinges made in Germany. The guard stops pacing and stands in the doorway. When Dixon throws the toilet brush at her, aimed at the left shoulder, she recoils in disgust. It's just enough of a distraction for Dixon to move forward and punch the guard on the chin. But the guard is too much off balance, already falling backwards, and Dixon feels that she doesn't make enough contact. And this is a bad mistake, because she only stuns the guard and doesn't knock her out as intended.

The guard attempts to fight back. She's slow on her feet and a front-foot fighter. Dixon knows she needs a little distance, to use the guard's weight to her advantage, but if she does get distance, the guard will just pull out her gun. So they wrestle, fighting awkwardly in the confined space and not landing any significant blows. Dixon manages to get a firm grip on the guard's right wrist, but then feels a fist jab her hard in the ribs. The left fist, not nearly as hard as the right would be. She shifts with the impact, getting to the side of the guard, then turning quickly with her hand still gripping the guard's wrist. She manages to twist the arm around the guard's back and shoves her face first to the floor. Her cap comes off as she struggles. Dixon puts a knee in her back.

Act now, she tells herself. Do it. Before she starts screaming.

She gets a handful of the guard's hair, making the pony tail come loose a little. Imaging the head is Schultze's, she slams it against the floor.

The guard's body goes limp. A trickle of blood seeps from under her forehead.

Dixon unhooks the holster from the guard's belt and tosses it into the corner. She flips the guard over. She's quite heavy now, as a dead weight. Dixon gets her boots off, then shimmies her out of her jeans. She swaps her tracksuit pants for the guard's jeans, which are rather baggy on her, and puts on the boots, which fit. She's panicking a little, making this swapping of clothes take longer than it should. The guard is also not helping, having put on several layers of tight singlets, intended to give her more support and lift. She gets these off, including the guard's bra. It's too big for her, but she puts it on anyway, suddenly feeling like she's twelve years old again and trying on her sister's bras. Back then, that one year between them had meant several cup sizes, and it meant that Misty was firmly the centre of everyone's attention.

She lays her own t-shirt, which still smells musty from sleep, over the guard's naked upper body, and does the same with her tracksuit pants over the guard's legs.

She feels guilty for leaving the guard in a humiliating position like this.

The guard starts to stir, her eyes blinking open slowly and her right hand reaching for her forehead.

"I'm sorry for this," Dixon says, taking the guard's head in two hands. "But you arrested the wrong girl. I'll be back when I've found Ole's killer."

And she knocks the back of the guard's head against the floor.

At the basin, she gets into the guard's jacket and looks in the mirror.

"Butch," she says to her reflection.

In the jacket's inside pocket is the guard's ID. There's also a set of keys, some cash and a mobile phone. She keeps the cash and ID, but leaves the keys and phone. She sweeps the cap off the floor and jams it on her head, tucking her blonde hair under it, so that she now looks seriously butch. She lowers the visor a little, shadowing her face.

She's about to exit the bathroom when a thought strikes her: the phone.

"Just to drive it home," she says to the guard.

She opens a text message on the screen and types: "I'm innocent and I will prove it." She leaves the message unsent, the screen still glowing.

At the door, she edges it open a crack. The hallway is relatively clear: a couple of people walking with files, the murmur of mundane office work, men mostly. She needs to walk with purpose, like she works here, and not break stride.

About twenty metres to the right, she sees the familiar green stairs sign hanging from the ceiling. It's the same sign she's seen in every German building she's been in, the same sign that totally detracts from a movie watching experience in a German cinema.

That bloody green sign, she thinks. Always catches your eye. I can see you now. And that stick figure on the run is entirely appropriate.

She waits for two men to pass. She sees Schultze come out of one of the offices. He's holding a blue dossier in his meaty fist as he lumbers down the hall.

The guard stirs on the floor.

Dixon grabs a paper towel and opens the door. As she walks quickly down the hallway, she pretends to dry her hands with the towel, as if she's far too busy to waste time in the bathroom doing that.

There's a man coming from the other direction.

She balls up the paper and lobs it into a waste basket.

"Guter Wurf," the man says.

"Danke."

Then she's bounding down the stairs, taking them two at a time.

"India has won the toss," the announcer says, his voice crackling through the old speakers, "and will bowl first."

Devan Marawar shakes his head.

"What's wrong?" Sara asks.

"A poor decision," he says, watching the captains walk off the field. Both captains look at the sky, at the grey clouds that have already delivered rain and brought the covers out. "But it probably just made someone rich," he adds. "Or poor."

"Please tell me you're not involved in that anymore."

"Amma," he says softly. "It's a lifetime ago. But I know how it works. And so do you. You're the one who got me into it."

"I never thought it would be that petty. I knew they were involved in results, winning and losing, but not in the small minutiae. I still don't know why they bother with it."

"Because anything with a possible outcome is open for betting."

Sara looks over the field. She smiles, because Lord's just before the start of play – with the crowd assembling and getting comfortable, the fielders warming up and showing off, the umpires striding to the middle with purpose, and all around the ground the tension building – is a sight to behold. It's a coolish day, with a brisk wind blowing down from Regent's Park, carrying with it faint smells of the zoo. She's glad she let Devan talk her into watching the morning session. She marvels that even from here, she can see the field's rather dramatic slope.

"In my opinion, they're not thinking big enough," she says. "Small bets for small minds."

"Playing the numbers. You'd be surprised how much people are willing to wager on the toss, or who will hit the first boundary, or who will take the first catch. All these bets make the game more interesting to watch."

"For some."

"Amma, I agree with you. It's the cricket that people should be watching."

"I guess the new version, what's it called?"

124

Devan smiles admonishingly. "Twenty-twenty. You know what it's called."

"That's not cricket at all," she says. "But I assume it allows people to bet on every ball."

"That's the idea. And there's a lot of money to be made."

"Dirty money."

Devan pats at the back of his hair. He moves his head left and right to check who may be listening. The members' section is scattered with people. Mostly retirees with small ear-pieces in place, tuning into the local commentary.

"Money is money, Amma," he says quietly. "It doesn't question where it comes from, or how it's made. And money is always just money, clean or not."

They lapse into silence, which is broken by modest applause; the crowd clapping the opening batsmen onto the field. When the clapping subsides, there's an increase in chatter, the murmurs rippling around the ground as a few thousand people discuss the weather.

"Are you betting today?" Sara asks.

"Certainly not," Devan replies, offended, and looking around again.

"Calm down. I was just checking. Gambling is a hard thing to shake."

He leans close to her. "I was never addicted, Amma. I was involved in the business. That's all. You should know anyway."

"You took it too far. You're lucky I saved you."

"Yes, yes. Always saving me."

On the field, the play begins. They watch an over in silence. When the play turns to the Pavilion End, Sara says,

"Devan, don't ever lose appreciation for all that you have."

"I appreciate it."

"You started at the bottom," she says, "and worked your way to the top."

"With a lot of help, I know." Devan shifts in his chair, to face Sara. He pats her hand. "I know my place, Amma. Success hasn't changed me."

"Of course it has. And so it should. I'm very proud of you."

"You made me."

"I saved you."

Devan nods. He gives the cricket his attention.

"No matter what happens to you in life," Sara says solemnly, "you can never separate yourself from your roots."

"I'm ashamed of them."

To his surprise, Sara puts her arm around him. "No. You need to use this to your advantage. Turn your shame into humility. You need to make it part of your story. Believe me, people will like you more when they know just where you started. Of course, you need to keep my part out of it."

"I will," he says, wanting to move closer to her, to feel both arms around him, but Sara's arm remains like a soft weight on his shoulders. He feels no love from her and this cuts at his insides. "I always do."

"Thank you."

Sara takes back her arm and picks up her cup of tea. She blows at it and sips.

Devan wants to leave.

"There aren't many Indians here today," she says.

"It's Thursday. They're all working."

"Good."

"They'll come out on the weekend, if the match is close."

"To bet or to watch?"

"To watch," Devan replies, hating this line of inquiry. "They don't have the kind of money that this sort of betting requires."

"And you? The freshly minted Lord's member?"

Devan takes out his phone. "I'm flying to São Paulo tonight. I'm on the Eurostar to Paris and flying from there. You?"

"I have my lecture tomorrow."

Devan can't resist himself: "It's all about the evils of organised gambling I hope."

Sara gives him a hard stare. "Don't talk like that to me."

"What then?"

"The Indian diaspora. From independence to the modern day. We finally fought ourselves free from the British only for everyone to start leaving. And many of them came here."

"Including you."

"Only temporarily," Sara says. "Because I wanted the education I couldn't get at home. India gave me no choice. I had to leave."

"Well, enjoy it while you can, because the trend you just described will be over soon. In fact, it will be turned completely around, and there'll be no diorama for you to lecture about."

"Diaspora."

"But then, you could just start talking about the trend of Indians returning home. The rise of the sleeping Bengal tiger."

She eyes him with a hint of warmth. "It's working, isn't it? They're coming home."

"They are, now that we have something to offer. That wasn't the case ten years ago. Even five years ago."

"Incentive is important."

"Yes."

"I'm so very proud of you, Devan. I knew you had potential, but I'll be honest and say that I never thought you would get this far."

"I'm glad I proved you wrong."

She nods slowly. "Please, keep doing that."

Devan watches some more of the cricket, but it's slow and ponderous, nothing like the exciting twenty-twenty version.

"So, Amma. Do you think it will rain?" he asks, bored.

"What odds are you giving me?"

He shakes his head.

"Oh, don't be like that. I'm just having some fun. I'm very happy to see you. And thank you for inviting me."

"And the rain?"

"This is London. You should bet that it won't rain."

"How did you put up with it?" Devan asks. "When you were studying here."

"I spent most of my time indoors. In libraries. I didn't feel entirely welcome on London's streets, back then."

"And now?"

"Now I realise what a scared little girl I was. All worried for nothing. I could've walked the streets. I just didn't want to. I was scared of things that weren't even there."

"It's hard to imagine you like that, Amma," Devan says. "Scared and hiding."

"It's true." After sipping some tea, "But that's where I started from, and I'm glad it's part of who I am. I can sit here and see how I've developed. This is why I keep telling you to embrace your roots. Stop avoiding that topic when people interview you."

"Is that an order?"

"Yes."

Devan is taken aback by the firmness of her voice.

"Think about that article in the *Economist*," she says. "You should've handled that better."

"I didn't read all of it."

"Devan, you need to have a greater awareness of what the world is saying about you. Unless you give the journalists a clear story, they will make stuff up. Or worse, they may go digging."

"They just want an excuse to badmouth India," he says defensively. "They're missing the point of what we're trying to do."

"So, tell them."

"They're scared of us. They want us to be the bad guys. The villains from the sub-continent. It doesn't matter what I say."

"It's up to you to change that." Sara lowers her voice to a whisper. "They should be scared. In a decade from now, India will be more powerful than England. We will be able to outsource our work to them. Move our production and factories to Manchester and Leeds. My word, we could even load up in some ships and invade, turn history completely around."

"Your next lecture?"

Sara shakes her head and whispers, "One day. The English deserve to pay for all they've done. My family ..." She trails off, looks over the field, then gathers herself. "Learn from your mistakes with the *Economist*, Devan. Get the story right. Make the people like you."

"All the journalists are hacks," he says. "They just focus on the weapons, that the navi can only be used for military purposes. And then it's just a short step to linking us with terrorism and the wars in Iraq and Afghanistan."

"Sounds like you read all of the article."

He nods. "They have an agenda."

"Then it's up to you to change it," Sara says. "You're the big powerful businessman, and the journalist is just some little pen-pusher. He's nowhere near the position you are in. So, you should set the agenda. You should be the one in control."

"Yes, Amma. I need you in there with me."

"You know that's not possible." She sips her tea. "When's your next interview?"

"Tonight, on the flight to São Paulo. The *Herald Tribune*."

"This is your chance to do what I say."

"What should I say?"

"Focus on the construction projects, the hospitals and schools.

And give him lots of numbers. Tell him how many people Nayakall employs. Tell him about the scholarships and the charities. The Nayakall Foundation. These are big positives."

"And they never get mentioned." Devan rubs his forehead. "It's always Nayakall the weapons manufacturer. Devan Marawar is a warlord."

"He isn't. He works for India."

"Yes, for my country."

"And not for Manmohan Singh," Sara says. "Keep him out of the discussion."

"Yes, Amma."

"You are a servant of your country, Devan. You want India to be a developed nation." Sara struggles to keep her voice down. "You want industry, jobs, clean water, sustainable transport and infrastructure. You don't want to blow up the world and you don't want to rule it either. You want our people to eat, to have a high quality of life. You want girls to go to school, to work and live independently. You want them to choose who they marry. And you don't want today's children of India growing up like you did."

"And then I tell my story?" Devan asks.

"Some of it. Humble beginnings. The life on the street. The inequality and chaos. You wanting more. And most importantly, not being selfish. You need to hammer this home. You are not in this for yourself. You're in it for all Indians."

On the field – and on cue – a wicket falls. India has struck. Devan and Sara both clap as the batsman walks off the field.

"Excellent," Sara says, and Devan's glad that she refrains from making a reference to betting. "And now you know exactly what you will say tonight," she adds.

Devan looks away. "There were thousands of kids on the street, but you helped me. You could've helped any of them, but you chose me. Shall I tell the journalist about that?"

"Keep me out of it."

"We were like a second country," Devan continues, reliving the memories. "All of us trying to survive. And then I get plucked from the crowd by an angel."

"That's not the story, Devan. I'm not in the story." Then her voice softens. "But I think it's more that you chose me. You stood out in that crowd. You were instantly recognisable as being different. Shining like a jewel. I couldn't leave you there on the street, begging."

"I'm the penny you picked up for luck."

"You are much, much more than that."

"Thank you," he says. Then in a lowered voice, "But you left thousands of others on the streets."

The groups are assembled outside, smoking in tight circles. They're talking in German and looking collectively dishevelled and depressed.

She locks her bike and greets the groups with a broad smile. "You guys are going to learn something good today," she says brightly.

But they ignore her, keeping their circles tight. As she takes the three flights of stairs, she wonders how she'll get through the day without shoving a blackboard duster down a student's throat. Heino is the one she wants to see choking on chalk dust. She's teaching the Kennedy class this morning, and Heino will be present, making trouble from the front row.

"Hi, Angelika," she says to the receptionist.

Angelika holds up an index finger, showing that she's on the phone, that the headset is not only for pinning back her wall of frosted hair.

Dixon goes to the filing cabinet and retrieves the Kennedy class card. She reads this as she walks down the hall to the teachers' room.

"Morning all," she says, closing the door behind her.

A few teachers mumble replies. Some just nod, looking tired and strained. The German staff are huddled together, sharing – and guarding – their thermos of coffee. Dixon thinks they give off the distinct impression of people who didn't quite make it in life; they set out to become teachers, maybe at high school or even university, but fell far short and the best they could do was teach German at a language school. She doesn't like sharing this room with people who let themselves fall through the cracks, who didn't have the necessary mettle and drive to realise their dreams, but who would have a list of excuses detailing why they didn't make it.

Externalising the blame, she thinks, trying to ignore the German teachers. Like all the students here too.

The handful of English teachers are spread out around the room and have their heads in the teaching materials, trying to extract some diamond they can wow their class with; or at least keep them amused and occupied for ninety minutes. They slurp coffee from cardboard cups and munch on rolls, all bought from the bakery downstairs.

She smiles at Seth, who smiles back grimly. The lanky doofus from Port Macquarie looks like he's been up all night.

Not a single person in the teachers' room looks like they want to be there. Dixon included. She quickly runs through a mental list of all the things she'd rather be doing today.

The list is dominated by things in Melbourne and Narooma. She feels homesick.

A soft buzzer sounds in the room, signalling that it's eight o'clock and that the first lessons start in fifteen minutes.

Ugh, she thinks.

A glance at the illegible hand-written reports in the Kennedy card just make her feel worse about the morning class. On Friday, Martha "worked on spelling and grammer" with the class. There's no page number given, as a reference to the teaching materials, and she has to go back to the afternoon session on Wednesday, to when Seth taught the group, to see that they are on page thirty-four. But that's not exactly helpful either, not even as a metaphor, because there's no way that she or Seth or any of the teachers can get twenty-seven long-term unemployed people on the same page.

"Hey, Seth?"

Through a mouthful of Franzbrötchen, "Myeah?"

"What did you do with Kennedy on Wednesday?"

"Tried to keep them awake on hump day," Seth says. "I had to confiscate one guy's *Bild Zeitung.*"

"Let me guess. Heino?"

"I'm a peace-loving guy, Dominatrix, but I want blood with fucking Heino. That guy is poisonous. He's ruining the whole group."

"I know. I'm with you. I was taught to never wish anything bad on someone, but ..."

"With Heino you can definitely make an exception." Seth takes another bite of his Franzbrötchen. "Check the page number," he manages to say.

She does so. "That's not helping."

"You lousy rookie. Well, I was trying to teach the past continuous. It was going badly right up until the bell rang."

"I hate that stupid bell. It's like we're back in school."

"Only difference here is that the students are older than the teachers."

She takes another look in the book, trying to make sense of the past continuous. She never learned any of this stuff at school. The book has a few diagrams and explanation tables, but it gives her nothing she can actually use.

"God, these are crap," she says, closing the book. "Who writes these things anyway?"

She checks the clock. She's got less than ten minutes to come up with a killer activity that will take up the whole lesson, teach what's required and keep Heino from making trouble, which would in turn keep her from feeding him chalk dusters.

"I want company classes," she says. "I want to work on-site."

"Then get in the trenches, Dominatrix. Do your tour, earn your keep and then they'll send you out for the cushy stuff. And when that happens, you'll discover it's not all that cushy. You'll end up dreaming of the Arbeitsamt groups."

"I doubt that. But when will I get these company classes? I've been doing this for four months already."

"Six is normally the minimum. It's the filtering system, to weed out the timewasters and those who don't cut it."

"Ugh. What about you? You've been here for years."

"I like the classes with the unemployed." Seth sits up a little straighter. "Most of the time. I feel like I'm doing something good for society. For the community. Getting these unfortunates back on their feet."

Dixon dismisses him with a wave. "Whatever gets you through the day, Seth."

"And it's regular work, good money, and I got a family to support. I'm finished every day at three. If you take those company classes, your life will turn into a donut. Classes early in the morning, like at six, and then late in the evening. With nothing in between."

"Sounds great. I can be a tourist during my time off."

"You'll spend hours riding the U-Bahn," Seth continues, "and crowded buses, to get to companies that are only reachable by car. Take it from a commuter. It's not any fun riding out to places like Billstedt or Harburg in rush hour. Deo is not on the average German's shopping list. Nor is mouthwash."

"Dat is not true, Sef," a German teacher says. He's tall and angular, with a salt-and-pepper beard and matching bushy hair. She's not sure why, but he's the one teacher at the school who really creeps her out, and she always makes sure she's never alone with him.

133

"It's true," Seth whispers.

Dixon sits back. Past continuous, she thinks, watching the hands on the clock move faster than they ever have before. She checks the book again. The explanation is long-winded and complicated, the illustrations ludicrous and with a context that's non-applicable. And if she refers to the book, bloody Heino will just call into question the grammar rule, and then spend half an hour searching on his phone for an explanation that proves himself right.

She turns to Seth. "Mate, lend an Aussie a hand. What's past ..."

Seth jumps in quickly, slapping the table for emphasis. "Action interrupted. And now listen very carefully. You were asking me about the past continuous when I slapped the table. Get it? Think of it as -ing stopped."

"More."

"Come on. That was great."

"Another example," she says, wanting to take Seth into the class with her. She thinks two teachers working together would be able to master the group. Twenty-seven is just too many students for her to handle. "You know the materials backward. You never even prepare. And the students love you."

Seth grins. "I get them to watch *Crocodile Hunter*. And then I tell them we're all like that. Rough and tumble crocodile wrestlers. They're all scared of me."

"Example please. I'm on the clock."

"Fine. I was standing on the grassy knoll when Kennedy was shot."

"I hate these presidents for class names. Always makes me think of *Point Break*."

"Oh, I love that film. 'We are the ex-presidents.' Johnny Utah. Ha-ha." Dixon laughs as well.

"Hey, do you two mind?" Martha says. "I'm trying to plan here."

"If you'd taught them the past continuous on Friday, like you were supposed to, I wouldn't be having this problem."

"It was Friday," Martha replies hotly. "We had fun."

"An orgy on the second floor?"

Seth laughs as Martha gives Dixon the finger.

"At least someone thinks there can be humour in this room," Dixon says, gathering up her materials. Then she's struck by an idea. "Another room. That's what I need."

"For what?" Seth asks.

"To split the class in half."

She stands up and goes out of the teachers' room. A few students are crowding the narrow hallway. They're all a bit overweight and bulky, and take up more room than necessary. She has to weave between them and push her way through. They're also talking in German, despite the clear rule told to them from day one that they shall speak English together, even outside of class time. Total immersion, that's the idea, but none of them stick to it. She's already discovered that during these two-month courses, none of them really learn anything. She thinks these people gave up learning anything new years ago, gave up trying as well, and now the grey cloud of loserdom hangs over them permanently, especially the ones who make it to the end of the course. Those who drop out early are the more intelligent and motivated students, the ones who could really benefit from the course, but who inevitably find jobs and have to pull out. Those who remain to the end, clutching their copies of the *Bild*, talking German whenever possible and smoking in the breaks, have long stopped even applying for jobs. And nearly every class has at least one prick like Heino who ruins the experience for the rest.

She gets to Julian's office and knocks. There's no answer, so she opens the door. On the wall is the room plan for the week. On this Monday morning, all the rooms are booked.

"Fuck," she says. But she thinks about last Monday, when she taught Kennedy. Then, the room next door had been empty.

"Morning, Dixon," Julian says, coming in. "Can I help you with anything?"

"Hey, DOS. I was just checking the schedule."

"You better hustle. Classes start in about one minute."

"I'm all over it," she says as Julian moves around to his chair and sits down at his disorderly desk. "What's up with room nine? Is that being used today?"

"Hameln," Julian says, without looking at the calendar. "It's booked for them."

"Yeah, but they weren't there last Monday. Did they take a field trip?"

In a low voice, Julian asks, "Do you want to use the room?"

"Can I? I need a second room for an activity I've got planned."

"Go for it. And if it works, remember to write it down and add it to the file of lesson plans."

135

"Thanks, DOS."

"Welcome."

Dixon goes out of the office, then goes back in. She stands in the doorway. A few late-arriving students brush past her.

"What's the deal with the Hameln class?" she asks. "Where are they?"

Julian looks at the monitor and starts tapping at the keyboard with his index fingers. "Permanent field trip. Learning by doing."

"Practical German, yeah?"

"Something like that. Now, if you don't mind." The bell rings. "Ah, there's your cue. And I've got about a hundred emails to read and reply to."

No need to be rude, she thinks as she walks down the hallway to the teachers' room. Glad I'm not the director of studies. What a miserable job.

But something makes her stop and turn. She weaves back between the students. They stink of cigarette smoke and failure, and are in no hurry to get to class. At the reception area, she fingers through the filing cabinet and finds the Hameln class card. Today's attendance has already been taken and the class report filled in. She looks through the list of names. Eastern Europeans mostly, maybe Russian, all present today. Thirty girls in one class. The room wouldn't be big enough for them.

"What are you doing?" Angelika asks in her halting English.

"Just checking something."

There's a photocopier next to the filing cabinet. She makes a quick copy of the attendance sheet, folds it and puts it in the back pocket of her jeans. She places the class card back in the file. As she rounds the receptionist's desk, now late for her class, the door to the school opens. Heino saunters in, wearing that huge puffy coat of his, with the fur-lined hood, that makes him look like a hip-hop star. Or a pimp.

A failed pimp, Dixon thinks. The forty-year-old failure of a pimp.

"Guten Morgen," he says slowly, completely bored and nonplussed by everything life has to offer. "Vat make we today?"

"Ben?"

"Yes?"

"Ben, wait up."

He stops pedalling and coasts. When she gets alongside him, he asks, "What's the matter? Why are you so slow?

"Look at this thing I'm riding. I feel like I'm pedalling a rickshaw with a couple of tubby Yanks in the back."

There's a pair of rollerbladers coming from the other direction. Ben positions his bike a little to left, almost in front of Dixon, to let them pass. The female of the pair, her elbows out and hands splayed for balance, goes within a centimetre or two of knocking Ben off his bicycle.

Dixon is just slightly disappointed it doesn't happen, especially given the amount of sheep poop on the ground.

"How far are we planning to go anyhow?" she asks.

"To Hohenhorst."

"Where's that?"

"At the end of this path."

She looks ahead. The dike seems to go forever. Up ahead, she can see yet another gate, and she's certain she will be the one who opens and closes it.

"Why are we going to Hohenhorst?" she asks. "All this pedalling better be worth it."

"Well, my dear Dix, it's nice just to be out, but we are going for apple juice."

"That's your surprise? Apple juice?"

Ben grins and nods.

"You get me out of bed on a Sunday morning to ride a couple of hours for apple juice?" she asks.

"I thought you liked the outdoors."

"I do." She swallows what she wants to say. "It's very nice. You're right. Good to be out. Bring on the juice. I hope it's the nectar of the gods you say it is."

"Another four or five miles and you'll find out."

"What's that in a real distance?"

"Seven kilometres or so."

Ben rings his bell and they weave between a large group that has been separated by the group members' various walking speeds.

"I'm glad we took the train to Wedel," she says. "Would've been a long ride otherwise."

"Maybe we can stop in Blankenese on the way back. You can meet my parents."

"And bring them flagons of apple juice as a present? How do you buy it here anyway? By the gourd?"

"The what?"

"I'm not carrying it."

Ben tilts his head towards her bike. "We could put it in your basket."

"No way. That would just make this rust pile even heavier."

"You need a new bike."

"This is Astrid's," she explains. "She never uses it. It's actually pretty good in the city, even with just one speed. And nobody would ever think of stealing it."

"But not quite the best for touring the glorious German countryside."

"Yeah, what he said." But she catches herself again and brightens her tone. "I want a bike like you've got. What did you call it?"

"A hybrid," Ben says proudly.

Dixon gives him a thumbs up. "Good for you."

"Excuse me?"

"Nothing."

They ride in silence. As she's not only struggling with the bike, she decides to change her focus, to take in the surroundings and enjoy herself regardless. So she smiles at the beautiful autumn colours in the trees, the flock of geese in one field, the cows and sheep in another, the swans gliding around a small lake, the whitish sun arcing around the side of the sky. It's very pleasant out, and yes, she thinks, nice to be out of the city.

As they approach the next gate, she snaps out of her thoughts and sees that Ben has positioned himself behind her. She reaches the gate first and is forced to hold it open for him. He nearly falls off trying to ride through, but compensates for this with a burst of speed, clicking through the gears and pedalling with his whole body.

"What a gentleman," she mutters, letting the gate fall shut. It thumps against an old car tire.

From a dead stop, it's an effort to get the bike going, and she stands up and puts in some work. But once it's going, it rides very easily. She knows Ben is just trying to show off: one more thing he can do, ride a bicycle. And she thinks that she might like him a whole lot more if he didn't keep trying to impress her. He just wants too badly for her to think that he's the greatest human being on the planet.

Is there a bigger turnoff than insecurity? she wonders.

Putting in the effort on the bike is making her hot. With a wool hat, scarf and jacket, she's over-dressed, even though the sun is only giving the illusion of warmth on this crisp, clear day. There are plenty of people out enjoying it. The clusters of families and groups of friends walk slowly, spread out, Sunday strolling and taking up the whole path. Every cyclist has to ring their bell to clear the way, and every cyclist has a bell to ring, and every cyclist uses it, and every walker jumps in shock and annoyance when they hear one. These high-pitched ting-a-lings, and the desultory conversations in reaction, are detracting greatly from the enjoyment of being out in the countryside. Dixon hears meanness and annoyance in the ringing of the bells, so it's no wonder that the walkers react in the same way.

"Come on, Dix," Ben shouts. "Put your back into it."

Challenged, she pedals harder and says, "All this for apple juice."

The bike path along the dike is littered with sheep shit. There are grubby, mud-covered sheep grazing on the dike's hill, which explains all the fences and gates.

She wants to turn her bike around and pedal back to Wedel.

"I really thought you were more of a sporty type," Ben says when she pulls alongside him.

"Let's swap bikes and have a race," she says. "Last one to the apple farm pays."

"It's called an orchard," Ben says. "Oh, let's just enjoy the ride. It's fabulous to be out. We have to work all week, but today we're free."

He tries to ride with no hands, but the bike tilts precariously to the left and he only just manages to stay on.

"Are you taking me with you tomorrow?" she asks.

"No. You start much earlier than me. When's your first class again?"

"At seven."

Ben scoffs at this. "My lord. You'll have to be on the ferry at six-

139

thirty. That means getting up, maybe, an hour before, depending on how long you need to get ready."

"Not long."

"I'll still be fast asleep."

They negotiate another group, Ben's bell a-ringing.

"Thanks for your support," she says when the path is clear.

"Who's in your class anyway? Can you say?"

"Don't know. Haven't checked."

"It's a huge company. Unless they're in NAG, I probably won't know them."

"I think they're HR people," she says, knowing exactly that they are HR people, and having already memorised the students' names and searched them online.

"What'll you teach them?" Ben asks, feigning interest.

"Not sure yet. It's kind of a test class. The HR folks want to be sure Multilinga is the right school for the company."

"Is it?"

Ben's pace starts to slow. Dixon wonders if he's getting tired, but then she looks up ahead and, sure enough, there's another gate approaching. She slows down as well.

"I think so," she says, now riding at almost walking speed. "The pressure's really on. My boss said as much. But I know I can do it."

"So do I."

But she thinks he doesn't sound convincing.

"The method is good," she continues, "but the materials are awful. You can't use them. I'm going to tailor my class to the HR broads. Talk their talk, use their language, get them onto topics that they already know about."

"Good idea."

"Yeah, and it's a confidence thing too. People feel more comfortable talking about what they know, especially when learning a new language." ·

They finally reach the gate. Dixon opens it. A man on a racing bike, ringing his bell madly, is coming from the other direction. She holds the gate open for him and Ben is forced to stop. The man doesn't say thank you. He's wearing a bright yellow jacket.

"Looks like someone is seriously lacking attention," she says.

"What?" Ben asks, walking his bike through the gate.

"The fluoro jacket."

"I think it's good," Ben says over his shoulder. "People can see him."

"And that's the whole idea," she mutters, pedalling again.

More sheep. Fewer people.

She thinks Ben looks awkward on the bike, like someone who seldom rides, or someone who was taught to ride by someone who seldom rides. His whole body is involved in every revolution, his back going from side-to-side, like a lumbering animal, his shoulders dipping, his knees splayed, his head bopping. He seems to will the bike forward with all of his strength. He grips the handle bars hard enough to turn his knuckles white, and he rings that bloody bell the way someone might hammer a gong.

"We're almost there," he says, puffing now, working hard. He looks behind to see where Dixon is, and the movement causes him to lose control and ride a few metres on the grass. A sheep bleats and struggles out of the way.

Dixon laughs.

"Good to hear you're finally enjoying yourself," he says, back on the path and slightly more red in the face.

"I'm just nervous about tomorrow."

"You'll be great."

"Thanks, Ben. And thanks for taking me out for a ride."

He smiles and nods. "All this, my princess," extending a sweeping arm, "it could be yours one day."

She laughs again. She likes him when he's like this, when he lets his guard down and plays the fool a bit. Unfortunately, it never lasts very long, because he takes himself way too seriously.

"I'd prefer this area to downtown," she says. "Great that there are no cars."

"You'd get bored out here. I did."

"Come on. Blankenese is not exactly the sticks. It's fifteen minutes by train."

"I like the city," he says flatly.

She does as well, but she's also enjoying this respite from it. The open fields and the lack of people. Hamburg's traffic drives her mad, especially biking in it. She's thankful for the numerous bike paths, but it can still be tough just to survive a ride. The traffic flows incessantly, throughout the day, perfectly organised and engineered. She spoke about this with Seth and a few other teachers at the last Multilinga staff meeting: what an incredible feat of efficiency Hamburg is, that the city can have so much traffic yet so few traffic jams. Last week, waiting for Ben, she stood on the pedestrian bridge near the Landungsbrücken train station and watched all the cars passing below. She kept a mental record. After ten minutes, she calculated that, excluding taxis, one in every eight cars had more than one person in it. All these cars, all in the city, but no jams. Amazing. Standing there, she also asked herself how the locals could afford it: to run a car, pay the insurance and buy the petrol.

"Thirsty, Dix?" Ben asks, snapping her from her thoughts.

"I've got a major hankering for apple juice. You reckon you can help me with that?"

He laughs. "What about having lunch tomorrow?"

"My classes are finished by ten. Two times ninety minutes, back-to-back. I'm not gonna hang around."

"Shame."

"Sorry."

They ride a hundred metres or so in silence.

Dixon can hear Ben breathing.

The sheep graze and wander over to the path for a pee. Birds glide overhead; they look like hawks.

She's glad they've left all the strollers and rollerbladers behind. They've got the path to themselves.

"Looks like we're the only ones who want apple juice," she says.

"Everyone else drives out, so they can carry it back as well."

"Ah." She pauses. "Hey, look, Ben, can you tell me a bit more about Flussair? So I can prep myself for tomorrow?"

"What do you want to know?"

"Tell me about your department. You have yet to say anything about what you do exactly."

"There's a good reason for that. Besides, the HR people don't know either."

"But what happens when I have a class from your department? Maybe you'll be in it."

"I doubt that," he says, offended.

"I'll still need to be able to talk on their level."

"Nobody in NAG will talk about what we do. Those are the rules."

Dixon presses the point, not willing to let Ben win: "But tailoring a class requires the students using their own language, the words they use at work. It's the same as talking about yourself." More coldly, and looking at Ben, "Everyone likes talking about themselves." Then in a lighter tone, "It's part of the needs analysis too, asking them when they use English, what they need it for and stuff like that. We have to do it in the first class."

"You'll have to clear that with Lessinger," Ben says with a shrug. "He's the department head. You'll probably have to sign something. Non-disclosure, we'll kill you if you talk. Something like that."

"A secrecy agreement?"

"Yes."

"Is it that top secret?" she asks, pedalling to keep pace with him. "Are you making, like, the ultimate weapon?"

"We don't build weapons," Ben says harshly. "The navigation systems are for aircraft. Passenger planes."

"Is it like sat-nav in a car?"

Ben grunts. "It's much more complicated than that. Too complicated for you to understand."

She just keeps herself from extending a leg and pushing him and his bicycle to the poop-covered ground.

"Anyway, you don't have a class with NAG yet, so there's no reason for us to even discuss it."

"I'm interested in you," she says, attempting to smile with sincerity, "in what you do. Sounds like really fancy stuff."

"It is." After a deep breath, and with Dixon seeing his guard drop, "What I do is not that much different from what a lot of other people do. I'm basically a salesman. I have a product and I have to get people interested in it, so they buy it, or they invest in the development. I'm sometimes involved in the testing, but that's just for education purposes, so I can talk about the products. The guys doing the real work are the engineers and scientists. That's not me."

"So why did you choose to work in this department?"

"Because this is where the real tech is. The amazing stuff. Tomorrow's technology. Any construction company with a pile of steel and a few engines can put a plane together, but the navigation equipment, the fly-by-wire, drone aircraft, this is where the future is, Dix. Imagine a plane with five hundred people on board and no pilot. The cockpit's empty. Or, or a rescue mission, something too dangerous to risk the lives of pilots. You send in the drone. It's cutting-edge stuff."

"Aren't the Americans using drones in Iraq?"

He turns to her, almost falling off the bike. "How do you know that?"

"I read about it."

She's annoyed by his surprise and disbelief.

"Well, they've got the tech," he says, "but it's a few years out of date. It's nowhere near as sophisticated as what we're doing, but yes, the principle is the same. What they can do is very limited. Short range too. We're a decade ahead of them."

"Also for use in Iraq?"

"No, Dixon. Not at all. Why do you say that?"

"Just asking. I wanna know what you do. I like the fact that you're really into it."

There are symmetrical lines of apple trees on the right.

"Here," Ben says. "This is it."

"Fabulous. I've got a camel-sized thirst."

Ben points down a side road and lets Dixon lead the way. She reaches the gate first and holds it open for him.

Babette Korner leans against the low counter of the kitchenette. With her long legs, she's almost able to sit on the counter.

She considers the morning so far, everything Dixon has said and hasn't said. All the truth and fiction, and combinations of the two. It's there she gets stuck, at the concept of fictional truths.

She's lying, she thinks to herself, sipping coffee from her large thermos mug. Lying about something. The question is what.

The coffee is her third of the day, which means she's already consumed a good litre of the stuff. Liquid diet, she thinks, liking it. What she wants is a cigarette, to inhale deeply and think, to hold the smoke inside her and let the joyous reactions take place. Yes, when you smoke it right, you can get a little high from a cigarette. From a good cigarette, hand-rolled, with some heavy tobacco that has texture you can chew on. Something with body, not something filtered or processed.

But this floor of the LKA, with its healthy, bookish nerds – guys who run forty-five minutes during lunch break – has a no smoking policy.

It's all right. She's trying to quit. But the extra caffeine hasn't quite dulled her need for nicotine. Worse, sipping a coffee is not nearly as meditative and relaxing. Nor is it as social.

She's not getting any clarity, any distance.

Dixon is lying, but she doesn't know why. And she doesn't know which are lies and which are fictional truths; the made up stuff and the conjectures that might turn out to be true.

She looks around. The LKA here is not nearly as busy as her section. It has the look and feel of an office. Very few people here are wearing guns. The desk-bound officers hunch over their keyboards and type expertly, like they've had training. They could be doing data entry for a bank, or some other bland office task. Not exactly world-saving investigations, but useful, certainly useful. She's reminded again how often some totally evil prick is brought to his knees not for murder or drug-running or something like that, but by a financial investigation. The bodies pile up, but he goes to prison for not paying his taxes.

She bets that the people working in this section live by the mantra, "Follow the money." It'd be the first thing they're told on their first day: "Here's your desk. Here's the target. Now, follow the money and see where it leads."

The Dixon Grace file is on the counter. She flips it open and checks the bank statements. A healthy balance, because Dixon never paid rent while living with Benjamin Steckdorf. Looks like she spent a lot, on flights and hotels, travelling around Europe. But why wouldn't she? Korner wonders. Isn't that what she's here for, the European experience? There's not a single thing suspicious about the statements. No cash deposits from unnamed sources. No money to follow.

She sips some more. The fingers of her left hand drum against the counter.

One possibility, she thinks, is to let Dixon go, then follow her, see where she runs to. And who she runs to.

"Saraswati Mittal?" she wonders out loud. She checks her watch. Schultze is taking a pretty long time trying to put together Mittal's file.

She doesn't like Schultze, the man and his type. But he does good work, as do the others in this section. Effective work. She admires the officers here, but is glad she's not one of them. She's also glad she'll never have to go into battle with any of them. An investigative wimp like Schultze wouldn't have her back in a tough situation, wouldn't come to her rescue when needed. He probably hasn't fired a gun in years, let alone killed anyone. But she also knows that it's the guys like Schultze – committed, clean and without scars – who rise up in the department. These arse-kissers go from one office to the next, moving slowly up the chain, working the numbers and staying out of trouble. They're politicians in the making, statisticians and mathematicians, out to make the right allegiances. It's the Schultzes who rule the LKA, especially at the top, and the Bundesnachrichtendienst, and the Kriminalpolizei, and every other civil service organisation in Germany; this massive family tree populated by men who never get their hands dirty. They're family men, clock-punchers, heading home on the six-fifteen train or taking the Autobahn to their big houses in Quickborn, Reinbek and Itzehoe.

She thinks she would also have a chance at promotion if she was willing to play the bureaucratic game, to work the levels and pamper the gents on high. Climb the ladders and avoid the snakes.

Reminded, she pulls out her phone.

It rings four times.

"Korner."

"Na, Mama. Wie gehts?"

"Ja-ja. Mit Marcus ist die Hölle los."

"Gib ihn mir."

There's a pause as the phone is passed.

"Mum?"

"Ah, my sweet little devil. Are you giving Oma a hard time?"

"Ist langweilig hier."

"Speak English, Marcus."

"I'm bored. When are you coming home?"

"Later," she says, but wishing she could walk out the door right now. "You're raising hell at home and there are plenty of people raising hell in the outside world as well. But I'll get back in time to read you a story. Okay?"

"That's hours away."

"I know. So enjoy it with Oma. And be nice to her."

"Okay." Silence. Then, "Mum?"

"Yes?"

"I want you to come home."

"Oh, sweetie, I miss you too. But we'll see each other tonight. We'll play games and read some books. It'll be fun."

"Why not now?"

"Mum's got bad guys to catch. The world to save. So be good. I don't want to come home and have to catch another bad guy."

"Okay. Bye."

"Bye, my little devil."

She pockets the phone. Bad guys, she thinks. Is Dixon really one of them? A spy, maybe. Out of ignorance, most likely. She probably didn't know what she was doing or who she was dealing with. Or is that the fiction Dixon wants me to believe?

Schultze is ambling towards her, blue dossier in hand.

"Zarasvardi Middle," he says, handing it to her.

"Danke."

She opens the file and reads, ignoring him until he turns and lumbers away.

"Wo ist Dixon?" she asks, making him stop.

Schultze shrugs his big shoulders. "Toilette," he says, and he continues to walk.

The dossier on Saraswati Mittal is very thin, like the one on Dixon. There's a profile from the Freie Universität in Berlin, and the records from the foreign office. The professor-doctor-doctor is clean, seriously clean. It appears Schultze has done some extra research online, because there are a few printouts of the organisations Mittal is connected to.

Korner groans as she reads.

Mittal is involved with a couple of women's groups in Germany and one in the UK. She sits on the board of the charity FeedIndia. There are a few photos of her with the Indian Ambassador, and what look like graduation photos. Schultze hasn't made a link to Nayakall, beyond the very thin connection of Mittal being born in Tiruvallur, which is inland from Chennai, where the headquarters of Nayakall is located.

She stops on one photo. It's a FeedIndia function, a fundraiser of sorts. A line of smiling people, well-dressed and professional. Mittal is on the end, looking small and frail. The rest are men. She checks the caption, reading through the names.

Devan Marawar, she thinks to herself.

She takes out her phone and searches the name. She discovers that Marawar is founder and CEO of Nayakall.

She sips some more coffee. Okay, she thinks, so they might know each other. That's still no reason to bring Mittal in for questioning. Schultze had already suggested that, before he did any research on her. But it would be a mistake. Mittal would have some serious lobbying power behind her, with her connections to the India Embassy and the Foreign Ministry and God knows what else. This dossier probably represents the tip of this Indian angel's iceberg. And if called in for questioning, Mittal would just as quickly come to the rescue of Dixon Grace. With that, the whole investigation would come crashing down. There's nothing fictional about that truth. That's the reality. If they've got nothing concrete on Mittal, then they can't go near her.

Korner understands that the fact Dixon Grace has been arrested must be kept a secret. For now. She needs to dig deeper, to think bigger.

She sips and contemplates. Bigger. This is all bigger than Dixon, she thinks, that's for sure. Murder and espionage, these crimes are beyond her. There's something larger at work and it involves big players. This all can't simply be the work of one English teacher from Australia, a former police officer at that. She's not capable.

Korner's suddenly struck by the overwhelming feeling that they've made a terrible mistake by arresting Dixon. Someone has made her to be the sacrificial goat. Dixon is taking the fall for a bigger player. She's a diversion, a time-waster.

So she decides to let Dixon go, and to follow her. Just for a day or two. But she'll need to be clever about it, will need to keep Schultze out of the room.

She checks her watch.

I just need to wait for lunch break, she thinks with a smile.

Then she checks her watch again.

She leaves her thermos mug and the two dossiers on the counter. Out in the hallway, a few men are wandering up and down, at work but in no hurry. She sees Schultze chatting with someone. They laugh. Schultze's head turns as she passes him.

She gets to the ladies bathroom and pushes the door open. The guard is sitting on the floor, pressing Dixon's t-shirt against her naked chest. She looks dazed. Her forehead is red with blood.

Korner sees the mobile phone on the counter next to the basin.

"I'm innocent and I will prove it," she reads. "You clever girl."

He sits at the bar. The purple stool is more than a little kitsch, like he's in a refurbished strip club on the Reeperbahn, or he's an extra in an avant-garde film. He chooses to run with that image, to keep his mind from falling back to some recent forgettable nights out in St Pauli.

He shakes his head viciously, to make the images go away, but they remain.

And he hates himself for it. He's been on this self-hate trip all day long. In this incredibly crowded city, he's a circus sideshow freak, two heads taller than almost everyone else, blonde-haired and fair-skinned, and sweating profusely. They all stare at him, talking behind their hands as they point at the damp sweat circles under his arms. He can't escape, feels exceedingly self-conscious, as if his every move is being watched, judged and ridiculed.

He'd thought Shanghai would be more international, more open, and maybe it is, in another part of town. But the whole day he's felt on display, an oddity brought back from the far west. That's why he's hiding in the hotel bar, enjoying the air-conditioning and drowning in this purple sea. He would prefer to sit outside on the terrace, but it's just too damn hot and humid, and he sweats too much, his forehead beading like a slow-motion sprinkler. Here in Shangahi, he has sweated more than any time in his life. He's already had three showers today, and gone through three shirts.

He drinks his weak beer, grimacing as he relives the day.

At the meeting, the blue shirt had been a mistake. By the end of his presentation, he looked like he'd just got out of a pool fully clothed. And all of them, unmoveable objects sitting there in their suits, had stared with shock, as if they never sweated at all.

He grunts, hating it here, and hating himself.

Like they did after the meeting, some slightly racist undertones work their way from the back of his brain to the front. He has a lot to say about Shanghai, about the people here, but no one to say it to.

He takes out his mobile phone and thinks about who he can call. Dixon? he wonders. No, because we barely talk any more. She's probably glad I've gone away on business again.

He decides on his mother, certain that she will lend a sympathetic, bigoted ear.

"Excuse me? Is this seat taken?"

Ben looks at the empty stools, that line-up of deep purple, perfectly angled and positioned. He wonders why the Indian-looking man wants to sit next to him.

"Go for it," he says, cancelling the call and pocketing his phone.

"English?" The man climbs onto the stool and gets comfortable.

"German, but I was educated in England."

"Ah."

The waiter meanders up to the man and raises his eyebrows.

"Vodka and cranberry juice, please," the man says. Then to Ben, "An American business friend got me onto that drink."

"Hmm?"

"The best of both worlds, that's what he said. Healthy and intoxicating."

"Right." Ben stares straight ahead, trying to avoid his reflection in the mirror.

"What are you drinking?"

"I think it's beer," he says with a look at the label. "But it tastes a lot like water. It's awful, but I do feel a bit more rehydrated."

The man laughs politely. "Not quite German beer."

"No. It's not."

The man smiles, keen to be sociable. "My name is Dinesh."

"Ben."

They don't shake hands. Ben starts to peel the label from his beer bottle. The waiter places Dinesh's drink on the bar. It has a purple umbrella in it. Dinesh takes the umbrella out and twirls it with his thumb and forefinger as he sips.

"Would you like one?" Dinesh asks.

"A tiny umbrella?"

"A drink. V and C."

Ben drains his beer. "Sure. Why not. But no ice. I had a bad experience with ice once. In Bali."

"Cranberry juice is good for the stomach," Dinesh says, beckoning the waiter. He taps the rim of his glass with the little umbrella and then holds the umbrella up, signifying one. The waiter complies and gets to work.

"Looks a bit like medicine," Ben says. "Cough syrup, or something like that."

They lapse into silence. Ben can hear piano music, a jazzy version of *The Wind Cries Mary*, coming from the lobby, or maybe from the restaurant. It could even be coming from the speakers above the shelf of bottles. He likes the music, and likes the fact Dinesh has sat down next to him.

Distraction is very, very good, he thinks.

"What brings you to Shanghai, Ben?" Dinesh asks. "Business or pleasure?"

"There's no way it could be pleasure."

"Maybe you're not looking in the right places."

Ben looks through the sides of his eyes at Dinesh, curious as to what kind of man he is, what road he may lead them down, if allowed. He's average height, a little plump, with a face shaped like a rectangle. He has a strange, childish smile. Ben doesn't even try to guess his age. He's wearing a well-cut, navy blue suit. Ben, who considers himself an expert on personal presentation, thinks the suit is tailor-made. Not quite bespoke, but made-to-measure. It fits the rounded Indian like a glove and yields in the right places when he's sitting.

Ben's drink arrives. He stares into it, seeing more past than future.

"It's been all business," he says at last, "and it will continue that way. I'll be all business tomorrow morning. I'll pack efficiently, get to the airport on time and fly back home. Unfortunately, not in business class."

"You sound keen to leave. I assume Shanghai hasn't worked her charms on you."

"Not unless by charms you mean the almost one-hundred percent humidity."

Dinesh laughs again, following through with his baby-faced smile.

"I'm not in the right frame of mind for being a tourist," Ben adds.

"It's not always easy mixing business and pleasure." After a pause, "Who do you work for?"

Ben sips his drink. To his surprise, he likes it. "Can't say."

"Ah, CIA?"

"Not quite."

"But dealing in secrets, am I right?"

"Just doing business," Ben says. "Or trying to. Cutting through the haze to cut some deals."

Dinesh talks into his glass, just before sipping: "Industry?"

"Aircraft."

"For transportation or destruction?"

Ben turns his head to Dinesh. "Excuse me?"

But Dinesh is all whimsical smiles. "Well, there are planes that move people from one place to another," he says brightly, "and there are planes that remove people from the face of the earth. Which are you involved in?"

"It's not that black and white," Ben says, taking a big gulp of his medicine-like cocktail.

"An answer like that leads me to conclude the latter."

"Actually, it means no answer at all."

"Or it means both." Dinesh is enjoying the innuendo. "All the aircraft manufacturers do both. Don't they? Diversify their business, go where the money is. Do what their customers want."

"There's no money in weapons."

"Oh no?" Dinesh sounds like he disagrees.

"Not directly," Ben says. "People who want to fight and blow things up normally don't have the money to do it. That's what my boss says, anyway."

"I think your boss has a very limited view of the world, if you'll pardon my frankness."

"Ha-ha. That's good. Frankness. My boss's name is Frank."

"A pun without even trying," Dinesh says.

"Frank's certainly a joke," Ben mutters into his glass.

"What do you think?"

"About what?"

"The money."

"You mean weapons, right? I'm not interested in them." Then, nodding thoughtfully, "Okay, some of our tech has military applications, I'll give you that. But it's not what we build it for."

"Interesting. And? Successful here in Shanghai?"

Again, Ben sees himself sweating in the presentation, then sweating during lunch, then sweating – through a fresh shirt and after a shower at the hotel – during the brief walking tour of downtown Shanghai.

"That depends," he says. "I've lost a couple of kilos already. I'd call that a success."

"I could use that too."

"But the business hasn't really gone as planned."

"Because?" Dinesh prompts.

"Because I'm not the one they want to deal with. I'm not ..." He trails off, hating himself. "I'm not high enough. I'm just the lowly messenger. They want to deal with the department head."

"With Frank?"

Ben gestures at Dinesh with his almost empty glass. "Yep. His royal Frankness."

"Perhaps it was the message, not the messenger."

"No. It was all about status. They didn't take me seriously. Because, for them, I'm just one of the minions. A blonde-haired freak of a minion."

Turning slightly to Ben and leaning an elbow on the bar, "I think you're being too hard on yourself. Doing business with the Chinese takes a while. Deals don't normally get done after one meeting."

Ben raises his eyebrows at Dinesh, liking what his drinking partner is saying.

"I don't think it would've been any different with Frank," Dinesh adds. "But I'm very curious to know what the message was."

"You really want to know? Are you CIA, or India Intelligence, or whatever it's called?"

Dinesh shakes his head. "No. I'm a messenger, like you."

"And what's your message?"

"What's yours?"

They both laugh.

"This is going nowhere," Ben says. He holds up his glass in the direction of the waiter. "I need another drink. You?"

Dinesh's glass is still almost full. "I'm good, for now."

Ben swivels the purple stool. "Let's make a deal. It's late. We're in Shanghai. We'll never see each other again. We don't know each other's last name. Let's both say exactly what we do and get it out in the open. You don't have to name any companies or organisations. Just say what it is."

"The message."

"Yes."

Dinesh smiles. "Deal."

They shake hands.

There's an awkward silence, before Dinesh asks, "Who starts?"

Ben looks around. "I will." Lowering his voice, "I'm involved with planes that fly themselves."

"Robotics?"

This catches Ben slightly off-guard. "Uh, not quite. But it sounds like you know your stuff. We're focusing on drones. Pilotless aircraft."

Dinesh is sufficiently impressed. "Fascinating. But most certainly effective for removing people from the face of the earth."

"Unfortunately, yes."

"Is that the message you're bringing to China?"

Ben's second drink arrives. He removes the umbrella and takes a sip. "Not the military part. More about the benefits and possible uses."

"Such as?"

"Emergencies, rescues, natural disasters, evacuations. That sort of thing. Situations that require removing human errors from the equation and keeping pilots out of harm's way."

Dinesh considers this. "I think you're going into dangerous territory when you're willing to put lives in the hands of machines," he says solemnly.

"About ninety percent of the world's already like that," Ben counters.

"True. The western world." Dinesh takes a small sip. "And? Were your clients interested?"

"Like I said. They didn't want to speak to the messenger. They just stared at him as he sweated a river."

"Very rude."

"Yes."

"Maybe it needs some time," Dinesh says. "Invite them to visit your company in Germany."

"Are you an expert when it comes to doing business with the Chinese?" Ben asks, a little jokingly. "Is that your message?"

Dinesh takes one last conservative sip and stands up. From the inside of his suit jacket, he pulls out a business card.

"There's no need for me to repeat everything you just said," he says, placing the card on the bar, next to Ben's right hand. "I think we should stay in contact, in case you're interested in being the boss rather than working for one."

Ben picks up the card and looks at it. "Wait a minute? Who are you?"

"Write me an email," Dinesh says, giving Ben that childish smile of his. "It was nice meeting you." To the waiter, "Charge his drinks to my room please." To Ben, "But don't overdo it. I wouldn't want you to miss your flight tomorrow."

Ben watches Dinesh walk the length of the bar, the brown fingers of his left hand sweeping lightly along the back of each purple stool he passes.

The business card is firm and stiff, with rounded corners. It's weighty too, like it's made of some metal-plastic composite rather than the usual cheap paper.

"Dinesh Prasad. Nayakall."

He looks into his glass, at the reddish liquid that tastes better with every sip. He racks his brain trying to recall where and when he heard that name.

The house is quiet. No one has come in today, but as Laz keeps saying, the day isn't over yet. The Christmas and new year period is normally high season at the café, a veritable revolving door of battered and suffering women. They arrive at all hours and in all manner of conditions. Dixon spent many Christmases working here, helping out.

"I'm done," Dixon says, pleasantly weary from working in the garden all day. It had been Laz's idea, to plant strawberries, so that Dixon would have good fortune in Germany. Laz had said that the success of the small berry patch would mirror Dixon's own success in Germany.

"That's how you spend Christmas," Laz says. "You plant something."

"Indeed."

They're sitting at the window, watching the evening sunset fade. The colourful lights on the houses are starting to dominate, but the scattering of clouds in the sky are still tinged slightly pink.

Looking at Laz, Dixon thinks her beautiful grandmother seems tired, just starting to age. She wonders if the work of the café, all the stress and troubles Laz deals with on a daily basis, is beginning to wear on her.

They're drinking blackcurrant juice from wine glasses. Dixon picks up her glass and swirls it.

"Ah," she says. "The illusion of alcohol."

"Thanks for your help today."

"Was nothing, Lazarus. It was good for me, to get my hands dirty and go all hippy again."

"Yes. Do some real work for a change." Laz takes a sip. "Are you nervous?"

"About the teaching?"

"You're about to set off on a big adventure. Europe, Dixie. I can't even begin to imagine it."

"It's gonna be wild. You can come visit me."

"I always wanted to go to Europe," Laz says with a thin smile. "Paris was this young girl's dream."

They drink a little. The silence is solemn. Some hoon in a suped-up car goes roaring down Bowen Street.

"Amateur night," Dixon says. "When all the idiots come out to play."

"And the night's just beginning."

"Welcome to the midnight Christmas vigil of Saint Lazarus. Hah. Sounds like a television special."

Laz laughs softly as she looks out the window. The street is quiet again.

"Tell me about what you're feeling, Dixie. We haven't talked about it at all today."

"You had me working too hard." After a sigh, "Look, I'm nervous. About living in Germany. And what do I know about teaching English?"

"When you can hardly speak the language yourself."

"Easy, Lazzle Dazzle. Your accent's not exactly localised."

"I think I adapted all right."

"You did." Dixon reaches out and strokes her grandmother's forearm. "You're amazing. This house. The life you've led."

"Don't get soppy on me."

"You're beautiful, and I want you to see Paris. I'll meet you there. "

Laz looks wistfully out the window. "Some day. I still say you don't know just how good you have it, Dixie. But Narooma was never enough for you. Same with the café. You always had bigger things in mind."

"Misty can have it," Dixon says angrily. Then in a more relaxed tone, "Maybe it'd be good for her. To deal with things. She hasn't been the same since Melbourne. And that was ages ago."

"She owes you. A lot."

"So do you, for all that garden work today. Twenty bucks an hour, at least."

"You're lucky to get a glass of blackcurrant juice."

They smile at each other, enjoying the moment, savouring it.

"Misty started a support group here," Laz says. "For attack victims."

"Yeah? She hasn't said anything about that."

"Maybe it's time you had a talk with her. About the attack. And about Rika too. Do it before you leave again. Who knows how long you'll be gone."

"I'm thinking about two years. Astrid's descriptions of the winters there, God, it sounds diabolical."

"You could always come back here for a few weeks of summer."

"Good idea."

"How is Astrid?" Laz asks.

"Pretty good. It's hard to get a read on her from her emails. She's studying to become a lawyer, and she's working part-time as a paralegal."

Laz fingers one of her hair bands loose. One plaited pigtail slowly unwinds. She has long, lustrous straight hair that's now a mix of brown and grey. The balance of the mix is slowly shifting towards grey.

"A tough girl," she says. "I knew that when she first came in. And I knew something was wrong."

"It'll be good to see her."

"Take some pictures of the lemon tree, the one she planted when she was here."

"I can't believe how much it's grown."

"The lemons are very tasty too," Laz says, pulling out the hair band from the other pigtail. "Do you remember what I said then?"

"This tree is meant to be here," Dixon says dramatically.

"Don't make fun of me. What about the photos?"

Dixon takes a gulp of juice. She'd much prefer a glass of wine, but there's no alcohol in the house. "Of the tree? I already sent them to her."

"On Facebook?"

With an expression of surprise, "How do you know about social networking?"

"Misty gave me some lessons. I'm in the process of building a website, for the café."

"You are?"

"The people coming in here get younger every year," Laz says, finger-combing her hair. "They're wired in and I should be too."

"You're amazing, Laz. Beautiful too. I can't imagine what a stunner you must've been as a teenager."

"Not stunning enough. And not a worthy possession."

"That life was never meant for you."

With a sigh, "I guess it all worked out for the best. If I was still in India, I'd be a great-grandmother by now. Or have you got something to tell me? You've been grinning stupidly all day, like you're in love or something."

"Just excited," Dixon says quickly. "My nerves bubbling to the surface."

"You're lying."

Defiantly, "I am not."

Laz's face falls flat, but her eyes remain caring and sympathetic. "I think after all these years of watching women dodge the truth of their own lives, I'd now be able to pick a liar." Pointing a finger, "You, girl, are lying."

"It's nerves, really." Dixon looks out the window to avoid her grandmother's eyes. "I'm heading into the unknown."

"I believe that part, but there's something else. All that doesn't explain the stupid grin."

Dixon sips her juice. "Give me something stronger and I might just tell you."

"The house is dry, you know that."

"You don't keep a bottle stashed away for emergencies? Port or brandy, to calm frazzled female nerves?"

"Alcohol's not the answer to anything," Laz says.

Dixon mimes locking her lips with a key. She tosses the key over her right shoulder.

"You could never keep a secret," Laz says. "I bet you're just dying to tell me."

"I've changed."

"That's also true. And it's about time too. You were such a little brat."

"Hey, steady on, Lazarus."

"You were a brat," Laz declares. "Out of control sometimes. Well into your twenties."

"You're making it easier for me to leave."

"I don't mean it in a bad way. But that kind of behaviour does inhibit personal growth."

Dixon crosses her arms. "You're starting to sound like mum."

Laz is thoughtful for a moment. She looks out the window and runs her fingers through her hair. "Rika was lost," she says. "Caught between two worlds. She always wanted something else, even when she had all the best things right in front of her. She went through life as if the solution to all her problems was just around the next corner."

"Or in a self-help book," Dixon says harshly.

"Hmm. Your father is such a good man, Dixie. And I'm glad to see you're a lot like him. But Rika never appreciated him. Sometimes, it was awful to be around them. I don't think she ever sat back and thought how lucky she was. She just focused on all the things she'd rather have, the things she thought she wanted more."

Dixon sniffs. "Poor dad."

"Poor Rika," Laz counters. "It was that attitude that took her to India, and then ... I hope Steve still doesn't blame himself."

"Of course he does. Wouldn't you?"

"He needs to let it go."

Dixon doesn't reply. She looks down at her hands. They're cracked and dry from the garden work.

"What about you, Dixie? Have you let it go?"

"What do you think?" Dixon replies petulantly.

"I think your time in the police changed you."

"It did."

"And you have a different concept of life and death. Different from me."

The shining beam of a car's headlights makes them both turn. The car stops in front of the house. A woman gets out, leaving the door open and the lights on.

Laz springs to her feet, her long hair trailing behind her as she runs for the door. Dixon follows her. Together, they unlock the two deadlocks and open the door. The distraught woman is a blur as she rushes past Laz and Dixon into the safety of the house.

"Close the door," she says, almost out of breath. "He's coming."

Laz moves forward and carefully embraces the woman, who begins to cry hysterically.

Dixon goes out onto the veranda.

"Anything?" Laz asks, now holding the woman tightly.

"Nothing," Dixon says, scanning the street.

"Come back inside."

"Close the door, close the door," the woman shouts.

"I'll just kill the lights."

Dixon walks down the short path and opens the gate. At the car, she leans inside and turns the lights off. She takes the keys out, closes the door and locks the car. With the headlights off, the festive lights on the nearby houses lend the street a colourful feel. Across the road, there is a large flashing display on the roof of the police station, replete with a Santa Claus in a blue uniform.

She goes back through the gate, but the rumble of an engine makes her stop and turn. A vehicle comes roaring up the hill from Princes

Highway. The four-wheel drive screeches to a halt next to the woman's car and the driver jumps down. The door stays open, the engine running and the lights on. A quick pick up and he'll be off again.

The man is big, solid-looking. A farmer, Dixon decides. He staggers with the first few steps. Dixon has the brief flash that he'll rip the gate off its hinges and toss it aside, but he pushes it open, rather delicately.

"Where is she?" he demands.

Dixon stands in the middle of the path, blocking it, her hands loose at her sides. "Go home," she says firmly.

"I said, where is she?"

"And I said go home," Dixon says, using humour to suppress her building adrenalin. "Wow, this is a fantastic conversation."

"Laura!"

"She's all right here. Let her be."

The man straightens up to his full height, well over six feet. "Who the fuck're you?"

"Constable Dixon Grace."

"Grace? You Gully's kid?"

"Yep. Glad to hear you know each other."

He moves forward. "Get outta the way."

She digs her bare feet into the grassy path and pushes him back. "No."

The physical contact and her defiance take him by surprise.

"Don't make me. I'm not in the mood."

"Look, mate," Dixon says, trying to sound reasonable, "just go home, have a good sleep and we'll sort all this out in the morning."

"Laura! Get out here!" With an index finger pointing at the ground, "She's coming home with me, right now."

"Don't talk to her like she's your dog."

Again, an expression of surprise, confusion almost. "Fuck off," he manages to say.

"That's exactly what you should do."

As he moves forward, his big farmer's hand reaches out to shove her aside. Dixon sidesteps it and grabs that outstretched arm. She pulls it, really yanks it hard trying to pull the arm from the socket, and uses the man's weight to flip him over her hip. He lands on the grass on his back, letting out an audible "Ooof" as the wind is knocked out of him. For a moment, he lays prone, with his knees half bent,

162

like someone with sciatica. Dixon sees him blinking in the darkness, wondering how he ended up on his back.

"Dixie," Laz shouts. "Get inside. Now. We'll lock the door."

But Dixon doesn't move. She waits for the man to get up, wanting him to. He complies, slowly getting onto one knee, then pushing himself up. Once on his feet, he sways a little and his breathing is laboured. He looks past Dixon at the veranda and heads for the steps, ignoring her. As he passes, she grabs the collar of his shirt from behind, pulling at it hard so the first button pops. She pulls again. The second button holds, catching at his Adam's apple. He gasps for air and grapples at the front of his shirt. She drags him backwards, twisting the collar in her left hand and getting him towards the gate. The second button comes loose, as does her grip, and the man gets himself free. He turns and takes a big swing, his arm arcing through the air. She sees it coming, but a little too late. She just manages to tilt her head slightly forward so that the punch connects with the side of her head. It sends her sprawling to the grass, her left ear ringing. She rolls on the grass a few times, to get some distance from the man and to shake the grogginess from her head. The man is furiously shaking his hand, and she bets that a couple of knuckles are broken. The satisfaction of that renews her strength and gives her clarity. She stands up, her bare feet gripping the grass, her strong toes making small, anxious fists. She feels blades of grass sliding between her toes. She has an acute awareness of everything around her. The headlights are incredibly bright. She can smell him, and he smells of fish. He's not a farmer, he's a fisherman. She can hear the engine whining and ticking. It needs tuning, she thinks, maybe a new fan belt.

In front of her, the man seems to move in slow motion. He's in an absolute rage, having forgotten whatever problems he and Laura have, whatever might have gone wrong. But he's sluggish and slow as he attacks. He lunges at Dixon in a fury, his arms swinging and cutting swathes through the headlights. She dodges each attempted punch, parrying the fists when they get too close and moving backwards to keep just out of his strike range. She waits for him to throw a big left, and when he does, she sidesteps to her right and gives the extended left arm a push. The man twists, off balance and shuffling forward. He has his back to her now, exposed, and she punches him as hard as she can in his left kidney. She hits the same spot three times, just above the man's exposed love handle, holding onto his right shoulder for extra leverage. He screams with pain and straightens like he's been shot in the back, his left hand reaching for the point of contact. She swings her left leg under his feet and brings him down to the ground. He falls like a tree, thumping against the grass. As he rolls onto his back, she sends her left foot into his genitals. She's sure to make a fist with her toes, to prevent any of them from breaking, and this is a smart move because the flesh she makes contact with is hard.

"Ugh," she says, stepping back from him. "You sick bastard. You get off on this?"

He's got himself into the foetal position, with his hands on his groin. She goes forward to kick him again, in the head, but Laz pulls her back.

"Leave him," Laz says.

"Gladly."

Dixon allows herself to be pulled backwards. Then Laz is pushing her up onto the veranda and into the house. The two deadlocks fall shut with resounding clicks.

"What was that?" Laz demands.

Dixon takes a couple of deep breaths. The adrenalin slowly starts to subside. Her head hurts.

"Answer me."

"Self-defence," she says, rubbing at the point of contact above her ear to see if she's bleeding. There's a lump, but no blood.

"Good," Laz says, to Dixon's surprise. "Very good. Not exactly non-violent like Ghandi, but effective."

"I learned a few things in Melbourne."

"You're full of surprises." As they move into the front room, Laz adds, "Please use your powers for good."

Dixon nods and smiles.

Laura is standing at the window in shock, having seen the whole thing.

"Did you kill him?" she asks.

"I can say with all certainty that blood is still pumping in his veins," Dixon says.

"Should we call the police?"

Laz goes up to Laura and puts a calming arm around her shoulder. They both look down at the man, still in the foetal position on the grass, but now not moving.

"No police," Laz says.

"But they're right across the street."

"Maybe we should tie him up instead," Dixon suggests.

"Leave him where he is," Laz says. "I'll take a couple of photos as well. Evidence that we can show, if necessary. The shame will be bad enough. Beaten up by little Dixie Grace."

Reminded, Dixon checks the toes of her left foot. Nothing feels broken. "What about his compensation strategy?"

"His what?" Laura asks.

"His car. It's still running."

"Leave it," Laz says. "The longer he's out, the more petrol he'll waste. Maybe the car will run out. The battery too." She turns to Laura. "Are you all right?"

Laura nods. "I hope you haven't hurt him."

Dixon is incredulous. "Are you serious? I just saved you."

With a gesture towards the table, Laz says, "Why don't we sit down and have a glass of blackcurrant juice. Laura, you can tell us what happened. You're safe in here."

She locks the bike and takes a seat. The small outdoor dining area faces the inlet. Across the water, she can see the soaring and zooming sails of kite-surfers.

Uncouthly, she uses the sleeve of her shirt to wipe the sweat from her forehead. She's early, but wonders if she's at the right place. For part of the bike ride, it seemed like she wouldn't get here at all. The climb from Pasai was punishing; she had to push the rental bike some of the way, when the road was too steep. But once over the peak, it was all downhill, and she got low on the bike, crouching down, streamlining herself and going as fast as the bike would go. She took the corners at dangerous speeds, whooping with the delight as the tires slid ever so slightly over the bitumen.

She looks down the promenade in both directions. Save for an old woman walking a minute dog, it's deserted, as is this dining area and all the other cafés along this stretch. When arriving, she passed through the old town, where lots of people were sitting in the restaurants and cafés. They were crowded in, sitting close together, talking loudly, and looking like they'd been there for hours. But there's nobody here by the water.

She finds that strange.

It's cooler here, quieter too, and the view is much nicer. The old town eateries have outdoor seating that faces, and juts, onto the streets, making people shout at each other as they inhale car and truck fumes. Still, they'd probably shout even without the traffic. She's only been here a couple of days, but she's already discovered that shouting is how the locals prefer to converse.

"Is this seat taken?"

The voice comes from behind and makes her jump in surprise. She turns.

"Sara."

Dixon stands up and they share an intimate hug.

"It's so good to see you," Dixon says.

"I didn't mean to frighten you," Sara says as they sit down. Thumbing behind her, "I came in through the restaurant. I took the honour of ordering too, while I was in there."

"Thanks. I thought I might be at the wrong place."

"No, you've got it. Early too." Sara shifts her wispy frame in the wicker chair, getting comfortable.

"There was a bit of luck involved." Gesturing towards the bike, "I rode here, from San Sebastian, including a brief journey on a little putt-putt ferry in Pasai. I totally underestimated the journey."

"In what way?"

"It was very hilly, but lovely. I went through some kind of national park. Fantastic views. And I flew downhill the last part, which is why I managed to get here early."

Sara swaps her sunglasses for her horn-rimmed spectacles. "You look beautiful," she says with a smile. "It appears that Germany is suiting you."

"The summer, yes."

"But it's over."

"I know. I'm here to get one last blast of it before settling in for winter."

They enjoy the view for a moment, both of them watching the soaring sails across the water.

Dixon breaks the silence: "Where have you come from?"

"Bayonne. I'm at a conference."

"Doing it all in French?"

"Yes."

Dixon clucks her tongue. "That's so amazing. I couldn't even do something like that in English."

"It's not that impressive. All rather boring really," Sara says. "All these stuffy academics. They spend their whole lives immersed in books and learning, but can't make interesting conversation. The worst thing is they think they're so superior. All that education, but they don't really add anything of value to the world. Just more words and ideas. Nothing practical."

"Easy, Sara. I'm a teacher now, too. Not quite at your level, but I'm an educator."

Sara smiles at this, but Dixon can't get a read on her reaction.

"How did you learn French?" Dixon asks.

"I studied in Toulouse. The language just seemed to seep into me. I think it was already somewhere inside of me and I simply needed to find it. I didn't need to sit in a classroom and conjugate verbs or repeat after the teacher."

"Lucky you."

"How's the teaching in Hamburg?"

"Good," Dixon says. "Now it is. I've done my tour of duty."

Sara is confused. "Doing what exactly?"

"Teaching crash courses for the unemployed. The school has some kind of deal with the employment office. People without a job can do a two-month course while they search for work. It sounds very noble, but it's hard work for us teachers."

"I see. As a teacher, it makes you or it breaks you."

"Yep. Basic training. Here's the book, here's a roomful of losers."

"They're not losers," Sara says admonishingly. "They're probably at low points, and what they deserve the most is your sympathy."

"Don't get me wrong, I liked a lot of them. But there was always one or two in every group who just made the whole class miserable."

Sara nods. "That's not just in your classroom. That's in classrooms all over the world."

"Now that you say that, you've reminded me of my schooling," Dixon says. "Every class had some attention-deprived dickhead who tried to sabotage every learning activity." Dixon is thoughtful for a moment, and regretful. "I feel a bit better about those unemployed classes now. I needed someone to tell me what you just said six months ago."

"So if you've done your tour and you're no longer teaching at the language school, where are you teaching?"

"At companies. I learned all the tricks necessary to teach the important clients, and I won over my director of studies." Boastfully, "I think I've become the best teacher in the school. I seem to be very popular with the students. It could just be the accent, because most of the other teachers are Brits and Yanks, but I like to think it's because I'm a decent teacher."

"I'm certain you are." Sara looks down the empty promenade. "Can you tell me about some of the companies?"

"Mostly local. Tchibo, Nordbank, some of the five-star hotels. I'm starting at Flussair in October."

"That's good to hear."

Dixon nods. "The first group is from HR. If that class goes well, then there'll be others. That's what I've been told. I intend to pull out the big guns, all my top-shelf material. I'm gonna go in there and wow them."

"Well, it sounds like you really enjoy the work."

"I do."

When Sara doesn't reply, Dixon looks around for the waitress. The restaurant doesn't even look open.

"I ordered grilled fish and salad," Sara says. "I hope that's all right."

"Sounds great. I'm loving the food here. But the menus are impossible to understand. This Basque language, all these X's. I can't even decipher it, let alone pronounce the words."

"You can normally get a menu in French, being so close to the border. That's how I ordered here."

"Still, I'm having a great holiday. Thanks for the tip."

Sara leans close. "Try to keep it a secret. This part of Europe is still relatively undiscovered. All the action is on the east coast of Spain, and on the islands. But here, it's possible to get away from things and enjoy the local flavours."

"San Sebastian's packed, especially the beach, but it seems mostly to be local people."

"Were you missing the beach?"

Dixon lets out a long sigh. "You have no idea. And the sun. I really miss the sun. I'm stocking up on as much vitamin D as my body can hold, in preparation for the long winter."

"It's not that bad," Sara says, the voice of experience. "Here's a good tip for you. Go to a wellness centre in the late afternoon, just before it gets dark. You spend some time in the sauna, relax, lie around, read a bit. Then you come out a couple of hours later and you don't notice that it gets dark early. You don't feel like the days are short, and a good sauna is invigorating."

Dixon is having trouble picturing Sara naked in a sauna in Berlin. "I'm thinking of joining a gym for the winter," she says. "I'll try to find one with a sauna."

"I recommend it."

"There's a gym where I'm living, but I haven't scoped it yet."

"How is your living situation?"

"All right. I'm down near the harbour, in the Portuguese Quarter, close to where all the ferries dock."

"I know the area. It's nice."

"I'm sharing with another girl. A friend of a friend of Astrid's."

Sara gives Dixon a look, her eyes peeking just over the rim of her glasses. "You don't sound very positive about it."

"Is it that obvious?" Dixon lets out a snicker. "The place is tiny. Too small for two people. There are two adjoining rooms at the front, with a kind of mini balcony. Silke has all that. I've got a big room at the back. But the window faces the crappy pigeon courtyard. I can't open the window because of the smell."

Sara laughs.

"The bathroom's a closet," Dixon continues. "And I mean literally. There's a shower and a toilet in there. You shower right next to the lav. But, I will say this, it makes it very easy to shave my legs. I can put my leg up on the closed toilet seat and reach my ankle without having to bend. I haven't cut myself once since I moved in."

"How convenient," Sara says, still laughing softly.

"It's not funny. Okay, maybe it is, a little bit. The rent's high and that's not funny."

"Because this is where everyone wants to live."

"Yep. Close to the city, right next to the harbour. Lots of cafés and restaurants. It gets packed on weekends. Boatloads and busloads of waddling tourists. You can't get a seat outside when the weather's good."

"What about your boyfriend?"

"Ben? He's not far away. Walking distance. He's got this sensational penthouse apartment overlooking the harbour. I've only been there a couple of times, but God it's fab. There's this big terrace with an incredible view. He told me his family owns it. I've made it my mission to move in with him, somehow."

"Sounds like a good idea. How are things going with him?"

Dixon is about to answer, but is interrupted by the waitress, who comes out carrying a large, cream-coloured tray. It has both meals on it. The waitress simply places the tray on the table and walks away.

"Uh, pardon?" Dixon says, getting the waitress's attention. "Cola, please." Dixon turns to Sara. "Do you want a drink as well?"

Sara nods as she moves the plates off the tray. She arranges the cutlery and paper napkins.

Dixon holds up her fingers and speaks slowly. "Two colas, please."

"Izotz?"

"Huh?"

The waitress mimes dropping blocks into a glass.

"Oh, ice. Yes. Si, si."

The waitress grabs the now empty tray and heads inside.

"A little mime goes a long way," Dixon says. "That's one of the things I've learned as a teacher. Your goal is to make yourself understood, anyway you can."

"That's right."

Dixon lays a paper napkin across her lap. "Actually, I'm fluent in Basque. I just didn't want to make you feel bad."

"How thoughtful of you."

They start eating. Sara takes small portions and chews slowly. Dixon is more aggressive, attacking the salad with appetite.

I've earned this, she thinks.

"Are you taking German lessons in Hamburg?" Sara asks.

"No time for that," Dixon says, through a mouthful. She continues negotiating her plate, pushing the thick crescents of onion to the side and squeezing lemon, with her fork, down the length of the fish. "This is good."

"What do you speak with Ben?"

"English. He went to school in England. No, no, no. Let me say it this way." In a snobbish British accent, "He was educated in England."

"Sounds like it's not going well," Sara says. "You wrote in your letter that you really liked him."

"He has his plus points."

"The apartment?"

"Hah. That's a good place to start. I reckon it's worth giving the relationship as many shots as it needs. Don't worry. I'll stick with him, work on him. I want to be sitting on that terrace. Soon."

The waitress delivers their colas. Dixon gulps down half of hers in one go.

"How's your fish?" Sara asks.

"Delish, but it makes me homesick. Great fish and chips in Narooma."

Putting down her knife and fork, "I remember going to a place in Gerringong, years ago. It's down on the beach. The fish and chips shop was just a little shack. It looked like it might fall over."

"Werri Beach," Dixon exclaims. "You know that place?"

"I was taken there, by a friend."

"Everyone on the coast knows it. We used to stop there all the time, on the way back from Sydney."

"Who knows? Maybe we'll end up having fish and chips there together."

Dixon points at Sara with her knife. "That's a date. It might not be for a while, but keep me informed of your whereabouts. You seem to get around all over the place."

"I'm starting to tire of the travel," Sara says, picking up her cutlery and eating some more. "That's the problem with specialising. You become the only person in the world for what you do."

"Can't you supervise PhDs online? Using Skype and email?"

"Yes, I can. I do that already." After a pause and a look over the water, "Maybe I still like the travel. It gives me the chance to meet up with friends in exotic places like this."

"Wild, isn't it?"

"When are you flying back?"

"Sunday," Dixon says through a mouthful. She swallows. "I'm gonna head down the coast, stop in a few villages and then get myself to Bilbao. I'm loving the beach time, but the water's a bit oily. And when it gets hot, there's not a speck of sand left. The beach is totally packed."

Sara nods.

"But you know what's really weird," Dixon continues. "There are all these people at the beach, just marching up and down at the edge of the water. From one length of the beach and back again. It's hypnotic. And it doesn't look like parading. It looks like exercise, or some kind of mobile social gathering. All the men walk together, and the women do, too. And there are some just pounding the sand, their arms swinging. They get to the rocks, turn sharply and head back down the beach. It's bizarre."

"Perhaps it's the local resistance," Sara suggests. "Separatists plotting as they walk along the beach, their voices and conspiracies lost in the wind."

"Those guys don't look violent at all. They can barely get up a decent walking speed. And the young people don't walk. They lie around on the beach in big groups and preen themselves. There's a lot of preening going on at the beach."

"I bet you get their attention?"

Dixon shrugs. "I haven't noticed. The guys are completely obsessed with soccer. And with their hair. Mullets galore."

Sara looks at her quizzically.

"You know, long at the back, short at the front," Dixon says, miming the cut with her own hair. "Very popular here. It looks like they cut it themselves, but given all the salons in San Sebastian, I'm betting their hair is professionally mulleted."

"I'm sure Ben would notice the attention you get."

"If he was here. He's a bit of a jealous type. He makes it out to be all chivalrous and noble, but it's just plain annoying. He's possessive towards me. And I don't want to be his possession."

"But you want his apartment."

Dixon gives Sara a smile. "We all have to make sacrifices."

"And compromises."

"Yep." Dixon eats some fish, but seeing that she's nearly finished and Sara's barely halfway through, she slows down and says, "I'm pretty happy to have this holiday on my own. After all the teaching, the talking and listening, it's nice to have a bit of quiet. And it's given me time to assess the year so far. My big European adventure."

"And?"

"And I'm really glad I came. Especially because I got to meet you. I'm discovering places like this, having adventures like a bike ride from San Sebastian to some little village near the French border."

"Have you taken any pictures?"

"Some. With my phone. Would you like to have a look?"

"The screen's too small for me." Sara rummages in her handbag and retrieves a small plastic case. "Here. You can just give me the micro stick from your phone and take this new one."

Dixon puts down her knife and fork and takes out her pink phone. She clicks the backing off and removes the micro stick, putting the new one inside.

"I hope you saved your photos on your computer," Sara says, sliding Dixon's micro stick into the small plastic case.

"I made prints yesterday in San Sebastian. You can keep the stick. Delete them all when you've had a good look."

They both resume eating.

She waits for the girls to arrive. They're late, again. But she lets this slide, because the girls have no reason to rush. Moving in haste requires having something important and necessary to move towards. The girls all know that little awaits them. Being a few minutes late for their German lesson will make no difference to their lives.

This makes her feel sad, for the girls and for herself.

Busana Isayeva inhabits a world where there is no tomorrow. There is only the past, which she can never escape, and the present. What lies ahead is what she is now experiencing; an endless succession of days exactly like this one, full with duties, worries and responsibilities.

She will not cry, not in front of the girls. As they start to filter in, she steels herself against her emotions. These girls, she thinks, they need to start believing that there is a tomorrow, or that there might be one. She needs to somehow fill them with hope. That starts with a foreign language, and through that language a foreign world opens itself up.

Maybe.

The girls look tired, with many of them having been up during the night to care for the infants and toddlers. They take their usual seats without requiring further prompting. Busana thinks her girls hear enough orders during the course of each day, and will continue to hear them the longer they stay here, which could be forever. The worst situation is that a girl might be taken to become the fourth or fifth wife of a man in his sixties who will treat her like dirt, as will his other wives.

"Guten Tag," Busana says to the class.

The girls echo her, but with strong accents: "Gooten Tahk."

"Sehr gut. Sollten wir anfangen?"

The girls seem disinterested, as they normally are for this lunch-time lesson. They don't see the point.

Busana turns to write on the scratched chalkboard, but a knock on the door makes her stop.

"Entschuldigung," she says, going to the door.

She opens it on two men: a soldier in a very crisp and clean uniform, and a man in a rumpled black suit.

"Frau Isayeva?" the man asks. His slept-in suit and greasy hair make him look like someone who got lost on his way home from a funeral, a few days ago.

"Ja?" Busana replies, eyeing the military man warily.

"Wunderbar. I found you. I came here yesterday looking for you, but you weren't here."

"We had," shooting a glance at the soldier, "an emergency. I was called away."

The man smiles dopily, as if he's hung over. "But I've found you now. There's something very important I want to ask you."

"I'm in the middle of a class."

"Yes, teaching your girls German, it's very good. That's why I am here."

He gestures for the soldier to go into the classroom and extends his hand to lead Busana out into the hallway.

"Leave the door open," Busana says.

The man nods at the soldier.

Busana crosses her arms as she and the man take a few paces down the hall. "May I ask who you are?"

"Yes, yes. Of course."

When he trails off, she asks, "And?"

The man seems reluctant to answer, or he's a bit slow on the uptake, perhaps pretending to be.

"You're not from Germany," Busana says. "Because of your accent."

"True." He thumbs towards the classroom. "I'm talking German because I don't want my escort to understand. He's far too miserable to be able to deal with good news."

"It's rare that good things happen around here."

Again that sad, drunken smile, "I think that's about to change."

"Oh, really?"

The man puts his hands in his pockets, spreads his legs a little. "It's impressive that you teach your girls German," he says. "How did you learn?"

"I'm self-taught."

"Great, great."

Busana thinks the man is flirting with her.

"You're also an orphan," he continues. "Like the girls in your class. Like all the girls here." Looking around the miserable hallway, "You spent much of your life here."

"Some."

"But you were married."

"Once. So?"

Now, the man's smile is sly and sober. "He beat you, didn't he? Brutally and violently. But you didn't stand for it. After a while, you started to beat him back. And then you couldn't stop yourself." Chuckling, "You're lucky even to be alive."

"Are you from the police?"

"No. I actually admire you for what you did."

"I think you're the only one." She walks a few paces away from him, trying to shake the memories from her head. They're still vivid; they have colour and smell, taste and texture. It's ten years ago, but the time hasn't given her any distance.

"Then I guess that makes me your most important admirer."

"That was in Grozny," she says firmly, trying to close the chapter. "I was just a teenager. A little girl."

"I know, I know. Sorry it didn't work out. Bad luck, I guess, for you and your husband."

Walking back towards him, "Yes. Luck."

"And now you're back here. You were in the army too, for a while, weren't you?"

"You seem to know a lot about me."

"Some. It's hard to know what's true." He gets closer to her. He smells of vodka. "Why do you teach these girls German?"

Busana looks at the man, hating him, but she can't help feeling he would be rather handsome if he had a shave and a shower. If he put on some clean clothes and lost the aura of old funeral.

"Frau Isayeva, I don't have all day."

She takes a moment to gather her thoughts. "I don't know," she says.

"You must have a reason." Chuckling again, so jovial. "It can't just be a time filler."

"They have more than enough to do during the day. They basically work here. They're not orphans anymore."

"Ah, they're volunteers?"

"Yes, let's use that word."

He nods, liking this idea.

"I teach them German to give them hope," Busana says. "I want them to know that there's more to life than this place."

"That's good of you." Spreading his hands wide in front of her face, "Expansive thinking. What else do you teach them?"

"Self-defence."

"How to kill a husband? Or just army combat?"

Busana's face is blank. "Self-defence," she repeats, more intently than before.

"Let's hope my guardian angel doesn't try anything in there."

"I hope he does."

"Hah. Hah. That's good. I like that. I like you."

"Can you please get to the point?"

His face hardens and goes slightly pale. "Be patient. Frau Isayeva, I am your saviour."

"You are?"

"You give these girls words, turn their hands into weapons, but I can offer them much more than that. I can offer you more."

She's listening now.

"Don't you want to go to Germany?" he asks. "Wouldn't you like to take your girls with you? Just think of what they might achieve there."

"What's the catch?"

The man smiles, again like he's a bit stupid; a messenger who doesn't quite understand the gravity or depth of his message. The grin comes across to Busana as a promise, one which may not be kept.

"I can take you to Germany," he says. "Your whole class. How old are they?"

"The youngest is fourteen, the oldest is seventeen."

"Excellent. The age limit is fourteen."

"Age limit for what?"

"It's a language trip," he explains. "For three months. They go to school in the mornings and work in the afternoons. I know that sounds hard, but the work is one way for the girls to stay. If they work hard, show some skills and get offered a job, they can get an extension on their visas. They can stay in Germany. And once in Germany, lots of good things can happen."

Busana is stunned by this offer. "What's my role?"

"This is why I'm talking to you. You are the one who can make this happen. It begins and ends with you."

He looks down at the floor, then runs a hand through his hair and raises his head, almost pulling it up by the hair.

Busana waits for him to continue.

"You're the tour leader," he says. "You'll be responsible for the girls. It's the perfect job for you because you're already their leader. They respect you. They look up to you. They will follow you and do what you say. And you speak German. This is your chance. This is what you've been waiting for."

"What kind of work will the girls do?"

"Waitressing, kitchen work, child care," he says quickly. "Nothing strenuous, but work that gives them the opportunity to stay, if they work hard."

Busana looks into the classroom. The soldier is standing upright, almost at attention. The girls are staring at him. To her surprise, she thinks the soldier looks nervous and self-conscious.

"Well?" the man asks, getting close to her again.

"I'm not sure."

"What can you not be sure about? This is the best offer you'll ever hear. I missed you yesterday and you're lucky I came back. We need you, Frau Isayeva. The girls need you." Gesturing towards the classroom, "Shall we go inside and ask them? I know they will say yes."

"Of course they will. They'll do anything to get out of here."

"And so will you?"

Busana pauses. She looks at the paint flaking from the walls. "These girls have more life ahead of them than me."

"So give them that life."

"First, tell me where you're from."

The man shuffles his weight from foot to foot. "Hamburg."

"Before that."

"It's good that you want to know things, but sometimes too much knowledge can be harmful."

"I don't want your life story," she says. "I just want to know what and who I'm dealing with."

"Okay. Okay." More foot shuffling. "You and me, we're not so different. In Hamburg, you will not be so far removed from the world you know."

"Chechnya," she says.

The man nods once.

"Were you born there?"

"I was."

"Were you a soldier?"

Another nod. "Aren't we all?"

"We've been fighting so long, we don't even know what we're fighting for any more."

"I'll tell you more when we're in Germany," he offers. "How's that? You need to trust me. There are people in Hamburg who will help. They will know and appreciate whose side you're on."

"I'm not on any side. Someone fighting for freedom can be just as barbaric and evil as someone fighting for oppression."

"There'll be no fighting in Hamburg. We won that war, long ago."

Surprised by this comment, it also makes her like him a little more.

"Shall we tell the girls the good news?" he asks, extending his arm towards the classroom.

"Just a moment."

"Yes?"

"You need to know that I'm not religious."

"I can see that."

"And I will not let these girls become prostitutes or mail-order brides. They are not items to be sold in the new world."

Shrugging, he says, "If you keep making demands, the offer might get taken off the table. You're lucky to have this chance at all."

"I don't want to sound ungrateful. I just wanted you to know that."

"Now I know."

"Good," she says, stepping aside. "You tell them. You strike me as a man who enjoys bringing people good news."

He smiles, then, strangely, hisses at her like an angry cat. Entering the classroom, he shouts out the news in Russian. The girls scream with delight, with disbelief. They push past the soldier and rush to the doorway. Huddling around Busana, they envelop her in a massive group hug. There are smiles she has never seen before.

Busana wonders who will care for the toddlers and infants.

Flight AF 456, Paris to São Paulo
21 July, 2011, 8:34pm

The take-off is bumpy with crosswind. Devan Marawar closes his eyes. The upward, shuddering surge of the aircraft makes him sleepy, makes him dream of more technologically-advanced airplanes.

Planes that fly themselves.

Energy-efficient propulsion systems.

Aircraft and fuels that make flying affordable for everyone.

Aerospace India as the global leader in passenger aircraft.

His Amma being very proud of him.

A loud ding makes him open his eyes again. They've reached cruising altitude and the seatbelt light has been turned off. He immediately unhooks the belt, letting both ends dangle over the side of the spacious seat. He manipulates the controls to his left, getting comfortable.

The man next to him takes out a yellow legal pad and an archaic recording device.

"Shall we begin?" the man asks as he lowers the tray and sets himself up.

"Is that a tape recorder?" Devan asks.

"Yes. A little old fashioned, I know. An old habit. It's what I started with."

Devan picks it up and looks at it. "This technology has been superseded. Why don't you use a digital recorder, or even the voice recorder on your phone?"

The man shrugs. "I guess I'm sticking with what's always worked for me."

"That's the wrong attitude," Devan says, placing the recorder on the tray. "If a better version comes along, you'd be stupid not to use it."

The man, aware he's being watched and judged by Devan, fumbles with the recorder. He switches it on and the tape starts turning.

Devan picks it up again and says, "Houston, we have a problem."

The journalist laughs politely.

"Okay. I think it's working. Just." Devan puts on a warm smile. "What did you say your name was again?"

"Armand Johanssen. From the *Herald Tribune*."

180

"May I call you Armand?"

"Of course."

With one hand tapping his heart, "Please, call me Devan."

"Sure."

Devan sits back in the seat and settles himself. "Thank you, Armand, for not talking during take-off. I normally nod-off. Did I?"

"I think you did."

"See?" Another warm smile, then, "So, Armand, what's your thing at the *Herald Tribune*?"

"This profile is supposed to be about you, not me."

"Yes, but I'm curious, that's all."

Armand writes the date at the top of the yellow legal pad, along with Devan's name and his company. "I cover technology and business. Call it the business of technology."

"And what will your article focus on? Business or technology?"

"I think a bit of both. It all depends on what you say."

"But you have an agenda. Right? Everyone who interviews me has an agenda. A very narrow one."

The man in the seat across from Armand, annoyed at their speaking, angrily jams his noise-cancelling headphones on his head and switches on the big screen in front of him. Armand leans over to apologise, but the man ignores him.

Devan laughs a little. "You don't fly business class very often, do you, Armand," he says. "It's not that different to economy. The seats are a bit bigger, the food is better, you've got some more space, but the people are pretty much the same. Who was it that said hell is other people?"

"Thank you for organising the upgrade," Armand says.

"I'll be very busy in São Paulo. I thought this would be the best way we could do the interview. So, what's your angle?"

"I'm interested in writing about Nayakall as a rising corporation. The new affluent, industrial, moneyed India."

"Looking to take over the world, of course. WMD and all that rubbish."

"You tell me."

Devan clasps his hands over his small belly. "No. You tell me."

Armand flips a few yellow pages back, to check his research notes. "Well," he says, "Nayakall has its tentacles spread rather widely."

"Tentacles?"

"Construction, hospitals, schools, charities, sports."

"Aircraft," Devan adds.

"Yes, aircraft. And weapons."

"No. We don't make any weapons." Devan picks up the recorder and says, "Houston, we don't make any weapons."

"But Aerospace India, one of your companies ..."

"One of Nayakall's companies," Devan interjects, gesturing with the recorder before putting it down.

"They make the guidance technology for weapons."

"The technology, but not the weapon. This is safety technology. That's its primary use. It has nothing to do with weapons."

Armand scribbles some notes. His handwriting is illegible. "Would you feel safer if the cockpit of this plane were empty?" he asks, still writing.

"Yes, and if it had been like that two years ago, that Air France crash might not have happened."

"And here we sit, on a France–Brazil flight, with pilots in control."

"They're not in control," Devan says. "That's the problem. That's why the technology was developed."

"Tell me more about that."

Devan lowers his voice: "Pilots today are overworked, undertrained and liable to make errors. Doesn't that make you nervous?"

"To be honest, now that you say that, yes. If what you say is true."

"It is, believe me."

Armand chews on his pen. "But I think I'd be more nervous if I knew this incredible hunk of steel was being controlled by a machine."

"No wonder you've got that tape recorder. And you're still working with pen and paper. You're living in the dark ages, Armand. Or you're in denial. Much of the world is already controlled by machines. This is just one more step in that direction. Why would flying be any different from everything else in life? Especially if the technology is there, and it works, and it makes a difference."

"Let's talk about the tech," Armand says, putting his left elbow on the broad arm rest between them. "How did Aerospace India develop such sophisticated technology in such a short time?"

"Good people," Devan says emphatically. He opens his mouth to say more, but stops himself. He thinks about what his Amma said this morning. The interview's not going as she would want it to.

"Care to elaborate?"

"If you've done your research, you'd know this already. One of the strategies of Aerospace India, and our other companies, is to utilise home-grown talent. And that focus is on young talent, university grads with ideas, ambition and drive. They want to make fantastic new things that also have a positive impact on the world. You probably don't know about the India diaspora. You probably think we're all taxi drivers and cooks, but we've been supplying technical workers to companies all over the world for over half a century. We're trying to stop this trend by bringing our young talent back home. Our goal is to put them to work on something that benefits their country."

"Fascinating," Armand says, not making any notes. "Sounds rather socialistic."

Devan turns to him. "Does it? Why can't India be an economic power? Is it so hard to imagine?"

Armand is unconvinced. "It seems more than a few years away."

"You're American, aren't you?"

"Yes."

"And you feel threatened by a powerful India. The same way you felt threatened a decade ago by a rising China. You want to secure your power monopoly."

"Not me personally," Armand says defensively. "But there are power enclaves that are wary. Let's say that."

"Is that your opinion, or did you get some of these powerful men on tape?"

"I was given this assignment a few weeks ago. In the time between, I asked other leading people what they think of Nayakall."

"What did they say?"

"They're wary, like I just said. It all strikes them as too fast, too soon and too localised."

Devan shakes his head. "You only spoke to Americans, I'm sure. Narrow the focus, get the quotes you want. That's great journalism. You spoke to champions of the competition economy who are scared of a little competition. They should stop looking at the threats and focus on their own problems. You Americans, you ruined your own economy by sending production overseas. Always global. Let's think global. You should be thinking local. No, send the factory overseas then sit around wondering why no one has a job anymore." He collects himself. "Excuse me. Those last sentences were very much off the record. I just wanted you to know that Nayakall is about improving

India as a country, and not about removing America from its power pedestal. And I wanted to give you a better idea of what Nayakall is about."

"And that is?"

Devan thinks about the morning session at Lord's. He misses his Amma and wants to make her proud.

"What is Nayakall about?" Armand pushes.

"Empowerment," Devan declares. "Localised empowerment. You see, what the world thinks about us is far from the reality. If you want to write a good article, Armand, take a closer look at what we do. In fact, you should go to India and see it for yourself. I can arrange it for you, business class all the way. You should go to Chennai and witness the changes. You can visit the production plant and the testing ground of Aerospace India. You'll see that they're developing the technology right there, making something great out of nothing. And that's just one of our companies. As you said, we build hospitals and schools as well. Go to India and have a look at them. Talk to the students and teachers, to the doctors and patients. Get a first-hand account of how things are changing there. Nayakall is behind so much positive change. In fact, there's not even much reason in talking to me. I'm just a businessman. That's why I'm sitting in business class. First class is for gangsters and politicians."

Armand smiles as he writes, the pen moving furiously across the legal pad. The tape recorder stops and he struggles with it as Devan starts talking again.

"My business is making India a better country," Devan says as Armand gets the tape recording on side B. "You all think that means turning India into a nuclear superpower intent on world domination. But you're wrong. You're all completely wrong, because you make those judgements from offices on the other side of the world. If you went to India, if you saw what was happening there and started to understand Nayakall's part in it, your opinions would change. You'd applaud our efforts. And you'd want something similar to happen in your own country. Local empowerment, that's what you need. From the street to the office, right up to the boardroom. Get rid of all those old bastions of power. Give your people some hope, Armand, from the ground up. That's what Nayakall does. It gives so many people in India a new hope. An entirely new kind of hope."

"A new kind of hope," Armand echoes. "That's good."

"If you like, you can come with me to Chennai. I'm flying there after my meetings in São Paulo."

Bizarrely, Armand checks his watch. "I don't think we'll have time for that. My deadline's too short."

"Then your article will be incomplete," Devan says, disappointed. "You'll do less than half your job. That's a shame. Not for me personally, but I would like just one journalist to tell the real story of what is happening in India right now."

"Well, we still have a long flight ahead of us."

"If the plane stays up in the air."

"Stop saying that." Armand takes a deep breath. "I can't go to India, but maybe you can tell me more about it."

"Do you have a bagful of mini cassettes?"

Armand laughs. "I have enough. Where do we begin?"

"On the street. Let's take your story to street level."

Armand turns a yellow page over. His pen is ready.

"I am a child of the street," Devan says proudly.

She gets out at the Rathaus U-Bahn station and heads up the stairs. She finishes the last of the roll she bought at the Lattenkamp station and dumps the paper bag in the trash can marked PAPIER.

On the street, there are lots of people about; the perennial shoppers who always keep downtown Hamburg busy. She wonders where they come from. There are tourists too, and the early lunch crowd. The market square in front of the city hall is busy. A few homeless people are gathered on the concrete steps of the Flaggenmastsockel, the empty cartons of wine at their feet. One man is curled up in the foetal position, asleep, with a small cup in front of him for loose change.

She ducks between two buses and crosses to Rathaus Strasse. Behind her, she sees the police cars gathered at the south end of the city hall. One car pulls up and two blue-clad officers get out.

She lowers the visor of the St Pauli cap to shadow her face. That's out of habit, not necessity. She knows that few police actually patrol the streets, except along the Reeperbahn, where they even get around on horseback.

It's a lovely day. She already misses Hamburg, but the city has betrayed her, meaning it won't be difficult to leave.

She takes the short hill towards the St Petri church, passing Café Paris. She glances through the windows, wanting to go inside: to have a coffee and a croissant, to stare at the art nouveau fittings, to sit in the salon that feels like an opulent, renaissance grotto, and to wonder how it all survived the bombings and fires.

But there's no time for that. Like others on the street, she's someone going about her business. She has things to do.

At the top of Rathaus Strasse, she waits for the green man to let her cross to Dom Strasse. On the other side, there's a new park, with freshly laid grass and low concrete pillars. Quite a few people are eating lunch, while others are sitting with their eyes closed, faces pointed at the sun; soaking up the rays they're starved of.

She scans the pillars, worried she won't find him, or that he's not here. But sure enough, there's Seth, slouched on a pillar in the far corner of the park, furthest from the road. As she heads towards him,

186

she sees he's got his orange lunch box open on his lap and a couple of class cards next to him. He leans to the right, reading, chewing, preparing for the afternoon session.

Bad boy, she thinks, for taking the class cards out of the school.

She weaves a little to her right, to come up from his blind side. Once close, she casts a shadow over him, making him turn.

"Dominatrix?"

"Julian will have a fit when he finds out you've kidnapped the class cards."

He gives her a broad smile. "What are you doing here?"

"Not much. Enjoying the day."

"What's with the cap?"

"Just keeping the sun off the old noggin."

He clears the class cards away so she can sit down. She does so.

Seth talks through his sandwich: "Don't worry about the cards. Julian and I are in cahoots now. He made me assistant DOS."

"No way. Since when?"

He leans towards her so their shoulders touch. "It hasn't been announced yet."

"Well, congrats. And good for you." She gives him a coy smile. "Maybe something unfortunate will happen to Julian and then you'll be DOS."

"Can that be arranged?" Seth asks, playing their flirtatious game that's been going on since they first met.

"For the right price."

"Ha-ha. But seriously. It's not a big deal, until something unfortunate happens to Julian. Still, I think he might be grooming me to take over."

"You want that?"

"You know full well I'd rather be on a wave at Flynn's Beach, but not everything works out the way we want it to."

"I'd be glad to have you as my boss."

"Then I could give you orders."

"Such as?"

Seth laughs awkwardly. He takes a bite of his sandwich and swallows down whatever he wanted to say.

A truck thunders past on the cobblestoned street behind them, briefly drowning out any possible conversation.

"What's with the cap?" he asks. "It looks ridiculous."

"I'm undercover."

"Oh, yeah? Doing what exactly?"

Dixon leans her elbows on her knees and sits forward, like a basketball played riding the pine, keen to get into the game.

"Come on," Seth says. "Out with it. You don't want to lie to your future boss."

She takes off the cap and gives her hair a shake. "Sorry if I look so awful."

"You don't."

"I got hauled out of bed this morning. Didn't even get the chance to look in the mirror."

"Trust me. You look as good as you always do." After some more sandwich, "Trouble in domestic paradise?"

"That's one way to describe it." She runs her fingers through her hair, pulling it back. "Look, Crystal Seth, I need a favour."

"Make it snappy." He checks the clock on the St Petri church. "My afternoon class starts at quarter past."

"I know. God I'm glad I don't do that anymore."

"It's fun. The current groups are really good. It's incredible. Not a dickhead among them."

"What about the German classes?" she asks. "Are there any crash courses at the moment?"

"The four-hour morning groups?"

"That's them."

"There's one, I think."

"Right. Good." She puts the cap backwards on her head. "I need the class card."

Seth stops mid-chew: "Wha for?"

"I just need it. Can you get me a copy?"

"Why?"

"I guess your exalted position means I now have to explain every little thing to you."

"Yeah. Exalted. Don't play games with me, Dominatrix."

She shifts a little, getting closer to him. "I'm gonna tell you something I haven't told anyone," she says in a lowered voice. "If you're gonna get in deep at Multilinga, then you should know about this."

"That the German classes are fronts?" Seth asks, also in the low voice of conspiracy.

Sitting up straight, "You know that?"

"Everyone does. It's not exactly secret. Herr Matthäus has been doing it for years, to generate revenue."

"Doing what?"

"Providing a visa loophole, for a price," Seth explains. "The people arrive, get three-month student visas to learn German, then go out and work for cash. Cleaning, gastronomy, that kind of stuff. The sort of work Germans don't like doing. When things work out, they get sponsored for real visas and can stay. But even when it doesn't, a lot of them just stay on illegally, working for cash."

Dixon is intrigued.

"Fantastic, isn't it?" Seth continues. "I was really impressed when I found out. I always thought Herr Matthäus was a bit of a git, but I'm full of respect for him now. He's working the system, putting himself at risk to help others out and give them opportunities."

"And make money."

"Yeah, that too. But good on him. The bureaucracy in this country is mind-numbing. He's fighting it, in his own way."

"What does Julian say?"

"He was the one who told me. He doesn't advertise it because he wants to keep the school out of trouble."

"And that'll be your job soon."

"Given the situation, I'd say it's one of the perks."

Dixon nods a few times, getting it. "Aha, a little kick-back for silence and support."

"You've seen the car Julian drives."

"Well, even with all that, I still want a copy of the latest class card."

Sandwich finished, Seth starts packing away his lunch. "I need a reason. A really good reason."

"I have one, but I can't tell you yet. I'll tell you later. Promise."

"Promise?" Seth echoes sarcastically.

"I don't wanna cry wolf too early, but I think there's more to those classes than what you just said."

"There isn't."

"There is, and I need more proof."

Seth stands up and shoulders his bag. "Why don't you get it yourself?"

"No time today," she says, standing up as well.

"Me neither. And no inclination."

He starts walking across the park, with that long, loping stride of his, shoulders dipping with each step.

189

She hustles to catch up and says, "Come on, Seth. You're my crystal, my diamond, the one guy in this whole town I trust. Copy the card and I'll buy you the biggest, most ludicrous coffee you want."

"Fine. Where and when?"

"Café Gnosa. On Lange Reihe. Three-thirty. After classes have finished."

Seth nods. "All right. I can't say no to you, but I guess you know that or you wouldn't have asked."

"Thanks, Seth." At Dom Strasse, the pedestrian light is green and she takes it. "Just bring the card and you'll be my hero forever."

Across the street, she watches Seth lope down Dom Strasse. His pace quickens as he realises he's late.

Back at the Rathausmarkt, she spins the cap around on her head and crosses the crowded square. A lot of people are having lunch on the move, but there are plenty of people standing in groups, looking at each other and seemingly wondering what to do next. The congregation of homeless men under the Flaggenmast has grown.

At the canal, she crosses the bridge, dropping a few coins in the hat of an accordionist, then heading towards the orange tower of the old post office.

Such a nice city, she thinks. It'll be a shame to leave.

She tries to meander, like someone with time on her hands, but keeps her eyes open for a bike with a combination lock. She finally finds one at Gänsemarkt, among the tangle of bikes outside the Passage shopping mall. The lock is a bit rusted and turns slowly, only in one direction. The bike has one of those red warning stickers on the frame, that it will soon be forcibly removed.

She saves the city the hassle, because she picks the lock and starts pedalling the bike up the hill of Valentinskamp.

She pushes a pillow behind her, to get more comfortable, and sits up. She closes her eyes very slowly, then opens them again.

"Do you happen to play golf?" she asks.

He shimmies across the bed and nestles his small head between her neck and shoulder. "No."

She moves her left hand down his arm, squeezing his shoulder and bicep. "But you played sport. You're trained. Or are you just another vain gym-junkie?"

"I played cricket. Well, I used to."

"No golf? Shame," she says, now running her fingers gently through his hair. "A sub-twenty handicap and you'd almost be the perfect man."

"Almost? Might be time for me to learn then."

"Take a lesson tomorrow. We're right next to Albert Park. People tell me it's a nice course."

"I guess you play. You can give me a lesson."

"My bag's at home," she says.

"Your home here in Melbourne?"

"In Narooma. Uh, should I really tell you where I'm from?"

"You already did. In the workshop. But I don't need to know it anyway."

"So, how much do we get to know about each other?" she asks.

"Not much."

"I don't even know your name."

"I could tell you, but there's a good chance I'd be lying."

"But you know mine."

"Dixon Treya Grace. It's the loveliest name I have ever heard."

"And this is the strangest start to a relationship I've ever had."

He lifts his head to look at her, propping himself on an elbow. He stares at her.

"What?"

"I don't think this can become a relationship," he says, and there's sadness in his voice. "At least, not the kind that results in dinner parties and moving in together and maybe getting married."

"Are you already married? Do you already have all that with someone else and that's why you can't have it with me?"

"What makes you say that?" he asks. When she just shrugs, he adds, "I don't have anyone. I travel the world, recruiting. Cricket was my better half and now ..."

"And now your job is." She moves onto her side. The movement causes the pillow to fall to the floor. "Oops."

"Don't worry. This bed seems to have plenty of pillows."

He hands her one and she folds it before putting it under her head. She almost drifts off.

"Nice room," she says with her eyes closed. "I was expecting one of the five-star places downtown. But I think I like this more. A little more lower class, but nice."

"My life is not as luxurious as you might think," he says, taking a pillow and folding it like she did. Mirroring her position, "We're on a budget. Limited expense accounts. Three-star hotels, seats in economy, cheap take-out. We work on commission too."

"Who's we?"

"People like me."

He pulls the sheet up, but she pushes it back. He smiles at her audacity, then starts lightly tracing a finger up and down her thigh.

"Do you mean there are other guys like you, flying around the world trying to recruit Indian students?"

Nodding, "Our work has already made a difference."

"How? Tell me about it."

He takes a moment, watching his finger on her skin. "When I was a boy," he begins at last, "I was full of dreams. And I was an unhappy child, because I wanted things I could never have. My grandmother said I walked around in a daze, miserable and dreaming all the time. I couldn't concentrate at school. I sometimes walked across the street without looking. I walked into things. Only when I played cricket, then I was able to focus. That red leather ball obsessed me. I slept with it in my hand. It was the sun I orbited. The centre of my universe."

She lets her head sink further into the pillow. She finds his voice familiar and soothing. It makes her feel protected, coveted and comforted.

"I was good," he continues, "but not quite good enough. People said I was unlucky. Born at the wrong time, during the golden age of Indian cricket, but that's no excuse. The problem was me. I didn't change. I went from being a dreaming child to being a dreaming adult. I was never really paying attention."

"I never would've picked you for a dreamer," she says slowly.

"Life changes you. Experiences change you. Dreaming all the time cost me my dream."

"How poetic."

"Yes."

"And just a little clichéd. You never played for India?"

The finger stops on her hip and starts tapping. "It wasn't meant to be," he says. "I should've stopped dreaming about it a long time ago. And now that I think about it, I realise that it was a very shallow, selfish dream. There are more important things in life than sport. And personal success can sometimes leave you empty, unless it's shared."

"Hmm."

"I'm happy now," he says, finishing his story. "Doing what I do."

She opens her eyes. "That's all good, but it's sport that gives you moments of transcendence. Like when you hit a perfect drive off the first tee, with everyone watching. You time it so well, you don't even feel the contact. And you don't even need to look. You know it's long and straight down the middle. Oh."

This makes him smile, his very white teeth shining in the darkness. In full agreement with her, he is unable to reply.

The curtains are open and the streetlights are powerful enough to cast some light up here on the eighth floor, providing the soft, romantic light that the energy-saving globes of the hotel's lamps can't. When they'd first come into the room, they hadn't bothered to turn on the lights. It had been more interesting, and pressing, to undress each other.

They only met a few hours earlier, but they feel very comfortable together. Dixon would like to talk about that, about what she's feeling and how it all seems just about right, but she's scared to. She would like to drift off to sleep, to wedge her body against the warm, dry skin of the stocky dreamer-turned-recruiter and let go. They could talk feelings in the morning. But after all that's happened today, she's never felt more awake, more open to the possibilities of the world. Her life view has been altered, her priorities shifted. She's been snapped awake. She knows she won't go back to being Constable Grace. That door has been closed, and in front of her are infinite doors. She wants to open all of them.

"A moment of purity," he says, finally breaking the silence. "Sport can make you feel like a god, if only for a moment."

"Tell me about your career. Would I know your name?"

"Probably not. I played tour games, but no tests. I carried the drinks in one-day games against the lower nations, but I never got into the eleven." After a pause, "At the time, it was very hard for me. I trained and trained, really worked on my game to get better. It was wasted time. I could've been doing other things."

"Like carrying a message and not the drinks."

He laughs. More precisely, he giggles, like a man impersonating a child's laugh. It's not exactly gallant and cool, but it makes her like him even more because he's being himself.

"Now, I'm happy with the way things happened," he says brightly. "The charmed life of a cricketing superstar in India wasn't for me. It never was, and I should've known that years ago."

Dixon sings: "'The dream is over. What can I say?'"

"What is that? A song?"

"*God*. John Lennon. My grandma's a serious Beatles fan. Had all of Lennon's later records too. In that song, he goes on and on about the things he doesn't believe in, and finishes by saying he just believes in himself."

"Also rather shallow and limited."

"Like orbiting a red ball?"

Another giggle. "Yes. Like that. You're quite funny."

"Thanks."

"A dream in a confined space," he says. "A person should think bigger than that. Think outside of themselves. The whole world is not only just about you."

She rolls onto her stomach. This pillow falls to the floor as well. She cradles her head in the crook of her bent left arm, like she's tanning her back at the beach. He starts stroking her back.

"Aah," she says.

"You are a gift from the gods."

"I bet you say that to all the recruits."

"Just you. You are the first I've touched." Sighing, "And the last. We're not allowed to do this."

"I'm a one-off? I feel so special." She lets that last word hang in the air, then asks, "What do you believe in now, if not cricket?"

He takes a deep breath and lets it out. "I've been thinking about that a lot lately, about my job and where I'm going. All the travelling gives me time to think, in departure lounges and hotel rooms like this one."

"And all that time you were plotting how to get your first recruit into bed."

"No, not at all."

"That's because they're all men."

"Yes, and that's something we want to change," he says. "We want women in India to step up. To be educated and independent. India shall no longer be a place where a woman wants to be the mother of a thousand sons."

"Oh, boy, would Laz like you."

"Who's Laz?"

"My grandma. She who is still recovering from Beatlemania."

"You make fun of her, but I can hear the love in your voice. You're very close to her."

"I am," she says, touched by this observation.

"I was raised by my grandmother. And so were you?"

"Hmm. Pretty much."

"What about your mother?" he asks.

"She was always more interested in some sick animal than me or my sister."

"Was?"

She sniffs and turns her head away from him. "She died, three years ago."

"I'm sorry."

"One that goes against the flow of your futuristic vision. She was an educated and independent woman who went to India and didn't come back." She turns back to him. "But we got off the topic. I wanna know what you believe in. Because you must have pretty loose beliefs to be in here with me."

"There's no way I could've resisted that temptation," he says. "You are beyond beautiful."

"Don't bore me with empty praise. Answer the question. Tell me about your epiphany in economy class. Your enlightenment in a two-star hotel."

More giggling.

"You certainly like to laugh," she says.

"I'm sorry. I can't help myself. You are very funny. A clever kind of funny."

"And there you were thinking this slut would be all smut."

"Excuse me?"

"Forget it. Beliefs, big boy. Let's have them."

"You, Dixon Treya Grace." Pointing at her for emphasis, "You are like no one I have ever met."

"Good."

"It would be very easy for me to say I believe in you." He turns onto his back and puts his hands behind his head. "I believe in change. You can take that however you want, however it applies to you. Actually, I'll be more precise and say that I believe in positive change."

"You want to change the world, positively."

"I want to change my world. India."

"Absolutely positively," she says, mocking him. "And you couldn't do that playing cricket?"

"I'm having much more of an impact now than I did then."

Grinning, "Maybe it would've been different in the national eleven."

"Ouch."

"Sorry," she says, trying to contain the laughter that's rippling through her body. "I thought you were over it."

"It takes a long time for a child's dream to dissipate." He smiles, rather ruefully. "What was your dream when you were a child?"

"Escaping Narooma."

"You did that. But I think you need to dream bigger."

"Escaping Australia. How's that?"

"No. You need to dream beyond yourself."

"Europe?"

He moves onto his side and shifts closer to her. "Getting there."

"Germany. Hamburg."

"A very good place to start." Kissing her shoulder, "I know someone in Germany who will help you. I'll write down her details in the morning."

"Hmm."

He moves and kisses her lower back, working his way up her spine, kissing the point of each vertebra.

"All right if I stay here?" she asks.

"I don't want you to leave."

"Good, because I'm too tired to make the trek home."

He kisses her shoulder blades, then smells the back of her neck, getting his face under her hair.

"You smell very nice."

"I'm sleepy," she murmurs.

"You may stay here," he says, lowering his body on top of hers. "But there will be no sleeping."

Ben's apartment, Hamburg
3 July, 2011, 9:16pm

She sits on the terrace, her chair facing south-west. After a pretty miserable Sunday, weather-wise – she got caught in the rain twice – the sun has broken through the clouds just as it's about to set. It's shooting hazy rays onto the cranes, making them look like giant, shadowy creatures, immobile at the water's edge.

She shifts her chair a little, to get in the line of one of those rays.

She has Ben's tablet in her hands. It's very easy to use, all swipes and index fingers. She does some online searching and jots down notes in preparation for tomorrow's classes; ideas stolen from teachers better than her. She's anti-confetti method – giving students endless printouts and photocopies – and prefers activities that get students moving around and involved. She thinks of it as putting the language into action: role plays, visual exercises, guessing games, fun stuff like that. She finds it fascinating how much the straight-laced Germans love to play, as if they've been denied this their whole lives. Or, they associate language learning with kindergarten and the fun they had then. So they sit there in her lessons, in their suits and ties and pressed dresses, keen to laugh and have a good time before going back to their offices for the rest of the day. For her, a successful lesson means making everyone laugh at least once.

That's something she learned early on at Multilinga when trying to animate the unemployed: make the classes fun and they'll enjoy themselves, learn something and like you. That last part being imperative. She's transported this to her company classes, where she has excellent attendance and is well liked by all her students, to the point that they bring their colleagues along, and ask her to join them for lunch in the company canteen.

She likes the popularity and respect. It was something she hadn't expected. But then, there's been a lot about Germany that has defied her expectations, mostly in positive ways. Looking over the terrace at the slow-motion movements of the harbour, the ferries and ships sailing at walking speed, she hadn't expected it to be this beautiful.

Ben comes out onto the terrace, bleary-eyed and yawning loudly. He pulls a seat up next to her and collapses into it.

"I'm so out of it," he says, yawning again and following through by rubbing his face with both hands.

She doesn't look up from the tablet. "You should've stayed awake yesterday like I told you to. Gone to bed at the right time."

"I couldn't. I was too tired."

He leans across to kiss her. She tilts her face a little towards him, proffering her cheek.

"Good morning," she says.

"Is it?" He takes a look at the sunset. "I wish it was."

"Your system's all out of whack. Your internal body clock's gone haywire."

"It feels like a ticking time bomb." After laughing at his own joke, "How long was I out?"

"About four hours."

"Really? What did you do?"

"Not much," she says, still fingering the tablet. "Worked a bit, prepping. Took a walk down to Hafencity."

"Without me?"

Ignoring his arrogance and neediness, "You know, I don't really like the new buildings in the harbour, but I like the old ones."

"The Speicherstadt. The old warehouses."

"That's it. Love the gothic turrets and towers. The ghostly canals. What an awesome place to dump a dead body."

"The new part is better," Ben says emphatically. "I want to live there, but the rents are so high. About twenty euro per square metre. Cold."

"I guess the price is better here," she says under her breath.

"What?"

"Nothing."

They lapse into silence. Ben yawns again, and when he does so, she feels his eyes on her, wanting her attention. She goes to the *Australian* website to catch up on the news from home.

"I'm awake now," Ben declares. "There's no way I'll fall asleep tonight. Maybe I should go for a run or something. Do you want to come for a run?"

"No, thanks. I had a pretty intense Pilates class this morning."

He laughs. "Intense Pilates."

She considers telling him it was actually aikido, but decides to let the lie stand.

"And I've got my usual seven in the morning class tomorrow," she says. "So it'll be early to bed for this worker."

There's an awkward silence, then Ben says, "Do you have Lessinger as well?"

She nods. "For lunch."

"I thought that was over."

"He's got one more lesson in his block, after tomorrow."

"Good."

"Why don't you like him? I think he's a fine fella."

"He's all right," Ben says unconvincingly. "It's the lessons over lunch that I don't agree with. The bosses do it just to show that they can. It separates them from their minions. And they do it right in the cafeteria so we can all see."

"He may yet book another block," she says, hoping to rile him up.

"What? No way. He doesn't even need it. His English is good enough."

"You said that at the start."

"He's playing with you. He's faking it."

"Why would he do that?" she asks.

Ben huffs audibly. "Because ... because he wants to spend time with you. And he wants to show me who's boss."

"You're jealous? He's an old man, Ben." When he just sits there in a huff, she adds, "You're probably more jealous of his position."

"I should be running that department." Then, more off-hand, "Maybe I should look elsewhere."

"Can you do that? You told me you know too much. You've got some agreement that stops you from changing jobs."

"Six months office duty," he says, nodding. "If I quit, I'll be sitting around the whole time answering the phone and making coffee."

"Girls' work, yeah?"

He nods. "My only chance is if Lessinger lets me leave. The old bastard probably would. Just to get me out of the way. I am his main competition, after all."

"Maybe you should be nicer to him."

But Ben doesn't hear her. "I met a man in Shanghai. From India."

He stops there, forcing her to inquire for more.

"And?" she asks, checking the rugby scores.

"He was from Aerospace India. They're a new company on the rise. Fast-tracking production to get into the Asian market before the

Chinese." He chuckles a little, remembering Dinesh Prasad and the cocktails they shared. "He called himself a messenger, but I think he was more powerful than that. Someone high up in the company."

"Did he offer you a job?" she asks.

"Sort of. I'm not quite sure." He digs a thumb into one eye and his middle finger into the other, screwing up his face as he rubs. "Could you imagine living in India?"

"Can you?"

"Not really, to be honest. It's too hot for me. But if the job was good, management level, then I'd definitely consider it. I'm going nowhere here. I'll make having an air-conditioned office a clause in my contract."

"So take it."

"Only if you come with me."

She shakes her head several times.

Clearly disappointed, he says harshly, "No, really, think about it some more. Don't answer so fast."

"It's got nothing to do with you, Ben. Not every little thing is about you. I promised my father I'd never go to India. Not even to visit. I'm a good girl and I intend to keep that promise."

"Why?"

"Long, sad story," she says. "You don't wanna hear it. So, did the Indian guy offer you a job or not?"

Used to talking about himself, Ben says, "He spoke about opportunity, when we met. I wrote him a short email yesterday, just to touch base with him, and he already replied."

"What did he say?"

"Not much, but he mentioned opportunity again, that he might have something to offer me soon." Another chuckle, "He hopes we'll have the chance to share a vodka and cranberry again."

"You don't drink vodka."

"I did in Shanghai."

She puts the tablet down. "Do anything else in Shanghai that you don't normally do here?"

Defensively, "What does that mean?"

"I don't know. Maybe," and she decides it's time to make her play, "take in some of the local nightlife. Like what we have here, around the corner, but Shanghai style. Did Mister Vodka-Cranberry Indian take you on a red light tour of Shanghai? Down the side streets where the little girls play?"

"He most certainly did not. Are you trying to be funny?"

She shrugs. "You do it here. So why wouldn't you do it there?"

He stands up quickly. The chair moves across the wooden slats a little. "What are you on about?" he demands. "No, what are you on?"

She feels the adrenalin surge, and the moment is just about as good as she'd imagine it would be. "The magic word to open all the doors is," pausing for effect, "Jelena."

"You've lost me," he says, but his body goes slack against the railing and his guilt is clear.

"I wish you'd told me last year that you've got a hankering for little Russian girls," she says viciously.

"No. Look, wait. It's not like that. But how ...?"

"As Astrid would say, Hamburg's a village. It doesn't take much for word to get around. I know someone who knows someone who knows Jelena. Lucky me, eh? And it just so happens that I ran into that someone this morning. The question is, what do we do now?"

Ben turns and places his hands on the railing. There's a massive white and yellow Grimaldi cargo ship passing, heading for the docks near Veddel. He watches it.

"Well?" she asks. "Silence doesn't exactly count as denial."

"It's not what you think," he says.

"What then?"

"You don't want to know."

"Fine, keep it all to yourself," she says, gathering up her papers and class cards. She drops the tablet on Ben's empty chair. "If you're not gonna to say anything, we've got a problem. But as you're not denying it, we've already got a problem."

He smacks the railing. "We've got a problem because you won't come to India."

"A promise is a promise." Standing up, "Unlike you, I'm loyal."

"Wait just a minute," he orders. "Sit down. Let me explain. It's more complicated than you think."

"Are you now gonna tell me about your weird fetish?"

He pats the air with his hands, to make her keep her voice down. "It wasn't me. It was a company thing."

Dixon raises her eyebrows at him. "Go on."

"It was Krüttgen's idea," Ben says, turning to face the harbour again. "It wasn't long after we started the new project. We did the drone test flight, with the new tech. Frank thought the plane would crash, but it worked. It really worked, and it was much better than the fly-by-wire tests last year. It was ... amazing. And he was like a little kid, all giddy with excitement and jumping around."

"Because it's his project," she says.

"Yes. He got all the credit. Lessinger too. Frank was the team leader," thumbing himself in the chest, "when it should've been me."

"And how does the team celebrate?" she asks. "Like any company does. With booze, underage hookers and violence on the Reeperbahn."

He shakes his head. "It was a mistake."

"I didn't think you had that in you."

"It wasn't me," he shouts.

As he leans against the railing, Dixon is overcome by the urge to push him over it. To grab him by the ankles and lever him over. She can almost see him spinning in the air, arms flailing, as he falls and lands on one of the Café Amphore's tables.

"I don't know what your friend told you," he says, "but at least hear my side of the story."

She pulls the chair back, further away from him, and sits, hugging her papers. "Let's have it. A bedtime story before I sleep on the sofa."

He runs his hands through his hair. "We all went out for dinner, on the night of the test." Pointing below, "Down there, at the Riverkasematten. It was Friday and we stayed on drinking. Frank said it was company money and we could drink all we wanted. He was in such good spirits. Lessinger was there for a while, but after he left, Frank started making all these promises. That he would get Ole's job and I would get his job. We would all move up, because of the drone project." His voice trails off as he adds, "He was so wrong about that."

"And how did you go from there to the Russian bordello?"

"It's not funny. Stop making jokes about it."

"I'm not. I'm totally pissed."

"Really, Dix. It wasn't me. Frank ... he wanted to go to the Kiez. We were the last ones left. It was really late. Frank came with me to the building. I even got my key in the door, but then he convinced me to go with him. 'Just a drink,' he said. A nightcap in a special place he knows. I didn't want to, but I thought then it was my chance to secure the promotion."

"Hah. That's good. Now it's men who are fucking their way to the top."

"I'm telling you the truth. Respect that, please."

"I'm all out of respect for you." Then, changing her tone, "So, this is about your career? You're trying to get ahead."

"I'm sick of being a team member," he shouts.

"So, take the job in India."

"I just might do that now."

"Good."

"But you won't come if I do."

Dixon shakes her head. "No, I won't. And not because of what I learned today."

"I didn't do anything." He struggles with the memory, then continues, "Frank beat up on Jelena. Something about her laughing at him, about his size, I don't know. Something made her laugh at him and then he just lost it. I went into the room to see what was going on. He was ... just pounding her. I pulled him back, then the heavies came in and Frank pointed at me, like I did it. One of the bouncers was a woman, but it was more like she was running the place. They threw us out, and took all the money we had."

"Poor you."

"Yes." Hitting the railing with a fist, "Yes. Because the woman took my wallet and kept it. I'm the victim here."

"Oh, right. This was when you came home saying you were robbed."

"I was robbed. My security pass was in there too. But then, when we were outside, Frank hailed a taxi. Just before he got in, he had the balls to say 'You take care of me and I'll take care of you.' Every time I see him at work, he always gives me this look. Like we're both traitors or something. In allegiance. I hate him."

"Great story," Dixon says. "But even with all that, you were in a Russian brothel, with a Russian girl."

"I couldn't go in and just have a drink. Frank expected it." He waves his hand at her. "Anyway, it was just this one time."

"Oh, yeah. That makes it all right then. All is forgiven." Standing up again, "Excuse me, but I'm late for my date with the sofa. I've got an early start tomorrow and I know you don't like being woken when you're not ready."

"Dix, wait."

"Goodnight."

As she walks inside, Ben says, "I won't get to sleep anyway."

She shouts back, "Maybe a Russian girl can help you burn off some energy."

"We should be looking for Frau Grace," Schultze says, his big hands gripping the dashboard of Korner's car.

"She'll turn up," Korner says. "Let the police do that."

The GPS tells her to turn left to reach the destination. She pulls her Audi into the driveway and stops behind a black Mercedes M Class.

"Oh great," she says. "Another soccer mum driving around in a tank."

"That would be much more comfortable than this little thing," Schultze says, hauling himself from the car. "Safer too."

"Keep talking like that and you might walk back. And that's rubbish about the safety." Out of the car, she presses the button on her key, making the lights flash once. "These monstrosities are dangerous. Get one of them in front of you and you can't see a thing."

Gesturing towards the Audi, "Well, you can't."

Korner stops. "Me, being a woman?"

"I meant the car," he says quickly. "The car is too low. Anyway, you only need to watch the car in front of you."

"Who taught you how to drive? You should be watching two or three cars ahead, but you can't with one of these in front."

As Schultze shakes his head, Korner considers scratching her key down the side of the Mercedes. She manages to contain herself, then decides to take out her anger on Schultze.

"You have one," she says. "Am I right? Your wife is also a soccer mum."

"My wife is much more than that."

"Good to hear."

"And my children play handball. A lot of your assumptions about me are wrong."

"Are they?"

"I would ask you not to think of me as a typical man." Looking away from her towards the house, "A typical west man."

"You're the one who went digging behind the iron curtain," Korner says. "Plus, you are such a typical LKA5 guy, I'm starting to think you're all genetically bred. Clones or what have you. Maybe even robots."

Schultze grumbles, but says nothing.

They get to the door. Korner's about to ring the bell, then stops and says, "Okay, fine. Let's start over. No assumptions. No reading of the leading investigator's file. Right?"

"I didn't do that," Schultze says, and he's both defensive and offended. "I just called your supervisor. I like to know what kind of people I'm working with."

"You mean the people you're working for."

"I'm a team player."

"Good."

Korner presses the bell.

Schultze peers through the door's frosted glass. "I don't think Frau Grace is here."

"Of course she isn't. But she escaped from the LKA just to prove that she's innocent. That's not exactly normal behaviour for a murderer."

"You think she didn't kill him?"

Shaking her head, "There's something bigger going on. Dixon's harmless. I don't think she's capable of these crimes."

"You're wrong. She's on the run for a reason." Schultze raps his knuckles against the glass. "She'll try to leave the country."

"She won't."

The door lock clicks.

"Whatever you do, Schultze, don't mention the affair," Korner whispers before the door swings open.

A tall, well-dressed teenager stands in the doorway. Korner observes that he doesn't look terribly sad.

"Ja?"

"I'm Kriminalhauptkommissar Korner and this is Kriminaloberkommissar Schultze. We'd like to ask you some questions, if we may."

"We spent the whole morning doing that," he says with a sneer.

"It will only take a few minutes," Korner says. "Can we come in?"

With a slouch, he gets out of the doorway, allowing them passage.

With the big M Class out the front, Korner enters the house expecting more. But apart from the large, flat-screen television, the interior is rather dated and disgustingly bourgeois. It's a big house, but it's crammed with stuff: more furniture than necessary, an excessive amount of knickknacks, every countertop and small table covered with something. There are stacks of magazines, small animal figurines, vases, plastic flowers and potted plants. Korner gets dizzy trying to take it all in. On the walls are cheap reproductions of famous art, behind glass and in thin frames. She counts seven lamps, all of them on. Every window is shut, the curtains drawn, giving the house a submarine-like atmosphere; a vessel continuing down into the depths. In this closed-in, over-crowded space, she thinks, one person's change in mood would affect everyone present.

There doesn't seem to be any air in the room. Korner is scared she might faint.

She has the brief flash of a basement room in Belgrade. The power's out. In the darkness, the women huddle their children close to them, getting two or three under each arm. The young NATO soldiers, baby-faced and yet to be hardened, look at each other wondering what to do, wondering how they ended up here, in this basement. In this war. Their torches illuminate the growing dust, and everyone starts coughing.

Korner coughs. She hits a fist against her chest.

"Excuse me," she says.

"My mother's in the kitchen," the boy says, and he points before drifting out of the room. His footfalls can be heard on the carpeted stairs.

Korner doesn't wait for Schultze, who's still taking in the living room, as if every item was a clue of some sort. But Korner thinks that all this room does – perhaps the whole house – is portray Lessinger's wife.

She finds Frau Lessinger standing next to the kettle, which is slowly coming to a boil. She's got her back turned, seems unaware of Korner's presence. She's middle height, round without being fat and without any feminine curves; the kind of shape that low-intensity Nordic walking produces in middle-aged women. A sort of rectangle with rounded corners, and arms. Her hair is cut short, in a bowlish bob, and dyed dark red, almost maroon.

Korner likens it to the colour of dried blood.

She stands with both hands resting on the counter, not quite gripping it as someone who is grieving might, someone who is struggling to cope, but like someone who is waiting. There's a slinky of bracelets on her right wrist, a large watch on her left and chunky rings on the third and fourth fingers of both hands. The rings have the glassy look of something found in an American child's cereal box.

The kettle starts to boil.

"Frau Lessinger?"

She doesn't turn around.

Korner steps further into the kitchen and says, louder this time, "Frau Lessinger."

The woman nearly jumps as she turns. "Who let you in?"

Her face is made up, her hair recently coiffed. She's got a volume bob look with the fringe blown back from her face.

Korner is surprised to see that she's actually rather pretty.

"Your son," she says, gesturing towards the floor above.

"Oh."

Korner feels the presence of Schultze in the kitchen, and sure enough, when she looks behind, he's leaning against the doorway, notepad in hand, looking very officious and self-important. Like a tax inspector, or a repo man. In the kitchen's bright lights, Schultze's yellow pullover almost glows.

"We're from the Landeskriminalamt," Schultze says.

"Have you found the murderer?" Frau Lessinger asks.

Schultze steps forward. "We have ..."

"We're still investigating," Korner interrupts. "Murders almost never get solved in a day. Real-life police work is nothing like it is on TV."

Frau Lessinger sniffs, and the action momentarily wrecks her beauty. Korner has a sense that Frau Lessinger watches a lot of television.

"When did you last see your husband?" Korner asks.

"Yesterday morning. When he left for work." Sniffing again, "He often went to his boat after work, to unwind and take a sail. His work was very stressful."

"Do you know if he was meeting anyone at his boat last night?"

Smiling bitterly, "Another woman?"

"Anyone. Did he ever have business appointments there?"

Frau Lessinger shakes her head. She turns to pour her coffee, the water going straight into the cup. It's instant, or some powdered concoction, and the smell of it quickly fills the kitchen.

"The boat was Ole's domain," she says. "He sometimes took the kids out, when they were younger, but I was never allowed on board. That's okay. I get seasick. I'll be very happy to sell that thing. I asked Marius to put it on eBay."

"Already?"

With a shrug, "Why not?"

Korner clears her throat loudly. "Is there a study in the house? Does Herr Lessinger have a computer?"

"He worked on the boat." Frau Lessinger stirs what looks like instant cappuccino. The spoon comes out covered in frothy yellow muck. She licks it. "He never brought work home with him," she continues. "He had a computer, but it always stayed at work, unless he was travelling."

"Did he travel a lot?" Korner asks.

"No. He was too high up for that. He normally sent someone from his team."

"I see."

Korner hears Schultze making notes. She also hears him breathing, the air whistling in and out of his nose.

"But it was definitely murder," Frau Lessinger says over the rim of her cup. "Wasn't it?"

"Excuse me? I don't follow you."

"It wasn't suicide."

"It was murder," Schultze says, making Korner turn to him with anger.

Frau Lessinger nods. As she smiles – or tries not to – she becomes pretty again.

"Thank you for your time," Korner says. "And I'm very, very sorry for your loss."

She pushes past Schultze and walks with her head down through that cluttered warehouse of a living room; that abandoned second-hand shop with the big television. She can't get out of the house fast enough. She's already in the car and backing out of the drive when Schultze comes running towards her. She stops at the gate so he can get in. He takes his time, entering the passenger seat back first, bumping the car out of gear, then swivelling his legs in. She's reversing before he has the door shut.

"Where's the fire?" he asks, belting up like he's crossing himself.

"Can you believe that woman?" Korner roars the car down the street. "Definitely murder? What the hell is that about?" Working the gears and squealing around the first corner, "I think Lessinger would've been well within his rights to kill himself. Imagine coming home to that every night?"

"Please, slow down."

"She's probably just popped a bottle of cheap sparkling wine," Korner says. "Drinking it from plastic glasses."

She takes a hard left, making Schultze grab the little handle above the passenger window with both hands, but he can't get all his gnarled fingers around it; just two fingers from each hand, like he's hooked onto it.

"That fucking woman," Korner says, seething. "What a piece of work. I'm surprised Lessinger didn't try to kill her." Turning to Schultze, "And you're an idiot for telling her it was murder."

"I'm not an idiot. It's all clear to me."

Korner weaves the car between the traffic. "You're not really used to field work, are you?"

"You're going the wrong way. This whole excursion was a waste of time."

"No, it wasn't."

Schultze now has his hands on the dashboard. "You just barged in," he says, face pale, "and reminded her of what she's lost."

"Or what she's gained."

"A boat?"

"More than that." Korner pulls into a bus stop opposite the Wedel S-Bahn station. "Out you get."

"What?"

Slowly, "Get out." She puts the car in first gear, ready to leave. "I can't do this with you. I'm sorry, but you're a desk jockey. You're unprofessional and you add nothing. You're not skilled for working outside the office. Come on. Out! I don't have all day."

"You're not leaving me here."

"Your fault. Take the train back. That's an order."

A ripple of anger goes through Schultze's moustache. He unclips the seat belt, clanging the metal fastener against the window in the process.

"Careful."

He swings the door open and levers himself out, gripping the door frame with both hands. Once out, he bends over the open door.

"You are the one who is unprofessional," he says.

"Yeah, whatever." She revs the car a few times. "When you get back, take a look at Lessinger's finances. I'm betting he had insurance, which is why his wife wants it to be murder. She seems a bit too keen on money. Could be an incentive there. And we need to find his computer. The company said he took it home last night. It's missing."

"It is? I wasn't informed of that."

"You are exceedingly uninformed, Schultze. Now, step back from the car."

Schultze lets out a loud, annoyed grunt.

"Something to say?" Korner asks.

"According to you, I add nothing." And he slams the door.

Just as quickly, Korner lowers the window. "Find the computer and I might just forget all your GDR comments."

She accelerates the car, making Schultze jump back. She gets onto Rosengarten and pulls off an ambitious u-turn, making a couple of cars break suddenly. She takes the next left.

There's a sign that says, "Wedel Harbour."

The car rattles over the wooden planks of Punkalla Bridge.

"Not so fast, Dixie."

"What? Why?" Accelerating out of the next corner, "We're joyriding, Ace. We gotta go fast. That's the whole point. The joy of it."

"But the scenery is so nice."

Dixon slows down a little. "The McDigiots haven't shown you much of the hood, have they?"

"No."

"All right. Then let's enjoy ourselves. We're on the scenic route, after all."

"We will get in so much trouble," Astrid says, but she doesn't seem too worried about it.

"Nuh. It's like I said at the Plaza. We'll just do a loop, up to Tobacco Pinch Road and back to Princes Highway. We'll take the car back to the Plaza, but park it in a different spot. That way, whoever owns this heap will know that she just forgot where she parked."

"Good plan. But what about the police?"

"Hah. They know fuck all," Dixon says. "I've been in the cop shop. The guys there use it for nap time, all day long."

"It will get reported."

"No chance." Sniffing loudly, "Smell that?"

"The perfume?"

"Yep. It's probably some old duck's car. A batty old biddy. It explains why she had a spare key in a magnet box under the rear wheel, and why the seat was way forward when I got in." Snapping her fingers, "That reminds me. I have to put everything back the way it was, when we're finished."

"Definitely. Otherwise she will know."

"Relax, Ace. She'll sit in the salon for a couple of hours, take another hour to do the shopping. We're set, believe me."

Astrid shrugs and perches her big feet on the dashboard.

It's a beautiful afternoon. The twisting and curving road is lined with trees. Up ahead, three kangaroos jump across the narrow road.

"Oh wow," Astrid says.

"Good thing you made me slow down."

Astrid turns her head to watch the bounding kangaroos. "They're awesome."

"I know. I've seen them my whole life and they still amaze me."

"All I saw so far is the inside of my host family's house," Astrid says. "And the school."

"And the café."

"Right."

"Are the McDigiots that strict?" Dixon casually leans an elbow on the open window. When Astrid doesn't reply, she asks, "You wanna talk about it?"

"I wanna keep driving, right across the country."

"Long way." Checking the gauge, "We don't have the fuel for that. Crap, I hope we've got enough to get back to town."

Astrid's face goes pale.

"Just kidding, Ace. We've got enough, just not to get to Sydney."

Astrid looks out the window, watching the scenery. She sighs. "When I was dreaming of Australia," she says, "this is what it looked like. I imagined I would go to school for part of the day and spend the rest of my time travelling and seeing the country."

"Nuh. It's all bloody school all the bloody time. We've earned this joyride."

"We're free for the next two days," Astrid offers.

"Not me. I've got a big competition tomorrow. Come watch."

"Okay."

A four-wheel drive with a caravan comes from the other direction. Dixon moves the car to the side of the road, scraping a few branches.

"Careful," Astrid says, ducking down.

"Oops. Glad it's not my car."

The car passes and Astrid sits up again.

"You're not totally into this, are you, Ace?"

"I like the scenery, but I don't like the car. Where did you learn to drive anyway?"

"Laz taught me. It took her, like, ten tries to get her license. She couldn't do a hill start, or a three-point turn. My dad gave her lessons and she finally got it together. Anyhoo, she decided I wouldn't go through the same process. She started teaching me when I was thirteen. It was fun."

"She's great."

"Isn't she? I reckon when she dies, she'll have her own personal cloud in heaven, if there is such a place. Old God will worship at her feet." She honks the horn to scatter some rabbits off the road. "I could pass the test tomorrow. Maybe not the written. I hate studying."

"School here is easy," Astrid says.

"Then you can do all my work too. I'm swimming in it and I don't even care."

"I had more homework than this when I was eleven. The classes were harder too."

Dixon laughs. "Glad I wasn't born in Germany. Hah. Never thought I'd say this, but I'm glad I was born here."

"It's great here. But the people ..."

Looking through the sides of her eyes, "What about them?"

Astrid runs both hands backwards through her blonde hair, combing it forward to cover the large bruise on her cheek. Dixon had asked about the bruise this morning, before school, but Astrid had said nothing.

"Just so you know, you've got total freedom of speech in this car, in English and German. Thanks for the help on the Deutsch test, by the way."

"Forget it."

"If only my other classes were so easy."

"You would need a friend for each subject, to help you."

"Hah, yeah, I would, but I'm totally happy with you, Ace."

Astrid smiles thinly. Dixon is unsure if Astrid values their friendship as much as she does.

The road seems to narrow as it bends and weaves. Dixon takes the corners slowly, just to be safe, in case someone comes from the other direction; another caravan pulled by a car the size of a tractor.

She decides to change the subject. "You still homesick?"

"Not right now."

"Excellent. We've created a diversion."

Astrid nods.

"It's nice, ay," Dixon says brightly. "My dad used to bring me out here when I was little, to fish upriver."

"It's lovely." After a pause, "I'm not homesick when I'm hanging out with you."

This makes Dixon smile so broadly she briefly loses control of the car. "Sorry." Regaining control, "I think it's really cool we met, Ace.

That's one thing I hadn't planned on. In the summer, I didn't know how I was gonna keep going to school. You did that. Of course, I hadn't planned on stealing a car either."

"That was your idea," Astrid says.

In a deep voice, copying her father, "Tell that to the judge, girly."

They both laugh.

"But seriously," Dixon says, "I thought I'd have to deal with all the same old dicks. You've kept me in school, and kept me from going berko. I mighta dropped out otherwise."

"To do what?"

"Dunno. Escape?"

"Where?"

"No idea."

"What about your golf?" Astrid asks.

"I don't think I'm good enough, to be a pro that is. Misty neither."

"Why would you want to leave? I think you're completely wrong about Narooma. I love it here. Well, I would if ..." She trails off again.

After rattling over another wooden bridge, Dixon pulls the car off the road and stops. She turns the engine off.

"What are you doing?"

Still gripping the steering wheel with both hands, Dixon says, "Right. Here's the deal, Ace. You're gonna tell me what's wrong. And we're not moving until you do. I'm tempted to leave you. It gets pretty hairy out here at night. All sorts of critters come out, of the animal and almost human variety."

Astrid gets out of the car. She walks back to the bridge and stands at the railing. Dixon gets out and joins her. They look down at the murky, greenish water.

"Everyone into the pool," Dixon says.

"It's tempting to jump in."

"Go for it. Just don't swallow any of it."

"Also tempting." Astrid looks at the sign. "Cobra Bridge? Are there snakes out here?"

"I reckon so. No cobras, though. Don't get them in Australia, I think. I always fall asleep during biology."

"Why call it Cobra Bridge then?"

Dixon nods thoughtfully. "Good question." She weaves her hand through the air. "Maybe it's because of the snaky road, or the snaky river."

"Or the slimy, snaky locals."

"What the hell is up, Ace?" Dixon shouts. "It's got something to do with that bruise, hasn't it?"

Astrid crosses her arms. She appears to be cold. She rubs her shoulders a few times.

"The McDigiots, right?

Turning to Dixon, "I think I need your help."

"With?" She's already imagining clocking Mr McDougall in the head with her driver. With that thought, something seems to happen inside her, like she's been suddenly sparked to life, and she wants to pound Mr McDougall's head in. Her hands even come together in an interlocking golf grip.

"I need to get out of that house."

To let out her aggression, Dixon picks up a stick and hurls it into the river, the way she's done with so many putters over the years. A straight arm heave, like she's throwing a grenade.

"Did he ...?" But she can't bring herself to finish. The idea is just so repulsive, and it makes her want to destroy things; pull up to the McDougalls' house with a mobile wrecking ball and smash the place to pieces, with Mr McDougall inside, and her laughing while she manipulates the controls and makes that ball swing wildly through the air.

"Not him," Astrid says emphatically, snapping Dixon from her thoughts. "Her."

"Her?"

"I don't know what to do. She hits me for every little thing."

"What? Mrs McDougall?"

"Ja-aa."

"Yeah? Does she say why?"

"I think it's because ... I think ... because I'm German. Something to do with the war."

"That's ridiculous. Mrs McDougall's a bit gaga, everyone says that. But she's harmless. I never heard about her hitting people."

Astrid pulls her hair back to show the bruise. "She hits me. I would not lie about this."

Dixon hugs her. Astrid starts to cry.

"It's all right," Dixon says. "It's all right. We'll figure this out."

"She comes into my room when I'm sleeping. I wake up and she's sitting on my bed, staring at me. So mean."

"That's totally fucked up." Stroking Astrid's hair, "Why didn't you say something earlier?"

"I was scared."

Astrid pulls out of the hug. Dixon lets her go, but keeps a comforting arm around Astrid's shoulders.

"Has this been going on since you got here?" Dixon asks.

Astrid nods. "What will I do?"

Dixon thinks for a minute. "It's good that you told me." Some more thinking. Then, "Lazarus! We'll go to Laz. She'll know what to do."

She starts to move, but Astrid grabs her arm.

"Wait. Mrs McDougall said she will get me deported. If I tell anyone."

"She's one fucked up bitch, but she can't get you kicked out of the country. Come on. We're near the turn off. We'll drive straight to Laz's." Raising a finger, "To the batty-biddy mobile."

They get in the car. On the drive back, Astrid opens up a bit more about her home life, how the hits started and how Mr McDougall was oblivious to it, or just looked the other way, and how she searched online to find some possible connection between Mrs McDougall and her hatred of Germany.

"Find anything?"

"No."

"You probably need her maiden name. Before she was married."

Astrid then launches into a long confession of her aborted attempts at running away. She would get to the point of departure each time, only to stop and go back to the house.

"Why?" Dixon asks.

"I had nowhere to go."

"You could've come to my house. Damn it, Ace, you should have. You should've told me all of this much, much earlier."

"Dixie, please. I was ... embarrassed."

"We could've done a lot to help. Me and Laz." Dixon keeps her head low as they cross the cage-like bridge over the inlet. "You could've changed your flight."

"I know. I'm sorry."

"Whatever. It's good you told me. I care about you, Ace."

"Thanks."

Dixon gets even lower as they enter town. "What about your parents? Do they know?"

"I can't tell them. I wanted to, but they're in Germany. What can they do from there?"

"They'll have to know now. Don't worry. Laz'll have it all covered. She's the one you want in your corner."

"I hope so. I feel so lost, so helpless."

"You won't be the first to arrive at the house of Lazarus feeling like that," Dixon says. "She'll probably make you work in the garden. Plant a tree, or something like that. Your little contribution to the Adamless garden of Eden."

Astrid is silent as they pass the shops, the caravan park and the tourist office. They're sights so familiar to Dixon, she doesn't even see them anymore.

She makes a right onto Bowen Street and stops in front of Laz's house. Three other cars are parked out front.

"Sorry to take the joy out of joyriding," Astrid says.

"Don't sweat it. All for the good." Dixon gives her a supportive smile. "You go in. I'll take the car to the Plaza and bus it back. Tell Laz everything you told me."

"Thanks, Dixie."

They hug. Astrid gets out and walks to the gate.

As Dixon watches Astrid go inside the house, it suddenly occurs to her that she's about to lose her best friend. And she hates herself for being more concerned about her own loss rather than what Astrid's gone through.

You selfish bitch, she thinks to herself. Just like your mother.

She puts the car in reverse. She's just about to back onto Bowen Street when a fist knocks against the window.

"Oh, shit," she says, recognising the blue shirt.

She leaves the zoo of alpha males on Grosse Freiheit and takes a right before the traffic lights. Away from the flashing neon of Hamburg's famous party street, it's quite dark and seedy. She's a bit surprised by how rundown and nasty the area is, especially given the gentrification that's taken place a few blocks south of the Reeperbahn. But here, St Pauli is showing its true self, its genital zone: as the host of nightly drunken rampages, with groups of men singing soccer chants and visiting strip bars, and sometimes venturing into a dank club to see what claims to be a tasteful show starring a girl and a donkey, and sometimes ending the night asleep in a doorway.

She's not scared.

Schmuck Strasse is not living up to its name. It's hardly the jewel of St Pauli, some decorative haven nestled within the sinful mile. It's foul. Next to the graffiti-covered buildings, there are dried-out splashes of vomit and acidic trickles of urine. On the footpath, there's an inordinate amount of dog shit and chewing gum, making her walk slalom-style. The dilapidated park on the left has a small soccer field enclosed by a high fence. The dirt is clayish red, like a tennis court. The goals are half the size and fixed to the fence. She sees the dark shadows of bodies, bundled up in sleeping bags in one goal and seemingly lying on top of each other. A dog barks loudly and comes over to the fence to bark at her. She hears the throaty cackle of drunken laughter.

Number fifteen is at the back of the Grosse Freiheit music club. Above the door, there's a yellow star with the number 36 in red. She looks back down the street and sees the flashing guitar at the club's front, casting colourful lights onto the grim facade of the St Pauli Church opposite.

There's a single letterbox. MÄRSH IMPORT-EXPORT is written on the tag in pen. The tape holding down the tag is lifting at both ends. The front door is behind a cast-iron security screen.

This is the address for all the girls registered in the Hameln class.

She presses the buzzer next to the letterbox.

She hears heels clicking on a wooden floor. The door opens. Through the screen, Dixon sees a scantily clad woman – in a thin robe over old-fashioned lingerie – smoking a cigarette from a short holder. Her hair is in curlers. She blows smoke at Dixon.

"Ja?"

She's come this far and now doesn't know what to do. "Guten Abend," she says.

"Sind Sie die neue Kellnerin?"

"Ja. That's me. Sorry I'm late."

"You're early." Eyeing her with disappointment, "And you're overdressed."

Dixon shrugs apologetically. "I wasn't sure what to wear."

"Come on in and we'll find you something."

The woman clicks the latch and swings the door outwards. She steps towards Dixon to lead her in. Now seen in the harsh light that's shining on the doorstep, the woman reveals herself to be rather old and haggard, despite retaining a certain kind of prettiness that's aided by expertly applied make-up. Dixon looks at her and assumes that this life has worn her down. She thinks the lines on her face – and all the covered up lines – are the opening sentences to a host of stories and experiences, few of them good.

As she enters, the woman offers Dixon a smile that's more grimace than anything else, as if she knows that a broad smile will crack even more lines on her face, and perhaps her make-up.

"Welcome," she says, locking the iron screen and the front door.

She leads the way down the short corridor, through soft, yellowish light made softer by the dense wafts of her cigarette smoke. She walks very slowly in her massive heels. They come to an open room, which has a small bar to the right. The room is crowded with a disorderly array of tables and chairs, with the chairs pushed up close so the backs hook onto other backs, lifting the legs from the floor; as if twenty people left this room in a hurry, all at once. Low hanging ceiling lamps cast circles of light on the bar and tables. The lamps have red shades with long gold tassels. On the far wall, the stage has a purple curtain for a backdrop; it looks like velvet. In the centre of the stage is a single, shiny pole.

It's an awful thing to witness, Dixon thinks, and an awful thing to be inside. A converted apartment, perhaps, with this the living room and with the bedrooms to the back, where the girls from the Hameln class supposedly live and study.

She works hard to keep her face expressionless.

"You spoke with Busana already?" the woman asks, casually leaning against the bar. Her robe drifts open on one side, revealing chunky legs in black suspenders and fishnets.

Nodding, "She told me to come by tonight."

"And you're actually here. Busana is always promising people, but they never show up."

"Maybe they're intimidated, by the area."

"Are you?"

"No."

"Ah, another girl who thinks she's tough." The woman stubs out her cigarette and puts a new one in the holder, which is smeared with lipstick and looks like it might be gold. "This place will sort you out."

"I have a black belt in aikido."

Raising her fake eyebrows, "Is that right? You might need that in here."

"I can handle myself."

"I thought you might be a dancer."

Dixon glances at the pole on the stage. "Two right feet, unfortunately," she says. "I'm much better working at the bar than dancing on it."

"Har. Humour, that's also good." She lights the cigarette. "Some of the girls who work here are dancers. They come to Hamburg with dreams of getting in one of the musicals, but they never make it. Eventually, they have to pay the rent and end up here. Not the good dancers." Thumbing behind her, "They're at the Dollhouse and Funky Pussy. We get the leftovers, the cast-offs. The real rejects."

"I see," Dixon says, preventing herself from being saddened and angered by the whole industry; what she assumes must be an exceedingly complex industry that extends far beyond these four putrid walls.

"But you don't dance?"

Dixon shakes her head. "I'm not built for it either, for that kind of stage."

The woman runs her eyes up and down Dixon's body. "You're too skinny. You're not a junky, are you?"

"Absolutely not."

"We get too many junkies in here. Still, we could get you some surgery." Putting the cigarette holder in the corner of her mouth and reaching out to briefly cup her hands under Dixon's breasts, the long

221

nails digging in, "Give you a bit more upstairs and then put you on the stage. That would look good."

"How about I start with pouring drinks and throwing guys out?"

"Har. I like you. You've got spark."

Dixon smiles.

"As for security," the woman continues, "Rake will be here soon. He mans the door. We're opening in about half an hour. That means we better get you into something more appropriate."

Dixon follows the shimmering train of the woman's robe. "Do you have a uniform?" she asks.

"You could call it that."

As she walks, Dixon gets glimpses through almost closed doors. The bedrooms. Again, she gets the feeling it's all converted, with a large bedroom split into two, with an extra wall and door.

"What is your accent?" the woman asks. "You're certainly not German."

"I'm Australian."

This makes the woman stop and turn, her robe billowing a little. "Now, what is a nice Australian girl doing in a place like this? Why are you even in this horrible country?"

"Need the money."

"You'll make more dancing."

"That's not for me."

"We pay cash. That all right for you?"

Dixon nods. "I don't have a working visa."

The woman starts walking again. "We could get you a residency visa," she says. "You just need to sign up for a German course."

"Cash is good."

The woman opens the door to the changing room. It's lit by the bright spots encircling the very theatrical dressing mirror; half of the globes are out. The rack of garments is mostly underwear and costumes: nurse's uniform, cowgirl, catholic school girl and other standard stuff.

"Take a revealing top," the woman suggests. "Use tissue paper if it's too big."

Dixon goes to the rack and fingers through the hangers. "Just a bra?"

"Yes. And hot pants. Or a mini. It gets hot in here later on. There's no ventilation, and the windows don't open."

Dixon continues browsing, her hands shaking slightly.

"Use one of the lockers for your clothes," the woman continues. "But I wouldn't put anything valuable in there. You can put your bag behind the bar."

"Thanks."

"I'll leave you to it. The girls will be arriving shortly." The woman starts to walk away, then ducks her head back inside. "What's your name?"

Dixon hesitates. Something girly and lower class, she thinks. Britney? No, too obvious.

"Sofie," she says, and it sounds unconvincing even to her.

"I'm Roswitha, and it's not my real name either. But Busana is definitely Busana and you don't want to mess with her. She's one very tough bitch."

Roswitha leaves Dixon with the rack of garments. She flips through, touching the hangers rather than the clothes. She'd like to go home and get some of her own stuff, but it appears she wouldn't have anything appropriate. Though, she thinks, it would be a good reason to escape from here before getting in too deep.

No. Something's going on here and she wants to get to the bottom of it.

She takes a silky red bra, which almost fits when put on over her own bra. She checks herself in the mirror, turning left then right. She stuffs in some tissues and the change is dramatic; she looks like Misty did in high school.

She removes her jeans and shimmies into a tight pair of gold lamé shorts. She pulls the thin back part of her underwear just above the shorts line to look slutty. She swaps her ballerina flats for some heels and checks the mirror again.

She laughs. "Gawd, look at me," she says to her reflection. "Miss Bogan, Miss Trailer Trash, Miss Hair Band Groupie, I'd win them all."

She manages to get her clothes into her bag, with her purse, phone and keys at the bottom. She shoulders the bag and walks down the corridor to the main room. She nearly falls a couple of times, but finds the rhythm and gets a bit of a strut going, like she's worked here for years.

Three girls come from the other direction, all in conservative street clothes and carrying big shoulder bags. They eye her competitively.

"Hi. I'm the new bartender," she says, hoping to lessen the hardness of their stares, to show she's no rival.

But they pass her, then split up, each girl going into a room and closing the door.

Entering the seating area, Roswitha gives her a clap, her hands extended far from her body. A few more girls come in and head down the hallway. Roswitha follows them, again walking very slowly.

Dixon moves behind the bar. She stows her bag on a low shelf and slips out of her heels. Her ankles already hurt with the strain, and she thinks this might turn out to be the toughest part of the evening: wearing these bloody lifters.

A girl enters and approaches the bar. "Can I have a coffee?" she asks in a heavy accent.

"Ah, yes. Hi." Checking the bar's set-up, "I think so."

"Behind those bottles," the girl says, pointing.

Dixon locates the coffee machine, hidden by half a dozen bottles of Smirnoff. It's a normal household appliance, requiring filters and coffee grounds, and not the café machine she expected to find. She disposes of the soggy filter and sets to work making a fresh pot.

"The coffee's in the fridge," the girl says, taking a seat at the bar. She lights a cigarette and blows smoke at the lightshades, making the gold tassels flutter.

"Yes, it is." Dixon gets back into her heels and goes to the fridge. She retrieves the coffee. Bizarrely, the filters are in there as well. She grabs one. "Milk?"

"No."

"Need to stay awake?"

"That's not funny."

"Sorry."

Dixon sets to work, leaning against the counter for support and positioning her body sideways so she can look at the girl and talk to her.

The girl's bleached hair is pulled back in a stiff, plaited ponytail. Her hair looks very long. She's pretty, in a small village kind of way. She'd get lost in the big city, swallowed up by all the average-looking girls, but would be the belle of the ball in a tiny farming town.

Under the bar's soft lights, Dixon thinks she's rather attractive; more so than the girls she saw earlier, which probably explains why she's come in alone.

"Are you dancing tonight?" the girl asks, exhaling smoke with the question. "You have gorgeous legs."

Looking down at them, her knees a little splayed because of the heels, "I do? No, I'm not dancing. I can barely walk." She steps out of the heels. "I'm the barefoot bartender."

The girl laughs.

"I'm Sofie," Dixon says.

"Olga."

She swipes the security card.

"Good evening, Mr Steckdorf," the computerised voice says.

The door swings open with a mechanical whirr.

Lax security, she thinks, for such an important area. No retina scan, no fingerprint or handprint sensors, no double security cards. Given more time, she'd like to have a shot at getting past the door without the stolen card, just to see if she could.

It's dark in the corridor. The only light is coming from the green exit sign, glowing above the door she passed through: one way in and one way out.

A perfect trap, she thinks.

But she's not afraid.

The hall ends at a closed door, which is locked. OLE LESSINGER is written on a small plaque next to the door. She doubles back, checking the other plaques, and finds Benjamin Steckdorf's office.

Sitting at his desk, she looks at everything: the ergonomic keyboard, the fluttering array of post-it notes attached to the screen, the photograph of Steckdorf and a girl. She stares at the girl, trying to place her.

She turns the computer on. It boots quickly, as if it were only hibernating. The log-in requires a username and password.

She grunts at the screen.

The cursor flashes.

She looks around the desk again, at all the little yellow pieces of paper. She checks the drawers, under the keyboard and under the phone.

Nothing.

The eyes of the girl in the photograph catch her attention. She grabs the frame and spins it around. There are small metal clips holding the backing on, and she needs her fingernails to turn these and get the backing off. Once free, a piece of paper drops on the table.

She punches in the username and password, labouring over each input to be sure it's right. It's difficult to type with the gloves she's wearing. But once in, the rest is easy. She jams in a USB stick and locates the folder DRONE NAV. On the screen, a green line tracks the progress of the file transfer. And that progress is achingly slow.

A noise in the hall makes her turn. She switches the monitor off and jumps to her feet. She positions herself against the wall, behind the door.

Footsteps. A man passing the doorway to Steckdorf's office. The footsteps stopping. The man turning, then entering office. The man looking at the flashing red light of the USB stick.

It's now or never, because he's already reaching for the phone to sound the alarm.

She steps forward, stomping down on the man's leg, just below his left knee. It bends in a direction it doesn't want to go. The man yells with pain. But in that brief moment, as the man goes down, she thinks he yells more with annoyance than pain.

Using his momentum, she pushes him head first towards the metal desk, catching the edge. He falls to the floor, looking at her before losing consciousness. She checks his wallet and learns that this is Ole Lessinger. She pockets his credit card.

With the monitor back on, she waits impatiently for the transfer to finish. The green line creeps towards the end. 96%. 98%.

Lessinger starts to stir.

100%. Done.

She rips the stick out and steps over the man. She runs down the hall, through the door and out of the department's main entrance.

The soccer-field sized car park is empty, but bright, the lights shining down like stage spots. No, she thinks, running, they're like prison tower searchlights, and there are guys in those towers with AK-47s. There's nowhere to hide and nothing to do but run.

So run. Fast.

The man's suit is baggy around her frame.

An alarm sounds, triggering a chain of alarms from one building to the next.

She sprints, the pants ruffling and catching the wind, making her feel like she's dragging something behind her.

There's a white hatchback speeding across the car park, and another one coming from the opposite direction. The cars manoeuvre themselves to cut her off.

She won't make it to the fence, so she slows down to a walk. She gathers her energy, letting the required adrenalin build.

The hatchbacks stop in a V in front of her. Both men get out. One guard is a little heavy and he's slow to move, still gathering his things while the other is already walking towards her.

She sees he has no weapon, apart from a baton and a single ring of plastic cuffs.

"Bleib stehen," he says.

Take him down, she thinks. Take him down now.

She raises her hands, to allow herself to be arrested.

The first rule of hand-to-hand combat she learned, many years ago, is that you can't fight two people at once. You need to get one down in order to fight the other, because two will always overpower one, no matter how good you are.

She takes a few steps towards the guard. From the corner of her eyes, she sees the heavier guard about twenty metres away, lumbering towards her and not expecting any resistance. He's talking on a phone. The alarms stop.

Seeing that she's actually a woman in a man's suit, the thinner guard says, "Meine Damen und Herren."

And his body relaxes, his arms loose at his side, assuming she'll be no trouble.

With the hand that's holding the cuffs, he reaches forward, perhaps expecting her to cuff herself. But she grabs the hand, twists the man's arm and flips him over her back so he lands on his back. The baton rolls from his hand. She picks it up and hits him in the head with it, in one swift movement, then spins, ducking just in time as the other guard swings his baton. He puts too much into it and is off-balance, opening up the right side of his torso. With both hands, she drives the baton into his ribs; she hears a couple of them crack. The guard doubles over, his hand clutching the point of impact. She follows through by whacking him in the head and he collapses to the ground, next to the other guard. She pulls their hands together, one from each guard, and secures the plastic cuffs.

No more cars are coming.

She runs across the car park, getting to the mesh fence near the runway. Once over that, she's in darkness, the long runway unlit.

It's a wide expanse and she's already tired from running.

Halfway across, she hears the faint sound of the alarm, but it gets fainter the further she runs.

At the security fence, she takes off the baggy jacket and flings it over the wire. The USB stick falls out. She fumbles in the darkness, feeling between the grass and weeds before locating it.

She puts the stick between her teeth, scales the fence and runs into the darkness.

She locks the bike to the railing of the St Annan Bridge. With a look at the old red brick buildings of the Speicherstadt, she has cause to stop momentarily; to let the other lunch-goers push past her while she enjoys this view.

She's feeling something, and chooses to ignore it.

She walks over to the stand-alone, double-storey brick hut. She doesn't see Astrid sitting outside, but she's definitely here. Because Dixon knows that Astrid's whole life is about schedules and plans, and she always has Thursday lunch at the Fleetschlösschen, alone or with colleagues. Dixon once met her here, for boring conversation and a tasty lunch. She has often come back since, sometimes with Seth, when he had the afternoon free, but never on a Thursday.

The doorway is crowded with a group of four, straining their necks to look at the menu scribbled on the chalkboard. The chalk's been smudged in some places, by people who have pointed at the board and touched it accidently. This group seems oblivious to people trying to get in or out of the café.

Through a gap between two men, she sees Astrid sitting alone at a table by the window. Now that she's found her, she's not really sure what to say.

Have to improvise, she thinks to herself.

Still waiting to get in, she observes Astrid, who is reading a magazine and sometimes looking out the window as she eats. Dixon once more marvels at how different Astrid looks from when they met at high school in Narooma. The whole sordid experience completely changed her, turning her from an adventurous blonde bombshell into a neurotic librarian whose life was all about schedules.

She feels sorry for Astrid, more so because what happened affected their friendship. Bunking with Astrid for the first few months had been an ordeal.

But even with all that, Dixon thinks Astrid will make it, and she hopes so too. Astrid will finish her degree and become a successful lawyer. She'll be able to plan her life accordingly, earn money, get married and live well, but Dixon wonders if Astrid will get any joy out of it.

Narooma sucked the life out of you too, Dixon thinks as she walks up to Astrid's table. She falls into the seat opposite.

"G'day, Ace," she says brightly.

"Hey. Dixie. This is a surprise." Astrid looks more annoyed than surprised; her Thursday routine ruined.

"How's it going?"

"You know, the usual." With a forced smile, "A lot to do."

Dixon tries to ignore the view out the window. "Uni or work?"

"Both. Up all night and then up early in the morning. Tired all the time."

"Poor you."

On the clock, Astrid continues eating her salad. "What's with the St Pauli cap?" she asks.

"I'm undercover," Dixon says, taking the cap off and giving her hair a shake.

"Not anymore."

"No one will recognise me in here."

"Why should anyone recognise you?"

"It doesn't matter." Smiling broadly and reaching out to touch Astrid's left hand, "I came here looking for you."

"Why?"

"Because we haven't seen each other for ages."

Astrid shrugs. "Sorry."

"Nuh, my fault. Completely. Just been, like, mega busy lately. And it's all fallen in a messy heap with Ben."

"Really? I thought you were good together. Ben told me earlier this year he wanted to marry you."

"What? Get out."

"That's what he said."

Dixon sits back in the chair. "When was that?"

"You were back home. In Australia."

"That was in March. You saw each other while I was gone?"

Astrid glares at her. "You were always so jealous," she says viciously. Then, lightly, as way of explanation, "We ran into each other in the Schanze. He was fully in love with you then."

"Well, he's not anymore."

"What happened?"

Dixon needs Astrid's sympathy. "The bastard cheated on me," she says, trying to sound hurt. "And then, get this, then he had me arrested."

"No way."

"Yep. This morning. I was woken up by a SWAT team storming the flat. They cuffed and hauled me downstairs."

"Don't joke, Dixie." Checking her watch, "I'm not in the mood."

Dixon holds up her right hand. "I'm deadly serious."

"You can't be if you're sitting here. Or did they already let you go?"

Dixon looks out the window at the murky brown water below. "I broke out."

"Of what? Prison?"

"Keep your voice down, Ace." Dixon leans close. "The LKA. In City Nord. That's where they took me."

Astrid smiles thinly. "Okay. You got me. Very funny. But I don't have time for your jokes, Dixie. I have to get back to work, and I've got a paper due tomorrow."

"Astrid, please. I need your help. I would never lie to you. Absolutely, cross-my-heart, Cobra Bridge confession, stolen cars and joyriding, I'm telling the truth."

Astrid allows her face to soften. That afternoon out on the Wagonga Scenic Drive, on what was perhaps her last day of innocence, it's a good memory for her.

"Yes," Dixon says, guessing her friend's thoughts, "I've also been thinking about that day, because it was the last time I was arrested."

"You set me free, but got locked up yourself." Astrid says. "Thanks for that, by the way, for taking all the blame."

"Forget it. It was all my idea."

"But you did it for me. You wanted to show me the places that ... that other people wouldn't show me."

Astrid checks her watch again and stands up. As she goes to the counter to pay, Dixon snatches a few fork loads of Astrid's salad and downs the half-drunk glass of orange juice. Having paid, Astrid motions for Dixon to follow her outside.

"My bike's over here," Dixon says, walking for the bridge.

"That's not your bike."

Dixon gives Astrid a cheeky smile. "I borrowed it. I'm planning to put it back where I found it, but in a slightly different place."

Astrid smiles thinly, as if she doesn't want to, but can't help herself. "So, you're on the run, with stolen property?"

"Yeah."

"You shouldn't be talking to me."

Dixon unlocks the bike and wraps the lock around the seat post. "I know."

"You're implicating me, putting my whole career at risk."

"Well, if you help me out, it might all actually give you a leg up."

Astrid starts walking towards her office. Dixon follows her.

"What did they arrest you for?"

"Brace yourself. Murder."

This makes Astrid stop. She takes a few steps back from Dixon. "What?"

"I didn't do it. Come on. It's me. Dixie. You really think I could do something like that?"

"Ben said you're a murderer?" Astrid whispers. "Why would he do that?"

"A girl at the cop shop said he maybe did it to break up with me."

Astrid starts walking again, very quickly, like she's trying to walk away from Dixon. Her large feet give her some serious walking leverage. She crosses the street to Am Sandtorkai. Dixon jumps on the bike to make up the lost ground.

"Who was murdered?" Astrid asks, looking straight ahead.

"Ole Lessinger. A former student."

"Why would you kill him? Where's the motive?"

"That's exactly what I said to the police. But they wouldn't listen to me. I broke out to prove my innocence."

Looking at Dixon, "That's not how it works here. Let the police do their job."

"They're terrible at it," Dixon says. "They already arrested the wrong person."

"Did you try to call me, or a lawyer?"

"They wouldn't let me."

Astrid stops again. "That's not right. If you shout lawyer, you're allowed to have one." Walking again and speaking over her shoulder, "Sounds like they're trying to build the case around you, to cut some corners."

"They've got nothing. That's why I broke out."

"Now you're playing detective."

Astrid is only focused on herself, Dixon thinks. She has been every since she left Narooma. There's got to be a way to make this about her.

"And you escaped the LKA," Astrid continues, berating Dixon like an angry mother. "How did you manage that?"

"I was in the police, remember? I took down the guard during a toilet break and ran for the stairs." With her free hand, she fishes in her pocket. "Look. I stole the guard's ID. She's got the cap on in the photo as well. And her skin's a bit darker, like mine."

"Tell me you haven't been passing yourself off as her?"

"Not yet. But I might."

"Don't," Astrid orders. "Impersonating police is a serious crime."

"The police here have given me serious circumstances to work with," Dixon replies.

They're outside Astrid's office, one of the Hafencity's new buildings.

"Are you going to find your student's killer?" Astrid asks.

Dixon is struck by inspiration. "No," she says. "You are."

"Me?"

"Do you have a pen?"

From her handbag, Astrid takes out a little notepad which has a pen hooked in the spiral.

Dixon kicks the bike's stand and takes the notepad. She writes in the first blank page she finds.

Looking at the page, Astrid asks, "Busana Isayeva? Who's she?"

"You need to find her."

"Is she the murderer?"

"Possibly. She's involved, somehow. And she's involved in something else, but I can't tell you about that now. We can bust that wide open too. Another big case."

Astrid's shoulders drop a little. "Dixie, I can't help you with this. I have to work. And I can't help an escaped criminal."

"This is your chance, Ace. We nail this and you can kiss this crappy job goodbye. You could become a prosecutor, spend your days sending bad guys to prison."

"And bad girls," Astrid says, liking this idea. "Bad women."

"You just need to find out something about her. Where she lives, what she's doing here, who she's connected to."

"Okay. Then what?"

"You're finished at three, right?"

Astrid nods.

"Come straight to Café Gnosa after work." Dixon jumps on the bike. "Bring whatever you have with you."

"Dixie, wait."

Dixon starts pedalling away. Over her shoulder, she shouts, "Find her, Ace. I know you can."

Astrid is left holding the open notepad. She reads the name again and goes inside.

Dixon rides down Am Sandtorkai. She takes a red light, weaving between two cars, which both sound their horns. She ignores them and stands up to pedal, heading in the direction of Landungsbrücken.

The stretched sedan comes to a halt at the end of Janaki Avenue. There's a huge construction site, with a great deal of activity and clouds of dust.

Devan Marawar opens his own door and gets out. In an instant, the air-conditioned comfort of the expansive back seat is replaced by heavy humidity and warm dust. With a gesture, he gets Nathan sliding across the seat and, reluctantly, out of the car as well.

"What are we doing here?" Nathan asks, standing next to Devan, but feeling no kinship with him; feeling very much like a dependent underling, a follower almost. He keeps his distance too, a good half metre, as Devan was a bit too touchy-feely in the car for Nathan's liking.

Devan takes a moment, his eyes scanning the site. "Do you know this area?"

"Not really." Pointing across the estuary, "That's Foreshore Estate, on the other side. I remember going there as a child during the Ganesh Festival. Every year in September."

"This September will probably be the last one."

"How come?"

"Because we own all of that," Devan declares. "All of this too."

"What about the people who live there?"

"If they're smart, they'll come work for us. It will be under development soon. We just need to get the people out of their shacks." Angrily, "We're getting all kinds of resistance from activists. Can you believe that? They want to save that trash pile."

"It's not exactly luxury living over there," Nathan offers, deciding to withhold all his happy memories of Ganesh.

"It could be, if we ever get started." Devan turns to Nathan and sweeps his arm back and forth in the direction of the water. "Forget Goa, Nathan. This stretch could be the Indian Riviera. A hot spot for luxury tourists from all over the world."

Swatting at the dust, Nathan coughs and disagrees.

"Follow me," Devan says, walking forward.

The sand is soft underfoot and chalky dry. As he walks, Nathan removes his suit jacket and hangs it over his right forearm. He resists the urge to wipe his forehead with the sleeve of his shirt, as some of the workers nearby are doing. A swivelling crane casts a shadow on the ground, offering respite. They manage to walk in the shadow, briefly, but then it moves too fast for them to stay in. Up at the control cabin, the crane has the same boxy N logo that's on the outside of Nayakall's headquarters, except that this N has arrows at the start and end of the letter: one pointing down, the other pointing up.

Nathan lets Devan walk ahead. The workers stop what they're doing and stare. Some of them tap the person nearest and point at Devan, whispering something as well into that person's ear.

Nathan is surprised to see that the workers look at Devan with respect. They are looking at him the same way too, because he's in a suit and got out of the same car as Devan. The workers are shy towards Nayakall's number one, but not towards Nathan. They come up to him and proffer dirty, sweaty hands to shake. He's forced to comply, grimacing as he tries to smile.

"Keep building India's future," Devan shouts above the noise of machines and generators.

Nathan is left shaking hands like a politician while the workers part to let Devan through. He jogs to catch up to his new boss. Once alongside him, the workers keep their distance.

"Is your company involved in all of this?" he asks.

"Yes, Nayakall Construction. A subsidiary of ours."

"What are they building?"

Devan walks with his hands in his trouser pockets. "Beach-side hotels. Luxury resorts." Pointing, "That will be a Marriot. And over there will be the Leela Kempinski. The Indian Riviera starts here, Nathan. Right here. This will change Chennai forever."

It is incredibly hot in the sun. Nathan notices that Devan isn't sweating. But Nathan, with his athlete's metabolism and enhanced ability to turn water into sweat at a rapid rate, feels his forehead beading, even when he moves with the least amount of effort.

Devan stops to take in some of the work going on: two dozen men, many of them shirtless, or in torn shirts, working in a hole. It all looks rather primitive, with planks on the ground to allow wheelbarrow access and a lot of men clutching rusty shovels. No one is wearing a hard hat. Some workers have sandals on their feet, their toes and heels yellow with dirt.

"Look at this, Nathan," Devan says, putting his right leg on a pile of wood and his elbow on his knee. "Do you see this? Indians at work. There's nothing that warms my heart more than productive people."

"They all look rather young," Nathan observes.

"They are." Devan seems happy about that fact. "They're teenagers. We'll take younger kids too, to keep them off the street and to give them the gift of a work ethic." Looking back in the hole, "They line up to work for us because they know the money's good, and they work hard because they also know we reward good workers. And we reward loyalty."

"I see."

Devan points at one shirtless teen in battered sneakers and pants ripped just below the knee. "You see him? He's working in this pit, but in his head, he's thinking about his future. He won't spend the rest of his life working like this, and he doesn't want to. If he works hard and shows aptitude, he can rise up, from a worker to a team leader to a foreman. If he really wants it, he can rise right up to a managerial position in the head office. This is what we're offering, Nathan. A future."

"It sounds like the army," Nathan says, unable to stop himself. "From private to general."

Devan takes his right leg down from the pile of wood and walks up very close to Nathan. "No," he says firmly. "Not at all. I'm shocked that you say that. This is about opportunity, about developing this great country. It's about progress and change."

Leaning backwards slightly, "I apologise."

"And so you should. You just insulted these men, and you insulted every Indian who went out to work this morning. What you see here is the spirit of the entrepreneur. People need to have this spirit, to know that you can rise up. You're not a slave. You can change things."

"Positive change," Nathan says, and he's very sorry for his army comment.

"Yes. Yes. This is what built empires. This is what built America. Teens who start in the mailroom and are running the company two decades later. People need to have that ambition, and they need to know that it's possible. They can go from pauper to prince. It's up to them to make it happen." Ruefully, "America has lost that spirit, Nathan. That's why the country's in the toilet, having to fight wars for profit. But here, we're building. We're working. We're growing."

Nathan nods. "Perhaps cricket is a better example of what I want to say. Any child can play for India, if he's good enough and willing to practice and make sacrifices."

"Yes. Go on."

Keen to redeem himself, "It doesn't depend on class or social standing. Talent is talent, but it needs to be matched by ambition and drive."

"But even with that," Devan says with a smile, "the young cricketer needs coaching and assistance."

"Like I got from Dinesh."

"Precisely. All those numbers add up."

As Nathan watches the men work, he returns in his head to his cricket analogy. He thinks the boys are working as if coaches are watching, putting in extra efforts to catch attention and maybe get out of this pit; working together, but still in competition with each other. He's very glad not to be down there, but in a few of the men, he thinks he can see parts of himself. And this makes him turn away.

Devan starts walking. Nathan is glad to follow.

When they're side-by-side, Nathan says, "You need coaches."

"And experienced players," Devan replies.

"That's what you want me to do. Find experienced people, to work here?"

"Yes. If one of these boys wants to be an engineer, he needs to be trained by an engineer."

Devan is leading them in a circle back towards the car. Nathan wonders if Devan is just now starting to feel the heat and humidity.

"Where do I start looking?" Nathan asks. "And just who am I looking for?"

"We can't get the people we want." Devan shakes his head. "They're entrenched, wherever they are, far too interested in themselves to come and work for their homeland. You need to get them before they settle, before they get brainwashed by empty dreams."

"Students?"

"And their families too. That's where the real opportunity lies."

"I don't follow you."

Devan stops and turns to Nathan. "Take a student studying in, I don't know, Australia. That boy doing his engineering degree, his whole family has made sacrifices for his education. They are putting all their hopes into him, and he has a responsibility to repay their sacrifice. Unless they're rich, but very few Indians are, and anyway, we don't want the sons of the rich, because they have no work ethic. They have no willingness to start at the bottom and work their way up. Do you see? We help the boy by bringing him home and putting him to work locally. But in the meantime, while he's still studying, we help his family."

"With what? Money, scholarships?"

"More than that. You don't think big enough, Nathan. That's something we'll change." Devan starts walking again, slowly. "If a boy signs a contract to work for us after graduating, we immediately put processes in place to improve the situation of his family. We find them better jobs, better housing, and get the children into better schools."

Nathan gets it now. "And in doing so, you lock the boy into his commitment."

Devan claps twice. "Yes. It's a very charitable and generous way to get security on our investment. But don't focus on that. Don't ever mention that. Focus on how this one act has so many widespread benefits."

"So, I travel the world, going to universities, looking for Indian students?"

"Boys and girls. Women have just as much to offer the new India as men. I think more."

"How do I know who to recruit?"

They reach the car. Devan opens the door and Nathan gets in first. The air-conditioning offers instant relief. Devan gets in as well and closes the door, but the car doesn't move.

"You'll be given briefings about where you should go and which students to target," Devan says. "It will depend on which companies need people. As an example, Aerospace India, one of our subsidiaries, is growing faster than we can keep up with. They urgently need mechanical and aeronautical engineers. Dinesh is on the road recruiting them."

The cool air helps Nathan relax a little. "At universities?"

"At companies. He's looking for interns, at Boeing and Flussair, and also at the major airlines around the world. Transport companies, automotive, military, you name it."

"Has he been successful?"

Devan smiles. "You know Dinesh. He could sell Christianity to Tibetan monks. He actually does more than necessary. You see, while he recruits Indian interns, he also tries to poach local people who want more opportunity. That's why Aerospace India has grown so fast. He's brilliant at sniffing these people out. Single, a low-level position, years going by without a promotion. He finds them and gets them working for us. And they bring all their knowledge with them. He told me he can pick them just by the way they move, by how they carry themselves."

Nathan laughs softly at this. "Dinesh said he picked me as a batsman by the way I walked. I had this hunched over, defensive walking posture. That's what he said. I looked like someone who wouldn't give his wicket away without a serious fight."

"How old were you?"

"Ten."

Devan shakes his head in admiration. "Diamond Dinesh. That man is eighteen karat brilliant."

"Do you think I can pick people like that?"

"You're sitting in this car, aren't you? Nathan, if Dinesh says you can do it, then you have my full support. It might be difficult at first, but we'll give you time to settle in. You'll start with students, the softest targets. My secretary has prepared a dossier for you. The road will be your home for a while."

"There's nothing for me here. I'm ready to start."

"Good. You'll get a list of places to visit, possibly with specific names of students. We're still building the research department. The research is important because we want to maximise your travel time. You'll get a Visa card, but you'll be on a limited expense account." Smiling at Nathan, "That's Dinesh again. He said you can't walk around like some moneyed fool. You need to be at the same level as the people you're recruiting. Rolex watches, fancy cars, five-star hotels and briefcases full of money will scare them off, make them suspicious. And, you have to make them choose you. It's not your job to convince them to work for us. You're just the messenger. You put the facts on the table and let them decide. If you target the right people, they won't think twice about it. Word's already beginning to spread. It's highly likely that by the time you get to a university, the students will have heard about us and that we're looking for recruits, and that we help out their families. One of our recruiters has probably already been through."

"Do you mean there are others out there doing this?" Nathan asks, keen to get started and be the best recruiter Nayakall's ever had.

"For about the last five years. Dinesh was one of the first." Devan points at the small, makeshift office off to the side of the construction site. "There are probably some of our early recruits working in there. University grads in their early twenties running this show. Good for them. A sister of one of them is probably working as a secretary in there. Someone's mother makes all the lunches. A father delivers the office supplies. You see? And when these buildings are finished, there'll be jobs available in the hotels. They are building the future."

"It's great," Nathan says, thoroughly impressed. "But how can I promise jobs if I don't have a direct line to Nayakall? I can't imagine I'll ever have that power."

"You'll have nothing to do with it. Once the student signs on, the agreement comes back to us and we do the rest. On the agreement, the student can write down ten dependents. It's written up as a contact sheet, but really, the student can write down all the family members he wants us to help."

"What about money?"

"They get paid when they work," Devan says flatly. "You never make promises about money. When people work, they get paid. This is not about giving people gifts. This is about putting people to work here in India. Real local change. Anybody needing more incentive than that is not right for us."

"And me?"

"You work on commission. You get a fixed amount for every recruit. We don't have prized recruits. Everyone is equal for us. Fifty thousand rupees a head."

"That's a lot of money." Nathan just stops himself from declaring that he would do this job for free.

"It's nothing to what Nayakall gets in return. It might mean we get one engineer and ten workers. And those people will be in our system, and their children will be in our system. Not only that, their children will get a better education and be more likely to become engineers than workers. Or they become doctors and teachers and so on. For a measly fifty thousand rupees, a large group of people takes a step up. We can't even begin to quantify the impact of one high-quality recruit."

Nathan looks past Devan, through the tinted windows at the under-construction Marriot. The building is already showing the cubicle signs of hotel rooms. He thinks it all sounds very good, and

Devan delivers convincing, almost hypnotic arguments. He wants to get started, but he still doesn't quite have the vision of India that Devan has.

"One day," Nathan says, "I want to be able to think as big as you, Devan."

"You flatter me, but it's an admirable ambition. So? What do you think?"

Nathan has never been more certain of a decision in his life. "I'm in. How do we start?"

"We head back to the office to sign some contracts and get you fully briefed," Devan says without missing a beat. "You're flying to Singapore tomorrow. Economy class. Dinesh will meet you there for some quick training. We've got a south-east Asia itinerary prepared for you, then down to Australia and New Zealand."

"You knew I'd say yes?"

"Dinesh knows how to pick them." Pressing the intercom button on the door's armrest, "Back to HQ, Ravi."

They stand on the side of the slanted field, close to the cluster of spectators and substitutes. With the westerly wind, and the slope, all the play is on this side of the ground. There's a lot of grunting and swearing. The play is slow and static.

"Which one's your colleague?" Ben asks.

She points. "He's standing down near the goals, at the other end."

"In blue and white?"

"In purple."

Ben folds his arms and watches the action. "What's the point of this sport? It's like twenty guys trying to catch a chicken."

"Hah."

"None of them can get their hands on it," Ben continues, "and if they do, they don't know what to do with it."

"At the highest level, it's very entertaining. But this is more the chicken league."

"You brought me all the way to the Stadtpark for this?"

"I thought you'd be interested," she says, peeved. "This is what I grew up with. It's the biggest sport down under."

"And you should be very proud of it." He takes his tablet out of his shoulder bag. "Good thing I brought this with me." Walking away, "If you need me, I'll be working under that tree."

She's glad he's left.

As Seth comes off for a break, another sub runs on for him, an enthusiastic sprint that lasts about twenty metres. Seth grabs a bottle of water and jogs towards her.

"Hey, Dominatrix, you made it."

"Looking good," she says, but she doesn't like the barbed wire tattoo he has around his left bicep, or the odd strands of hair on his shoulders.

Munich kicks another goal. The spectators clap sombrely. Some of them jeer.

Seth takes a drink. "When did you get back?"

"Weeks ago. Middle of March."

"Haven't seen you at the school."

"I'm a field operative now. All company classes. Living the donut dream."

Seth chuckles. His eyes fall on the action, which is happening very close to them. A minor scuffle breaks out, stopped by the umpire. Dixon is amazed to see the umpire is the same Aussie from Ben's cricket team, in the same blue Scarborough Beach hat he always wears. Now, with a whistle in hand, his barrage of orders and encouragement never ceases.

"How was it?" Seth asks. "Being back home?"

In a sing-song voice, "Sounds like someone wants to go-oh."

"You have no idea."

"It was awesome. I sat on the beach, grilled some snags, swatted some flies, played golf every day. I even got to watch my dad make a half century."

"He plays cricket?"

"Yep, he's not as good as he used to be, but he's still handy with the bat." She smiles, a little sadly, missing her dad. "His latest half century was a bit more personal. He turned fifty. That was why I went home. For his surprise party. And no, I didn't jump out of a cake."

"What an image," Seth exclaims. "What present did you give him?"

"A shirt. Written on it is 'The older I get, the better I was.' He loved it."

Dixon feels an arm around her shoulders. She turns. "Oh, Ben. This is Seth, my colleague from Multilinga."

Ben puts down his shoulder bag to shake Seth's hand.

"You the cricketer?" Seth asks.

"Yes. I guess Dix has told you a lot about me."

"Yeah. Right. A bit."

The action comes close again, the Aussie umpire shouting himself red in the face. Dixon takes the chance to get out from under Ben's arm to get a better look at the play. The guys are aggressive with each other, and little wrestling fights keep starting; spot-fires the umpire can't control, except by yelling from afar. She thinks the players are better at getting their hands on each other than the ball.

Ben and Seth don't talk until she comes back.

"Brutal," she says to them both.

"What kind of jumper is that?" Ben asks.

Seth folds his arms, getting his fists under his biceps, to bulge them a little. "It's the Fremantle jumper." When Ben looks a little lost, he adds, "The Fremantle Dockers. One of the AFL teams based in Perth."

"Great colour."

"You wanna say that a bit louder, mate? Maybe you can say it to all my teammates at quarter-time."

Dixon steps between them. "He's kidding, Seth. He didn't believe me when I told him fifteen minutes ago that the L.A. Lakers wear purple too."

"They do," Seth says.

Ben's arm is around her shoulders again. He pulls her close. "I find it very hard to believe."

"Nothing wrong with purple," she says, just stopping herself from shrugging out from under his grasp and putting a leg behind him to trip him over. "The colour of royalty."

"That's right." Seth looks around. He waves at the coach, who beckons him. "Looks like I'm back into it."

"Get into it," Dixon shouts.

Seth runs awkwardly back onto the ground. He's immediately into the action, fighting for the ball, then wrestling with the opponent who had it. The umpire pulls him off and yells at both players. As everyone runs after the ball, Seth stops and looks directly at Ben.

"This is barbaric," Ben says, looking at Dixon.

"We breed them tough down under," she says proudly.

"Isn't he married?"

"Yes."

"Then why was he hitting on you like that?"

"He wasn't hitting on me." She starts walking away. "We're friends. We work together."

He follows her. "It looks like he's more than that."

She stops and faces him, again fighting the urge to bring him down. "He was the first Australian I met in this town. And he taught me a lot about being a teacher."

"Your mentor, right?"

"Ben, let it go. Jealousy is not attractive. You told me that once."

She starts walking again. Ben keeps pace with her.

"Look," she says, trying to be reasonable, to sound like she's willing to meet him halfway, "I get homesick. All right? I came to the footy hoping to meet some more Aussies."

"Are there any here?"

"Your friend from the cricket club is umpiring."

Ben looks at the field, squinting a little. "Oh, yeah." Then, snidely, "He plays in the second team."

"The rest of the Aussies are pretty much bogans and deadbeats. Seth doesn't belong out there with them."

They walk around the makeshift boundary, towards the goals at the south end of the field. Most of the small orange witch's hats, outlining the boundary, have blown over.

On the field, a young couple is spreading a blanket about twenty metres out from goal. A player runs over and tells them to move. The couple watches the game for a moment. As the play is happening at the other end, they spread the blanket anyway. Their dog starts running around.

"Do you see him a lot at the language school?" Ben asks.

"Who?"

"Seb."

"You mean Seth. Not anymore. Not since I started doing company classes. He only teaches at the school."

"Were you together last year?"

"What? Are you crazy? He's married, Ben. Don't you understand that? Seth is a friend." With emphasis, "A friend. You know, I can have friends who are men."

"Not when they flirt with you."

"He was being friendly. That's how friends are with each other." Shaking her head, "You're really one to talk like this."

"What do you mean?"

"Come on, Ben. Every time you visit your parents, your mother gets that tramp Ingrid over as well. Like they're conjugal visits. You think that doesn't make me jealous?"

"You never want to come with me," Ben counters.

"Because your mother wants to burn me at the stake."

"You don't give her a chance."

"Why should I? She told me, in these exact words, that she wants to burn me at the stake."

"You're exaggerating again."

"I'm not. Sorry, Ben, but your mother is full of hate."

He stops at the goalposts. "That's an awful thing to say."

"Does that hurt? Because it hurts me when you think my friends flirt with me."

"Don't make this about Seth or my mother," Ben says. "This is about us."

The goal umpire, a substitute player with a luminous yellow vest over his jumper, turns his head to listen to their argument. A few players are listening as well.

"No," she shouts. "This is about you. It's always about you. The whole mother-fucking world is about you."

She walks off.

"Now hang on a minute," he orders.

She turns.

"Wait." Ben looks in the direction of the spectators. "Dix, wait right there. I forgot my bag. I'll be back in a second."

He runs in front of the goals and cuts across the field of play. He runs awkwardly, like his knees don't really work. The ball is coming in his direction, having been kicked to open space. Foolishly, he picks it up and looks to give it to someone. A few players descend on him, with Seth leading the charge and bringing him down in a hard tackle.

Smiling, she turns and walks down the path in the direction of Landhaus Walter, to where her bike is locked.

The tide has gone out, exposing many of the rocks, which are black and glistening, but drying to metallic grey. Seagulls are perched on the rocks.

The beach is deserted. The two of them lie close to the water, where the sand is firmer and there are few shells. Lying on her back, her knees bent, Dixon feels the damp sand just starting to come through her towel. With the sun high and hot, the coldish sand is actually rather refreshing.

"Aaah," she says, looking up at a sky that's freckled with tiny white clouds. "Whatever happens, don't let me fall asleep."

"I bet you've missed this."

Dixon yawns. "Misty, you have no idea. The winter was so grim. When I was at the airport, it felt like I was breaking out of prison."

Miranda laughs softly.

"Seriously, sis," Dixon continues, wading through the jet-lag to muster her enthusiasm. "From October, it was like the sun packed her bags and headed south. It was grey from then on until I left."

Miranda rolls onto her left side, an elbow propped, her head cupped in her left hand: a model's pose. An hourglass tipped on its side. Dixon feels a pang of hate as she's reminded how so many of Miranda's positions are modified – or blatant – model's poses.

Miranda's hair is short and straight, and Dixon thinks the look suits her. She's also lost some weight, and now resembles a coffee coloured nymph rather than their mother. Dixon is glad the similarities went with the shed kilos, and the new hairdo is helping as well. She thinks her sister looks gorgeous, and she wishes she didn't hate her for it.

"What about those letters you wrote," Miranda says. "The Christmas markets, the snow and the fairy lights. That hot wine."

"Okay, that's all pretty good. The markets are fab. But Christmas ..."

"The disaster Christmas."

"Don't remind me." Dixon rolls her head slightly to face her sister. She's missed her much more than she will admit, more than she'll ever say. "Ben's mum is a beast. She has claws and fangs and breathes fire."

Miranda laughs. "Is his dad the same way?"

"Total opposite. He's a ghost. It's like he doesn't exist, except as financial supplier. Frau Stinkdorf just dominates and he can't get a word in."

"She snipped him?"

"Long ago. Maybe on their wedding night. Cut his balls off and now keeps them in a jar beside her bed. Or in her trophy cabinet." In a posh accent, "She hunts, you know."

More laughing.

"I had one conversation with him, when I went out into the garden for some air. He was out there smoking a cigarette."

"Not a pipe or a cigar?" Miranda asks.

"He smoked like a guy in prison does." Demonstrating, "Holding the ciggie with his thumb and index finger, with the burning end near his palm. I thought he was about to tell me was gonna break out that night."

Miranda turns her head slightly to look at the water. "What about Ben?"

Dixon grunts.

"Okay. We'll come back to that later. The teaching?"

"It's great. Sometimes, the lessons are just gossip sessions. We talk movies and music and books. The Germans are a pretty cultured lot, more so than us."

"So, definitely going back," Miranda says, sounding disappointed.

"Sure. This is just a holiday." Sighing, "Well-earned."

Miranda takes the hand that's resting on her hip and draws small circles in the sand. "Playing any golf?" she asks.

"Nuh."

"Shame. I'd beat you now. You were way better than me in high school. It was that German friend of yours. She wrecked your game. Total bad influence."

"Astrid? Are you for real? She was a saint. Still is, though now she's more nun than saint." Dismissing it all, because it was so long ago, "Anyway, I was just trying to get attention."

"Mine?"

Dixon sits up quickly. "God, Misty, not everything is about you. Even if in high school there were plenty of boys who worshipped you."

"It wasn't like that," Miranda replies hotly.

"You've got a pretty selective memory."

Calmly, "What I meant is, I wish it hadn't been like that. I hated being the centre of attention."

"You loved it."

"Maybe I did then," Miranda concedes. She rolls onto her stomach. With her head cradled in the crook of her arm, she closes her eyes. "I've changed."

Dixon feels a throb of envy. "The new Laz. You and her are pretty close now, so I've gathered."

"Hmm. Since I started working more at the café. We want to buy the house next door, turn it into a kind of retreat. More aikido and self-defence classes. Yoga, spas, saunas, pregnancy classes, that sort of thing."

"Maybe your first brat will be born in that house."

"At the least the kids won't get polluted."

"Bullshit. Our dad was always great. Even when I fucked up royally, he kept his head. It was mum who was doing the polluting."

Raising her body quickly, moving backwards so she's sitting upright on her bent knees, "I can't believe you just said that."

"Whose attention do you think I was trying to get?"

"Mum was all over you," Miranda says.

"Please. Did we experience the same childhood? Lazarus was there for us. Dad too. But mum was always off trying to save the animal planet."

Miranda digs her hands into the sand and looks like she might cry. "You just remember it that way so you don't have to deal with it. Same with joining the police, and the same with going to Germany."

Dixon shakes her head. "Wrong, wrong, wrong."

"You're all over the place, Dixie."

"I am not. You are."

Miranda's voice is hard and vicious: "I was for a while, but that was not my fault."

"No. Just born this way."

Miranda gets two handfuls of sand and throws them at Dixon. The sand sticks to the sunscreen.

Stunned, Dixon jumps to her feet, the adrenalin building like mad. "Are you trying to pick a fight with me?" she shouts.

"Sorry," Miranda says, not moving.

Dixon goes to the water to wash the sand off. There's a small pool between the rocks. The water is cold, and this takes some of the heat out of her head. She gets down on her knees, then sits in the water. She feels refreshed. The adrenalin slowly subsides. When she looks up, Miranda is standing in the pool as well, her hands on her hips.

Sitting down, Miranda says, "I came here in the summer, when it was packed with toolies and schoolies. I saw all the guys on the beach, with their eskies and their drunk games of beach cricket, and I turned around and went home."

"At least that hasn't changed."

"No, but people change, Dixie." Miranda leans back, putting her arms behind her and sticking out her chest a little. "You've changed."

Dixon plays with her hair. "It's the bimbo rinse, isn't it?"

"No." Miranda gives her a studied look. "It's something in your eyes. You've hardened up."

"Yeah? Maybe it was the whole Christmas experience. That woman, I wanted to strangle her."

They lapse into silence. The seagulls squawk. The water laps against the rocks.

"Ben likes it," Dixon says at last. "The combination. Blonde hair and brown eyes."

"It sounds to me that it doesn't really matter anymore what Ben thinks, or wants."

Dixon cups some water and splashes her face. She goes to do it a second time, but flicks the water at her sister.

"Hey."

"That's for the sand," Dixon says. "Be glad I didn't throw you face first into the sand."

Rubbing her eyes, Miranda says gently, "Dixie, it's great to see you."

They smile at each other, sharing a rather pathetic moment that makes them both laugh.

"But there's something you're not telling me," Miranda adds.

"There's not much to say. I get up, I go to work. I try to stay in shape. Okay. If you want me to share, I will tell you this. I'm glad I'm not Constable Grace anymore."

"That was never the right thing for you."

"God, you sound like Laz."

Miranda shrugs her slender shoulders. "Is that so bad?"

"Just as long as you don't sound like mum, talking about destiny paths and personal journeys and saving hamster souls."

Miranda offers Dixon a sad smile. "Tell me about Ben."

"He's a softcock. A real mamma's boy. I'm nearly through with him."

"But you're living together."

251

Dixon stands up. "I think that fantastic flat is the one thing keeping us together."

Standing as well, "You're still holding back."

Sarcastically, "Must be the new hard me. Tougher than ever, able to keep secrets." Then, feeling some emotion, "Okay. Fine. Here it is. I miss you guys. You and dad and Laz. But I don't miss this place. This teeny tiny limited little world."

"That's not it."

They start walking out of the water together. Dixon stops. She reaches out and grabs Miranda's arm to make her stop as well. They stand with the water gently covering their feet.

After a long breath, "This stays between you and me," Dixon says, "because I don't want dad and Laz worrying about me. It's all under control."

"What?"

"Last year, I got into a bit of shit," Dixon says, and she can't help but put a little pride in her voice. "My own fault. I went snooping when I shouldn't have."

"Like you did in Melbourne, and got kicked off the force for it."

"Not kicked off," Dixon corrects. "Forced out. Technically, I quit."

"More."

With her left foot, Dixon flicks water at Miranda's legs. "It's a bit messy," she says, "which is why I wanna go back. To clean it up."

Miranda has her hands on her hips again, her feet apart. "Get to the point."

"It's like this. My language school, Multilinga, they're into something really heavy."

"What?"

"Organised prostitution."

"Oh god, tell me your snooping didn't go that far."

"I just worked a few nights bartending in a club in St Pauli, and I got to know one of the girls there. We became friends and she told me what had happened to her. She was brought from Russia to be a prostitute in Hamburg, all under the pretence of being a language student at Multilinga."

"So, go to the police."

"Olga won't let me. She doesn't want to get in trouble, or get the other girls in trouble."

"Olga? I think you better start from the beginning."

He limps down the pier, loosening his tie as he goes. His left knee makes a sickening click every time he tries to bend it or put pressure on it. The brace is not helping.

Posterior cruciate ligament, he thinks, and he wonders if he'll ever run again.

"We can fix it," the doctor had said, "but it's a bit risky at your age." Then, pointing at the imaging scan, "The problem is all your cartilage has worn away."

So, there'll be no running, not for a while. There'll be surgery, rehab, learning to walk again, possibly injections to help the cartilage grow, but certainly no more marathons.

Why even bother trying to get the knee right? he asks himself.

It feels good to have the tie loose, to release the top button and breathe a little. Because everything is a bit harder these days, more complicated; the world a whole lot less inspiring. Just getting out of bed and standing up has become an ordeal.

In front of him, the workdays stretch towards his retirement, which might come sooner if someone starts asking more questions about the break-in at NAG a couple of weeks ago. The days are exactly like this one, with nothing really relevant to do except point the actual game-changers in the right direction, blame them if anything goes wrong, take the credit when things go right, and prepare to move aside so they can step in and replace him.

What was all so important a month ago doesn't seem that way anymore. All those relationships he maintained, all the impressive projects, all the miles he logged. It amounts to nothing. He's now an old technology about to be superseded, and he's got himself a wrecked knee in the process.

But, with all of that, he can't imagine not going to work. Once retired, he'll be forced to spend a lot more time at home.

The pier seems longer than ever. Each step compounds his misery, each click in his knee, each flash of pain.

He can't believe that a few weeks ago, the world had throbbed with promise and possibility. He'd skipped down this pier, youthful and exuberant. Then, she'd rolled up and told him it was over.

And he had walked away, without argument, without a fight. That's what hurts the most. He just conceded. Dropped out a long way from the finish line.

The gangway has been pushed askew by the rising tide. It's an effort to realign it, to close the gap. But he's not strong enough. He's forced to leap the gap, using the railing for support. He has a brief flash of falling down through the gap, to the water below. Holding his attaché case for weight, letting the computer and all those papers take him to the bottom of the river.

Or, he thinks, standing on the gangway, untie the boat and sail out to the North Sea. Never look back. Make the deal, pocket the money and sail away. Alone.

The deal. Will it be the same girl? he wonders.

He gets himself down into the boat, his knee clicking sickeningly. In the low-roofed cabin, he places the attaché case on the table and sits down. He'd like to swap his suit for a pair of shorts and a fleece, but it requires too much effort, and he's not staying anyway.

He looks around the cabin. The boat is all he has, and he finds that depressing. His river raft, as Dixon used to say, that nearly capsizes in the wake of container ships.

He smiles, sadly. One day, he thinks, life is great and you're really looking forward to things, then nothing has meaning anymore. Going forward, then standing still and now going backwards. From colour to black and white. Talkies to silent. 3D to 2D to no D. Nothing. A void. Sailing in circles, around and around on the river because the boat's too rickety and cheap to handle the North Sea. It's a floating garden shed, Ole, only useful as an escape from the house.

He feels exhausted.

He takes out his notebook and flips it open. He stares at it, watching it boot, one screen switching to another as the machine runs through its usual process. The same start-up, every single time. Over and over. Day after day.

He swipes the fingerprint sensor and enters his password. From the desktop, he opens his private email program.

The cursor flashes on the blank email. He doesn't know what to write, so he just starts typing; two index fingers buzzing around the keyboard like flies around a carcass. He opens with a confession: he never needed English lessons. He just wanted the chance to meet her and spend time with her. Those lunch lessons were the best part of his day, of his week. And that goes for any time they spent together. It wasn't about sex, he writes. It was about companionship, friendship and togetherness, being with the one person you know you're supposed to spend your life with, even if your life is two-thirds over or one-third begun. What mattered was the moment. Being together. Having the feeling of completion. The overwhelming sense that this person is the only thing that truly matters. Now, that's gone. There's nothing left. No point in continuing.

He doesn't bother reading through the email, to correct mistakes or fill in missing words. He hits send before he can change his mind.

At least she knows how it is, he thinks. Or how it was.

The sound of footsteps on the pier make him look up. He struggles to his feet. Outside the cabin, he sees a woman stepping down into the boat. This time, she's wearing a short coat, pants and black gloves. There's a large black sports bag in her right hand. He sees that she's wearing boots under the slacks, and he likes that. He thinks boots over pants is a disaster, and makes a girl look like a cheap hooker.

"Sie sind früh," he says.

"Ja."

They go into the cabin. As she gets close to him, he inhales her scent, liking it; not a perfume of any sort, but her natural scent.

"So, how's this going to work?" he asks, sitting back down.

"I need the latest project," she says, standing over him, her head just under the roof. "The latest technology."

"Was that what you were looking for in Steckdorf's office?"

She nods once. "I'm sorry. About your knee."

"So am I. It's wrecked."

"There was nothing on that computer."

"Steckdorf's? No. It's all old stuff. Who told you to look at that?"

"He did. I heard him talking at the club where I work. A lot of drunk boasting."

Ole smiles thinly and shakes his head. "What a fool. But that's why you got into contact with me."

"I've been watching you."

"Really?" He finds this strangely comforting and flattering.

"I knew you would want to do business."

"Me? Why me?"

"Instinct," she says.

"You're not exactly a pro, are you?" He chuckles a little and adds, dismissively, "Instinct." Then, in a friendly tone, "Would you like a drink?"

"I only want to do business."

"You Russians toast everything, including business deals. Or is this deal going to turn into a robbery?"

She places the bag on the table next to the computer.

"You can have the notebook," he says. "Everything's on it, even stuff that's still at the drawing board stage." Gesturing towards it, "Take it."

She looks at it. "The deal was a USB stick."

"I've prepared that too," he says, taking it out of his jacket's inside pocket and placing it on the table. "But not everything's on it."

"What do you want?"

"How much is in the bag?"

"What we agreed on."

"In cash?" he asks.

With a thin-lipped smile, "Paper money, yes."

She closes the cabin door and pulls back the zip of the sports bag. He looks inside, at the pile of newspaper.

"What the hell is that?"

But before he can protest any further, her gloved hands are around his neck, both thumbs pushing with incredible force against his throat.

What strong hands, he thinks.

She gets her weight over him, one leg pinning down his thighs. He tries to pull the hands away, but the gloves are slippery and her grip is too tight. He feels that she's actually wearing latex gloves over her gloves, and he wonders why he hadn't noticed that earlier.

In these final moments, he wonders many things. He thinks about his life, but lets all those thoughts and images pass, not giving them any attention.

He kicks his legs a little. His left knee clicks. But his resistance makes no difference. It starts to feel like the boat is listing, going further and further until it might flip altogether.

With her close to him, he gets a good look at her face. Her mouth is hard, her lips pale and thin, but her eyes are soft, almost apologetic. She's not terribly pretty, but he has a strong and sudden sense of attraction to her. Those brown eyes are hiding something and he wants to know what.

He wants to kiss her, to stroke her cheek.

She presses harder and he knows he's done. There's no reason to struggle. It really was all for nothing, but he does have this moment, being strangled by an inexplicably sexy girl on his boat. A girl with familiar eyes who has the class and style to wear boots under her slacks.

It's an intimate, very personal way to die.

He admires how easily she has taken control of this situation, and regrets saying that she's not a pro.

And he realises that this is what he's always wanted: a woman who would take control, who would come on board and take the helm.

Rather than trying to pry her fingers loose, he lets both his hands lightly grip her wrists. There's a gap of skin between glove and sleeve; he can feel slithers of hairs under his fingers. He strokes them and tries not to gasp.

But he's sinking. Down, down.

His final vision as his head tilts to starboard is of her boots. Shiny, black and hidden. She's got class, he thinks. She doesn't have to put it all out on display.

Then, he's gone.

She's careful to catch his head, to stop it from hitting the wood. She straightens him up and smoothes his clothes. His hands are smaller than hers. She takes his hands in her own, lining up the fingers so they fit around his neck, with the thumbs over the red marks left by her own thumbs. She presses hard, and is sure to push his fingers against the back of his neck as well. Satisfied, she tilts his head backwards so it rests against the top of the bench. His eyes are open, his mouth agape and almost smiling.

She snaps the notebook shut and slides it into the sports bag. Out on the pier, she tosses the USB stick into the water and lights a cigarette as she walks.

The play is incredibly slow. They're all experienced cricketers, competitive too and eager to show off, but they're also old university friends who haven't seen each other for a while, some not for ten years. There's a lot of talk on the field. Between overs, the players sometimes gather in small groups and crowd around the tiny screen of a phone: photos of babies, weddings, holidays, or something like that. She can only assume. It could be a recent buck's night from one of the guys, where they all ended up in a club like the one on Schmuck Strasse.

It's three months later and she still doesn't know what to do with Olga.

Ben is batting. It's a twenty over match, where the batsmen try to hit everything, but Ben is letting a lot of balls go.

The few WAGs that have come all have small children. They've set up a kind of makeshift day-care spot; an adjoining square of four blankets that they're collectively guarding. On the blankets are half a dozen toddlers and a pile of food. It's all in plastic containers, bought straight from nearby supermarkets, with the price tags scratched off. Baby-less and pre-packaged-food-less, she feels unwelcome on the blankets. She stays long enough to ask the necessary questions about each baby and listen to the mum's bragging. But even with that, they answer her questions talking to the other mothers, like she isn't there.

So she gets up and walks away. She circles the field slowly, watching the play when it happens and enjoying the solitude.

This'll take all day, she thinks, as Ben attempts a risky single on the last ball of an over in order to retain the strike. He just makes it.

She wonders if it will rain.

The sky is overcast and the air is cool. The poor conditions have kept people out of the park, save for joggers and dog walkers, and that meant Ben and his university pals could take over the all-weather synthetic cricket pitch and have their reunion match. At the start, there had been a long argument between Ben and Neil, or Nyall, about who would be captain. A vote was held. Ben lost.

On the adjacent field, another match is in progress, with what look like two all Indian teams. She can see they're playing on a turf pitch.

Her dad used to say a turf strip made cricket a completely different game. The boundary on that field is ringed by picnicking groups of spectators. There are a lot of them, as well as spontaneous games happening with children. A few men are slowly doing laps of the field, pausing to watch the play and discuss.

She stands between the two fields, able to watch both games. She's not willing to have Ben see that she's gone. She watches one ball of Ben's game, two of the other. The quality of the cricket is much higher on the turf strip.

A very light rain starts to fall. She moves under a tree for protection.

Ben takes a few runs and hogs the strike. His batting partner, clearly frustrated, takes a big swing when he gets the chance to bat and skies the ball to long-off, who juggles the catch. The players cheer.

"Dixon Treya Grace," a voice says.

She jumps, then moves around the tree just enough to see a man standing with his back against the trunk, directly behind her.

"Oh. Well, hi there."

"It is wonderful to see you."

"You scared the hell out of me."

"Sorry."

"My Melbourne messenger," she says, suddenly short of breath. "What are you doing here?"

"I promised I would find you."

"The world is small."

"It is, when you know where to look."

She stares straight ahead, but reaches her hands behind the tree. She feels him. He takes his hands in hers.

"What are you doing here?" she asks.

"I'm watching the cricket. What about you?"

"Same."

"How is it?"

"Boring. Big time boring. Twenty-twenty cricket has reached a new low, if that was possible."

"At least they look the part. Even if they can't play, they've got the right gear."

"Clothes don't make the cricketer," she replies. When he says nothing, she asks, "Are you on a recruiting drive?"

"I'm here to see you."

"How did you know I'd be here?"

"I have my sources."

"Sara," Dixon says in a gentle, thankful voice.

"And I'm also recruiting, at the University of East London, but ..."

"But what?"

"The recruits aren't exactly the best. A few of them are out there playing. More talent for cricket than engineering, and that's not saying much. The university is one of the worst in England."

"Really?"

"They'll take anyone, and that's not how we operate. We're far more selective. I guess there was hope I might pull a diamond out of the rough."

"Doesn't sound like there's much chance of that."

He squeezes her hands. "I think I just did."

"Well, that's nice of you to say, but this jewel is kind of taken."

"Kind of? By?"

Pointing at the field, "The one on strike."

He leans around the trunk to watch. "Terrible technique," he says. "Diagonal bat. That's the kind of thing they stop you from doing when you're six. And he pokes at the ball away from his body. No footwork. A good bowler would get him out first ball. I could."

"I'd love to watch you try. Winner gets me."

He moves back behind the tree. "Do you love him?" he asks.

"What kind of question is that?"

"A professional relationship then. Score a free trip to London."

"I'm paying my way." Pausing, then, "He's nice, but I'm not at the love stage yet. Do I have to be?"

"That's up to you. And nice is nice, even if he can't bat."

"I would've eloped with you in Melbourne," she says, "but you had other plans."

"So did you."

"And here we are in merry old England."

"On another recruiting drive. Scraping the bottom of the barrel."

"Careful. Ben went to the University of East London. They all did. They're having their ten-year reunion."

"With a game of cricket?"

"And dinner tonight." She pounces on the opening, keen to take a risk. "But it's guys only. None of the WAGs are invited. They all have kids and someone has to stay home and take care of them while the boys booze it up."

"That means you're free tonight."

"Maybe."

This time, he reaches behind the tree, the hands sliding behind her back. "Have dinner with me," he says.

"Done. But no Indian food."

"Where are you staying?"

"With one of Ben's friends. Neil or Nyall. I can never remember it. It's the tiniest flat you can imagine. A hovel. With two kids and two adults, plus us on an air mattress in a converted laundry. There's no window in our room. It's like we're all living on top of each other."

He giggles. The familiarity of the sound, and the memory that comes with it, makes her skin tingle.

"And the plumbing is awful," she continues. "Six people and one bathroom. It sounds like the toilet is constantly flushing and loading, flushing and loading."

"My hotel room's not much better."

"Where is it?"

"At the Viking. Around the corner from here. Out on the main road. What is it? Romford Road?"

"Like I'd know."

"It's very loud."

"It's loud everywhere in this city. But I'm guessing you're still on a budget, right?"

"Yes." Giggling, "Yes."

"Well, I think I need to see the inside of this room," she says. "Just to be sure you're keeping to your expense account."

"I think that's a very good idea."

She feels a card slide into the back pocket of her jeans. "A room key?"

"I can't open the door with no clothes on."

"Hmm."

"Eight o'clock," he says. "I'll be waiting."

She pushes herself off the tree and starts walking for the field. After a loud shout from all the players, Ben is trudging off the field, looking very annoyed. He stops and turns to shout at the umpire, who is someone from Ben's team taking his turn at umpiring. Ben remonstrates, pointing his bat. Some of the players laugh. A few lie down on the wet grass, still a little hungover from last night.

The other batsman isn't quite ready, so Dixon takes the break in

261

play to walk straight across the field. A couple of the players – married men, all of them – whistle at her.

"Streaker," one shouts.

"Dickhead," she mutters under her breath. She turns around to spy the tree and sees the messenger walking around the other field, his hands in his pockets.

She's led into the conference room. There's a large, square table, with the chairs facing the white screen, which is one of those fancy white boards you can write on and then print what's on it. Three students are already in the room, waiting, notepads in front of them. They all have yellow German–English dictionaries, all the same size. Like Manuela, who met her at the gate and ran her through the long list of dos and don'ts and cans and can'ts, and who organised her security and visitor passes, the women are nicely done up; a conservative yet stylish collection of pantsuits. There's not a hair out of place, not a smudge of lipstick on a tooth, not an unfiled or unpolished nail among them. Dixon wonders when they got up this morning. That kind of presentation takes time.

"Hi," she says, waving overzealously. "I'm Dixon."

The women nod politely. Manuela takes her place at the table, her notepad and dictionary in front of her, perfectly aligned.

One woman says, very formally, "Good morning, Frau Dixon."

"Good morning. But, please, Dixon is my first name, and you can call me that."

"Pass say Grace Dixon."

She looks down at it, pinned to her blouse on a slant. She lifts it up with a finger, reading it backwards. "So it does," she says, annoyed. "Well, it's wrong. My name is Dixon. Shall we get started?"

The women sit in schoolroom poses, expecting to be instructed rather than involved. Dixon decides to change that straight away by sitting down at the table with them and getting them to introduce themselves. Forced to speak, the atmosphere in the room thickens. It's clear that Manuela is the boss; eyes fall on her when any of the other three speak. The hierarchy is respected even in the classroom. Dixon knows the class would be a whole lot easier without Manuela.

The women avoid using each others' names. The introductions are self-conscious and repetitive, as the women already know each other and what they respectively do.

Dixon makes notes.

Their fluency is terrible. They get stuck searching for missing words and hands reach for dictionaries, only to be stopped by Dixon. They talk only when asked a direct question, and the answer is normally not longer than one sentence. She hears that their levels are very different, which complicates matters further, but lets them speak, not willing to take shots at their confidence just yet by correcting them. Getting them to talk is hard enough.

Manuela the boss, the difference in levels, the early morning hour, the fact that this is a test class with a lot of future classes relying on it: because of all this, Dixon finds herself sweating during the introductions. With those done, the next step would normally be the needs analysis. She thinks this would be pointless until the women have accepted that they will have different needs because of their difference in ability. She decides to do it at the end of class. She needs them talking, so she gets the women to ask her some personal questions, going around the group so each woman can ask one question in turn. They keep it superficial: background, why Germany, travel, work. They are sufficiently wowed when she describes Narooma, its beaches and landscape, but all are shocked to hear she was a police officer in Melbourne. But that information has the added impact of giving her more authority in the room, especially as Manuela was starting to dominate. Dixon picks her as someone who thinks she's always the smartest person in the room.

This inquiry done, she decides to introduce one of her favourite activities: the premises exercise. She wants to get them talking about things they already know, starting with the place they work and their department. It's a big company, so the activity could last the whole lesson. And as they work in HR, they should know pretty much everything.

She takes a blank piece of paper and puts it in front of them.

"This is your company," she says. "We're going to draw a map of the company, the premises, and say what happens in each area."

"Draw?" one asks.

Dixon mimes with her hand, an artistic flurry. "We're going to make a picture. A very simple one. The map of your company."

"Malen," Manuela says.

"Ich kann nicht malen."

The women laugh awkwardly.

"English, please," Dixon says. "We only speak English during the lesson. This is not a translation course. You don't need dictionaries. If you want to know what a word means, we need to describe it, not translate it." Taking pen to paper, "Now, here's the entrance. This is the south entrance gate, for visitors."

"And deliveries," Manuela adds.

"Okay. Yes." She slides the paper towards Manuela. "What is next to the entrance gate?"

"That's easy. Car park one." After a prompt from Dixon, Manuela draws it, her fingers around the pen in the shape of a bird's beak. "Car park one is for visitor parking and top management."

Manuela passes the paper to the woman next to her and the exercise continues.

An hour later, they have five sheets taped together in the centre of the table. Everyone is standing, pen in hand, drawing, talking and discussing. Manuela is putting the final touches on a crude plane, positioned at the start of the runway. They've got all the departments, marking the ones in red that require a special security clearance. They've even drawn the fences, having argued over which fences have barbed wire and which ones don't. They're all so into the activity, Dixon has to use her hands, like a conductor, so each of them gets a turn to speak.

She brings it to an end five minutes before the lesson is over.

Manuela draws a little head in the plane's cockpit and looks at her watch. "That was ninety minutes? Es war ja schnell."

"I hope you all enjoyed it," Dixon says brightly. "You did great, all of you. But we need to talk for a minute about what we want do in the lessons."

They give the usual demands for grammar and vocabulary, but Manuela takes the floor.

Pointing at the papers, she says, "We need to do more exercises like that. For our department and all the others. We must talk about what we do, professional and correct. All classes must be like this, because we make the classes by department."

"That's a very good idea, Manuela," Dixon says, hating her. "That way, all the participants will already know each other. And they're all into the same topics."

"We make the decision soon," Manuela says. "We contact school in the next week."

"But this class will meet next Monday."

Manuela dips her head slightly left, then right. "I believe so. I need to talk to the head of HR."

"Well, I'll be here."

"Please keep your security pass for now. I want not to meet you at the gate every week. Can you find the room again?"

"I think so, yes."

"Bring your handy, in case there is a room change. And now you also know that you can't bring a computer onto," with a look at the headline on the five taped-together papers, "the premices."

"Premises," Dixon corrects.

"You can pick up the computer at the entrance gate," Manuela says.

"Thanks. And thanks for the great lesson."

Manuela stands up and walks out. The three women follow her, whispering among themselves.

"Have a great day, everyone," Dixon says.

She gathers up the papers, folding them carefully, and puts them into her shoulder bag.

She weaves the bike between the collection of homeless people standing in front of the Enka 4 kiosk on David Strasse. They watch her pass, bottles of beer in their scabby, swollen hands. Reminded of Schultze, she wonders if the police are out looking for her. She presses the cap lower on her head, fitting right in and even getting a smile hello from a man in a St Pauli jersey coming from the other direction.

She locks the bike at the corner of David Strasse and Kastanien Allee. Through the window, she sees Olga working at the coffee machine. As with Astrid half an hour ago, now that she's here, she doesn't know quite what to say. But during the course of her English teaching tenure, she discovered she had a gift for improvisation. So, she enters the café with confidence, knowing she'll say the right things at the right time.

The café is empty, save for one man sleeping on his folded elbows at a table near the window.

She snaps her fingers and points, trying to be cool. "Oligarch."

Olga turns around. "Hey, Dixie. What are you doing here?"

"Looking for a fine coffee, mother."

"The usual?"

"Yes, and make sure it's hot."

Olga gets the machine gurgling. "Where were you? You wasn't here since last week."

"You weren't here," Dixon corrects. "But the correct grammar is, you haven't been here. Since last week is unfinished time."

Olga's keen to get it right. "You haven't been here since last week. Why?"

"Busy."

"That's not excuse. You live around the corner."

Shrugging and wondering when inspiration will hit, "Lot of things to take care of. New classes starting. Relationship collapsing. I just tried to do my regular stuff, but kept getting sidetracked."

"Hat shopping?" Olga asks with a smile.

"Hah." Dixon takes it off. "This is my hunting cap. I'm people hunting." And there's her entry point, "Looking for your mother superior."

Olga lowers her head over the coffee glass, pouring the frothy milk with care. One long, brown pigtail slides over he left shoulder, the splayed ends below the tight hair band almost landing in the forth. She flicks the plaited pigtail back.

"You need a hair net," Dixon says. "If they can find one big enough for you. A converted fishing net maybe. Or you sew together an old pair of fishnet stockings. I bet you still have some."

Sliding the coffee along the counter to Dixon and then playing with her hair, "I think I cut it."

"What? No, you can't. You have such beautiful hair, especially since you stopped bleaching it."

"Was not my idea. The blonde."

"I know. Busana, mother superior." She sips the coffee. "Hmm. That's good. Do you know where she is?"

Olga shakes her head. "No."

"Come on. It's me. Please. I know you're still in touch with some of the girls. I know you help them sometimes, like you did with Jelena."

"It is hard life."

"Don't forget your articles. And contract. Sound like a native speaker."

"It's a hard life," Olga says, copying Dixon's accent a little.

"It is. Hard and unfair. Illegal too. But at least you've come out on top."

"Because of you."

Sipping the coffee some more, "You can repay me by telling me where Busana is."

"I don't know. I never know. She never lived anywhere. Uh, I couldn't tell you that last year."

"I couldn't have told you that last year."

"Yes."

"But she's in Hamburg?"

Olga shrugs.

"Come on. Work with me."

"Every day," Olga says, leaning across the counter, "I think Busana come in here and take me back."

"She can't do that."

"Or she send me back to Dagestan. I was one of the first."

"She can't send you back. You're set. In fact," with more inspiration hitting her, "you're the one who could bust this wide open. Yeah. You could have Busana arrested."

"No. Then girls sent back too. They want that not."

"I know, I know. We've been down this road."

"The girls," Olga confides, "they like it here very much. Will do anything to stay."

"Well, that's clear. Still, it's a hell of a price to pay."

"Is better than home. At home, they just get raped."

"And here they get money for it."

"Yes, and live better."

It's not going well. She forgot what a tough girl Olga is, but admires her for it. She drinks some more coffee, and thinks.

"You are good friend, Dixie," Olga says.

But Dixon disagrees. "Look, I've got the language school," she says. "I can prove that they're giving the girls visas. I want to shut those bastards down and stop this."

"Why? It all works. We got out of Russia."

"That doesn't stop this from being wrong," Dixon shouts.

The man at the window stirs and shifts his position. He settles again and starts snoring.

"Look, Olga. I'm tired of walking away from bad stuff. Ever since we met, I've been trying to think of a way to stop this. You didn't want to go to the police last year, and we couldn't, not after what happened. But now we can. With your help, we can link Multilinga to Märsh."

"How?"

"I've got a man on the inside," Dixon explains. "At the school. And he's definitely on our side."

Olga folds her arms. She looks tired from so many early starts. The morning shift that no one wants to work.

"Well?"

"Is risk, Dixie," Olga says. "Girls have nothing to go back to. No family."

"Yeah, you told me that. They take the girls from orphanages. I think that's the worst part. Get them young too, and then throw them in the trash when they're twenty."

"Or they work hard, get better job. Become escort."

"Move up a rung on the food chain. Stop trying to rationalise this, Oligarch. It's not right. It's got to stop."

"You stop it not," Olga says flatly. "Close this hole, another opens."

"Ugh. You're disappointing me."

"Sorry." With another shrug, "Is life."

Dixon drains her coffee and decides on a different tact. "What about Jelena? Is she still staying with you?"

"She back at Schmuck Strasse."

"How old is she?"

"Fourteen. Maybe. She says she know not exactly."

"What about the date on her passport?"

"Is probably wrong. Maybe she is twelve."

"So, this kid gets beaten and all you do is patch her up and send her back in for more?" Dixon asks, losing patience.

"I feel bad for Jelena. I do. I think she would help you. Jelena very unhappy."

"Are you still in contact with her?"

"We Skype. Is cheap and safe."

"Do you have your netbook with you? Maybe she's online now."

Olga reaches down and pulls out her small computer. She flips it open. "We talk not on Skype," she says. "Only send messages. Don't want other girls to hear."

Dixon's fingers drum against the counter. "I'm sorry, Olga. I don't want to put any pressure on you. I just want to help."

"Is okay. You good person. I see that in you first time. You behind bar. Good person in wrong place."

"Given the chance, I'd do everything the same."

Olga uses the track pad and types a little. "I also want to stop this. But this, much bigger than you and me. Many people involved. We too small."

"It only takes a pin to burst the biggest balloon," Dixon says. "My father used to say that."

Looking at the screen, "She's on. What now?"

"Tell her to meet you at Café Gnosa at three-thirty."

"Today?"

"Yes."

Olga types, waits, then nods. "She come. I too. I be translator for you. Like last time."

"Good. Thanks, Oligarch. If I'm not there, make sure you find Astrid and Seth. You met them both at my birthday party. Remember?"

"Yes."

Dixon reaches out her hands for the netbook. "Can I quickly check my email?" she asks.

"Sure." Olga spins the computer around. "Another coffee?"

"Better not. Gotta fly in a minute."

"Maybe you come over tonight. Tell me about relationship. You need sofa?"

Dixon looks briefly at Olga, feeling a little guilty. "We'll see. I might be detained."

Olga nods.

It's a fast internet connection. Dixon gets her email open and sees she has two new messages: one from Ben sent this morning, and the other from Ole sent last night.

"Meine Güte," she says, reading.

"What?"

"My crumbled relationship just got hit by a hurricane. It's in ruins now. Ben's got a job in India."

"Oh."

She clicks open the message from Ole. While reading, she says "Oh, you bloody idiot."

"What is it?"

"Men are so pathetic sometimes."

Olga smiles at this comment. "Born that way."

"Right you are, Oligarch. No sympathy for them."

A quick internet search lands her on the Hamburg LKA website. She doesn't bother trying to find the direct email address, but does get a contact for LKA7, Staatsschutz. She forwards Ole's email to that address, putting "ATTN: Babette Korner" in the subject line, and does the same with Ben's email.

"That'll give them something else to do for a while," she says, handing the netbook back.

"You wait?" Olga asks. "My shift finish soon."

"Sorry. Gotta go." Putting the cap back on, "Listen, Olga. If I don't make it to Café Gnosa, make sure you stick around for a bit. It could be a detective might come in my place."

"Police? No."

"Don't take your passport," Dixon says, heading for the door. "Tell them everything, but don't let them take you in. Same goes for Jelena."

"What? I not understand."

"And when it's over, you run and you don't look back."

"Dixie, wait."

But she's out the door and back on the bike.

271

She slouches boyishly in the chair, almost lying on it. Legs extended, feet pointing upwards, arms folded, chin resting on her chest. It's as much defiance as she can muster. But she's also scared, getting down this low in the chair so the two policemen can't see her.

Those two have desks pushed together. One sits with his hands behind his head, looking very pleased with himself. He was the one who arrested her, and his eyes shine with the pale glee of revenge. His mate mumbles something, making him laugh, and when he opens his mouth, his teeth are moist.

She sees a large stapler on his desk and wants to shove it into his mouth. Maybe staple his tongue to the roof of his mouth. For sure, she feels the strongest urge to fight back against these guys, but doesn't know how to. The best she can do is her posture of defiance.

"Ugh."

"Quiet," the arresting cop says. "I don't wanna hear one more word outta you."

She raises an arm above her head, like a girl in school.

"What?"

"Can I ask a question?"

The two men share a glance, enjoying themselves, ready for more amusement.

"Let's have it."

"It's like this," Dixon says. "I borrowed a car to help my friend. Her host mother beats her up, right? I got the car in order to save her. So, really, I think I should be rewarded for my heroic deed, and you guys should go arrest Mrs McDougall, like, now."

"Is that your question? That you should be rewarded?"

She sits up a little. "One of them, yeah. But, it's also, you know, I guess ... out there," pointing, "a whole lot of bad stuff is happening. Maybe a girl's being raped right as we speak, or there's a pedo luring a kid into a van with a bag of sweets. Or, or there's some dirtbag drunk of a husband beating up on his wife. But you two sit in here really proud of yourselves for nabbing some teenager who was trying to do a good deed."

"Get to the point."

"So, my question is this. Don't you guys, as policemen, have better things to do?"

Both men frown at her. The arresting policeman slaps his hands on his desk and stands up. He flips up the counter door and approaches her, with almost violent intent.

"If you weren't Gully's kid," he mutters.

Dixon sits up straight. "Then what? You'd hit me? That's brave. Maybe I'll tell my dad you touched me in an inappropriate spot. He won't stand for that."

This makes the policeman step back. "You'll go into JD for this."

"Jack Daniel's?"

"Juvenile detention."

With both hands in the air for emphasis, "For helping someone in trouble? For rescuing a friend?"

"You stole a car."

"Borrowed," Dixon replies. "Anyway, I learned at school this country was founded on stealing, and that we should be proud of our convict ancestors. I'm just being true to our roots."

"How do you know how to hot-wire a car?"

"I don't. The key was in it."

He leans against the counter. "Olive said she had the keys."

"Who's Olive?"

"The woman you stole the car from."

"Who's a champion listener then? I keep you telling you, I borrowed it."

He raises his right arm across his body, as if readying to slap Dixon with the back of his hand. She cowers in the chair.

The door opens.

"I wouldn't do that if I were you," Laz says, entering.

"Help, Laz. This is police brutality."

"It is not," the policeman says. "I didn't touch her."

"Good."

"Laz, get me out of here."

"Dixon Grace, shut up."

"Where's Gully?" the policeman asks, backing away. He gets himself behind the counter. "He said on the phone he was coming. Only a parent or guardian can sign for her release."

Laz sits down next to Dixon. "I'll wait until he comes. Just in case you decide to do something foolish." Looking at Dixon, "That goes for you as well."

"Let it go, Dale," the other policeman says. "They're not worth it."

"Dale?" Laz taps her chin with her index finger. "Dale Connell?"

"Yeah?"

"Dale Connell," Laz says slowly. "Your wife planted a beautiful white rose bush in the garden when she stayed with me. That was last year, wasn't it?"

Dale shifts his weight from foot to foot. "I don't know what you're on about."

Laz talks to Dixon: "Katie Connell. Lovely girl. Showed up in a pretty bad way. But she hasn't been back since, which means everything is all right." To Dale, "How's your home life?"

Dale snarls.

"Oh, yes," Laz says brightly. "I remember now. She came by to see me just before she left. Took the kids down to Merimbula, where her parents live. You know, she still writes to me. I think in the last letter she said something about meeting someone, and he treats her very well. Do you see the kids often?"

Dale doesn't reply. He crosses his arms and stares at Laz with hate, but Laz is far from intimidated. Dixon watches with awe.

"No, she got full custody, didn't she? And this new man is good with the kids. They're all happy together, so everything worked out for the best."

Dale points at Laz. "You're poison in this town, you know that? How many marriages have you wrecked? How many families have you broken up?"

"I'm sorry you feel that way, Dale. We've saved a lot of marriages, but no one ever talks about them. And the fact that your marriage ended is your fault, not mine."

"Bloody boat people," Dale says, sitting down at his desk.

"Yes, we're the reason for all your mistakes and problems," Laz says. "Don't ever think that you're to blame. It's always someone else's fault." Turning to Dixon, "You stupid, stupid girl. What is the matter with you?"

"I just wanted to help Ace. How is she? All right?"

"She's pretty shook up, from holding it all in for so long. I got her settled in one of the rooms."

"Maybe you can make a report against Mrs McDigiot while you're here. You know, two birds."

"The police can't help her, and they wouldn't if they could. I called Astrid's parents. She'll fly home as soon as possible. She's staying with me until then."

Dixon is incredulous. "You're just gonna let it drop? Then some other girl will stay there too."

"Calm down, Dixie. I'll report it to the organisation that runs the student exchange. It'll be up to them what happens."

"And justice is done."

"It is."

"You're way wrong, Lazarus."

"Not everything deserves punishment. Maybe it's an isolated incident. Still, Mrs McDougall will have to live with this for the rest of her life, and the whole town will know."

"Ugh." Dixon goes back to her slouching-lying position of teenage defiance. "Unsatisfactory."

"Sometimes you have to work the system," Laz says. "But poor Astrid. She suffered all this time without saying anything."

Sarcastically, "Suffering is good, isn't it?"

"It is. Maybe this will be a formative experience for her. People are different after they've suffered. It's up to her how she'll come through it."

"And I lose the only friend I have in the process."

"Don't be so selfish. You helped her. Astrid strikes me as a bit of a dreamer. Maybe this will help her focus, bring her down to earth."

"Ugh."

"Maybe you'll get the same from the experience."

"Don't you start with all those future questions," Dixon says. "What do you wanna be? What do you wanna study? I'm sixteen. I don't know any of that."

"You can always change along the way. What you start off doing in life doesn't have to be the same thing until the end. It took me nearly forty years to find what it is I want to do. That's half a life. But in the meantime, I had all those experiences that made it possible for me to do it."

"The magic keys to open your personal doors of discovery."

"Don't make fun of your mother like that."

"Is she coming? She'll be majorly pissed, I bet. Crap on about how I've ruined my future. Taken a sledgehammer to my path."

"Rika has her own problems," Laz says. "She always did, and

she never tried to deal with them. Always looks somewhere else for answers."

"Is she coming?"

"I don't know, Dixie. I'm sure they contacted her."

"Maybe she's got a cow to milk."

Laz smiles. "Her work is an escape, you know that. It's a distraction."

"Get her to work in the café."

"She never wanted that. I think she resents it a little bit, that I'm messing with people's lives. She thinks I should leave it alone."

"That sounds like something she'd say. Don't meddle with destiny."

"Oi," Dale shouts. "Will you two shut up?"

"This is public property," Laz says. "We can talk as much as we like." To Dixon, but lowering her voice, "Your mother's lost. A lot of it's my fault. You should stop trying to get her attention. Because you'll never get it."

The door opens.

Steve strides in. "What the hell is going on, Dixie?" he demands.

Dixon stands up. "Dad, I can explain everything."

"I hope so."

"Where's mum? I wanna explain it to her too."

"She's on her way."

"Steve," Laz says, touching his arm, "let's just sign the release and discuss it all at home. I know she'll take whatever punishment is coming. She made one mistake. Let's not ruin her life because of it."

"She'll go to court," Dale says. "Then to JD. She's stuffed."

"Careful, Dale," Steve says. "That's my daughter. I know she has a reason for this."

"I just wanted to help Astrid," Dixon says, almost crying now. "To save her from Mrs McDougall."

"Hang on, Dixie. Slow down."

"Just sign the release, Steve," Laz says. "This is being blown way out of proportion. We'll go home, Dixie will explain her actions and we'll all get on with our lives. She won't go to court."

"There's mandatory sentencing for this sort of thing," Dale says.

"Yes, for repeat offenders," Laz replies. "Steve, we need to get Dixie out of here, before they beat her to death and try to pass it off as suicide."

"Oi, fair go," Dale shouts. "Where the fuck do you think you are?"

Steve turns his back on Dale. "We're gonna have words, Dixie," he says. "At home. And there'll be no golf for you until the spring."

"Oh, da-ad."

"Maybe that way you'll learn." Steve turns around. "Give us the form, Dale. Where do I sign?"

The form is on the desk. Dale pushes his swivel chair over and slides the paper onto the counter. "Here. You playing on the weekend, Gully?"

Steve signs. "If I get picked. You? How's the shoulder?"

"Another week I reckon." Dale takes the form back. "No hard feelings, mate. Just doing my job, you know."

Steve knocks the counter with his fist. "Righto. Let's go."

Laz and Steve head for the door. Dixon doesn't move.

"I'm not going anywhere until mum comes," she says.

The solid wooden pier makes her homesick. The sound of lapping water, the wafts of diesel in the air. Masts swaying ever so slightly. The clunkity-clunk of boats jostling and softly colliding.

She's glad her mother moved to Hamburg to help take care of Marcus, but a part of her wishes she'd stayed in Darss. Then, they could visit every weekend, and stay in comfort rather than in the tiny cottage on the garden allotment her mother still has; the one given in exchange for some party favour her father did years ago.

She doesn't ever want to know what that favour was.

Now, in mid-September, it would still be warm enough to swim in the Baltic and lie naked on the sand. She feels a pang of guilt, for denying Marcus the coastal upbringing she had. Sure, it was communist East Germany, and it was hard, but they lived by the sea and that was special. She knows Marcus is a city kid who'll grow into a city teen. So much of his character will be shaped by this urban landscape.

She also thinks some more sun and salt would make the boy look a little less Slavic.

She reaches Lessinger's boat. The tide has gone out and the boat is tilted a little on its side. The muddy brown sand of the riverbed is exposed.

She crosses the gangway thinking the boat is a rather dismal affair, something to putt around in, or on, rather than something you could seriously sail. On board, it feels smaller than when she first saw it from the Sailors Inn. While eating a quick lunch, she'd pointed at the boat and asked questions of the men seated at the bar. They didn't really know Ole, as he seldom came in for a drink. It was the bartender who said Ole was a typical weekend boater; more interested in his own boat than being part of the marina's community, and not a very good sailor at all. They joked and laughed about how Ole struggled with tides. You could often see his boat stranded near the marina, the bartender said, with Ole scratching his head and looking at his watch. But Ole was dead. The fish was good at the Sailors Inn, but Korner thought the company wasn't. Murder wasn't funny. And even if Ole had been a poor sailor, he had risen up to a very high managerial position, and that was a lot more than the barflies in the Sailors Inn could say. She was glad to remind them of that.

She runs a key through the police sticker on the cabin door and edges the door open. Inside, it feels cramped and innocent, and rather unappealing. Not exactly a place for illicit affairs with much younger women, or the scene of a murder. It seems too plain for that, too ordinary. The fittings have a rustic nautical taste which might become comforting after a while, but Korner finds the sparse interior not to her taste. She does, however, conclude that Frau Lessinger was never here. And in that line of thought, the interior suddenly seems a little more comfortable. A refuge of sorts. It wouldn't be so bad to sit on this boat, drink a beer and wait for the tide to come in.

She wonders if Lessinger stranded himself deliberately, to buy more time and give him a reason not to go home.

She stands in the cabin for a good fifteen minutes, just standing and looking. Then, she opens everything she can find: small cupboards, stiff drawers, the bar fridge. In the freezer of the fridge, iced over, there's what looks like a log book. She sits down, brushes the ice away and flips this open. The pages are frozen stiff. There are sketches: of the river, container ships, trees, birds, other boats. She's no expert on art, but she's sure these are not bad. They show skill, aptitude and application. None of the sketches are dated. To her surprise, there's a sketch of Dixon, lying on the narrow roof of the cabin in a bikini. Korner thinks Dixon looks happy, or Lessinger drew her with a very happy pencil.

She finds it annoying that the investigating team went through the whole boat but didn't find this sketchbook. Schultze had already told her there was nothing incriminating found on board. No clues or leads, nothing untoward. Only the fingerprints were the link to Dixon Grace. That means she was here, on the boat, and the sketch proves it, but that didn't necessarily mean she was here last night.

Motive, she thinks. Murder requires motivation. Why would Dixon kill Ole? If Dixon is a spy and Ole was her source, then she killed him to cover her tracks. This is what Schultze believes, but what murderous corporate spy lies on the roof of the guy's boat in a bikini while he sketches her?

More plausible is suicide. After the meeting with Frau Lessinger, Korner considers the balance has been pushed in favour of that theory.

But for some reason, she doesn't think suicide is in Lessinger's make-up. Plus, self-strangulation, by hand, is not exactly the most common form of suicide. And he's on a boat, she thinks; use some rope, not your hands.

Leaving the cabin, she hopes that the autopsy results will give a better indication of what happened on this boat last night. A murder passed off as suicide is what she considers most likely.

Her phone rings.

"Ja, Korner."

"Schultze hier. I have some interesting news for you."

She stands at the back of the boat, looking towards the Sailors Inn. "Let's hear it."

"Lessinger owns the house."

"So?"

"No mortgage. He bought it. It's worth over half a million euros. He had that money when he bought it fourteen years ago."

"Get to the point, Schultze."

He clears his throat loudly, a double syllable, like a tennis player grunting. "They don't pay a mortgage," Schultze says, getting excited. "But they have no money. Lessinger made a big salary and they spent all of it. You just need to look through the bank statements to see how they were spending it. The money just runs through Frau Lessinger's fingers. You can see their whole life in their bank statements."

She walks to the gangway and stands on the pier. "Good." Forcing herself to say it, "That's good work. Anything else?"

"Yes. Lessinger has a private Swiss bank account," Schultze says, his voice brightening with the compliment, "opened in August, just a few weeks ago. But there's nothing in it. Balance is zero."

"Waiting for a payment?"

"Or he was tired of his wife blowing all their money and wanted to put some aside that she couldn't touch."

"Hmm. Maybe." She paces the pier a little. "What about the insurance?"

"It'll come through, when it's clear that it was," another loud clearing of the throat, "murder."

"You still shouldn't have told Frau Lessinger that. But she'll get the insurance. And she'll sell the boat too. I don't think she'll get much for it. It's like a decked-out row boat."

"How do you know that?"

"I'm looking at it."

"And?"

"I've got something to show you, when I get back. And I need the autopsy report."

"They said by late afternoon," Schultze says.

"We need it sooner than that."

"No, we need to find Dixon Grace."

Annoyed, Korner stops pacing. "Well, I don't think she's going to walk back to LKA on her own, Schultze," she shouts. Then, more calmly, "But if she's investigating, she'll probably hit her old haunts, call in favours from friends. The usual stuff. Check the apartment, the language school. Chase after any people she knows. Go talk to that friend of hers, Astrid someone. And ..."

"And what?"

She walks to the edge of the pier and squints down at the sand.

"Hello? Frau Korner?"

"I think I've found something."

"What is it?"

"I'll call you back."

She pockets the phone and stares at the purple USB stick nestled in the sand. There's a ladder nearby, but it doesn't go all the way to the riverbed; the last rung is about a metre short. She takes the boat hook that's hanging next to the ladder and climbs down.

She can't reach it. She tries to rake the sand a little, to cut a path for the stick to fall into, but this doesn't work. A shallow wave of water washes over the stick, the tide coming in, putting it further out of reach.

She has to go in, she knows it.

Back on the pier, she removes her shoes and socks and rolls up her pants. The rusted rungs of the ladder hurt her feet as she climbs down. The sand is much softer than expected, and cold, really cold. She sinks in up to her knees and has to lift her legs out of the sand to make any progress. Each step takes a while, but she edges closer to the stick, even as the water tries to wash it further away. But in doing so, the stick is getting cleaner and becomes more exposed. It's easy to pluck from the sand and she rinses it a little, flicking the water out of it.

Turning, the stick in her hand and still up to her knees in the riverbed, she looks back to the pier. For a moment, it feels like she's stuck, but she lifts her left leg out and begins the slow trek back to the ladder.

She's woken by the minivan jerking to a halt. She shifts in the seat a little. Her back is stiff. The seat is comfortable, but cramped. It afforded her some sleep, even if she made herself wake up every half hour or so just in case the driver tried something funny, as had happened two days ago, while waiting for another vehicle to arrive. Somewhere on the road back to Grozny, there's a man driving an empty minivan with a pair of black eyes, an ice pack on his groin and severely wounded pride.

This driver has kept to himself. He drove and said nothing.

She looks around the van. All the girls are still sleeping, with heads resting on others' shoulders, jackets for blankets, and some girls with their arms around each other for added warmth. She goes from face to face, wondering what the future will bring for each of them.

She hopes this is another van change. It would mean waking the girls, which she doesn't want to do, but it would mean a more comfortable ride. The minivans have been getting progressively better since they drove out of Makhachkala in a Soviet-era death-trap. That first van was a converted military transporter with no suspension or heating, and it had a leaky radiator that needed to be refilled every two hours. She didn't think they would make it to Grozny, but they did, eventually, and continued to make slow progress north until the first minivan change in Rostov and the fight with the driver. Then west, further than any of the girls had ever been, passing through towns that time had forgot and cities they'd never heard of. During the cigarette and bathroom breaks, or the hours waiting in the cold for another minivan to arrive, the girls talked incessantly about Hamburg, bombarding Busana with questions. But she only knew Germany from books, and also didn't know for certain what was in store for them. Already though, deep within her was the feeling that what awaited them in Hamburg wouldn't be what they expected, and this feeling had grown the further west they went. She hoped that it could be balanced against what they've left behind; that perspective making whatever situation they are forced into bearable by comparison.

She has never been to Germany. It seems strange now to be so close, and to be so far from the place she always wanted to leave. Life has completely changed in a week. It's not the first time that has happened for her, but for once she would like to be the one doing the changing, and not simply be the victim of outside forces.

She wants control.

She slips her arms into the sleeves of her jacket. The left inside pocket is weighed down by the girls' passports. The stiff, fresh rectangles press against her ribs, a burden that knocks against her heart.

At the very least, she thinks, if it all turns bad in Hamburg, there'll be no one to explain things to, no crying mothers or vengeful fathers. And they will have tried to escape, even if it ends in failure. She thinks that's better than the life they had.

The girls have no one and neither does she. That's sad, but they do have each other. Again, she promises herself to look after the girls, no matter what.

She rubs the mist from the window. Outside, there are women about, all of them old and pulling little trolleys for their shopping. They cross the car park, walking with effort, to get to the train station or to line up at the stops for the first buses of the morning. They have dour expressions, perhaps with several thousand mornings just like this one already behind them. There seems to be a point to their activity, to being up so early, but they don't exactly move with purpose. They also don't talk with each other.

She wonders if they have all day to complete a few simple tasks. She feels sorry for them, and jealous.

The Polish driver stands over her. He gestures for her to follow him.

"Jetzt?" she asks.

He nods.

"I'll wake the girls and get them moving."

"No," he says. "You."

Out of the cosy minivan, the air is biting cold. The dawn is just starting to light up the sky towards the east, from the direction they've come. The driver points at a long black sedan. As Busana walks towards it, her legs feel weak from three days of sitting, but she tries to walk with confidence and intent. She puts her hands into the pockets of her jacket to keep them warm and to hide the scabs on her knuckles.

As she approaches, the back door is flung open from the inside.

283

She lowers herself into the car and closes the door. There's a smallish man slouched in the other seat, half hidden by darkness. She sees the heads of the driver and another man in the front passenger seat.

"Frau Isayeva?" the man next to her asks.

"Ja?"

His smile lights up in the shadow. "Welcome to Krakow. I wish I could say welcome to Germany, but you're not quite there yet."

"How much further?"

"To the border? A few hours." In a conversational tone, "The Polish highways are awful, but they'll be silky smooth compared to where you're from. It'll be a long haul from the border to Hamburg, but you've already come this far. What's another thousand kilometres?"

"The girls are tired."

He holds up a calming, gloved hand. "Don't worry. They'll have plenty of time to rest when they arrive. The first few days will be light, I promise. It all starts on Monday."

"Are you from the language school?"

Pausing, "I'm a representative. This is all quite new, you see. Your girls are the first to make this trip. You're pioneers. And you're all very lucky."

"Why did you choose them?" Busana asks. The comfort of the car, especially the strong heating, makes her feel sleepy. She feels herself almost melting into the seat.

"Why do you think?"

"The man who came to the orphanage said it's because they're already learning German."

"That's one reason."

"And the other?"

He lowers his head so his face catches the beam of a streetlight. He smiles at her, but without showing his teeth this time. It's a cunning smile, mischievous. He has sharp features, she sees, placing him as Nordic, possibly Russian. His blonde hair is cut short and parted to the side. He's well dressed in a black suit. She's not sure of his age, because the pale, stiff skin of his cheeks is pulled tight over a pointy jaw, leaving his face lineless. Not even that sly smile cracks a line next to his eyes.

"You," he says. "We want you."

She's surprised by this. "My German is not that good."

"That's not what I mean." Reaching out his gloved hand, "But first, the passports. Please give them to me. We'll drive ahead and organise the visas. We'll have everything set by the time you arrive. You don't have to worry about a thing."

She hesitates, her hand already inside her jacket. "What about the border?"

"Poland's in the EU," he says lightly. "Anyway, the driver knows what to do. He'll detour through Görlitz."

"But how can I trust you?" she asks, pulling out the stack of passports. "You could be anyone."

"We do all this to bring you to Germany and you still don't trust us? We can just as easily turn the van around and take you back."

"I'm sorry. I mean no disrespect."

"Good."

"Some of the girls are very young," Busana says. "They're my responsibility."

"Mine too. We can share the responsibility." His hand extends further. "It's also your responsibility to ensure the girls have the right visas. Give me their passports so I can take care of that for you."

She hands them out to him, but there is a brief moment where they both hold onto the stack before Busana lets go. There's an audible snap as her fingers release.

He counts the passports. "You're one short."

"Liala decided not to come at the last minute. Her brother is in the orphanage."

"That's disappointing. But it's a good lesson for you. For next time."

"What do you mean?"

"For the next group of girls," he says, assuming his conversational tone of before. "If your group does well, we want to expand the program, get more girls to Germany for language lessons and possible work placement. A lot is riding on the girls in that van. And on you."

"I was told it's just three months."

"It is, it is. But the ultimate goal is to get these girls settled in Germany. Isn't that what you want?"

She looks at him in the shadows, a small, slight man with plenty of leg room in the back seat. He thumbs through the passports, looking at each photograph in turn.

"Sascha was right about the girls from Dagestan," he says. "They have a completely unique look. The fault line of where east meets west. Kaboom!"

285

"Some of them are Chechen."

"Like you? That's fine. This is about language, not religion."

"How do you know I'm Chechen?"

The sly smile again. "I know all about you."

"That depends on where you get your information," she replies. "The state files and police reports are all wrong. In Grozny, there are the ways things actually happen, and then there are the ways they're reported and recorded."

"My information is correct. That's why we chose you. You're loyal. Don't ever underestimate the value of loyalty."

"Where do you think my loyalty lies?"

He holds up the passports. "To me. To your girls. And to your roots."

"Chechnya?" She scoffs at this. "Not after the Moscow Siege. The whole thing has become more about God and power than freedom and independence."

"Agreed."

"What do you care? You're not Chechen."

He speaks to the men in front. "See? I told you she had fire inside." To Busana, "No, I'm not Chechen, but I do have an interest in the result. And I have an interest in you. Born a Terek Cossack, but put into an orphanage when your parents were killed in the First Chechen War. How old were you?"

"Thirteen."

"Mistreated, I bet. A Cossack princess thrown to the lions. And forced into marriage not long after."

"Not just me."

"But you never agreed with it," he says with admiration. "Never relented."

She sits up a little straighter. "Men only ever want to keep women down. Make them slaves."

"Is that what you think I'm trying to do?" When she doesn't reply, he says, "This is why you're here. You fight back, when you have the right motivation. What I don't understand is why you joined the separatist movement. It goes against everything that happened. You joined the enemy. Why?"

She looks down at the passports held in his hands, trying not to remember. "I wanted to learn how to fight," she says. "No one was ever going to fight for me, so I decided to do it myself. I went to Makhachkala once I'd had enough."

Shaking his head, "I would ask you never to lie to me. The separatists recruited you. After what happened with your husband. They wanted to use you, but you escaped to run an orphanage instead. You killed people."

"Depends on what report you read."

"I guess it does." He chuckles softly. "You have no intention of going back?"

"No."

"Meaning your loyalty is really only to yourself."

"To the girls."

"That's why you beat up the guy who got too friendly."

"He brought that on himself," she says, sliding her hands into the front pockets of her jacket.

"Yes," more chuckling, "but allegiance is a tricky thing. You change teams whenever it suits you."

"Do you want me on your team? I don't even know who you are."

"My name is Yorma."

"Where are you from?"

"Finland."

"Finland? So what do you care about rescuing Russian girls?"

"I want the right girls on my team. Including you."

"To do what?" she asks.

"Call them ... special assignments. Your first task is to get the girls settled in Hamburg."

"Tour leader. That's what I was told."

"Come now, Frau Isayeva," he says smoothly. "You know what's happening here. You knew when you first agreed to come along. What I'm offering you is the chance to not have to do what your girls will have to do."

Busana is unable to reply.

"I own these girls now," he continues, waving the passports in the air. "I own you. Don't look at me like that. You got out of Russia. That's what you wanted, and you knew there'd be a price for it. It's what you want for your girls too. And they can get it, if they work hard. Fuck the right man in the right way and they might end up married to a rich German."

"Watch your mouth."

"It's happened before and it'll happen again. So, why not get involved?"

287

"They're kids," she says, but she hears that the fire has gone out of her own voice.

Pointing at her with the passports, "You've got a choice. East or west. Forward or back. But we both know what you'll choose. You're a smart woman. You know exactly what you're getting into. It's why you brought the passports into the car with you."

"What do you want from me?"

Yorma leans across slightly and places a gloved hand on her knee. "I want to trade," he says.

"You've got the girls already."

"There'll be more girls. More work for you."

"Special assignments?"

"Far beyond the small world you're picturing." He leans closer. He smells of cigarette smoke. "What happens to the girls will be directly linked to your own performance."

"You mean, if I do what you want, they'll get treated better?"

"Yes. A fair trade."

Busana looks out the window. To her own surprise, she's not repulsed by Yorma, nor does she hate having his hand on her knee. She actually finds something soothing in his voice. His calm demeanour appeals to her, and it seems out of character with the business he's in.

She's suddenly aware that he's right: she knew all along what they were getting into.

Outside, the morning light is stronger than before. She watches a minivan pull up next to other van. This one is a shiny white Mercedes with Germany plates. The girls are tired and slow as they move from one van to the other. She sees Olga struggling to carry a girl asleep in her arms.

"Do I have a choice?" she asks, knowing that she doesn't.

"Of course you do." He looks out her window as well. "But it looks like they've already decided. And so have you."

She lets out a long sigh, which Yorma seems to make an effort to inhale.

"This is slavery," she says softly.

"No. This is business," Yorma replies, his voice no longer conversational or soothing. "It's opportunity in the open European marketplace." Then, brightly, "Frau Isayeva, this is cross-cultural exchange."

She walks up the beach, the red, white and green pareo wrapped around her waist. The hot sand pushes through her toes as she walks, making her hop a little.

Baby feet, she thinks. A whole year in shoes and socks. But, at least it will be spring when I get back to Hamburg. Then summer. Then what?

A part of her doesn't want to go back. Because life is easier here, more sedated, and she can be herself. And she can be with Laz, Miranda and her dad.

She gets on the narrow path heading for the road. Two guys come from the opposite direction with surfboards under their arms. They've got elaborate torso tats, and both have their boardshorts very low, the tied bow of the cords immersed in unattractive tufts of pubic hair. They block the path.

"G'day," says the one with the Southern Cross tattoo on his shoulder.

"You're not leaving, are ya?" asks the other. He's got "Forever Young" tattooed in a half circle of gothic writing just below his neck.

She pushes past them, resisting the urge to shove both over the path's fence. As she gets past, she sees the ugly crevice of bum-crack poking out the back of their boardshorts. Both of them, completely without arse; they're surfboard flat from head to heel.

"Oi, what's your problem?" Southern Cross demands, pulling up his boardshorts and letting them fall down again. "Can't even say hello?"

Talking over her shoulder, "Sorry, but I don't speak Neanderthal."

Forever Young crudely grabs his crotch, not really getting much of a handful, and shouts, "Suck this, bitch."

They both laugh, high-pitched and uncouth.

She stops, turns and takes a few steps towards them. It's tempting, very tempting. Both guys look at her chest, making it even more tempting. She imagines taking down one guy, then the other, by letting them come at her and using their momentum. She could break their surfboards over their heads. It would be easy. They move slowly, without athleticism. They're scrawny guys, lined and leathery, and only look muscular because they're so thin.

But then she catches herself, thinking that these guys don't look brave enough to hit a girl; dropping a pill in her drink would be more their speed. Suddenly, she feels sorry for them, and sorry for everyone who comes into contact with them. Something makes her think they live in a van, perhaps together, or they squat in an abandoned beach shack, do labouring work for cash, when there is any, and smoke too much dope. They drink more than they eat. Two worthless guys living worthless lives. Why waste time on them? And she doesn't need to pass this test.

"Have a good surf," she says with a smile.

As she walks up the path, she hears them shouting, but the words get lost on the wind, and she's not listening anyway. She walks across the grass. The blades feel spiky. She has to look down at her feet, to avoid the broken glass and rusty bottle tops.

There's quite a lot of traffic on Pacific Avenue. Nearly every car is a sports utility, with surfboards on the roof, or fishing rods. One has a boat lashed to the top. All the guys coming home from work now heading out for some leisure time. And they're all guys.

A few horns honk at her, so she pulls her t-shirt out of her bag and slips it on. She's forgotten how primitive Australian males can be and realises that her year in Germany has changed her.

And so it should, she thinks.

It also reminds her that things haven't changed here. Waiting for a gap in the traffic, she wonders why she'd thought it would. No, she thinks. Misty has changed. Definitely, and in a good way.

She sees Sara sitting at a table underneath a blue beach umbrella. She's wearing sunglasses that cover almost half her face. There's a foam cup in front of her. Dixon is impressed that Sara managed to get a cup of tea from a fish and chip shop. The other tables are all taken, with families enjoying an early dinner, eating straight from the unfolded paper. Seagulls lurk nearby and squawk. One kid throws a chip and there's a brief frenzy as the flock fights over it. This makes the kid laugh.

Tired of waiting, she ducks between two speeding cars, the bitumen hurting her soft feet, and scampers across the road. She attempts to enter the fish and chip shop's garden area with a bit more style, striding a little, proud of herself.

Sara stands up to greet her and they share a hug.

"Look at you," Sara says, pulling back. "Beach girl."

"It's so good to see you."

"Don't you look beautiful." Reaching out and feeling the pareo, "This is nice."

"I bought it in Bilbao. Not long after we met in Honda-whatever."

They both sit down.

"Hondarribia. Was that really the last time we saw each other?"

Dixon nods. "Can you believe it? And here we are in Australia."

"I think I've found a very happy place," Sara says, looking towards the water. "It's just lovely here."

"I'm so glad I escaped the winter. I spent the whole afternoon on the beach."

"You certainly look the part. You have a lovely figure."

"Thank you, but I think dinner here might ruin it. Did you order already?"

Sara picks up the foam cup and blows on it. "Just this tea. And it is awful."

Standing up, "Let me do the ordering this time."

She takes her purse out of her beach bag and heads for the little shack. Inside, she inhales the familiar smells of oil, vinegar and fried batter. She feels ten years old again, standing next to her dad and pointing at the chalkboard, wanting to try everything; her ears full of sand and her hair matted flat; Miranda outside, flirting with some of the local boys; and her mum elsewhere, called out to work and never interested in going to Sydney for the day or even up the coast.

She orders battered snapper, grilled bream and a small portion of chips. She declines, when asked, having vinegar on the chips as this makes them soggy and heavy. That's what her dad always said, and he'd said it two days earlier when they'd gone for fish and chips at Montague's in Narooma. She also gets a couple of packets of tartare sauce and a can of lemon squash. She takes a fistful of plastic cutlery with her and sits back down at the table with Sara, moving her chair slightly so she's in the umbrella's shade.

"Rustic dining," she says, placing the cutlery and sauce packets on the table.

"I'm fine with that. I've done rustic many times." Looking at Dixon and smiling, "You're so tanned."

"In just three days. It's like my body was starved of the sun. And

291

I've been lathering the sunscreen on. I need a scraper to get it off at night."

"Have you missed it that much?"

She pops the can of squash and sips. "Sure, but I don't need it all the time. It's good to have a holiday, to get away from Hamburg for a bit."

"I thought you were enjoying it there."

"I am, but ..." She lets out a long sigh. "Sara, do you remember when we first met, you told me never to hold anything back. That I could tell you anything, and that I should."

Sara nods.

"All right." She's been thinking about this all day, about how to explain her actions. "Some stuff happened," she starts, "just before I left. I got in trouble, helping out a friend."

"Who?"

"Olga. It's a long story. A Russian epic."

"Tell me the most important parts," Sara says flatly.

Dixon sits forward, leaning over her crossed legs. Lowering her voice, "Olga's a prostitute I met in Hamburg. I found out my language school is in deep with importing girls, bringing them from Russia to work as hookers in St Pauli."

Very annoyed, "The last thing you want in Germany is to have trouble with the authorities."

"I know," Dixon says, taken aback by Sara's tone. "It hasn't got to that point. Not yet. And it won't. I just wanted to get Olga out of it. That's all."

"What happened?"

After another sip of squash, "I met Olga last summer. At the school. They've got these dummy German classes set up, full of students that are never there. I wanted to know what that was about."

Admonishingly, "Dixon."

"I just looked around. I liked Olga and wanted to help her. Anyway, I ended up in this dive of a bar, dressed like a teeny pop star and serving drinks to horny old men. When I saw Olga there, I knew I had to get her out."

"This is not what you went to Hamburg to do."

"I didn't think it was that deep, but I was wrong. It's an economy. Olga told me everything. They ship the girls in by the busload. Country girls and orphans. Tell them they're coming to learn German and then imprison them in a brothel. I couldn't believe Multilinga was involved."

"Are you still working there?"

"At the school? Yes. I have to."

Sara stares at Dixon, but with those massive sunglasses, Dixon can't get a read on what Sara might be thinking.

"How did you free Olga?" Sara asks.

"I just needed her passport. I set Olga up in a friend's apartment, and I helped her get a job in a local café, but it was all useless unless we got her passport. I broke into the apartment of her handler and got it back."

"That easy?"

Dixon swallows, and lies: "Yes."

"Why didn't you take all of them?"

"Olga told me not to. She said they might lose one girl and let it go, but they wouldn't let all the girls go. All hell would break loose."

"So, no one came looking for you, or for Olga?"

Dixon shakes her head. "And it was good timing for me. Dad's surprise party, a quick trip home. I couldn't get on the plane fast enough."

"Hmm."

"That's it. I'm sorry. I've learned my lesson."

Sara takes her time before saying, "Dixon, you can't bring attention to yourself. Not in Germany. It sounds like you were lucky. Don't make the same mistake again."

"Yeah."

"Did you go to the police?"

"No."

"Good."

"That was Olga again," Dixon says. "She was scared she'd get deported, and all the other girls would too."

"That means it's all still happening."

Dixon nods. "Except without Olga."

Sara is thoughtful for a moment. "Sit on it," she advises. "It might be useful at some point."

"Okay."

"And keep Olga close. You might need her." Sara sips her tea. "It's good you told me all this. And it explains why you look a little different."

"I do?"

Sara puts her hands together and rubs them like they're cold. "Now, how was the birthday party?"

"Awesome," Dixon says brightly, glad for a change of subject. "Dad nearly had a heart attack. The whole town was there, pretty much. You should've come."

"I'm on too tight a schedule."

"At the University of Wollongong?"

"Yes, and leaving in a few days. What about you?"

"Another couple of weeks. It's such a long way, I didn't want to come for just a week."

"What about Ben?" Sara asks. "I bet he's missing you."

Dixon looks towards the beach. "I think I've just about had it with him. I'm getting nothing from the relationship. I almost walked out at Christmas. His family ... I sat there thinking, is this really worth going through all this? And I was getting a resounding no."

"Please, you need to continue. Don't give up on him just yet."

"Well, there is the apartment. It's fantastic."

"You sent me the pictures."

"A micro stick in the mail. Old-fashioned, but it worked."

"Yes, but the pictures weren't that good. I need better ones."

Dixon is taken aback by this, by Sara's critical tone. "Really?"

"In that letter, you said Ben's starting a new project."

"As a team member. He'll never get a position of importance, as much as he wants it."

"This is the new drone navigation, isn't it?" Sara presses.

"Yes. But Ben's not high enough. And he doesn't talk about it either, except to say that it's world-changing and he's got a lot to do with it."

"And his boss?"

"Frank Krüttgen. I had him in a class last year. He's one closed-off dude. Bit of a beast as well. There's something creepy about him. He wouldn't talk about anything work-related, even though that's how the classes are set up. Every lesson is talking about their work. He stayed for one lesson, then dropped out."

"What about the next level up?"

"That's Ole Lessinger. I met him at the company Christmas party. Nice man, a few years from retirement. Married. And too high up to sit in a class with his lowly department lemmings."

"I think it might be worth getting to know him," Sara says.

"Twenty-six!"

Dixon stands up, ticket in hand. "That's us. I'm starving."

He stands at the kitchenette, one hand leaning on the short bar, the other holding a small tea cup. He sips and thinks.

There's a pile of work to do. It might keep him here very late, again, and no amount of delegating can reduce the load, but he's stopped for a cup of tea. It was his Amma who taught him to always take a moment in the afternoon, to drink some tea and reflect.

His schedule has him sharing the pot today, but Dinesh is late. That's no surprise, he thinks. A flight back from Riyadh is bound to have delays.

He sips some more. His mind jumps from one thing to another, all the things he has to do. He lets these thoughts come and lets them pass.

It is normally during afternoon tea that he feels moments of sadness. He can't explain them, and the thoughts aren't really that bad. For some reason, he feels sad from the inside out; all the things he wants to do but is not able to. And there's no one he can share his feelings of sadness with.

The door sweeps open. Dinesh enters, carrying a small paper bag with string handles.

"Alo, Dev," Dinesh says as he heads for the bar with a noticeable spring in his step.

Devan raises his cup. "Indhaa."

"I'm very sorry I'm late."

"Would you like a cup?"

"Certainly."

Dinesh takes a stool at the kitchenette's bar while Devan pours the tea.

"You weren't shopping for me, I hope," Devan says, looking at the bag. "Buying Christmas presents in the duty-free shop at Anna International."

"Very funny. I know your opinions about Christmas."

"It's not our holiday. Simple as that." Devan gestures with his cup. "What's in the bag anyway?"

Dinesh takes a sip of tea. "Dates," he says. "The most incredible dates you've ever tasted."

"You go all the way to the Kingdom and all you come back with are dates? How did the meeting go?"

"Oh, good. Very good. They want to come here, to meet you."

"And to buy. We need this Dinesh. India only has so many rupees. We need a big injection of foreign capital."

"You need to be patient. Everything will come in good time."

Devan frowns. "We need better people. I need a hundred Dineshes. Out there on the road, finding the people we need, and doing the deals that get us forward."

"I can't be everywhere," Dinesh says. He opens the package of dates. "I try, but the world is large. Here, this will make you feel better."

"I'm not unhappy," Devan says loudly. "I'm just ... frustrated. I want more than dates. I want you to come back from the Kingdom with briefcases full of money."

Used to Devan's outbursts, Dinesh calmly says, "I told them to bring all the money with them. I didn't want to carry it."

"I guess we better get the trumpets out, for their big welcoming." Devan eats a date. He chews and nods. "These are good. They're not going to pay us in dates, are they?"

Dinesh laughs. "They have more money than they know what to do with."

"Liquid assets." Eating another date, "A desert gold mine."

"But I wouldn't want to live there. And I suggest you never visit."

"Why not?"

"Because I know your opinions about women."

"They're the future of India," Devan says matter-of-factly.

"Well, in the Kingdom, they're close to nothing. I think after a few days, you'd start a revolution. Or try to."

Devan sips some tea. "You know what I think, Dinesh," he says. "The Saudis could become a global superpower if they involved their women more. Instead, they're stranded in time, not going forward or backward."

"Apart from the fancy cars. And the air-conditioning."

"Small western comforts that money can buy. Cultural change is a little different."

"But I'll tell you this," Dinesh says, getting off his stool and walking around a little. "The rich men there, they really live it large. Complete and utter luxury."

"That's also a mistake. They have all that money and they still wear bedsheets."

"You're awful, Dev. You better be nice to them when they're here."

Devan eats yet another date. "I will shower them with fruity compliments. How about that?"

They both laugh.

Pouring some more tea, Devan asks, "Will I need a translator?"

"All the people I met spoke English. They were educated abroad."

"Isn't everyone these days?"

"Not me. And not you."

"The exceptions." Devan sips, and when Dinesh doesn't reply, adds, "What else do you have to report?"

Dinesh sits down again. He takes a deep breath, arranging his thoughts. "In the last year," he says, "I've had a lot of time to think. On planes and in hotels. I have a lot of free head space."

"In a very large head."

Dinesh smiles through this. "It's been a bad year for recruiting, and for research. I'm sorry, Dev. I did my best, but we don't have anything to offer. Not enough at least."

"I know," Devan says, rubbing his forehead. He pushes the dates away. "A lot of wasted effort. And money. You're the only one who actually did any recruiting. What went wrong with the others?"

"It took me a while to figure it out. Believe me, Dev, our recruiters are doing their best, but the people just aren't receptive. Then, I had a flash of inspiration. I was at the Smithsonian in Washington, at the exhibition of human evolution."

"This is how you spend company time?"

"Sometimes, yes." Feeling he needs to justify his actions, "Not every minute is given over to work. I like to see the places I visit, beyond hotels, lobbies and airports."

Devan nods. "I guess I would to. Now, get to the point. Tea break's almost over."

"The Smithsonian is an amazing place. It's rather strongly biased towards America ..."

"As you would expect."

"... But you can see what we've achieved. The human race." Excited, Dinesh stands up and walks around again. "While I was there, I learned about hunters and gatherers. Early man, thousands of years ago. The men did the hunting, taking down big animals and so on. The women did the gathering, getting firewood and finding edible plants. They divided the work based on ability."

"No," Devan counters, "they divided the work based on pride and ego. There was more pride in killing some fierce beast than picking fruit. Men are still like that."

"Yes, yes, yes. But I realised that this applies to what we do. A lot of the recruits are men. It's a simple, unfortunate fact that they don't listen to female recruiters. We have to send men to do that."

"Hunters?"

"Correct. Now, the women are much better at blending in and adapting. They quietly get information without bringing attention to themselves, especially in western countries, and they're very effective."

"The gatherers," Devan says, getting it now. "Like Amma."

"Plus, an Indian woman can look like a local in many places, if she dresses and acts accordingly. They can go where men can't."

Devan strokes his smooth chin. "You want to apply Stone Age society to Nayakall's recruiting and research?"

"Yes."

"You're mad, Dinesh. And I love you for it. How do you suggest we proceed?"

"We change things, starting from January. We turn the female recruiters into gatherers, with more training of course."

"It's the recruiters I'm worried about," Devan says. "We're going to need new people. More like you. Consolidate our efforts somehow. Send a handful of good people out into the world rather than dozens of mediocre people. The best hunters we've got. People who we know and trust."

"I have someone in mind."

"Who?"

"A local boy," Dinesh says. "From Chennai. I coached him when he was young. Nathan Channar."

"The cricketer?"

"Yes."

Devan likes this idea very much. "Bring him in for a chat."

"Well, he's rather devoted to his cricket."

"How old is he?"

"Nearly thirty."

"And he still hasn't played for India. His time has passed."

"I don't know, Dev. He's all about cricket. Incredible eye, especially once he gets set. Could've been a star if he'd had the chance."

Devan shakes his head. "Too old now. He'll turn into one of those players who never made it, then finds himself in his thirties with no possibilities apart from the sport he failed at. He'll end up as a taxi driver, if he's lucky."

"There's more to Nathan than that."

"No, there isn't. You either make it or you don't."

"I always thought he was good enough," Dinesh says, rather sadly, "but there's a big difference between being good and being really good. You're right, Dev. Nathan had his chance and now it's too late. My feeling is that he has excellent potential as a recruiter, but I still think it'll be hard to pull him out of cricket. The game is his love."

"Maybe we need to put the odds in our favour." Devan drains his cup. "And help out Nathan in the process. He'll have much more of a chance to succeed at Nayakall than with cricket. We simply need to get him to understand that."

"How?"

"By making his love turn against him."

It's a bit of an effort – and no one offers to help – but she manages to turn the heavy two-seater basket chair so it faces the sun. As it moves, it makes a loud, scraping noise. Everyone turns to look at her, including a few of Ben's colleagues, who are up early and hunched over tablets and notebooks, working diligently during this bonus weekend holiday. She sees Frank Krüttgen punching away at his notebook. For some reason, the guy totally creeps her out. There's something instinctive about it, that she knows he's a rotten egg, despite his appearances of normality.

Comfortable in the basket chair, and with her face getting some weak sun, she starts in on her breakfast. She makes half a roll with smoked salmon and cucumber, sprinkled with dill. She takes a bite, chews, and manages to swallow. Despite the fancy dishes and cutlery, the fabulous view, the formally dressed staff and the five stars adorning everything, the hotel's breakfast disappoints. It's average food in luxury packaging. The coffee is thin and lukewarm, and the food from the buffet has a rubbery, processed feel, as if it's come out of supermarket packets.

She continues eating because she's hungry, and because she doesn't want to be a snob.

Behind her, the hotel looms like a criminal mastermind's lair; boringly cubic, and all wood slats, metal and glass. With a few clicks of buttons and removing of roofs and panels, a rocket launcher might rise up from the hotel's bowels, or a huge satellite dish. The hotel's position next to the water provides a similar domineering, exclusive feel; purpose-built by someone who wanted it exactly in this spot, away from the village, a small world unto itself, one that could be quickly dissembled, or set to self-destruct.

She yawns and chews. She's slightly hungover, because all she could do to be social last night was drink. And she'd slept poorly because of it. The night started with dinner at the Gosch in Wenningstedt, the whole party. They sat at a long table facing the water, meaning half of them looked at the water while the other half looked at other eaters. The thick plastic panels shuddered with the wind and made conversation impossible. So, they shouted, and ate, and drank, but she couldn't keep up with the rapidly-spoken German. Nor could she keep up with them in drink, despite her efforts. They were nine people in all. Three couples and three men whose wives couldn't come. The food was good. Seafood fare, fresh. From the Gosch, they piled into two taxis and went to the Sansibar south of Rantum, where a table had been reserved and they were able to bypass the long line outside. But it wasn't much of a change; they still sat around drinking and shouting bland conversation. Ben didn't even try to include her. He spent most of his time hovering around Ole Lessinger and Frank Krüttgen, standing front on and close like he was trying to sell them something they didn't need, or convince them of something they didn't believe. It was pathetic to watch, and she didn't want to look in Krüttgen's direction. So, she drank to kill the time, to fill the void of no one talking to her. The other two women huddled close together, elbows linked while sitting down, clearly thinking that Dixon – as an unmarried girlfriend – was some kind of threat. She wondered if they considered her just an anomaly who would soon be gone; the short-term foreigner who didn't need to be factored into any equations or conversations, and who didn't speak German.

Only Ole Lessinger was friendly to her, kept trying to talk to her in his bad English.

She abandons the half-eaten roll with the gummy smoked salmon and pokes at the bowl of fruit salad. The bananas are slightly brown and have stained the chunks of apple the same colour. The peach wedges have the glassy look of those that come out of a can.

Not terribly appetising.

She takes a spoonful, chews, and puts the bowl back on the table.

It's a lovely day, not yet warm, but very bright. The sunlight is careening off the water and straight into the eyes of everyone breakfasting on the terrace. There's not a single person without sunglasses. The women have massive designer fly goggles while the men sport thin shades with metal frames that are too small for their faces. She gets the sense that the people are trying to be fancy, trying to show off; to be at a five-star level when they actually live a two-star life. That might explain the thick smears of lipstick, the walls of big hair, the copious amounts of gel to spike up receding fringes, the orange-shaded tans earned in winter sun studios, the conscious efforts to keep elbows off the table and to not hold a spoon in a fist.

She sips her pathetic excuse for a coffee and looks at the water. She wonders what the plan is for today. Krüttgen, with his bloody schedules and stopwatch, is sure to have something organised. It was like that yesterday, with every minute of every hour accounted for. Last night, she'd heard talk of golf and would like to play, but she doesn't have clubs with her. She could ask Ben if it's possible to borrow his sticks, but that would require having a conversation with him. And anyway, she knows how possessive Ben is of his toys.

It's nice to have this moment of peace, away from Ben and the group.

"Good morning, Dixon."

Annoyed, she turns and sees Ole standing next to her table. He's in running gear, his face shiny with sweat. She thinks he looks youthful and spritely, and she admires that he's up early and into the day while the rest are sleeping, moaning with a headache – like Ben – or working.

"Morning," she says, smiling through her own foggy haze of wine and champagne.

On the drive north, Ben had urged her to play nice with Ole, to put in good words. Ben said this trip was his chance, as he was the only team member invited along. All the other men are several levels higher than him, and it's why he was certain he was being groomed for some kind of promotion.

"Been out pounding the paths?" she asks.

"I train. For marathon."

"Wow. Impressive. Where's your wheelchair? I'm just kidding. You look totally in shape."

"Ich laufe jeden Tag."

"What?"

"I run every day."

"Maybe you should learn English every day."

Smiling, he says, "Best would be both."

"Multitask. Good idea."

Ole picks up the jug of water that's on the table. It has large, circular slices of green apple in it. He pours a glass and drinks.

"Have you fun last night?" he asks.

"Well," moving her head a little, undecided, "yes. Thanks for trying to keep me involved. For talking to me."

"It was fun." More drinking. "Sorry, that my English is so badly. Maybe you give me lessons."

"You know I already teach at your company. And I had Frank in a class last year. Briefly."

Ole glances towards Frank. "Hah. Was Hänschen nicht lernt."

"Pardon?"

"He hated it, no?"

"He walked out of my class," Dixon says, very glad that Krüttgen did. "I was offended."

"It was not about you. Frank, he has much on his mind."

Lowering her voice, "It was actually for the best. Having the boss in the class changes the dynamic. They all relaxed when he left."

Ole nods and drinks more apple-tainted water.

"You certainly dress the part," she says. "As a runner."

"Good gear make difference."

"How about you run inside and get me another coffee?"

"You want one?"

She shakes her head and smiles. "I'm joking."

"You joke a lot."

She reaches out and grabs the hem of his shirt, rubbing it between her thumb and forefinger, and lifting the shirt slightly. She gets a glimpse of taught, leathery skin.

"What material is this?" she asks. "Developed by NASA?"

"Not quite."

"Feels fancy."

Looking behind him, "Hotel also fancy. You like?"

"It's nice. But I'll confess, Ole. I keep expecting Sean Connery to walk out of the water, peel off his wetsuit and have a tuxedo underneath. You know, he's adjusting his cuffs and bow tie, all suave like, as he takes the steps up onto the terrace to bring down the bad guy and save the world."

He smiles, then seems to stop himself. After drinking some water, "I not follow."

"The hotel's great," she says. "It's very generous of you to bring everyone here, including me and Ben. Thanks for that."

"We still have budget left, from last year. I invite other team members, but only Steckdorf can come."

Dixon smiles gleefully as she realises Ben is simply making up the numbers.

"You have very nice smile," Ole says.

"So, you spend the budget and reward your team," she says, ignoring the compliment. "Zwei Fliegen mit einer Klappe."

"Ah, you do speak German."

"Just that idiom. I like it a lot. We say two birds with one stone in English, but sometimes flies are more exact. Birds are nice, but flies are dirty and annoying."

Ole laughs. "Steckdorf said not that you be funny."

"Well, he doesn't know me as well as he thinks he does."

"Oh no?"

"I already said too much." She waves her hand dismissively. "What's on the schedule today?"

"The schedule?"

"The plan. The minute-by-minute set of events."

"Ah. Golf, this morning. Nine holes. But it not really work. I want to play three against three. But Frank, he play not. We are short one."

"I play."

"Really?"

"I grew up on a golf course," she says. "And no offense, a much nicer one than this one. More difficult too. And about a quarter of the price."

"We pay everything here." Ole mimes a swinging motion and nearly drops the jug. "Have you, um, your Schläger?"

"Nope. And I don't have this stupid license either."

"Is okay. I know the hotel manager. We go to school together."

"Still?"

"Went to school together."

"Where was that?"

"Mulheim. In Ruhrpott." He smiles and nods a few times, liking the golf idea. "I get you on course today. You good player?"

"Like I said, Ole, I grew up with sticks in my hands." She stands, takes a glass from the table and lets him pour her some water. "You want me on your team, if you want to win. I played off single digits when I was a teenager. I haven't played much lately, but I shot eighty-eight when I was home in March."

"Then you play on my team," he says. "We put Steckdorf on other team."

"I'll need sticks, men's sticks. Don't you give me any ladies clubs."

He laughs again. "Good. We start in half an hour. We talk more on course. Maybe you give me golf lessons as well as English lessons."

"Maybe."

Ole's eyebrows go up once. He places the jug on the table and walks away, still drinking from his glass. He weaves between the tables, talking to no one, and heads inside.

Dixon sits back down and starts plotting all the ways she's going to kick Ben's arse around the links.

She walks into the Sailors Inn, her pants still rolled up, her legs filthy from the knee down. She has her shoes in one hand and the USB stick in the other.

All the barflies look at her. The bartender smiles dourly and points to where the bathrooms are.

She couldn't give a damn what these idiots think. So she walks straight past them, even as they laugh and comment. One guy is especially rude, and his comment makes her stop and turn. She walks up to him and wipes the USB stick on his white shirt.

"Hey, was für eine Scheisse," he shouts.

"Stimmt," the bartender says, pointing at the long, brown stain.

In the ladies bathroom, she sits on the counter and washes her feet in the basin. The water is nice and warm. Her feet feel rather soft from the sand, like she just had a brief mud treatment.

She uses paper towels to dry her feet and gets her shoes back on.

Back in the bar, the man with the stained shirt is waiting and he gets in her way. She doesn't break stride as she pushes him roughly aside. She hears laughter behind her, and the man remonstrating loudly, but she's already out the door and jogging towards her car.

She opens the door and sits behind the wheel. The package of tissues in her glove box allow her to clean the USB stick more sufficiently, but she still thinks there's a good chance it's damaged. The tech team might be able to extract what's on it. In her experience, she's learned that these sticks can survive a lot.

She lowers the window and places the stick on the roof to dry. She boots her tablet and opens her email, breezing through her inbox, deleting and filing, but not really reading anything. A lot of the messages are protocol; copy circulated ad nauseam. After all that, she's left with two emails, marked to her attention. She sees that the messages were forwarded to her.

They're from Dixon Grace.

She reads what might almost qualify as a suicide note from Ole Lessinger, and the two-line message from Ben to Dixon saying that he's leaving for a new job in India and that their relationship is over because she doesn't want to come with him. Checking the time, she sees that Ben sent the message this morning, while Dixon was in custody.

"India," she says, reaching for her phone. "Aerospace India."

She dials. It rings a few times.

"Schultze."

"Wir müssen Steckdorf finden."

"What? Why?"

"Steckdorf is heading to India. I need you to find him and bring him to the LKA for questioning. His new employer must be Aerospace India. He could be the leak."

"No," Schultze says emphatically. "Someone from a family like his would never do that."

"I don't care what you think, Schultze. Get him. Go to his work. If he's not there, go to his apartment. Get as many involved as you can. We need him."

"We're trying to find Grace Dixon."

"Maybe you should start by getting her name right. Where are you now? Do you have her yet?"

"Hafencity. I'm going to talk to Frau Thielen."

"Forget her. Steckdorf is the priority. Find him."

"But ..."

"Dixon knows that Ben's leaving. She'll probably go to the apartment. I'm on my way, but you're closer. Go there now."

"Yes. Okay."

"Quick. She might try something."

"What?" Schultze asks, giving the clear impression that he doesn't think Dixon would ever be able to overpower or outsmart her now ex-boyfriend, nor does he believe that Steckdorf might in any way be guilty. And in that one word, its sound and intonation, Korner wants to rip out Schultze's tongue and slap him in the face with it.

She manages to calm herself before saying, "You idiot, Schultze. Steckdorf could be behind all of this. The leak, Lessinger's murder. And now he's trying to leave the country. Go and arrest him."

"I don't believe it."

"I don't care what you believe. Just do as you're told. Go to St Pauli now."

"Yes, Frau Kriminal*ost*kommissar."

Now she's really angry. "How dare you take that tone with me. I'm going to report you, Schultze. I'll make sure you spend the rest of your days breathing dust in the basement archives. Now get to work. That's an order."

The line goes dead as Schultze hangs up. She tosses the phone on the seat.

"Fucking amateur," she shouts.

She starts the car. She works the gear stick into reverse and accelerates backwards. The USB stick slides down the windscreen, across the bonnet and onto the ground. It lands in a shallow puddle.

"Fuck!"

She jumps out and retrieves it. She gives it a few flicks to get the water out of it.

Back in the car, she sees the man with the stained shirt coming across the car park towards her, looking keen to remonstrate some more. She jams the car into first, executes a sharp turn and drives past him, through the puddle in front and splashing him with muddy water.

She roars her Audi out of the car park.

They hug on the dock.

"How long is it to Dubrovnik?" Dixon asks.

Sara sweeps her sunglasses into her shortish hair, pushing the fringe back. "A couple of hours, but I have work to do. The time will pass."

Dixon sniffs.

"Don't be sad. We'll see each other soon. We'll have to. This isn't the end."

"I know. But where? When?"

"I'll contact you. Just enjoy your last couple of days here, then go back to Hamburg and get everything sorted out. You've also got some work to do."

Dixon nods. "I'm not sure if I'm ready to move on."

"From what you've told me, and all that you've accomplished already, I think you've been there too long."

"It's just ..." Dixon looks at the water, then back at Sara. "I thought I was doing good work."

"You are. You've come so far since we first met. Do you remember that? In Waren?"

"Sure," Dixon says, well on her way to storing all those Germany memories and to go some place new.

"It's time to spread your wings, to take on a new challenge."

"New Zealand?"

"We still need to talk more about that," Sara says. "I'll be in touch about it. With dates and plans and what not. But don't worry about that now. You need to concentrate on Hamburg, cleaning things up there. Make sure you pay all your taxes. Don't leave anything that might catch up with you."

"Yes, Sara."

"Try to fix things with Olga too." Sara grips the handle of her wheelie carry-on. "We can't have that following you."

Dixon nods again. All these orders are making her feel less sad about Sara leaving. A part of her is now urging Sara to board the ferry so she can have some peace.

"Be patient," Sara continues, "but also be active. Don't sit around waiting for things to happen. You're the one in control, so stay in control."

Attempting closure, "It was great to spend some time with you here."

Sara looks over Dixon's shoulder at the creamy sand towers of the old town. "Beautiful place, isn't it? They say Marco Polo was born here. There's no proof, but it still leaves the door ajar for one's imagination. He set sail from here to explore the world and find out its secrets."

"I've never been to New Zealand."

"You'll be closer to home," Sara offers.

"Oh, I'm well over the homesickness."

One of the ferry workers motions Sara to board the catamaran. She does so, pulling her small suitcase behind her.

"Take care, Sara."

"You too. I'll be in touch."

She's the last on board and the door closes in front of her. The windows are misted over with salt, but Dixon's sure that Sara can see her. So she remains on the dock, her hands in the pockets of her shorts, the sea breeze blowing her blonde hair back.

She's no longer sad. She wants to move forward, to have a new challenge. And with leaving Germany, she can stop dying her hair.

She pulls that hair back into a ponytail and ties it with an elastic band, attempting to give herself a scruffy, unattractive look in order to deter the old town's males, both locals and tourists.

The catamaran powers up and pulls away from the dock. She has no idea where Sara is sitting, but waves anyway, in the general direction of the departing ferry.

She gets moving as well. Rather than walking into the old town, she skirts the wall, following the direction of the ferry and getting to the tip of the thumb of land that is Korcula Town. She takes her time, stopping to enjoy the view; the crystal stretch of water leading across to the hilly peninsula to the north. There are plenty of mangy cats around, moving like they're sedated, and she resists the urge to sweep each diseased and scabby feline into her arms.

Around the other side of the tip, blessedly in the shade of the old town, she takes a seat at one of the pizzerias. The table is up against a low wall, looking towards the water. On the other side, she can see Orebic, which from here looks like a tiny settlement but is actually a rather large village, and an attractive one. That's where they'd met yesterday, her and Sara, and they'd sat on a bench, talking for hours. Then, Sara had surprised Dixon by coming back to Korcula on the ferry to spend the night. It was nice, having all that time together. Dixon feels like she knows Sara a little better now; knows more of what's in store.

An old waiter waddles over, his apron wrapped high around his belly. She orders a bottle of water. As he walks away, she wonders how long it will be before some local men start propositioning her. Or worse, the love-starved English backpackers, who hover from bar to bar in groups of five or six, like hyenas looking for a carcass to feast on. At least when she was with Sara, the men had stayed away, except for that one embarrassing father–son combination.

It's the hair, she decides, trying to mess it up, to make it even less attractive. The blonde getting everyone's attention; some pornographic code all the guys understand.

The bottle comes. She pops the top and starts drinking straight from it. She sits with her back to everyone else, including those strolling around the city walls, in the hope she'll get left alone. Yet, she thinks it wouldn't be so bad to have some company, someone to talk to again; just not someone whose sole ambition is to get into her shorts.

She thinks of the messenger, wishing he might stroll out of the old town and sit at her table.

Feeling the presence of men, and their prying eyes, she drops some kunas on the table and takes the bottle with her, drinking as she walks. She ducks up one of the alleys that lead to the main street of the old town. A lot of laundry is strung across from one building to another; frilly nothings that flutter like flags in the wind. There's a telephone shop opposite the Cathedral of St Mark. She goes inside. Booth four is free. She closes the door, sits down and dials.

The phone rings and rings.

It's late in Narooma, after midnight probably, but she knows Laz will answer.

"Hello?"

"Misty?"

"Dixie? Do you know what time it is?"

"What are you doing there? Where's Laz?"

"There was a bit of a crisis. Nothing spectacular. It's great that you called. How's life in Hamburg?"

311

"Coming to a close. But right now I'm in Korcula."

"Where's that?"

"Croatia."

"Croatia?"

"Yeah, I'm on a bit of a holiday. Back to Hamburg in a couple of days. It's amazing here." Thinking of all the men, "But probably not the best place for you."

A hand muffles the phone: "It's just Dixie, Laz. Go back to bed."

"No," Dixon says. "I wanna speak to her."

There's a pause, then Miranda says, "That's not a good idea. She hasn't been sleeping well lately."

"What's wrong? Is she all right?"

"She's fine. The café got damaged by some high winds. A few broken windows."

Dixon hears Laz: "Don't lie to your sister, Misty. It was vandals. Tell her that."

Speaking distantly, Miranda says, "I don't want her to worry, Laz. You know what she's like. She'll fly back here thinking she's Wonder Woman and can save the day."

"I will not," Dixon shouts. "I'm not like that."

"Anyway," Miranda says, her voice clearer, "it's too late now. There's nothing you can do."

"Give me the phone," Laz says. There's some squeaking and crackling as the receiver is passed. "Dixie?"

"Lazarus. What the hell?"

"Calm yourself. It was just some kids. A few rocks through the windows."

"I tell ya, Laz. That town will never change."

"Yes, and unfortunately those kids will grow up to be men whose girlfriends and wives might end up seeking help here. And the cycle continues."

"The snake eats its tale. How are you?"

"Good. I miss you. We all do. Miranda talks about you all the time. My sister is in Germany and all that."

"No, I don't," Miranda shouts, her voice echoing.

Dixon suddenly feels a very real kind of sadness, completely different to when she hugged Sara on the dock.

"Are you coming home for Christmas?"

"That's the plan." Dixon pulls herself together. "Not quite written in stone, but I think I'm just about done in Hamburg. I might be back earlier. I can make up for lost golf time."

"But you're not moving back here," Laz says slyly. "To the town that never changes?"

"We'll call it an extended visit. I need some time to put my feet up and reassess. I'd like to travel some more, work in another place. I like this living abroad business. It's fun."

"You're always welcome here."

"Thanks, Laz. I think I've just about worn out my welcome in Hamburg."

"I guess Ben's not coming with you."

"Nope. It's pretty much over. I'm just trying to figure out how to end it without him blowing a fuse and going mental."

"Yes, you said in your letters that he's a jealous type. I would've thought that meant you were made for each other."

"Hey, steady on. I've matured. I'm over that jealousy thing."

Laz laughs a little. "I'm sure you can handle him, Dixie. Knock some sense into him if you have to. More self-defence."

"I'd happily have a wail at his mother."

"You know, from your letters and the way you described her, it's just uncanny how much she sounds like my first mother-in-law. Maybe she died young and was reincarnated as Ben's mother."

"Don't get all mystical and religious on me, Lazarus."

"Never. Two feet planted firmly in reality."

"Good. So that hasn't changed either."

"Now, what've you called for? You never call without wanting something."

"I wanted to say hi. That's all. To hear how things are."

"Life is as it normally is here. Misty's doing a great job. But your berry garden's gone I'm afraid. It was only good for one crop. Then the birds got to them. And once they got in the garden, they went for everything else. That was a problem for a while."

"Damn. Were they tasty, that first crop?"

"Very bitter. We threw them away."

"What do you think it means?"

"It's time to come home. To plant something new."

She leans the bike against the low wall and sits down. The stone is warm. She lowers the visor of her cap to shield her face from the sun.

She glances behind her, at the building she's lived in since January.

Probably should start using the past tense, she thinks. Because it's over. Done.

That upper class apartment in the lower class neighbourhood, it was never home. She always felt like a visitor.

She knows the rents are high in this area, as Ben considered himself a real estate expert, but further down Bernhard Nocht Strasse, people are squatting for free, and living in very old campervans up on blocks.

Across the street from Ben's apartment, left-wingers had smashed the windows of a flash new café and tormented the owners until they closed up and left. The place was still vacant.

Such a weird area, she thinks. Just a couple of blocks from the Reeperbahn.

From the terrace of the apartment, she'd often looked down on this spot directly below, but had never sat here, like now. It was always very busy during summer, especially when the weather was good. Then, not a blade of grass was vacant, not a chair at the Café Amphore left untaken. People barbecued using throwaway grills, which were left in a blackened pile next to the already full garbage bins. Guys did tricks on BMX bikes, skateboards clattered and dogs chased balls around. People drank beer and lined up the bottles along the Plexiglass wall that was deeply scratched with graffiti. Sometimes a bottle was dropped, or thrown, to busy Hafen Strasse below, to see what mayhem it might cause, but it was so late at night by then, there was barely any traffic to obstruct. The only damage would be some poor cyclist getting a flat while commuting to work the next morning.

When Ben was away on business or working late, she had spent a lot of time on the terrace, and had watched the activity, much of it decadent and pointless, unfolding below. A lot of people simply sat around with nothing much to do: street urchins sitting on benches in front of the St Pauli Church's iron fence, drinking beer after beer at all hours of the day, and staggering to their feet to gather the empty bottles left by other park patrons, with each bottle worth eight cents, and hauling the bottles away to cash them in and buy more beer. Dogs taking a shit wherever they damn well pleased, and the owners letting it sit there. People sitting outside the Amphore for hours, talking and talking until other tenants in her building came down in their pyjamas to tell the café's owner to close. Guys walking back from the Reeperbahn after midnight to fall asleep face first in the grass and get their pockets picked of whatever money they had left.

She wonders if she'll miss it, this strange neighbourhood. It was Ben's apartment and she never got settled. They'd lived here for nine months, but they hadn't spent much time together in the flat. And things had gone very much downhill since she confronted him with the Jelena story in July.

I'll definitely miss the harbour, she thinks, turning away from the building to look towards the red and blue cranes across the water.

From the terrace, it had been more interesting and calming to watch the slow-motion movements of the harbour than to get involved with the crowded, overly-dramatic frenzy of Park Fiction. But the shouts coming from below and the endless talking always got her attention, demanded it, and made her peer over the railing.

Police do the rounds here on foot, she knows that, sometimes on horseback. So, things never really get out of hand. A neighbour had said that it was very messy and dangerous on May Day, but she and Ben had been on Sylt that day. When they came back, everything was normal.

It's probably a waste of time to sit here, because there's little chance that Busana will walk past, and there's a very high chance that Schultze or some other cops will come looking for her at the apartment.

Let them come, she thinks.

What she is getting is a kind of closure. She'd like to go upstairs and pack up her stuff, even though she doesn't have much. Clothes mostly, a few books. After coming back from Croatia, she'd sent a box of stuff home, because she likes travelling light. The police have got her passport, purse and phone. Everything else she has is replaceable, but she wants those three items back.

To get them, the police will have to set her free.

It's nice to sit here in the sun.

She'd never thought that a passport would be so valuable. Back in high school, Astrid's red passport had seemed like a kind of novelty item, a small book to record thoughts and write dumb poetry. Not exactly a ticket to the world. She'd got her passport for the trip to Hamburg, because her family holidays had only ever been domestic, up and down the east coast and that long boring trip to West Australia. Despite all her forays around Europe in the last eighteen months, her passport still had a lot of blank pages, and she couldn't leave Germany without it.

Like Olga. No passport, stuck.

She sits up a little straighter and looks towards the corner of Pinnasberg and Heidritter Strasse. They're street names she will never forget. Down there, in one of the low-rent SAGA buildings, something attune to government housing, the girls lived in several apartments, two or three to a room. When she visited Olga the first time, she saw the cramped rooms, with the single beds separated by racks of clothing; cheap sexy stuff, like what was on the racks at the club on Schmuck Strasse. For house calls, she assumed, fingering through the clothes. And Olga explained that more girls were being farmed out for individual assignments, some of them as live-ins.

Sold into slavery. It was then she decided to help Olga. The only way Olga could be free was if she got her passport back.

When asked after Christmas, Olga had said, "I know who has it."

"Who?"

"The Finn. He carry passports everywhere he go. In briefcase."

"Do you know his name?"

"I know Busana. Sometimes, I see them together. Go together to apartment, organise girls."

"What is her full name?"

"Busana Isayeva. She hard woman. But she not always so. I remember very nice Busana."

"Write her name down. What does she do exactly? Is she your pimp?"

"She watch over, like hawk. The Finn, he has passports."

"Then he's the one I need to find. And I'll need a photo of him."

A few days later, Olga gave her a grainy print taken with a low-resolution phone camera.

Then, Dixon's vigil began. From the terrace, she braved the February cold, looking down to Pinnasberg and hoping to see the Finn, using Ben's opera glasses. The month passed and there was no sign of him, or she'd missed him. Some afternoons, she sat there with

Olga and got more of her story out of her. Olga said the Finn was perhaps out recruiting, getting more girls from Russia, expanding the business.

An awful thought.

It was in early March, while eating dinner with Ben on the terrace, that she saw a car stop at Park Fiction's dead end roundabout. Three men got out. Ben was talking, but she leaned over the railing to get a better look. She saw a suited man walking towards Pinnasberg, carrying a briefcase. It wasn't that she recognised him from the photo. It was instinctive. It was all the pieces fitting together: the black stretched sedan, the front-and-follow bodyguards, the confident strut of the small man, the slight, jaunty swing of the briefcase. She put down her knife and fork.

"Where are you going?" Ben had asked.

"I'll be back in a minute."

Now, sitting on the stone steps, the memory is vivid, like it happened last night. She looks at her building and sees herself coming out. There she is, slinking down the stairs. She's got one of Ben's woollen hats on and his driving gloves. She's wearing ugg boots, with her jeans tucked into the boots for added warmth. The handle of the bread knife is in her palm, the blade concealed by the sleeve of her pullover. She can see the intent on her own face, the clarity of purpose; mentally running through a list of what to do and how to do it.

She sees that she's afraid, that she's steeling herself for the task ahead.

Distract the two bodyguards. Get the Finn away from them. Isolate him somehow, so he can't call for help. Get Olga's passport, and only Olga's passport. Do it all without being seen. Remove hat and gloves and walk back to the apartment. Explain absence to Ben.

She shakes her head. A simple plan, but it didn't go like that. The memory makes her wince. Rookie mistakes, she knows that now. It would be different if she attempted the same thing again. Cleaner, more professional, with less damage. She wants to try again.

But she's deep inside the memory, and the cold March evening pulls at the skin on her face. The westerly wind blows off the river still chunky with yellowish ice. It gets down the back of her pullover and makes her shiver. The darkness is helping, providing cover. She's down low, then behind the car. She waits until all three are almost at the building, a good fifty metres away. She jams the bread knife into the

317

rear tire and pulls it out again. The loud hiss makes the bodyguards turn, and the car sinks slightly to that side. She's around the corner and over the St Pauli Church fence before they can see her. Crouching against the wall of a small garden house, she watches the two guards jog back to the car, guns bouncing in shoulder holsters under their suit jackets. They talk in Russian, sounding more annoyed than angry. One inspects the tire while the other opens the boot for the spare. She moves along the fence, sliding her uggs in the snow. She gets to the end of the fence and scales it. She's on the cobblestones of Heidritter Strasse, moving towards the corner, but Pinnasberg is deserted.

He's inside, she thinks.

She moves into the shadows and waits.

The minutes pass.

A car drives by, the wheels hitting the cobblestones like low-pitched machine gun fire.

Then she sees him, coming out of the building, briefcase still in hand. It's definitely him, and he's better looking in person, more like a trader of stocks than a trader of people. There's a girl following him, reluctantly. She's struggling in a tight mini-skirt and very high heels. She has the narrow hips of a girl not yet halfway through puberty, possibly even pre-pubescent. The Finn walks ahead. The girl attempts to keep up, clicking her heels with short steps.

It's now or never.

She picks up a bottle top and flings it at the girl's legs. It makes her stop and look. Out of the shadows, she catches the girl's eye and raises her index finger to her lips. She shows the blade of the knife and points towards the Finn.

"Ich hab mein," the girl stammers, "Geld vergessen. No money."

The Finn stops. "Mach schnell," he says glancing at his watch.

The girl goes into the building. She sees the girl standing just behind the frosted glass of the front door.

Walking drunkenly, she staggers towards the Finn, her left arm behind her back to conceal the knife. As she gets close to him, she suddenly realises she'll have to kill him. Her body seems to throb with adrenalin.

"Ja?"

"Do you speak English?"

"What do you want? Go away."

"You have something I want."

318

"What's that?"

"A passport."

"I don't know what you're talking about."

She pulls out the knife and holds it in front of him. "The briefcase. Open it."

"You're making a very big mistake."

"Open it."

"Who are you? Police?" Looking at her boots, "That's quite an undercover outfit you've got on."

"I'm a friend."

He looks towards the car, but it's parked just around the corner and out of his line of vision. He raises a knee to balance the briefcase.

"I will find you," he says, thumbing the combination locks on both latches, then opening the case. "You don't want all of them? Surely not."

She sees several stacks of passports, bound together with elastic bands. Each stack has a yellow sticky label on it and a date.

"Just one. Olga."

"Olga who? Do you know how many Olgas I have?"

"She was one of the first."

"Well," he says, picking up a stack, "she must be in here then. You know, you could just buy her off me. Everything's negotiable."

"She's a person, not a product."

"I'll still find you." He releases the elastic band and thumbs through the passports, checking the front page of each. He holds up one. "Is this her?"

"Yes."

He hands her the passport, and this distracts her long enough for him to pull a gun out of his briefcase. But before he can get a grip on it and negotiate the briefcase balanced on his knee, she swings the knife towards his left arm, making a deep gash and sending the gun flying towards the apartment door. The briefcase falls to the ground, the passports scattering like a spilled deck of oversized cards.

The Finn clutches his bleeding arm and shouts, "Hilfe!"

She's stuck to the spot.

The girl edges through the door and picks up the gun. She holds it with two hands, raising it, her hands shaking. She slips out of her high heels to have better balance and is very short without them. A little girl, barely a teenager.

"Warte," the Finn says, holding his arm as he walks towards her. His right hand is red, the blood seeping through his fingers.

The girl fires the gun, hitting him in the stomach and making him double over and fall. The blood starts gushing out of him. The girl drops the gun and rushes forward. She bends down to find her passport. Some are already floating in blood. She picks a lot of them up, bundling them together.

Dixon moves backwards, into the shadows. "Nein," she says, trying to get more distance. "Nur deiner."

The girl does as she's told, dropping the other passports and clutching her own. Dixon sees her run down Pinnasberg in the direction of Fischmarkt. One bodyguard follows her. The other stops to check the Finn, who points down Heidritter Strasse, in Dixon's direction.

She starts running, slipping a little in the boots and panicking. She takes a left onto Hamburger Hoch Strasse, then veers down a parking entry. She drops the woollen hat and knife in one of the large communal garbage bins and comes out onto Trommel Strasse. She hears the footsteps of the guard following as they echo in the parking entry.

The gloves go into another garbage bin. She runs as fast she can.

There are more people here. More cars. She could get lost amongst them, if she's clever. She runs down Lincoln Strasse, looking over her shoulder to see the bodyguard in pursuit, about thirty metres behind and gaining. At the Reeperbahn, she ducks between the traffic and crosses the busy street. A bus passing gets her briefly out of the guard's sight and she sneaks into the Veermaster, the ship-themed joint with the mast in the façade. Inside, it's in full swing, with the accordion band playing and a few busloads of tourists on the way to getting drunk. She hears English speakers and takes a seat at that table. She playfully takes the pirate hat from the guy next to her and jams it on her head. The guy responds by smiling and offering her some greenish liquid in a shot glass. She throws it down.

The bodyguard comes in and stands at the doorway. He scans the room. She turns away from him and starts chatting with the guy next to her. The guard rushes out, to check the other bars and restaurants nearby.

She gives it two more shots of greenish liquid. Parrot juice, they're calling it. Then she's walking in the shadows, back to the apartment, wondering how to explain her absence to Ben.

A tap on her shoulder makes her jump to her feet, ready to defend herself.

"You come with me," Schultze says, plastic handcuffs in his right fist. "We go back to LKA."

Dixon tries to shake the thoughts from her head. She manages to say, "Ell, car, aah? Gerd, we really need to work on your English."

"Yes, we talk more. Turn around."

She looks at him closely, fully in the moment now and determined not to make the mistakes she made in the past. He has a holstered gun clipped to the side of his belt, but she thinks he's never used it. And it's holstered too far back to be grabbed quickly. He's powerful, heavy-set, but slow. A single blow in the right place from him would knock her out, but if she were to do the same to him, to make a dent in that massive head of his, she would need something solid. Interestingly, he appears not to be in any way afraid of her, even after she took him down so easily in the interrogation room.

"Turn around, Frau Dixon."

"You still think the file's right, huh? I guess you still think I'm a spy, too, and that I killed Ole."

He nods. "It is clear to me."

"Great. Look, there's no need to cuff me. I'll come with you. Quietly." She takes a step towards him, her hands in the air. "But what are you doing here?"

"I must not answer that."

"Looking for me, or looking for Ben?"

"I found you. Now turn around."

Up close, about half a metre from him, she again finds it interesting that he's not intimidated. He's not expecting any resistance, doesn't think a woman can overpower him, or would even try. She hates him for his arrogance. But that's her advantage, because he's not ready, not prepared. That's the weakness she will target.

"You know, Gerd," she says, softening her voice. "I picked up on the way you were looking at me in the interview room. Maybe you and I can find a solution to our problem. Go someplace where no one's watching or recording."

"I do not know what you are talking about."

But she's got him now, made his body relax, made him take a step backwards before he lunges at her clumsily. He tries to grab her with his extended right arm. It's a simple side-step to avoid the grasp. In the same motion, she puts her left hand on his right shoulder and pulls his right arm backwards, getting a sufficiently sickening pop and making him yelp in pain. He stumbles a few steps sideways to get his balance and keep from falling. It's enough time for her to jump on the bike and start pedalling for the pedestrian bridge that goes over Hafen Strasse. He lumbers a few steps after her, clutching his right shoulder as he runs. He tries to unholster his gun with his left hand, but can't. So he stops and turns. As she carries the bike down the stairs on the other side, she sees him running for his car. She rides hard for Landungsbrücken, smiling as she pictures Schultze getting lost in the maze of streets that fan out from Hein-Köllisch Platz, and trying to drive with one hand. She decides her best option is to get to the landing bridges, down to the ferry docks where no cars can reach, and possibly down the elevator to the old St Pauli Elbe Tunnel.

But there are police cars coming from both directions on Hafen Strasse. Schultze's put the word out and the cavalry has come to his rescue. She slows down, cornered. Her first thought is her dismay that she won't make the meeting at Café Gnosa.

The cars cut off her at the Strand Pauli Beach Club. The cops get out and draw their guns. Schultze's big BMW pulls up as well. He gets out, the cuffs now in his left hand. His right arm is cradled in his yellow pullover.

"That was not smart," he says. He pulls the cuffs very tightly around her wrists and walks her to his car.

She doesn't struggle.

"You make a lucky shot," Schultze adds. "That was my bad shoulder."

He waits outside the civil and mechanical engineering building, trying not to lurk, loiter or seem suspicious. He's dressed like a student. There's still about half an hour before the last class of the day finishes. As it's Friday afternoon, the students are bound to be in good spirits and open to offers.

Through the trees, he sees an expanse of green and decides to head towards it. In the centre of the university's cricket field is a turf wicket, with a rope around it to keep people off, and little orange flags fluttering on the corners. There are also turf cricket nets to the right of the field, with the netting tied back, plus a couple of all-weather nets. The field is littered with birds of various colours and sizes: pink and grey galahs, magpies, rosellas, white cockatoos.

What a lovely setting, he thinks.

It's sunny out, not particularly warm. After the tropical heat of Singapore, Kuala Lumpur and Hong Kong, he's really feeling that cool breeze which is funnelling between the buildings and hitting him in the back. He walks up the stairs to the Victorian-style clubhouse and takes a seat on the veranda, out of the wind.

Looking at the field, a game of cricket appears before his eyes. The players are all dressed in white. It's summer. They have broad, stiff white hats on, to protect themselves from the sun. Some have long sleeve shirts, the collars turned up. The play is of a decent quality. The players are good enough for first grade, but not quite good enough for state or national level. He sees one teenager out there on the boundary, lanky and athletically awkward, but oozing talent and energy; he might have a chance to make it at the next level, but he's also forced to do a lot of donkey work in the field, because he's the youngest on the team. His teammates resent his ambition and are jealous of his ability.

The play unfolds in front of him. The bowler bowls, the batsman bats, the fielders walk in. Then it resets, and they do it all over again. The simplicity of the sport, its rhythm and cadence, are hypnotic.

He wants to play again, would give everything, all of the money he's earned in his first six weeks recruiting for Nayakall. He'd give every cent just to spend the whole day standing under the broiling

323

sun in the gully, waiting for a sharp catch; a thick-edged bullet that would smack into his palms and really sting, maybe enough to split the webbing of his fingers. But he'd hold the catch and hurl the ball in the air in celebration, and all his teammates would crowd around him. He missed that the most: being part of the team. The status of being one of a select group. Chosen, in the first eleven.

Now, he's the one doing the choosing, for a whole different kind of select group.

The clatter of shoes on the wooden veranda snap him from his thoughts. The players on the field disappear.

"Dinesh?"

"Alo, Nathan."

Dinesh smiles and sits down next to Nathan.

"What are you doing here?"

"Looking for you. How are you?"

"Good. Pretty tired, from all the travelling."

"It's hard to get used to, but you will."

Both men look briefly at the field. Nathan would like to bring the players back, but he can't. He wonders if Dinesh is also picturing a game.

"Are you here to check up on me?" Nathan asks.

"Well, it's been nearly two months since we had our recruiting crash course in Singapore."

"I'm doing all right. I've recruited some people."

"You have." Dinesh folds his arms. "It takes a while for the game to get out of your system, doesn't it?"

"Especially if it's the only thing you've known your whole life."

"There's much more to life than cricket, Nathan."

"Is there? When I was a boy, you told me to live the game. Sleep in my whites and dream of playing for India."

"I would teach you differently now." Turning slightly in the chair to face Nathan, "Devan is impressed with your work so far."

"Is he?"

Dinesh nods. "I know how much you want to impress the head coach."

This makes Nathan smile a little. "Don't misunderstand me. I'm glad to work for him, but I still have my reservations. I'm not quite sure who Devan Marawar is."

"You back-foot player. Defensive and cautious. Always were.

324

When you got on the front foot, that's when you really took control."

"I'm not sure I trust him."

"You will," Dinesh says. "Devan is a great man. And he will become one of India's greatest men."

"What do you know about him?"

"Enough to understand why he likes you." Dinesh puts an arm long the back of Nathan's seat. "You had similar upbringings. Similar starts. But I think he had it harder than you. If you can believe that."

"Is that your message? You came here to convince me about Devan?"

"You need to decide that for yourself. But Devan is the one you want to have in your corner." After a pause, "He sent me here, Nathan. To talk to you. We've decided to change things a little, and these changes affect your work. I know Devan comes across as being focused on money and development, but his priority is people. That's why you've been going from university to university and will keep doing that."

"I like it. The work."

"I knew you'd be good at it. In the first few months, you've landed a number of solid recruits. Devan is very pleased."

"I'm not doing it for him," Nathan says. "I love my country."

"So does Devan, and your love comes from the same place. You want to make the country better. As small boys, you looked up at everything. You both wanted to climb out of the gutter. You did it with cricket. Devan, well, he chose a different path."

"Sports gambling?"

"But you both went forward with the same ambitions," Dinesh continues. "To get more for yourselves. Now you want the same for India, for a billion Indians. You and Devan have a lot in common. Your ambition is born from struggle. You're fighters. You both have debts to pay. You're both about the same age."

"Really? I thought he was older."

"Experience has aged him."

"Tell me about him."

"I only know what he's told me."

"You don't believe him?" Nathan asks.

"Of course I do. You can't make up a story like that. A street orphan, taken into the care of a kind woman who gave him his start. To this day, he can't explain why she did it, but she did, and that's why he survived, why he sits in that big office and runs a multi-million dollar corporation. She's the reason why we're sitting here, and she's the reason why all the Indian boys studying engineering at this university and others will have jobs to go home to. And their families will be looked after as well. She is the reason India is changing."

"Who is she?"

"He calls her Amma, but she's not his mother. He doesn't know who his real parents are. I know that they always speak English together. He said she wanted him to learn the world's language, in order to become a citizen of the world. It's her generosity and kindness that he's put into his business. He wants to take people in and help them, the way it happened to him. He has already influenced so many lives in India, all for the better."

"Not including the families ruined by gambling," Nathan says in order to counter the gushing compliments from Dinesh, which come out as dramatic and forced. Nathan wonders how many times Dinesh has made this speech, or said something similar.

"The people Devan wants to help don't have the money to gamble," Dinesh says.

"What about the subjects of the gambling? The players."

"I wouldn't expect you to be so naive, Nathan. The results of sporting events have been manipulated since sports were invented. The Roman Emperors deciding if a gladiator should live or die. There's no such thing as a fair contest and there never has been. You know that. You were inside that world. Think of all the prestige and money involved. The drug-taking and advances in equipment. People cheat any way they can."

"You've become very cynical, Dinesh."

"I would say I'm more grounded. Seeing the world has opened my eyes. And I saw how I could change things. You're doing that now, too."

"I'm just recruiting."

"You're doing more than that. And that's why I'm here. Because we want you to do more than that." Dinesh pauses, taking a long breath and letting it out. Speaking in a low voice, "Nayakall wants to influence the result."

Nathan is taken aback. "With gambling?" he asks, sitting up straight.

"With information. And knowledge."

"How does that apply to business? Are you talking about insider trading?"

"Not exactly. Devan wants to level the playing field. We have people, some already set up in various locations, doing this kind of work. They're like researchers. Field researchers. They gather knowledge and information that is brought back to Nayakall."

"Do you want me to do that too?"

Dinesh shakes his head. "We want you to find the people who do that. Women. Good looking, preferably of Indian descent, able to adapt to different locations and blend in."

"Hang on, Dinesh. Gathering knowledge? You mean spying, right?"

"Don't look so shocked," Dinesh says calmly. "We're not the first company to do this. And how do you think Aerospace India got ahead so fast?"

"By stealing the ideas of other companies." And the analogy puts a sour taste in Nathan's mouth. "Like asking a player for his opinion on the condition of the pitch."

"That's a bad comparison. Aerospace India is building planes, not trying to win a bet on some pointless cricket match."

"Sorry."

They both look at the field in silence, until Dinesh prompts, "Well?"

"Is that my job now?" Nathan asks. "Recruiting engineers and spies?"

"The first part, most certainly. The second part is more about having your eyes open. It's been my experience that you can't go out looking for potential researchers. You need to spot them when you see them. That's why I know you'll be good at this. You always had a very good eye. Watchful, careful, able to quickly identify strengths and weaknesses."

"What am I looking for? And why only women?"

"Men stand out too much," Dinesh explains. "And women are more likely to earn trust. The best candidate is someone young, but experienced. A pretty face is always useful. Devan wanted you because you're good looking. That's what he said. People are more interested in hearing a message if it comes in fancy packaging."

"He said that? Is he gay?"

"Does it matter? You just need to find the potential candidates

327

and put them into contact with me or another handler. We've got handlers in place for our researchers in Europe and North America. The network's small, but we plan to enlarge it."

"A whole network of government agents."

"No," Dinesh says emphatically. "This is not the government. And I think you're getting the wrong idea. This is about knowledge. There's no stealing involved. The researcher settles in a city and goes about her work. She has a job, makes friends, builds relationships, all the while gathering information that we require. Maybe one task is to get close to a certain person. A target if you will. That's all."

Nathan thinks Dinesh is holding back. "And I'm supposed to find these girls?"

"To be more exact, I feel these girls will find you. You just need to keep your eyes open."

"What if I don't find anyone?"

"You will," Dinesh says. "Perhaps it needs a while. Some luck. Get your eye in first before you get on the front foot."

"All right. I'll give it a try."

"In the meantime, keep doing what you're doing." Dinesh checks his watch. "Class is just about finished, I think. It's your turn to bat."

Getting to his feet, Nathan asks, "Are you staying in Perth?"

Dinesh remains seated. "At the Hyatt. You?"

"An awful place in Northbridge. Near the train station. Why do you get to stay at the Hyatt?"

"Different levels. It's good that you're keeping to the budget, and to the rules. You'll get to the Hyatt soon enough."

"And do your job?"

Dinesh frowns. "I think Devan has bigger plans for you."

"Has he?"

"Come by my hotel for dinner."

Dinesh stands up. The two men walk down the clubhouse stairs and stand on the edge of the field. There's a faded white line on the grass, outlining the boundary.

"We've got more to talk about," Dinesh says. "I can tell you about some of the researchers I recruited, and how I found them."

"Okay."

"Have you walked around the campus?" Dinesh asks, sliding his hands into his pockets.

"A little. It's very nice, but a bit too nice for me."

"Still the boy from Chintadripet." Looking over the field and starting to walk, "I think this is the most beautiful university in the world. Can you imagine being a student here? How would you get anything done?"

Nathan watches Dinesh stroll towards the roped-off turf wicket. But the sounds of voices make Nathan turn. There's a trickle of students coming out of the engineering building. He heads towards it, seeing the Indian students keeping to their groups.

As the taxi drives down the leafy boulevard, Devan Marawar drums the rear seat's armrest with his fingers and looks out the window. He hasn't been to Berlin since his Amma moved into the new house from the apartment in Schöneberg, and he's happy to see she's settled in such a nice neighbourhood. It's suburban, but affluent, he thinks, and fitting for her. This kind of area never depreciates in value.

The houses are large, with big front gardens and tall trees. The lack of fences between the properties makes Devan think there is a strong sense of community here. He hopes so. For many years now, he's been worried that his Amma gets lonely in Berlin.

The taxi pulls up in front of a white box-like house, with a design that might have been futuristic when it was built twenty years ago. It now looks rather dated. Looking at it through the window, he wants to tear down the house and build something more worthy of his Amma.

He pays the driver and gets out. He hooks the fold-over suit bag in an index finger and flings it over his shoulder; the briefcase he carries in his other hand. Approaching the house and seeing his reflection in one of the front windows, he's glad to see he looks very much like a business traveller. The only thing that separates him from the herd is the bespoke suit he's wearing – and the second one he's carrying – but most people don't have the eye for such details. For many, he's just another man in a suit.

She must have seen him through the blinds, because she has the door open when he gets to it.

"Devan? What are you doing here?"

"Hello, Amma."

He bends down and hugs her.

"Get inside," Sara orders. "Where is everybody?"

"I left them in Frankfurt. I can do this in Germany. Nobody recognises me here."

Sara checks the street, then closes the door and locks it.

"Especially in Berlin," he adds. "The anonymous city. Anyone can disappear in Berlin. You told me that once."

He walks into the house, surprised to see that none of the furnishings are the same. He finds the interior comfortable and tasteful, but not very welcoming, and in no way familiar. There's something transient about it, as if a lot of people have lived in this space. It doesn't have the small touches that he recognises as his Amma's.

"It's not my house," she says. "I'm just renting it. All of it."

"Renting? Why don't you buy? Let me buy you something better than this."

"Devan, you know the rules."

"What about your apartment in Schöneberg?"

"I've still got it. I'm subletting it to a visiting professor."

He hangs the suit bag on the coat rack in the short hallway. "Oh, good."

"I'm trying suburban life for a while, to see if it suits me. Now, what brings you to Berlin?"

"Business and pleasure." Moving into the lounge room, still carrying his briefcase, "It's always a pleasure to see you, Amma."

"But it's business that brings you here, uninvited. On a short trip, I assume, because you don't have your entourage with you."

"My entourage? That's only in India. I get mobbed otherwise."

She sits down on the L-shaped red sofa, sliding up towards the one armrest and leaning on it. Devan paces the room a little.

"Devan, get to the point."

"I've only got a few hours," he says, still pacing. "Then I have to get back to Frankfurt. This trip wasn't part of my itinerary."

"That's right. Because you only come to Berlin when I tell you to."

"Yes, Amma."

Looking towards the hallway, "Why are you carrying a suit bag if you're just here for the day?"

"Cover. For the airports. With it, I look like a travelling businessman. With just a briefcase, I look suspicious."

This makes her smile thinly. "You always were a good student."

"It's also a time-saver," he says, gesturing with his briefcase towards the suit bag. "I don't have the time or patience to deal with the hassles of extra attention."

He sits down on the sofa, putting the briefcase between them.

"A present?" she asks as he thumbs the locks and flips the case open.

"A problem. A very big problem." Pulling out a green folder, "Someone contacted Dinesh. I'm not sure how she got his name.

Maybe from someone else, another deal. Dinesh meets a lot of people. And we've been doing more business with former Soviet states."

"I'm well aware of that. Go on."

He opens the folder and turns it around so she can see it. "We put this together yesterday," he says. "That's the email Dinesh got. There's also a transcript of the phone conversation between Dinesh and the woman. We recorded it, but there's not a lot in it. And her English is terrible. But as you can see," pointing at the page, "it's a Germany number."

"Zero, four, zero. That's Hamburg."

Devan nods solemnly.

"I don't recognise the number," Sara says.

"Why should you? This woman has nothing to do with us. She's someone else, a third party. She's got her hands on the new drone tech, and she wants to sell it to us."

"We already have it," Sara says evenly. She takes off her slightly horn-rimmed glasses and gives them a brief wipe. "But it means we're compromised."

"I know."

"It's good that you came here, Devan." Taking the folder, "You did the right thing. Now, leave this with me."

"We have to pull our researcher out. She might already be in danger." He closes the briefcase, stands up and starts pacing again. "This woman might have stolen the information from our researcher."

"I don't think so."

"She could wash up on the river's beach."

"Devan, calm yourself."

"You still need to contact her."

"Of course I need to contact her," Sara shouts. Then, more quietly, "I will, tonight. It normally takes a while, because we've been very careful about it."

"Whatever happens, she can't be exposed. It could result in a whole lot of trouble if she gets linked to Nayakall. It would put the whole network at risk. Everything we've built."

"You're overreacting." Studying the folder, "We don't really know who or what we're dealing with. I need to meet with this woman."

"And you need to pull your researcher."

"Don't tell me what to do. My researcher is very well established. In a short time, she's become the best we've got. I have some serious plans for her. And I spoke with her a few weeks ago. She's ready to move."

Devan's voice is barely a whisper, "Get her out, please."

"Let me take care of this. It's not your concern."

"Yes, it is," he says, his voice louder and firmer. "This will all come down on me. When you contact this woman, I want to know who she is and who she's working for."

"Why? To get revenge?"

"I want to know who we're dealing with and why they've tried to make this deal. It's wrecked what we set up in Hamburg."

"What I set up in Hamburg," Sara corrects.

"Yes, Amma."

"Do you have a name?"

He reaches out and closes the folder. The name is written in black pen.

"We tracked the email address. Her name is Busana Isayeva."

She's back in the rectangular room, the upside-down swimming pool, with Schultze, cuffed this time, hands behind her back. She sits forward in the chair, trying to get in a position that eases the pressure on her wrists.

Probably a good thing, she thinks, being cuffed. If my hands were free, I'd slam that arsehole's pumpkin head into the table. Again and again.

She looks at him. His right arm is in a sling.

"Someone pop it back in?" she asks.

"Ruhe."

"Is that caveman for yes?" When he doesn't respond, "What's gonna happen to me?"

"Ruhe."

"Are we waiting for your boss?"

With disbelief, "She is not my boss." He puts the thumb and forefinger of his left hand close together. "She is one very small level higher. That is all. But she is a woman and ..."

"Come on, you can tell me," Dixon says, feigning compassion. "No one's listening."

"Everybody is listening."

"Did she harass you?"

"Harass? I do not know this word."

"Put pressure on you, make life hard for you. Maybe slap you on the bum when it wasn't appropriate."

"Belästigung. Yes, but no slap."

Dixon laughs.

"Is not funny."

"Yeah, it is. A man claiming harassment. But not sexual." Laughing some more, incredulously, "And all because the woman does the job better. Hah. You men just can't take it, can you? That a woman can be your boss, be smarter than you, be much, much better at the job than you."

"Ruhe."

"I hope that shoulder hurts."

"I do everything in this investigation," he says, voice rising. "I do all research. I catch you, second time. I find more evidence in the apartment."

"What about Ben? Did you catch him?"

"There is no reason."

"Are you insane? Didn't you read the email?"

"What email?"

Dixon struggles against the cuffs, wanting to move her hands for emphasis. "The one I sent to Babette."

"Babette?"

"Korner," she shouts. "You numb-nut. Kriminalhelpwhatever Korner. Ben sent me an email this morning, saying he's got a job in India. The relationship's over and he's leaving. He's got to be the leak."

"Frau Korner say something about this. I do not see the connection."

"Now that's funny. No connection? So all that India stuff from this morning, that was only a connection because it was me, yeah? But now that Ben's going to work for Aerospace India, there can't possibly be a connection." She wants to clap her hands sarcastically. "You have got to be the world's dumbest detective."

"Ruhe!"

"Ben's so clearly the spy," Dixon continues. "He's the one you want. He sold the information to them and now that the shit's hit the fan, he's gone off to work for them. It's logic, Gerd. Surely you can see that. Even an idiot can see it."

"No. No. Not his family. You," he says, pointing a finger at her, "have affair with Herr Lessinger. You steal notebook. You kill him in cool blood."

"Cold blood," she corrects.

"And you escape from LKA. Beat up my colleague and leave her to die."

"I did not," she counters. "I didn't even take her gun."

"You have done all these things. You go to prison."

"Forget it. Your tiny mind is closed."

"Ruhe."

She looks towards the door, then at herself in the mirror. She's shocked by her reflection. She looks hideous, cuffed and hunched over like this, clumpy strands of hair falling around her face, and no free hand to push them back. All she can do is blow at them, to get them out of her eyes. She looks wild, dangerous.

She thinks it's amazing that this is the same day, barely the early afternoon of the same day. Only a few hours ago, she was in this room trying to get them to understand the truth, and a few hours before that, she was sleeping soundly.

She keeps looking at the mirror, trying to look through it. She hopes Korner is standing on the other side.

"What evidence?" she asks.

"Pardon?"

"In the apartment. You said you found evidence."

Schultze grins, his moustache extending. "I find big map of plane company," he says, gesturing with his free left hand and trying to move his right. He winces. "Made by hand, many papers sticked together."

She laughs softly.

"Is not funny."

"God, you're an idiot," she says, shaking her head. "That was an English lesson. My premises exercise. It was the first class with my HR dragons. They drew that, because I wanted to get them talking about stuff they know, like their company."

"Ah. But, you still have map."

She decides to ignore Schultze, to save her energy and will for when Korner arrives. She thinks Schultze is also waiting for Korner.

Dixon looks at the mirror again and bites her lower lip. There are things about Schultze that remind her of her mother, and she forces the connections together. His stubbornness, his unwillingness to hear something he doesn't want to hear, his weak body. The fact that solving a logic problem is more important than spending time with his kids and solving their problems.

And she's got it.

A couple of tears start to fall. She leans forward a little, tilting her head so the tears fall straight down onto the floor, dropping near the bolt holes.

The door opens.

"Schultze," Korner says, dropping a folder on the table, "get out."

"Pardon?"

"Get. Out!"

"Nein."

"Fine, but if you end up with a buggered left shoulder as well, it'll be your own fault. You're part of furniture in here, all right? An inanimate object. You don't talk."

Korner takes a pair of scissors from her back pocket and cuts through the plastic cuffs. Dixon immediately starts rubbing both wrists.

"Thank you," she says.

"You're welcome." To Schultze, "Didn't you listen to what I said on the phone? The emails. Benjamin Steckdorf is up to his neck in this."

"No, that is not correct."

"Shut up! You're a chair, Schultze. Chairs don't talk." Turning to Dixon, "Why did you leave?"

"Because you wouldn't listen to me," Dixon says, wiping away the last of the tears.

Korner paces the room. "You went out there to do something very specific. What was it?"

"Check my emails."

"You could've done that here. But why did you think there would be any emails?"

"I don't know. Instinct. Women's intuition? I thought Ole, or Ben, I thought maybe they might try to explain themselves. Ben especially. I couldn't believe he'd just give me up without an explanation."

"There is no point to this," Schultze says. "She is clearly ..."

"Shut the fuck up! You are really on thin ice, Schultze. And someone of your weight should stay far, far away from thin ice. Last warning, or I'll have you reprimanded."

"What? Reprimanded? What is this word?"

Korner looks like she wants to dislocate his left shoulder. "Think of it as setting a chair on fire," she says, standing over him. "Putting useless old furniture out on the street." Calming herself and pacing the room again, "Dixon, you have to tell me exactly what you did in the last couple of hours."

"Okay. I went into the city to check my email. I also contacted Multilinga to tell them I was sick."

"Did you contact the Australian Embassy?"

"No."

"A lawyer?"

"No."

This makes Korner stop pacing. "Why not? That's what I would've done."

"I guess ... I respect that you want to keep this secret. Under wraps, you know?"

"You didn't say that this morning. Then, you were all lawyer and embassy."

"Things were different this morning," Dixon says.

Korner walks around again, thinking.

Dixon looks down at her wrists, rubbing the welts left by the cuffs. Her first thought is that she will have trouble explaining those away, depending on how long they last. But, she thinks, at least now they go all the way around her wrist, when this morning they looked like the scars of a recent suicide attempt.

Pointing at the folder on the table, Dixon asks, "Is that the autopsy report? Of Ole?"

"It is," Korner says.

"And?"

"They say it's suicide. Self-strangulation." Korner laughs at this. "Ludicrous, but they found his fingerprints on the points of contact around his neck, including bits of skin under his nails. But the important thing is that there were no marks on his body. No sign of a struggle or a fight. If someone had tried to strangled him, he would've fought back somehow. He'd have marks. For the guys in the basement, that case is pretty much closed. And they're happy about it."

"Why?"

"It's their first ever self-strangulation." She laughs again, incredulously. "A guy strangled himself on a boat surrounded by rope."

"I cannot believe it," Schultze says.

"Come on," Korner says, flipping the folder open in front of him. "You believe everything you read in a report. When it's in a nice folder like this one. Here. Read it for yourself. And, you can have the wonderful task of contacting Frau Lessinger to tell her that she's screwed. She can put her whole life on eBay now, because there'll be no insurance coming through."

With difficulty, Schultze takes his glasses from his shirt pocket and puts them on. He starts reading.

"Good," Korner says to Dixon. "That'll keep him busy for a while. Now, why would Ole Lessinger supposedly want to kill himself?"

"You read the email he sent."

"He took his own life because you broke his heart? I thought the affair didn't mean that much, to either of you."

"And the rest," Dixon says. "He hated his wife. He was about to retire and lose the one thing he loves, his job. I guess he couldn't see the point in going on."

"Without you."

Dixon shrugs. "Maybe I'm just the focus," she says with as much innocence as she can muster. "He puts it all on me. But I think it's more about his life. Otherwise he would've done it weeks ago, when the affair ended."

"Did he contact you at any point during those weeks?" Korner asks.

"No."

"Emails, phone calls?"

"No."

"Do you know he has a Swiss bank account?"

"What? No. Why would I know that?"

"Do you think he was selling company information?"

"Do you believe me when I say I didn't kill him?" Dixon fires back.

"The autopsy says it was suicide."

Schultze closes the folder. "It does," he says.

"I can't believe he'd be the leak," Dixon says. She's feeling a bit of kinship with Korner, like they might now team up to solve the case together. "That wasn't in Ole's make-up. My opinion. He wasn't that kind of person. But Ben ..."

Korner shakes her head. "Why would he sell them information, then go and work for them? It doesn't fit. If he's onto a good thing, there's no reason to stop. You get arrested, he continues as before."

"Or he covers himself by leaving," Dixon counters.

"No. I don't think so. He's too small a fish. Same with you."

"You believe her?" Schultze asks.

Korner turns to him. "There is something much bigger going on here. Can't you see that? It's right in front of your face. We've got some English teacher in here when the big bad boys are out there running around."

"But why would Ben contact the police saying I'm a spy?" Dixon asks.

"He didn't. The anonymous caller was a woman." Korner pulls out a chair and sits down. She runs her hands through her hair and says, "I'm ready to let you go."

Dixon pretends to be stunned. "Really?"

"Moment, moment," Schultze says.

Korner claps her hands together once. "I think Lessinger was behind all of this. He was the one high up enough to get his hands on the information. And I'm still not convinced it was suicide, despite what the report says. Someone killed him for that information."

"I don't believe it," Dixon says.

"Did Lessinger ever talk about leaving his wife?"

"Sure. A lot. I mean, we only knew each other a short time, and we never talked about our personal lives during the lessons."

"He drew pictures of you. On the boat."

Dixon allows herself to smile. "Yes. He did."

"And did he talk about leaving his wife then?"

"He wanted to run off with me. A dumb idea, I kept telling him that. And he knew it too, because it would never fly with his conservative company. He talked about maybe leaving her when he retired, but it would cut him in half financially. He wasn't prepared to do that."

"That's right."

"And in the end," Dixon says, "he gets nothing. He's gone."

"But you see where I'm going. Maybe he was out for a big payout so he could leave his wife. That's what the Swiss account was for. Sell the information, get paid, retire, divorce the bitch and run."

"That doesn't explain why he would kill himself."

"Right," Korner says. "But it would explain murder. And it creates a pretty interesting scenario." Reaching in her pocket and pulling out a USB stick, "I found this near his boat. Someone threw it in the water."

"What's on it?"

"It's damaged, so I don't know yet. But I've got a pretty good idea."

"Can it be fixed?" Dixon asks.

"I'll give it to tech later. Schultze, you want to run it down? No? Stuck to the chair? Okay, there's no hurry." To Dixon, "There's something you're not telling me. In fact, I think there's a lot you're not telling me."

"And if I tell you, will you let me go?"

Korner nods.

After a deep breath, Dixon says, "All right. I knew Ben was leaving. That's why I checked my email. To see if there was anything from him, if there might have been a connection to this."

"You knew?"

"I found the contract. It was in a drawer that wasn't terribly well-locked. His start date is the first of October. He's probably sitting on a plane right as we speak."

"Schultze, check that out." When he doesn't move, she shouts, "That means now!"

Schultze slowly gets to his feet and lumbers from the room. "Ich glaub's überhaupt nicht," he mutters on his way out.

When the door is closed, Korner sits back and folds her arms. "So all that could mean that this had been coming for a while. He never said anything about it when he was interviewed this morning. Maybe he was the leak. Maybe he got someone to call you in, to cover himself so he could leave the country."

"If that's the case, you can bet the farm it was someone called Ingrid. But do you really think he killed Ole?"

Korner taps the folder. "Suicide," she says, clearly not believing it. "Maybe there are just sailing photos on the stick. Or, or photos of his drawings. Useless stuff."

"I can't believe that Ben ... that I was living with a spy and a murderer all this time."

"Slow down. It's just a theory," Korner says. With fingers rubbing at her temples, "I'm getting lost in all this theoretical stuff. But it wouldn't surprise me if Ben was acting all this time. That's the thing with people. You think you know them, but all the time they're putting on a show."

Dixon looks at herself in the mirror, glad to see she's a little less wild than before. "And what happens to me?" she asks.

"You're still holding back. I'll trade you freedom for your information."

"I just gave it to you."

"I want more."

"Hang on a minute. Where's your apology? You've narrowed it down to Ben or Ole, which means it's not me. But you arrested me, twice, and interrogated me, and treated me like dirt. Why should I do anything for you?"

Korner tries to smile, but with her long, oval face, she looks a little like a horse neighing. "Because I'm asking you to," she says. "You know we have to let you go, but I'm asking you to share with me."

"Share?"

"You didn't go out to find Ole's killer."

Composing herself, "No, I didn't."

"Well?"

Dixon pauses. It's just her and Korner in the room, but she feels plenty of eyes on her, feels like she's on some sort of stage. She decides it's time to rise to the occasion.

"I wanted to help a friend," she says. "I didn't know what was going to happen in here, but I knew I had to help her, whatever it took."

Korner crosses her arms and waits.

"Have you ever heard of Märsh Import-Export?" Dixon asks.

"No."

"It's a front company. They own strip clubs and brothels in St Pauli. There's one on Schmuck Strasse. I met a girl who worked there."

Korner is interested. "How did that happen?"

"Look, uh, I don't want to get people in trouble, innocent people, or cost them their jobs."

"But you escaped from here to help this friend. It was pretty impressive how you took my colleague down, and got out of here without getting caught."

"Aikido. Black belt. I didn't mean to hurt her, but I had to get out. I couldn't leave Olga."

"Olga? Olga-two? From your phone?"

Dixon nods. "And the others."

"What others?"

"The girls, working for Märsh."

"Prostitutes?"

"Yes."

Dixon fights the tears, the wave of held back emotions flooding forward. Suddenly, she wants to go home, to Narooma. She wants to sit on the veranda of Laz's house and have a good talk with her. She wants to plant something new in the garden. She wants to play golf with her dad and birdie that bloody par three third hole. She wants to have a heart-to-heart with Misty.

"They're just kids," she says, her voice breaking. "They ship them in from Russia, from way out in the east. Chechnya or somewhere. They take their passports and force them into prostitution."

"Who? Märsh Import-Export?"

"Yes, but Multilinga is involved as well, and that's how I got involved. One day last year, I needed an extra room for teaching and I checked the board. There was a class scheduled, but the room was empty. It was always empty and I wanted to know why. So I took a copy of the class card and tried to find some of the girls."

"Why would you do that?" Korner asks. "It's not your problem. It's got nothing to do with you."

"Well, I've got a bit of a history for sticking my nose where it's not wanted. That's what ruined my police career. I saw the class card and had this feeling that something wasn't right. I wanted to know what it was. I couldn't walk away without trying to do something. So, I tracked down the girls and got to know them. I even worked a few nights at the bar in Schmuck Strasse. Olga was one of the girls I met. We became friends, like, instantly, and there was no way that I could abandon her."

"So, Multilinga had language classes with no students. Why?"

Dixon looks at Korner as if the answer is obvious. "For the visa. The girls get brought here to learn German and Multilinga organises some sort of short-term student visa for them. But the girls are put in brothels and clubs and continue to live here illegally. They can't leave because Märsh has their passports. They're basically slaves. If they go to the police, they get deported."

"What about their families?"

"Olga's an orphan. A lot of them are orphans. They've got nothing to go back to. And the really sad part is, a lot of them are happier here. They know that they're better off in Germany."

"As enslaved prostitutes?"

"Really. Believe it or not."

"What about Olga?"

"She's not in it anymore. She escaped. She works in a coffee shop in St Pauli now."

Korner runs her hands through her hair again. "A hole in the system," she says softly. "What do you think we should do about it? Why tell me all this?"

"Because I want to do something to help these girls," Dixon says. Then louder, annoyed, "And I had it all arranged until you guys fucked it up. It's taken me ages to convince Olga to go to the police. She and another girl, Jelena, they were ready to tell their stories and close Märsh down. And I had a contact at the school who would blow that part wide open, too."

"I'm impressed. You had all this set up, but then you got arrested."

"Yeah, so thanks a lot for that. That's why I was so pissed this morning. I'd put a lot of work into this, and I wanted to keep my promise to Olga."

343

"She might get deported," Korner says. "The other girls too. From what you say, you won't help them at all if that happens."

"I was hoping, given the circumstances, that the police might be more lenient, a bit more humane, because most of the girls are minors. But after today, I'm not convinced the German police have a shred of humanity among them."

"Hey, don't judge all of us on Schultze. He's just one bad apple."

"Whatever. You want to know what I did while I was gone from here?" Dixon asks. "I set up a meeting with everyone involved. I even got Astrid to track down the woman I think is behind the whole thing."

"Who's that?"

"Busana someone. Olga wrote down the name for me. I thought I'd have enough time to get it all ready, but then your bloody colleague found me."

"Right outside your apartment."

"I was looking for Ben."

Korner gives Dixon a friendly smile. "I bet you enjoyed dislocating Schultze's shoulder."

"Yeah. I did. But I'm starting to think he deserves more sympathy than punishment. Maybe you should be nicer to him."

"I hate his type." To the mirror, "That's right. And being nice gets you nowhere in the LKA. It's all about scratching the back of the right pig, isn't it? It's all politics."

"I had the same experience in Melbourne," Dixon says. "You have to be willing to play the game. You're screwed if you don't. And you have to understand that the game has nothing to do with fighting the good fight."

"No, it doesn't." Korner stands up. "It's good you told me all this. I knew you were holding back. When's the meeting? The one you set up."

"What time is it?"

Checking her watch, "Three-fifteen."

"Then it's in fifteen minutes. At Café Gnosa in St Georg."

"Who'll be there?"

"Astrid, Olga and Jelena. Gnosa's a gay hangout, so you shouldn't have trouble spotting three girls. There'll be a tall Aussie doufus named Seth there as well. He's from Multilinga. They all know each other, so they'll be sitting together. Waiting for me."

"You can't come," Korner says.

"I know how it works. There's normally a long pause between being told you're free to go and actually walking out the door."

"I better get moving."

"If you raid Märsh," Dixon says, making Korner stop with the door half open, "do it late at night, when all the girls are there."

Schultze appears in the doorway. "Benjamin Steckdorf flew to Chennai this morning."

She walks towards the apartment. The backpack's not that heavy, but it's been a long twenty-four hours of travelling. From Hvar to Split on the crowded ferry last night, then a fitful sleep in a hostel that was a converted apartment, with the owner standing in the doorway and leering at the girls assembled on the bunk beds in what was his living room. She'd imagined peep-holes in the shower and hidden cameras, the owner perving on his guests any way he can. In the early morning, there was that hairy ride out to the airport in a taxi that wasn't really a taxi. While waiting in Split, the car pulled up and the driver planted the taxi sign on the roof. They negotiated the ride – in euros, not kunas – and off they went at break-neck speed. Two flights to get back to Hamburg, with a long, no-frills-airline-type delay in between. Two flights that didn't have an empty seat. But she'd made it back and could now have a greedy mug of tea and a long bath to wash away the dirt and grime of the journey.

A few people are sitting outside the Amphore, many of them with empty cups in front of them. It's a nice afternoon, with the sun sometimes breaking through the scattered clouds.

She gets between the tables to reach the door of her building. As she reaches the first step, the man reading the *Herald Tribune* lowers the paper and blocks her path with it.

"Nathan?"

"Hello, Dixie."

"God. What are you doing here?"

"Being a tourist."

"Not recruiting?"

"I'm here to see you."

She drops the backpack and sits down on the building's steps. She reaches out and strokes his face. "You can't be here," she says.

He raises the broadsheet again, hiding them both. "I'm under cover," he says.

"You can't just keep showing up like this."

"Well, this might qualify as an emergency."

"What happened?"

"Not past," he says. "Future. What is going to happen."

"And what do you see in your crystal cricket ball?"

"An opportunity. For you. But we can't talk about it here."

She pulls her knees under her chin. "That's right. We can't talk here. But I also have no intention of being hauled off to some dive of a hotel in St Pauli. Some place with hourly rates."

He giggles, and the sound is such a pleasant reminder that she wants to curl up in his lap.

"There are some absolute hovels in this area," she adds. "Like the place you took me to in London."

Looking at her, "That was still wonderful. But you'll be glad to know I've gone a little more upmarket on this trip. I'm spending my own money. Taking a holiday, if you will."

"Oh, I will. But it still sounds like business."

"I'm here to see you because I want to see you," he says.

"So you should."

"But not here."

"Where then?"

"I'm staying at the Le Méridien. Suite on the top floor. I decided to spoil myself, and you."

"What makes you think I'll come with you?"

"You'll come all right."

"Because it's a better place to talk?" she asks slyly. Then, looking behind her, "The problem is, I'm expected. My lamer half will be home soon. Nothing will happen, but I'm still expected."

"Send him a message," Nathan suggests. "Some kind of delay. Technical problems. Tell him the plane's navigation system is broken."

She laughs.

"Do it," Nathan presses, folding the paper away. "He's dumb enough to fall for that, isn't he?"

"He's not dumb. But you are for coming here."

"Then let's leave."

Dixon stands up, as does Nathan. He reaches down to pick up her backpack, but she grabs it first.

"I got it," she says, looping her left arm into the strap.

"Okay."

She crosses the cobblestone street and gets up on the narrow stretch of grass opposite the Amphore. She can see from Veddel downriver all the way to the cranes of the western part of the harbour.

"My suite also has a fabulous view," Nathan says.

"I'd like to see it, just to compare."

There's a small sandbox for children, with a scattering of half-buried toys. An incredible number of cigarette butts and bottle tops are nestled between the blades of grass, and the grass itself is patchy, much of it dead, or dying. Those patches are deformed circles, the remnants of where people have taken a piss at night.

"What's this all about, Nathan?" she asks.

He lets out a sigh. "It's about your lamer half."

"Ben? What about him?"

"He's ... complicating things. But maybe you can use it to your advantage."

"What are you talking about?"

"Someone's got to Ben," Nathan says. "He's been recruited. By Aerospace India."

"What?" Dixon can't believe it. "Why would they want him?"

Sliding his hands into his pockets, "Sometimes it's not the catch, but just showing that you can catch. If we can get him, then we can get others too. People higher up."

"He's useless. Worthless. The whole thing with him has been a painful waste of time."

"Do you really think that?" Nathan asks. "I think you got from this relationship exactly what you needed. And I know that you know that, too."

"Well, now it's over. Ben's going to India. Why aren't I happy about it?"

"Maybe a glass of champagne in the Le Méridien will help you."

"Stop that!" Then, calming herself, "When's he leaving?"

"End of the month, I assume. He's due to start in October. So maybe earlier."

"That son of a bitch. He hasn't said anything about it. And he was just going to leave without saying anything. What a soft-cock."

"Maybe it's the easiest way," Nathan offers.

"For him, yes."

"And for you."

She considers this, still taking in the sweeping view of the river and harbour. "I guess it is," she says. "But I don't like just being this thing that gets left behind. Or simply thrown out. You know, he comes to me at the end of September and says, 'Oh, by the way, I'm going to

348

India and you don't want to come with me so we're finished and you can pack your stuff and get out.' No way. I won't let that happen. I'll dump him first."

"That makes it sound like he already asked you."

"He did. In July, after he came back from Shanghai. He said he met some guy there, in the hotel bar, and he offered him a job."

"That was Dinesh Prasad," Nathan says. "And believe me, that meeting wasn't planned. That was Dinesh getting lucky."

"Well, back in July, I said I wouldn't go to India, because of the promise to my dad, and Ben got all in a huff, like a spoilt little kid, and we never talked about it again." Shaking her head bitterly, "All this time he was getting ready to leave. The contract's probably upstairs in that locked drawer of his."

"You don't need to see it. He's going, so let him go."

"What's his position?" Dixon asks. "Tell me it's not management."

"I'm not exactly sure. Middle-management perhaps?"

"That'll end in disaster. Not even a group of lemmings would follow him over a cliff."

Nathan giggles. "You never know. India might bring out a whole new character in him."

"He's not that adaptable. Or that surprising. And he's not willing to change. He'll get the runs, and he'll hate it there and come running back home to his satanic mother."

They stand in silence for a moment, staring at the harbour. A couple of ferries pass. There are small yellow boats ferrying people across the river to *The Lion King*.

"But you see the opportunity," Nathan says at last.

"I do. To sleep in the penthouse suite of a five-star hotel."

"That too."

"Lead on."

"You're the local. You show me the way."

Shouldering the backpack, she starts walking up the short hill to the pedestrian bridge. Nathan is at her side, his hands still in his pockets.

"We'll get a taxi down on Hafen Strasse," she says. "And be naked in the jacuzzi in fifteen minutes."

"Don't forget the message to Ben."

"Fuck him. I'm not going to let him screw me over like he wants to. Not again."

"The prostitute? I thought you set that up?"

This makes Dixon stop, halfway across the bridge. "How do you know about that?"

"Why do you think I'm here?"

"Sara."

"And you still need to send Ben the message."

Dixon takes out her phone and does as she's told.

"You've got to play the role to the end, Dixie," he says. "You can't just run away. I know you want to, but you've got to leave properly. We've already lost some people who tried to run when they should've walked."

Dixon pockets the phone. "Okay. I get it now."

They take the stairs down to Hafen Strasse and hail a taxi at the bus stop.

It's crowded, tourists mostly. She waits for them to step aside, as they all seem to be in a group, following some guy with, rather appropriately, a red umbrella. When they're gone, she takes a photograph of both tanks with her old SLR. She's got black and white film in the camera, and thinks the memorial will come up fittingly well in those shades.

She doesn't photograph the statue, as she's completely nonplussed by Soviet realism, particularly that garish memorial in Treptower Park. But the tanks she likes, and she works the angles, trying to get some good shots.

The memorial is close to Brandenburg Gate, in an area that was once a war zone and later a decisive borderline.

Rather easy to believe, she thinks, and to imagine. A soldier driving that tank. More soldiers hiding behind those trees. So many people dying for nothing. People destroying things simply because destruction is fun. Like a child stepping on the sandcastle he spent hours building, enjoying the destruction far more than the construction.

It's a lecture Sara Mittal has given many times: war as enhanced child's play with increasingly dangerous toys.

Turning towards the main road, Strasse des 17. Juni, she sees a woman walking towards the steps. She's well-dressed, in pants and heels. Her hands are in the pockets of her short coat, balled into fists. She has a leather shoulder bag hanging from her left shoulder.

Sara discretely takes a photograph of her, then moves towards the woman.

"Hallo," she says.

"Sind Sie Sara?" the woman asks, surprised by the diminutive Indian in front of her.

"Ja."

"I'm Busana. Thank you for meeting me today."

"You're alone?"

"Yes. And so are you."

With a slight shrug of the shoulder, "You can think that if you like."

Busana looks around the memorial.

"Shall we sit down?" Sara asks.

There's a low concrete bench to the side of the memorial. They sit on it. Busana sits with her back perfectly straight while Sara takes a few more photos of the tanks.

"Please, don't take any pictures of me," Busana says.

Sara ignores this. "It's good that you came alone. That makes things a little less complicated. For you."

"Why do you say that? I have what you want."

"Do you? How can you be so sure you know what I want?"

"Not you personally. The company you represent. Aerospace India."

"How do you know you have what they want?" Sara asks.

Busana pulls her hands out her jacket pockets and spins the leather bag around. She flips it open and pulls out a notebook.

"Put that away," Sara says.

"This belonged to Ole Lessinger, a man high up at Flussair."

Sara opens the notebook. "That's tremendous, but it has a fingerprint sensor. And possibly some other security mechanisms in place. We can't get through that. The notebook's useless."

Busana's face goes flat with disappointment.

"I'm sorry." Sara says. "Let's talk a little bit first. Tell me how you got this notebook and tell me about who you're representing."

Taken aback, Busana asks, "Aren't we waiting for Mr Prasad?"

"No." Crossing her legs, "But I would like to know how you know him."

Busana unzips her jacket and reaches inside. She pulls out a business card and hands it to Sara.

"Where did you get this?" Sara asks. "Did Mr Prasad give it to you? Because I know that he rarely gives his card to people, except when that person is of great importance to him."

"I have the card. It came into my possession. It doesn't matter how I got it."

"Yes, it does. If you want my trust, I suggest you tell me the truth."

"Where is Mr Prasad?" Busana demands.

"He's not currently in Germany." Sara's voice is calm and even. "He wouldn't meet with you anyway. He's too high up to deal with amateurs like you."

"Excuse me?"

"Don't shout. I know you've never done something like this before. So, talk to me. Tell me your story."

Busana crosses her arms defensively. "I want to meet with someone from that company. Someone important."

"Not some old woman?" Sara asks with a smile.

"Are you Mr Prasad's secretary?"

Sara laughs. She takes a moment to look closely at Busana, at her almost Asian features ruined by a very Russian frown. There's a bleak winter written all over her face. But that face is also flexible and adaptable, and saying so much. Sara thinks Busana is the borderline, a woman of four corners: where European west meets Asian east meets Arctic north meets sub-continent south. With the right clothing and manners, there would be so many places where she could easily blend in.

"I can assure you," Sara says at last, "that Mr Prasad would more likely be my secretary. So, let me give you my card."

She takes it out of her handbag. As she hands it to Busana, she pulls it back.

"But first tell me how you got Mr Prasad's card. I assume you're working for yourself. You're a thief trying to sell a stolen necklace. I want to know why."

"You don't want the notebook?"

"We don't need what's on it, because we've already developed our own drone technology. Aerospace India never steals a competitor's secrets. And, we don't do deals like this."

Busana's head drops in disappointment. Her shoulder length brown hair falls forward and hides her face. "So, why meet with me?"

"What do you need the money for?" Sara asks.

"Why does anyone need money? To spend."

"Or to pay off a debt. Maybe to buy your way out of something."

Busana is just keeping herself from crying. "How much do you think a person's life is worth?"

"Depends on the person," Sara counters. "Are you in the slave trade?"

Looking at notebook, "I waited years for an opportunity like this, but now it appears I have nothing trade."

"That's where you're wrong. You have yourself." Sara looks at her and smiles. "Tell me more about yourself."

Busana wants to stand up and walk away, but something keeps her on the bench. She likes Sara: the soft tone of her voice, her calmness, the fact that she seems so caring, supportive and understanding.

Even though they've only just met, Busana trusts her. More, she wants to trust her, to have someone in her life she can trust.

So, she remains seated and begins to talk.

He piles the trolley high with his luggage: his cricket bag, the matching set of leather bags his mother gave him for his twentieth birthday, embossed with BS, and his computer bag. He has to steady it all with his right hand as he wheels the trolley towards the customs exit, with nothing to declare.

No, strike that. He has something to declare: he's very excited to be here.

Through three flights, crossing continents and time zones, he'd had the overwhelming feeling that something important is about to start. In coming to India, he'd made the right decision, and he'd toasted that several times with the free alcohol available on the plane, putting him in excellent spirits.

The nervousness that came with signing the contract has been superseded by a sense of beginning. After toiling for years as a team member and arse-kissing just to make small steps forward, he's now got his management opportunity. This is his chance to build a small empire; thrive as a manager here for a year or two, then get headhunted back to Hamburg. Or, do the job so well, he works his way to CEO before he's forty.

That's the scenario he likes the most.

He's through the screen doors and enters the arrivals hall. It's very loud. He walks slowly, balancing his luggage on the trolley while scanning the signs held up by the shabby collection of drivers. His name isn't on any of the signs. But there had been no mention of an airport pick-up, and he considers himself a nimble enough traveller to be able to get a taxi to the city centre, or to Aerospace India's headquarters.

He heads for the exit. As the door opens, he's hit by an intense wave of heat and humidity. It's like entering a very crowded sauna.

There are people everywhere. He tries to pick his way through the throng. People come up to him, their hands out and the mouths muttering something.

"No, no," he shouts, trying to shoo them away with his free left hand. "Go away. I give you nothing."

But this makes the people push closer. They smell and have bad

355

teeth. Incredibly, one beggar is talking on a mobile phone, his other hand held out for whatever he might be given.

He pushes his trolley harder. It runs over someone's foot, sending that beggar hopping to the side. With a clearer path, he jogs a little, heading for the disorderly row of taxis. The beggars trail behind him, pulling at his shirt. He feels hands reaching into his pockets and swats at them, like they're flies.

An old car stops in front of him, with one wheel up on the curb. The driver jumps out, leaving his door open even as the traffic passes perilously close to it. The engine whines and clunks, the whole of the car shaking as it idles. The driver is middle-aged, short and plump. He has a very big smile on his face.

"Mishta Stackdoof, Mishta Stackdoof," the driver shouts. He shoves the beggars away and they scatter, in search of other targets. "Mishta Stackdoof I am Sri. I drive you to office I do."

Sri grabs Ben's left hand with both of his hands and pumps it up and down.

"Welcome to India. You are here first time you are I know you are. You have first time look on face. Ha-ha-ha. Everybody here first time have first time look on face always the same it is."

"Are you from Aerospace India?" Ben asks.

"Yes yes yes that is me I am that."

Sri opens the boot and starts throwing the luggage in, really throwing it, giving the bags a bit of spin like he's passing rugby balls, employing a deft flick of the left wrist.

Picking up the cricket bag, "Ah you play clicket Mishta Stackdoof you do. That is very interesting. I also play clicket am left-arm orthodox bowler I am. I very very good player in company team maybe you also play in company team we have many teams all very good."

"Can you be careful with that?" Ben asks. The sweat is beading from his forehead. He slides an index finger across it and flicks the sweat to the ground.

"Yes sorry so many apologetics yes. I say you are batsman because batsman always want careful to be with bats. Break not the bat my lucky lucky bat." He hurls the bag in the boot and slams it. "Get in please please get in."

Ben opens the back door.

"No no you sit in front with me," Sri says, wagging a finger. "The back wheels they have no bounce bounce they do very stiff."

356

"No suspension?"

"No yes no suspension very hard on your anus. Sit forward please."

Ben gets in the front passenger seat. His knees are pressed against the dashboard. He feels under the seat to move it back. He gets his hands on the lever and pulls. It snaps.

"Seat no move please be comfortable."

Wiping the sweat from his face and neck with his handkerchief, "It's like Shanghai all over again."

"What say you?"

"What's your position at Aerospace India?"

Sri lurches the car forward and pulls away from the terminal. "Yes I am Sri and I work for Aerospace India," he says, switching quickly through the gears and weaving the car between parked and moving vehicles. "I work there since company start. My son is engineer he is very very important boy build big big plane. I get job first as cleaner and I work very very hard and now I have car make me driver they do. Was very good idea to buy this car now I can do many things with it everybody know I have car make me important man."

"They don't have company cars?"

"Yes yes yes of course Mishta Stackdoof company have many big cars with air fresh and windows dark you cannot see can you. The men in American suits they ride in these cars talk on phone all the time but cannot see them through window dark. I get others from airport drive my small car very good car and me good driver but not bounce bounce in back."

Out on the main road, the traffic is hellish, a veritable kaleidoscope of vehicles and mayhem. Ben grips the dashboard with both hands. He feels the back of his shirt is already drenched and stuck to him.

"My city Chennai I grow up raise my family here work work work save money send son to engine school in Australia and he call one day and say he got good job in Chennai my city so I also get good job and now whole family work for Nayakall company we do. Yes wonderful my other children go to engine school law school doc school school school every kind of school."

All the while, Sri drives like a maniac, working the gearstick with force and sometimes steering with his knees so he can gesture more with his hands.

"Why didn't I get a big car?" Ben asks.

But Sri appears not to hear. "And so because that's why I very happy man Sri very happy with many good things in life because I work work work send first son to Australia and light shine on him we have good luck lucky boy." Turning to Ben, "You very lucky boy also to work for Aerospace India maybe you work for my son he is manager now he do."

"Watch the road!" Ben shouts.

Sri narrowly misses a truck, then veers to avoid clipping three guys on a motorbike.

"Is no problem Mishta Stackdoof. Please be comfort enjoy drive I very good driver."

"I'm in management," Ben says, wiping more sweat away. "It's more likely that your son will work for me."

"No no that cannot be possibility because big manager get big car to airport black windows they have. And last night they come to me say Sri go to airport get Mishta Stackdoof from Germany and I write name down I do so as to remember me."

"There must be some kind of mistake."

Sri furiously shakes his head. "No no no no mistake never ever you are new worker like other workers I get from airport some time to time come with big bag of books from engine school."

"I'm not a worker," Ben says, unable to look at the road.

"Yes please yes you also clicketer." Sri slams his hand on the horn and shouts something that Ben doesn't understand. "There can be no mistake," Sri continues. "I have car be good at job drive to airport pick up boys come home to work. You lucky boy to work in Chennai my city."

"No, I'm in management. Look, can you please slow down."

"Yes sorry I slow for you people say I talk very fast."

Sri plants his hand on the horn again as Ben shouts, "I mean your driving. The car. Slow down, please."

"I very good driver first in my family to have car I do because my son get good job and I get good job and whole family me get good job and we all live in better houses very lucky we are."

Ben looks out the passenger window, but the city's a multi-coloured blur. He feels the jetlag coming on already, all those celebratory drinks on the plane. It feels like a heavy weight at the front of his head, pulling it forward and sticking his eyes together. Sweat drips from his chin onto his pants. He reaches for his handkerchief again, but slides his hand into the wrong pocket. He moves his hand inside.

"My wallet," he shouts. "My wallet's gone."

"Yes please someone at airport take wallet happen many times it do take when not looking very fast you never see wallet again."

"Turn around and go back. Now!"

"You never see again never ever." Sri makes a flying off motion with both his hands, gripping the steering wheel with his thighs. "Wallet gone far far way."

"Damn it. Again? But I had everything in there."

"Ha-ha-ha. You get everything back make call new wallet new cards more credit and more credit. Everything come back again what you lose so be life."

Ben tilts his head back and rubs the sweat out of his eyes. It stings, as if his own sweat is poisonous. The car brakes suddenly, jerking him forward. The seatbelt nearly dislocates his shoulder. He's thrown back into the seat as Sri accelerates.

"Nobody drive so good like me in Chennai my city." Turning to Ben, "You very very safe here."

Ben closes his eyes, wondering what the hell he's got himself into.

She zips open the tent and bends down to go in. Marcus already has his sleeping bag pulled up to his chin.

"Wo warst du so lang?"

"English, Marcus."

"Where were you?"

"My little munchkin, you are getting so good in English," she says, zipping the tent shut to keep out the mosquitoes. "I was with Oma, just catching up on the last few days. Your mum's had a hard week."

"What happened?"

Lying down on the double air mattress, on her back, "You don't want to know. People, Marcus, they sometimes make mistakes."

"Made you a mistake?"

"Did I make a mistake?" she corrects. "No, not me. But I had to spend a lot of time cleaning up other people's mistakes." She turns to him and smiles. "That's my job. Righting the wrongs of other people."

"Like a superhero?"

"That's one way of looking at it. But even superheroes have to do a lot of paperwork."

Marcus slides over and rests his head on the crook of her shoulder. She puts an arm around him and feels his taut small body against her side, his warmth coming through the sleeping bag. His hair smells of salt.

"Tell me a story," he murmurs.

"Okay." She closes her eyes and considers how to approach the situation. Make up something connected with the events of the last few days? Or just tell him exactly what happened? Here, munchkin, this is how life is, and these are the kinds of people I deal with every day, and that's why you need to be careful who you trust in this world.

But it wasn't just an ordinary couple of days. The experience with Dixon Grace has changed her.

"Mum? Are you awake?"

She opens her eyes. "Yes, munchkin. Did you enjoy it today?"

"Oh, yeah. I like the beach."

"Me too."

360

He nestles closer to her and she savours the moment, knowing the time will soon come when he will be too big for such cuddling, for excursions like this, and for sleeping together on a double air mattress in a tent. And he won't want to either. He'll rather go with his friends for camping trips, to drink alcohol and cuddle with other girls. That's all a few years away, but she knows the time is running.

Even though Marcus is her son, her goal is to have a relationship with him where they are both equals, especially as he becomes an adult. Part of that is always being honest with him, keeping him in reality. She feels it's important that he's grounded, from an early age. She doesn't believe in sugar-coating the truth or excusing away things just so he doesn't feel bad. The idea is to give him the best tools possible for navigating what is becoming an increasingly complicated and dangerous world.

So, she says, "On Thursday morning I was given a very difficult case. A girl had been arrested and I had to ask her some questions to find out if she was guilty or innocent."

"Was she a princess?" Marcus asks.

She makes a mental note to talk with her mother about reading Marcus fairytales. "No, she wasn't a princess. She was normal girl. She was from Australia."

"Wow."

"She was a long, long way from home, and it seemed that she was in a lot of trouble. They said she was a spy."

"Really?"

"That's what they said. My colleague Schultze was convinced about it. But in the end, she was just caught up in things that were much bigger than her. She wasn't a bad person and she wasn't a spy. In fact, she even helped me solve a very big case. After all that happened, she still wanted to help me."

"Hmm."

She feels Marcus's head sink against her chest as sleep starts to set in. His soft breath goes through her shirt and tickles her skin.

"It's amazing how much can happen in one day," she continues, but she already has the sense that she's talking to herself. So, lowering her voice, "I spent Thursday morning with Dixon Grace. I know about her whole life now. About her work, her relationship with her boyfriend, her background. And I think it's unfair that I know all that, because she wasn't the person we had to talk to. We arrested the wrong person."

She trails off, aware that Marcus is snoring softly.

The wrong person, she thinks. But that person led me to Märsh and to closing a case that will probably get me promoted. It's already on the news and in the papers: Märsh running a prostitution ring with over a hundred girls, Multilinga to be shut down, a complete revising of student language visas, all the girls being deported back home to Russia.

From Thursday night's raid of the club on Schmuck Strasse to Friday morning's press conference, she became the star of the Hamburg LKA. There were meetings with superiors, reports to write, photo opportunities, and in all that fanfare, her colleagues forgot about Dixon Grace, about how they had ruined her life.

But she hasn't forgotten about Dixon. She just doesn't know how to make amends. Because on Monday morning, she'll be back at the LKA with new work to do, possibly higher profile cases, more pressure and longer hours.

She smells the salt in her son's hair, and then smells her own hair. It's a little matted from the salt, but in a good way, and her skin feels pleasantly dry from a day in the sun.

Dixon Grace, she thinks. Going home to Australia to play golf and sit on the beach. Will you come back to give Germany another chance?

I doubt it, she thinks to herself. You can't even speak German.

And she also doubts that she can face the LKA on Monday, to deal with more Schultzes, right the wrongs and clean up other people's mistakes.

Her thoughts drift to the Russian girls, all of them heading for home as well – those who had been caught – and none of them wanting to go. That had been the hardest part: putting the girls into detention to await deportation. And they're teenagers, all of them. Orphans.

What will they go back to? she wonders. In trying to help them, I've made their lives worse. In arresting Dixon, I ruined her life as well. How does all that make me a superhero?

She closes her eyes, wanting to sleep.

"My career is over, Marcus," she says.

She clears security and walks through the maze of shops, heading for the gates. It's Saturday night, and the airport's pretty quiet. That is, there's not nearly the kind of crowd on those mornings when she took her short flights around Europe. Then, the airport had been full of suited men with wheelie carry-on bags, as if the terminal was a factory where such men were mass-produced.

She lists the places in her head: Spain, Croatia, England, France, Denmark, Switzerland.

I'm going to miss that, she thinks, country-hopping in Europe. But there'll be time for that again, one day.

She's glad to be heading home. Laz, Misty and her dad, they all promised to meet her at Kingsford Smith in Sydney.

To her surprise, she thinks she'll miss the suited men as well. There's something about a suit that makes a man look a little more than he is; gives him a bit more in the shoulders and hides the bulk in the belly. It straightens him out and lends him some import. Ole had looked good in a suit, and he had always worn very nice suits.

Poor Ole, she thinks.

But Ben had also struck a fine pose in a suit, except for those stupid vests he wore, as if the three-piece suits were further proof that he was educated in England.

She won't miss him, but she will miss the apartment. And Hamburg, and the harbour.

"Let it go," she says to herself.

Because there's more to do. New jobs, new challenges. She wants them. She wants to be pushed, to see how good she can be. Hamburg is just the beginning.

At one of the empty gates, she takes a copy of the *Herald Tribune*. On the front page, there's a short blurb about the busted prostitution ring in Hamburg, with more on page four. She folds the paper and puts it in her shoulder bag.

She's sorry for Seth, but she hopes he'll find a new job, probably as director of studies at one of the other language schools in Hamburg.

At least Astrid is happy, having made some good contacts to get her into criminal law.

She wonders where Olga is.

She hears her phone buzz and flips open her shoulder bag.

The text is from Sara: "Have a good flight home. I'll be in touch very soon. S."

She deletes the message, turns off the phone and drops it back in her bag.

It's good to be travelling light like this. Just a shoulder bag. Ben will be left to deal with what remains of her stuff, if he ever comes back from India.

She's early for her flight and walks slowly, stopping to look at the displays of the souvenir shops. On this journey, she's got time, to wait in departure lounges and sit in planes. She can catch up on all the films she's missed. She's on hiatus, for the time being.

Sabbatical, she thinks to herself, liking the word very much.

She gets to her gate. There are two immigration guards, each in their own little box. Beyond them, the people who will be on her flight are scattered around the departure lounge. There aren't that many, which means they should all be able to stretch out a little and enjoy the space. She's got seven hours to Dubai, three at the airport there, then thirteen to Sydney. It seems like a lot, a whole day of travelling, but it's all right, because she's going home. It won't be long before she's standing on the first tee with her dad, chatting with Laz over a cup of tea and a muffin on the veranda, and diving into the surf at the beach with Misty. Summer has ended in Hamburg, but it's spring in Australia.

Nobody's waiting at immigration, so she takes the guard on the left.

"Guten Abend," he says, his hand reaching for the passport she slides under the glass. He flips it open. "Fliegen Sie nach Hause?"

"Ja. Ich bin wie eine Fisch ohne Wasser."

This makes the guard smile. "Vielleicht nehmen Sie mich mit?" he asks.

"Sind Sie bereit?" she replies coyly.

The guard laughs. She gives him a nice smile and walks towards the departure lounge.

"I'm ready," she says.

Travel Page (cont.)